Annie of Ainsworth's Mill

Katie Hutton is Irish but now lives in northern Tuscany, with her Italian husband and two teenage sons. She writes mainly historical fiction on the themes of love and culture clash. *The Gypsy Bride* was her debut novel in this genre, with *The Gypsy's Daughter* following. Katie is a member of the Irish Writers Union, the Society of Authors, the Historical Novel Society, the Irish Writers Centre, and the Romantic Novelists' Association, and reviews for *Historical Novel Review*. In her spare time she volunteers with a second-hand book charity of which she is a founder member.

Also by Katie Hutton:

The Gypsy Bride
The Gypsy's Daughter

Annie of Ainsworth's Mill

Katie Hutton

ZAFFRE

First published in the UK in 2022 by
ZAFFRE
An imprint of Bonnier Books UK
4th Floor, Victoria House, Bloomsbury Square, London, England, WC1B 4DA
Owned by Bonnier Books
Sveavägen 56, Stockholm, Sweden

A CIP catalogue record for this book is
available from the British Library.

ISBN: 978-1-83877-583-4

Also available as an ebook and in audio

1 3 5 7 9 10 8 6 4 2

Typeset by IDSUK (Data Connection) Ltd
Printed and bound in Great Britain by Clays Ltd, Elcograf S.p.A.

Zaffre is an imprint of Bonnier Books UK
www.bonnierbooks.co.uk

In memory of:

James Hutton
Killyleagh, 1905 – Barrow in Furness, 1977

and

Louisa ('Louie') Hutton
Killyleagh, 1908 – Cleator Moor, 1910

CHAPTER ONE

Moneyscalp Townland, 1897

'The half Barony of Mourne, so called from its smallness, is for the most part incumbered with mountains, and is coarse and rugged . . .'

Walter Harris, *The Antient and Present State of the County of Down*, 1744

Saying goodbye to Polly was the hardest, because it was the first time Annie Maguire had seen her father cry. There would be no space for the shire horse in a back yard in Comber. The child climbed two rungs of the gate and rested her face on the long white star on the animal's nose, the ridge of the skull hard against her forehead, her glossy black hair falling forward. The horse's breathing was thunder in her ears. Polly was the last animal to be sold.

Her father put his hand on her shoulder. 'Patrick's here.'

Annie caressed the horse's stiff ear one last time and climbed down to greet the man who farmed the neighbouring fields. Patrick and Agnes were childless, so their farm would never have to be divided. Patrick might even be buying this one. Thomas Maguire's riches, his three sons, had already departed for Canada, to work on farms so vast you'd never see end to end of them, not even if you were a bird. But here in Moneyscalp there was no halving the farm any further for an eldest son. It was only twenty-two acres. Yet that still meant it was too big for him to work alone.

As the thud of Polly's hooves on the grassed lane died away Thomas Maguire leaned on the fence, his head on his arms, his shoulders heaving.

'Are you laughing, Dadda?' asked the child, distressed. He didn't laugh often, and this hardly seemed the moment. Thomas turned, a flailing arm pulling her close. She buried her face in her father's old waistcoat. Like all the farmers below the slope of the Mournes, Thomas wore old, 'good' clothes to work in, garments once made for funerals or weddings, but which would end their lives like a horse sent to the knacker's yard, dismembered into strips for rag rugs. He smelled of tobacco, old sweat and horse manure. Annie loved that smell. She did not love his gulping tears. The child had never witnessed her father weeping.

At last Thomas recovered himself and, still holding his daughter in one arm, he fumbled out his handkerchief and blew his nose loudly.

'Come away home,' he said.

'We'll not see Charlie again, either, will we?'

'We will not,' said Thomas. 'Though Polly might. I told Patrick they harness well together.'

'Not bad for a Protestant horse,' said Annie, repeating the words her father had said every year at ploughing time. Charlie was the property of a Presbyterian farmer near Downpatrick. Her father laughed briefly.

'It's not her ploughing I'll miss most,' said Thomas, his face clouding over. 'It's the Sunday afternoons I had on her back over there in Lord Roden's woods when his lordship was away in England. Your brothers thought I was a pure eejit, you know. Keeping a horse all year to pasture when I cudda hired her only when I needed her.'

'Maybe we'll be let go to see her at Patrick's sometimes.'

'Maybe. We're not going as far as Roden's timber, after all. Mulligan told me that wood goes to Belfast for to go in the big ships they build for America. Carved staircases and panelling and that.'

'How far is Comber, then?'

'Two hours on the cart, so it is.'

Annie was silent. They might as well be going to Canada, then.

*

Annie cried out on entering the house. Her mother had taken down the picture of the Holy Family, the profile photograph of the Rosary Pope, whose fluffy hair had always reminded her of the sheep in the back field, and the Sacred Heart – an image she'd always found frightening but knew she could never say so. It wasn't just the marks the pictures had left on the walls

3

that distressed her. It was the thought of helping to unpack in their new home and suddenly encountering Jesus's reproachful eyes and glistening, pulsing heart in one of the fruit crates. The picture always reminded her of the bloody afterbirth in the grass during calving season – and now, thinking of it again, she knew it was yet another sin she'd have to confess to a strange new priest. Her breath caught. She might never see another calf born, nor the shearing of the sheep. 'They'll take you at Andrews' Mill,' her father had told her, 'as soon as you turn thirteen. *You'll* have a job indoors.' Annie clung to the hope that they'd take her mother too – provided the foreman didn't get to hear that cough – so she wouldn't be entering a world of strangers alone. Though she'd have to face the last days of her schooling at a new place first; surely there'd be other girls who would go with her from school slates to spinning?

The reek of the mutton and potatoes in the black-ridged pot hanging over the hearth was the only thing in the room that remained unchanged. Would the pot come with them too? It seemed so much a part of the paraphernalia hanging over the peat fire that Annie thought it would be wrong to take it away.

*

'Them Orange boys got their man on the council, so they did,' said Thomas, wiping a heel of bread around his plate to soak up the last juices.

'When do they not?' said his wife.

'Mr Harris says there'll never be Home Rule in Ireland as the Orangemen will never let it,' said Annie. Both her parents stared at her in astonishment.

'What do you know of that?' said her mother. 'Harris is half an Englishman and the other half's cracked.'

'He said every time there's a Fenian out . . .'

'Outrage,' supplied her father.

'Explosions and that. Says they only help the Orangemen to have everything the way they want it. No Home Rule. Only the way he said it, he was sorry it was so.'

'He might have something there,' said Thomas, looking at his child with interest.

With renewed confidence the girl added, 'He told me the main men in the United Irishmen were Protestants. That if it hadn't been for the Orangemen and the militia the rebellion might have won.'

'That's all history,' cut in her mother, irritated, 'a hundred years or more old. Peels no potatoes, so it doesn't. All you need to know is your writing and your arithmetic and your catechism. Don't fill your head with things you can do nothing about.'

'The child is interested, that's all, Mary. And maybe she's right – or Harris is. If the rebellion had gone another way then it mightn't be the Presbyterians deciding who gets voted in, who gets to work in what mill, who gets the best of a land deal – all them things. Anyway, he's coming the night, so he is.'

'Is he now?' said his wife.

'I'm giving him the wills, so I am.'

She stared at him.

'He says he's putting them in a library in Dublin. They might as well be there as we'll not be here,' he said through a mouthful of bread.

'We'll not be seeing Mr Harris again either, so?' said Annie.

'Not after this time, we will not.'

Annie's eyes welled up for the second time that day.

'I'll miss him,' she said. 'I remember more he's told me than any of them teachers.'

'He wasn't needing an education, so he wasn't,' said Mary. 'He needed a trade, like a poorer man, not to be digging around disturbing what's dead and buried and putting ideas in a child's head. Making your father take him up Slievenalargy in the rain to see the Mass Rock. Sure what does a Protestant want with one of them?'

Annie remembered that day. The sky had cleared by the time the three of them had got up there. Mr Harris had given her his tripod to carry, not, she knew, to burden her but to give her importance, as he told her about how the faithful – not *his* faithful, he'd added apologetically – had been forced to hear mass in hidden places, all through the penal times. He'd hopped about, this man of sixty, as excited as a boy as he set his camera up, delighted as he ran his fingers over the marks grooved in the granite, and guided hers until she too could trace the shape of the cross, the chalice and the three letters 'IHS' which Mr Harris had explained was a short way of writing Jesus in Greek. Annie had answered with pride that she knew where Greece was, for she'd seen it on the linen-backed wall map in the school room, and Harris told her he'd been there.

'He's been seen in the old burial grounds writing down all the tomb names. And telling your father the lumpy field where the trough is was a fort.' Mary Maguire clattered the plates together, and went out to wash them under the pump. Annie got up, knowing she was meant to go and help her, but hesitated behind her chair.

'What are the wills, Dadda?'

'There's no worth in them, Annie. They were made I don't know how many grandfathers ago, when the farm was taken and given to his lordship, whoever he was then, and the Maguires had to pay rent to live and work on it. There was two Maguires got the priest to write down that if the land got given back then to be sure it was to go to their sons.'

'But it's yours now.'

'For all the good it's done us. Too small now to split further. There's no living in it. But Harris told me there's men in Dublin would love for to see old writings like the wills, though I can't think why. And you'd best go out to your mother before she shouts for you.'

Annie obeyed, her head full of confused images: Comber, Greece, Canada, America, Dublin. There was England too – Mr Harris said it was England made him speak the way he did, even if he'd been born in Newry, because, unlike his sisters, he'd been sent there to school. Annie knew that Mr Harris attended the Church of Ireland. This was another mystery to the child; how could it be 'of Ireland' if the Quality went to it, when all of them sounded English to her? Listening to the stories the antiquarian told her about landless men, United Irishmen swearing oaths on Cave Hill, famine, and Trevelyan and the potato blight, she thought England couldn't be a good place. If Englishmen had done bad things to Irishmen in their own country, whatever would they do if she was ever to go to theirs? But the problem was, to hear Mr Harris – and the distant drums and fifes in marching season – that home in County Down pretty well belonged to the Orangemen, whatever documents the Maguires thought they'd signed their names to.

CHAPTER TWO

Killyleagh, 1895

'Archibald Hamilton-Rowan, of Killyleagh Castle, devised
his fortune to his grandson . . . "in the hope that he should
become a learned, sober, honest man . . . zealous for the
rights of his country; loyal to his king; and a true Protestant
without bigotry to any sect."'

John Burke, *A Genealogical and Heraldic History
of the Commoners of Great Britain and Ireland, Enjoying
Territorial Possessions Or High Official Rank: But
Uninvested with Heritable Honours,* 1833

'Robert!'

The child wriggled to the edge of the bed, ignoring the
snuffled protests of his two companions. He dangled his feet
over the side, then gently lowered himself onto the dusty rag
rug. He felt for his boots beneath the bed, pushing his feet into
them without tying the laces, and shuffled out of the room to
the head of the stairs. He didn't know what time it was, or why
he was being called. The steps looked vertiginous to him in the

flickering glow of the oil lamps below. He was afraid of falling over his laces on the way down, but more afraid of keeping Mrs Lamont waiting.

But it wasn't Mrs Lamont who'd wanted him woken. She'd always complained about how difficult it was to get him 'down', to the degree that Robert had early on learned the wisdom of pretending to be asleep when he wasn't. There was a visitor, James Cairncross, the land agent at the Big House, the man who had brought Robert to the farmhouse two years earlier and who turned up at unsociable times to ask gruffly how he did. It was only years later that Robert learned the man did this deliberately, to catch his foster parents out, and later still that he discovered why this mattered to Cairncross.

The land agent was standing proprietorially with his back to the fire. A big man, he absorbed much of its heat, and the child was convinced that if he moved, clouds of peat smoke would come billowing out of the folds of his coat.

'Come here, Robert.'

The boy shuffled forward, the nails in his boots scraping the flagstones. Cairncross patted his head awkwardly, then let his hand rest a moment on Robert's hair. The boy didn't know what to make of this. His foster parents didn't touch him, except to skelp his arse if he broke something, and their children only to kick him to make space on the heaving straw-stuffed palliasse or in their fights in the bracken.

'What would you say to a new home, Robert?'

The child stood silent for a moment. He wasn't used to being asked questions, except by the master at the National School, and those weren't good ones. The way the teacher asked them, it sent the answer out of Robert's head even though a moment before he'd known it, and it invariably came to him as he nursed his smarting fingers after the master had used his cane on them for forgetting.

'Are you not going to answer Mr Cairncross?' said Mrs Lamont behind him.

'Thank you, sir.' Then realising something more might be required of him, he said, 'Will there be boys?'

'It'll just be you, so it will. You – and herself. And a few cats.' There was a twitch at the corner of Cairncross's mouth.

Robert digested this. Cats were all right. He liked to talk to Patsy, the farm's mouser, when the Lamont children weren't looking. He'd miss Patsy. 'Herself' though? Would he share a bed with this person? There was in fact a lot he wanted to ask, but knew there wasn't much point. Things had always been decided for him.

'There'll be other wee gossuns, like yourself, so there will. Not in the house with you. In the other houses. You'll be in the town. Nearer your mammy that way.'

Robert felt his heart jump in his puny chest like a trapped bird. *Mammy?* He'd seen her twice in the last year. She'd brought him fresh bread from the kitchens which he'd eaten before Cairncross took him back to the farmhouse, where he was sure he'd have been made to share it. His mother. The only person who had ever kissed him. *What name would 'herself' have?* he wondered.

'I'll come back for you at the end of the week,' said Cairncross. Looking over the boy's head, he added, 'That's when yous'll be paid.'

*

On that last Friday at the old school, Robert hung back and let the Lamont children go in ahead of him. They didn't even look round or question why he didn't follow them. He walked instead through the whin[3] bushes and the bracken up to the top of the hill above the farm, eating his piece of bread as soon as he'd counted twelve reverberations of the bell of the Englishmen's church. Afterwards he picked a bouquet of bog cotton. Something to give his mother. Or perhaps 'herself' and the cats would like it?

He was hiding behind the byre, where he found a piece of twine to tie up the cotton stalks, when the Lamont children came shouting their way home. They barely looked up when he came in though, his present hidden inside his shirt. He went upstairs and gathered his very few belongings into the small canvas bag he'd brought to the farm: some greying small-clothes, a frayed shirt too small for William Lamont, a speckled stone he was sure he could see a face in, a gleaming bird skull, and his slate. He gazed for a while on a dusty-pink pamphlet entitled 'The Catechism for Children', published in Philadelphia, a place he hadn't known existed and still didn't know where it was, distributed by a visiting preacher's lady assistant. He'd meant to read it in case the lady came back, as she'd smiled at him, but he never did see her again. Eventually he put it in with the other things. It wasn't the heavy Bible with the clasps and the copper-plate inscriptions the Lamonts kept on the recessed shelf next to

---

[3] Gorse

the range, but then Samuel Lamont senior was a large man with shovel hands and an adult's bellow. Such a man would have a huge Bible, whereas Robert was merely a boy and so merited only that pamphlet.

He went downstairs, to where William, Samuel and Sarah were playing noisily with marbles on the hearth; he noticed that the little girl alone glanced up before returning to the game. He could hear Mrs Lamont out the back making cooing noises to the hens, more affectionate with them than he'd ever heard her with anyone human. Something bubbled in the black ribbed pot hanging over the fire – mutton by the smell of it. Robert took up a position on a rush-seated chair in the corner, his feet hooked behind the crossbar, clutching the bag on his lap. From this vantage point, with the top of the half-door open, he could see who came up the lane. He screwed up his eyes, willing Cairncross into view.

'Robbie!'

He looked round.

'Are ye deaf?' said Sarah. The others had paused in their game, watching him sullenly.

'I'm not.'

'I was asking ye is it today ye're going?'

'It is.' Agitated, he turned his face back to the sight down the lane, ignoring both Sarah's presence and the thump of Mrs Lamont's boots coming in the back, for something was shifting in the distance, resolving itself into a figure driving a trap. Robert stood up.

'Where're you going? You've not ate your dinner yet.'

But the boy had already unlatched the door. He stumbled on the cobbles of the 'street' in his haste but recovered, hurtling along the path to meet the trap.

Cairncross got down, leaving the reins dangling, knowing his pony was too lazy to go anywhere he didn't have to.

'What's this?'

'Can we go, mister?'

The man's eyes flicked up the path to the farmhouse. 'Wait on me here, then. That oul' hoor'll be wanting her money.'

Robert stroked the pony's nose, though the animal took no notice, too busy cropping the grass that grew rank between the wheel ruts scored in the earth of the lane.

*

The village, not much more than a cobbled street of single-storey dwellings, was coming into sight. Robert felt important, sitting up on the trap beside the land agent. He wanted the people to open their half-doors and lean out to see his progress.

'Don't say much, do you?' said Cairncross.

Robert paused. 'Naeb'dy wants to hear what I say.'

This made Cairncross shout with laughter, to the boy's surprise.

'Your woman'll make up for that. Where you're going, I mean. She's a powerful talker, so she is.' The man twitched the rein with his left hand, and the pony ambled to a stop. The trap shuddered as Cairncross jumped down. Then he turned to lift the boy, though Robert was sure he could have managed alone.

His thin body tipped forward into the man's arms, making him physically closer to Cairncross than he'd ever been; he could smell peat smoke, tobacco and horses on the man's overcoat. Robert stood wordlessly clutching his little bag as Cairncross dusted the greasy cloth of his shoulders.

'She's a seamstress, so she is. Mebbe she'll get ye better claethes than these.'

Robert glanced round. Their visit had garnered the attention he'd wanted only moments ago, but somehow it was less welcome now he had lost the vantage point of the trap. Three or four faces looked unsmilingly in their direction above folded arms resting on half-doors.

'And a good day to yerself too, Ma Henderson,' called out Cairncross to a woman two doors along. The face retreated and the half-door banged shut.

'Oul' bitch,' muttered Cairncross.

Robert stored up this expression where he had deposited 'oul' hoor'. He knew what would have happened to him had *he* spoken that way before Lamont or the schoolmaster. Cairncross seemed blithely indifferent. He wondered what the man thought of the woman they were going to see. Then, as if able to read his thoughts Cairncross said, 'She's a taig, our one. But no harm in her, for all that.'

This, for Robert, was the most astonishing thing of all. A papist! He'd never met one, though he knew who they were and why they were to be avoided. There'd been none in the National School, of course, a fact he'd never questioned, assuming they were corralled in some other school, or behind an impenetrable convent wall, or didn't go to school at all. After all, didn't he know that theirs was a religion based on superstition and ignorance? That's what the preacher with the nice lady assistant who'd given him the pamphlet had told him and his companions, and a man with a collar that starched would of course know such a thing. And now Cairncross, in broad daylight, with others looking on, was knocking fit to wake the dead on the door of this house, and he, Robert McClure, would go under the roof of a taig. What would Mammy say? Did she know?

A bolt was drawn and both parts of the door swung back. Looking shyly downwards, holding his cap in his grubby fingers, Robert first saw a woman's ankles encased in small side-buttoned boots, around which a black and white cat furled itself. His eyes travelled slowly upwards, past a rusty-looking black dress. Robert found it hard to say how old women were, but this one was younger than Mrs Lamont, and perhaps younger even than Mammy. She was smiling.

'Come away in, wee man.'

'What about me?' said Cairncross.

'You too,' she laughed. 'When aren't you in here?'

Robert marvelled at the clean smell of the flagstoned room. It was a pure scent, laced with vinegar, as if the space were a smaller version of the kitchen at the Big House. Then he became aware of four pairs of eyes intently watching him; none of their owners feared him. The cats were simply assessing him. Their presence was a surprise; Patsy at the farmhouse had lived in the outbuildings. One day Lamont had come in to find Sarah playing with the cat on the hearthrug and had chased the animal out with such roaring that Robert had been convinced Patsy would be gone forever. But no, going out to school the following morning, he'd stepped over the remains of a mouse.

'Sit yourselves down till I make yous a cup of tea,' said the woman. Robert wondered where he should sit: there were two chairs, one either side of the fireplace, each carrying a crushed-looking cushion made of some busily floral material. He looked round at Cairncross seeking permission; the land agent was hanging his coat and hat on a hook by the door.

Does he live here, so?

'Sit down, boy, as the lady told ye.'

Robert did so, wondering where it was Cairncross got his confidence. Was it something that came to you when you were big, and if it didn't, had you to pretend you had it and hope you'd not be found out? Did it come when you'd a horse to drive in a trap?

The woman came back with a jug of water. Taking a poker from its hook by the fireplace, she lifted the lid of the black kettle hanging there and topped it up. Robert was close enough not just to hear the hiss of steam but to feel its damp heat. As the woman bent over, the boy glanced up at something pinned to the chimney breast: a small four-armed cross made of reeds, plaited at the centre and its limbs tied with thread. He was aware there were other things adorning the whitewashed walls of the room but he hadn't the courage to stare at them just yet. He had an impression though of garish colour, of moon-pale faces gazing down at him. In the Lamont household the only pictures had been framed sprays of flowers or cottages of a kind he'd never seen bearing legends like 'GOD is our refuge and strength' and 'The Fear of the Lord tendeth to Life'. He didn't feel fear in this room, just some bewilderment.

'I'll learn you to make them, so I will,' said the woman, lifting her head in the direction of the little cross. 'You can gather the reeds for me.'

Robert remembered his gift then, and scrabbled inside his shirt to bring out the bundle of bog cotton. He held it out wordlessly, but his face heated when he saw how many of the stalks were bent. This didn't seem to matter to the woman.

'Aw, God love ye,' she said. She took the offering, stroking the fluffy heads. 'I'll get a jar for them.'

As the woman clattered behind a door, Cairncross came and leaned on the mantelshelf.

'I'll have to keep my eye on you,' he said, smiling. 'A rival.'

Robert couldn't think why.

'An' teaching you her popery already.'

The woman returned then, with the bog cotton in an old bloater-paste jar, which she placed on the windowsill overlooking the yard – Robert realised the house was only one room deep with a scullery built on out the back, though he could see doors that must lead to other spaces, and wondered where he would sleep. The pale sunshine lit the bog-cotton heads from behind and the boy saw that they were beautiful. In a flurry of movement on the other side of the glass a ginger cat appeared on the windowsill, looking through first at the bog cotton and then at Robert.

'How many cats have ye?' he asked.

'Oh . . . six or seven maybe. They keep moving so I've never thought to count them. That's the first thing ye've said since coming under my roof, child. Will you not tell me your name at least?'

'I'm Robert James McClure.'

'Sure you are. Your mammy's at the Big House.' She glanced up at Cairncross, and looked back at the boy. 'I see it now, right enough. How could I not have done?'

'When will I see her?' Robert asked.

The adults exchanged looks over his head but, instead of answering him, the woman spoke to Cairncross instead.

'She'll not be wanting to see *me*, James.'

Robert watched Cairncross with renewed interest. He hadn't known the man's first name.

'I'll take him,' said Cairncross.

The black and white cat jumped into the boy's lap, turning round and round to make itself comfortable, claws kneading his scrawny thigh muscles.

CHAPTER THREE

The Big House, Crossgar, 1895

> 'The Irish landlords continued to be colonists. The very building of their houses, the planting of their trees, the making of the walls around their estates ... they lived within their demesnes, making a world of their own, with Ireland outside the gates.'

> Elizabeth Burke Plunkett, Lady Fingall,
> *Seventy Years Young*, 1937

Three weeks later Robert sat up alongside Cairncross, feeling his heart lift and lift, so much so he was afraid his whole body would levitate and float away. To calm himself he gripped the edge of the studded leather seat of the trap with both hands. He wore new clothes, or at least new to him. Kathleen, as she'd told him to call her, had reshaped them for him from another boy's garments. Robert didn't know who this other boy was though he had asked himself if he'd grown out of them or had died wearing them. The grimmer thought of the two had come to him when these marvels had been brought home from the dealer, and

Kathleen had insisted on hanging them several days outside on the washing line. There they had flapped and careened like the crow corpses Lamont would tie to the gate of the field where the young lambs were, and forget about until they fell apart.

Cairncross's reassuring bulk sat to his right, close enough that Robert could smell that peculiarly male scent of his. Kathleen, the boy had noticed, smelled of the lavender bags he'd seen her folding into her carefully pressed linen whenever the angry little flat-iron had been put by and the cats and himself warned not to go near it until it was cool. His mother, whom Cairncross told him he would see in about a quarter of an hour, he remembered as smelling always of whatever she had cooked last for the people in the Big House. Whenever he thought of her, it was with flour ingrained in the creases of her knuckles and dusty in her neck when she picked him up and swung him about: 'My own wee darlin'.' His mother always cried when she saw him, even though she kept telling him how pleased she was he was there.

His excitement wasn't dampened when Cairncross drove past the Lodge House. Robert caught a glimpse of the avenue and wondered again why the Big House people had wanted it so much wider and straighter than the road the trap travelled if they didn't want people coming up it. Cairncross followed instead the curve of the demesne wall, though the reins were so loose in his hands that Robert realised it was the horse who really knew where they were going. Indeed, the animal turned his head without being told and entered the more modest entrance that led quickly to the Offices, or as Robert had heard the family's terrifying English footman mysteriously call these outbuildings, 'the

Home Farm'. As they approached, a bow-legged man emerged from one of the stables and touched his hand briefly to his cap before he disappeared into another doorway.

The horse ambled to a halt in the middle of the courtyard. 'Wait there and I'll get ye,' said Cairncross, swinging down from the trap. 'Can't have ye falling and getting your new clothes dirty.'

Standing by the trap, Robert reached out a hand to stroke the flank of the horse.

'You remember where to go, so?' said Cairncross.

The boy nodded.

'I'll be back for ye at five, so I will. I'll get away now before yer woman sees me, then.' He flashed his strong white teeth at Robert, who was wondering why the man wouldn't want Mammy to see him. The only people *he* never wanted to see were those he was afraid of, and Robert couldn't imagine Cairncross ever being afraid of anyone.

Cairncross hauled himself up in a rattle of tack and, with a few companionable sounds to the horse, turned the trap around. Robert looked across the courtyard and saw the woman standing in the doorway, wrapping her hands in her apron. Calling, 'Mammy,' he was on her in seconds, his face buried in her midriff. At eleven years old he still awaited the height Kathleen said would come on him when he wasn't looking. Yet his mother appeared and felt smaller than he remembered. She held him there for what seemed an age but couldn't have been, for he could still hear the wheels of the trap on the pitted asphalt. Eventually she relinquished him and stood gazing at him, her hands on his shoulders, then stroking his face and hair.

'You're a fine wee man, so you are. He should be proud of you.'

'Who, Mammy?'

'Never mind him, though. Come away in.'

*

Robert loved the warm fug of the big kitchen, the vast black range that he was convinced only someone as big and strong as Cairncross could work the handles of, the copper saucepans gleaming on their hooks, the row of blue and white delph along the mantelshelf, each plate looking as if it had been spaced from the next with a ruler. And here on the big table, a plate of still-warm soda farls was pushed towards him and he was told to eat as many as he wanted. Other servants came in and out: that intimidatingly liveried English footman, a housemaid who looked not many years older than himself, but old enough for him to think her a grown-up, though the girl smiled shyly at him. The ostler who'd touched his cap to Cairncross came in, vigorously scraping his boots before he crossed the threshold, though the day was dry, and looked intently at Robert before saying, 'Sure he's grown, Meg, a fine wee man.' Robert's mother got up then, to pour the man a cup of tea. The boy didn't notice when he left.

'So you're with the seamstress now?' she said when they were alone, though Robert sensed from the way she spoke that she'd known this for some time.

'I am so. She altered these for me,' he said, holding the lapel of his jacket.

His mother's eyes flickered over him in silence, but to his disappointment she made no comment.

'The shirt's brand new, so it is. I saw her make it. I help her a bit, so I do.'

'Making you work, is she?'

'Oh no!' he said. 'I asked. She's this machine. Sure it's the best thing I've ever seen. Black and shiny with gold flowers painted on it – real gold paint – and wee silvery bits that move up and down. I wind the bobbins for her only I've to stand up for to do it because if I'm sitting my foot won't reach the treadle. She's only the black thread and white for shirts and linen and sometimes some dark blue but it's the black mainly. For the funerals and that. She gets awful tired then because she says sure nobody knows when somebody's going to die and they've not the weeds ready, or if they do know, they're too busy with the poor sufferer to think about it and you wouldn't want to go ordering your claethes anyway with the sick person still breathing as it'd be like you want them gone, wouldn't it?'

'You've found your tongue in that house!'

'I talk to the cats, so I do. The machine's on a wee table of its own in the room I sleep in, and if I fold myself up small I can get under it and Ricky – he's my favourite of all them cats – comes in with me and I tell him about how I'm going to sew too for the fancy people in Belfast and get rich and have a big house with a kitchen like this one and you can live there with me and Kathleen.'

His mother drew her hands back a few inches.

'She'd not want to live with me, that one.'

Robert hesitated. 'So I'd need two houses. She'd maybe want that for the cats, right enough.'

'More tea?'

'Yes please.'

'I'll make it fresh.'

Robert went on eating, his eyes following his mother around the room.

'What's a by-blow?' he asked.

'Don't speak with your mouth full, Robert, I can't hear you properly.'

He hadn't, but he repeated it anyway.

'Why do you want to know?' She came over and took his cup to refill it, not looking at him.

'I heard the teachers at the school say it. They were look-ing at the register with all the names on and one of them went, "Another of Cairncross's by-blows if I'm not mistaken," only the other one went, "Shh," but not in a way she was cross. More like a laughing way.'

'Do you like him?'

'Mr Cairncross? I do so. Kathleen does. But the neighbours won't smile for him. Maybe it's because he calls them bad names, though he doesn't do it to their faces. But he never bothers his head about them, so he doesn't.'

'He wouldn't. I'm going to see if Albert wants another cup, seeing as it's fresh. When he comes in, let's not talk about Mr Cairncross.'

She opened the door and called out. Albert turned out to be the ostler, and yes, he would have another cup, thank you. Robert wasn't sure about the way the man put his chair close to his mother's, but he'd seen Cairncross do the same in Kathleen's house, so he supposed it was just what grown people did. When the man rose from the table – Robert noticed that he could never be still for long, even when seated – he reached across and pumped the boy's unsuspecting hand and said, 'Well, I'm pleased to make your acquaintance again, Robert. I hope you'll come back to see us soon.' Robert was impressed. Was it something about living in the Big House that made people talk that way?

*

When Cairncross's trap got back to Kathleen's house, he left Robert to climb down himself. He seemed anxious to be gone, muttering something about 'She'll have seen enough of me for one day.' Robert pushed open the door and went in, and stopped. He was sure he could smell the land agent's presence, and wondered if Cairncross had been there while he'd been sitting in the kitchen of the Big House. Kathleen came through from the little scullery and ruffled his hair. She smiled, but he thought she looked sad nevertheless.

'Did you have a nice time, wee man?'

'I did so,' he said, and threw his arms around her, feeling that he shouldn't have been gone so long if she wasn't happy too.

CHAPTER FOUR

Andrews' Mill, Comber, 1898

'I give my heart to any wee girl
What lives to be a spinner
That has a discontented mind,
From breakfast-time to dinner.'

Nineteenth-century traditional song, Ulster

'I think I'll never get used to it, Mother! The noise ... and I'll
never get good at picking off them bobbins.'

'The doffing, you mean?' said Mary Maguire.

'Yes – them other girls are so much faster, even if some of them
aren't as big as me.'

Her mother pulled the trembling child closer. The girl was
shivering with tiredness as much as from the crisp cold of the
morning. The shift would start in an hour's time, at six.

'They're half-timers, that's why. There's a woman on my
floor told me. They'll have been in the mill two years already,
some of them, a day in school, a day in work. That's how. You'll
catch up with them, my blue-eyed girl. And never forget, you've
something they don't have.'

Annie sniffed, looking up. All she could think about was yesterday's shame of dropping the full bobbins, three or four of them rolling away beneath the machine, and how one of the women had pulled her back sharply by the waistband of her skirt. 'Wantin' to kill yerself, are ye?' Annie wasn't going to tell her mother that. The foreman had come, and with a stick poked the bobbins out. The noise had been too great for the man to have heard her tearful thanks, but she'd said them anyway.

'There's precious little schooling they'll have had, them half-timers, if every day they know they'll be in the mill at six in the morning the next day and out at six at night. Sure their teachers'll not bother much with them. You've learned a good hand, and your numbers. Some day you'll find a use for them.'

Annie couldn't think how. All she could think was that she missed school, and was angry with herself for not liking it enough when she'd still been there. Today the terrifying combination of boredom and exhaustion would start all over again, and stretch into an immeasurable future. What use was a good hand if all that was needed of her now was to dart from row to row and feed the remorseless machines with bobbins?

'Even if we could work together, that would be better. It's like going into the workhouse – being separated.'

'Ssh!' said her mother. 'We all of us have work, and don't have to be out in all weathers to do it. And we've a roof over our heads.'

'Dadda's out in all weathers, so he is.'

'He likes it that way, even when it rains and the days are long.'

'It's not just the work,' said Annie tearfully. 'It's Comber.' She thought she would never get used to the clatter of horses and carts, the having to walk around people on the pavements, the feeling of being observed from upper windows when going out to hang the washing in the back yard. The call of peewits and yellowhammers could not be heard in this street, only the cackle of laughter from the women leaning over their half-doors, the stumbling and slurring men coming home late at night. Her father though had found work at the distillery, delivering the bottles as far as Belfast sometimes, and at other times distributing the potale, the grain waste, as animal feed to the neighbouring farms. He'd told his daughter so many times that it pleased him to go to the farms 'but not to have the bother of one myself anymore' that she'd realised eventually he was only trying to convince himself.

'Go and wash, child,' said her mother. 'I've to make our breakfasts and our dinners for to take with us.'

Breakfast, thought the child, *with all them others. Is there nowhere I can be alone?*

*

Yet unexpectedly, that day was better. Annie was at breakfast with the others, huddled on stools at the end of the hall because rain was beating mercilessly on the yard outside, when there was a scuffle behind her, and she turned to see a cloud of auburn hair, a drift of freckles and a pair of widely spaced grey-green eyes smiling at her.

'I'm Teresa Nolan,' said the apparition through gappy teeth. 'You the new one then?'

Annie nodded, her mouth full of bread and jam.

'Terrible, isn't it now?' said Teresa. 'You'll be thinking you'll never get used to it. Peel off a bit of that crust for me?'

Annie looked down at what remained of the bread and, tearing back the crust on the upper slice, gave it grudgingly to Teresa. She had been planning to eat the crusts last, and wondered how she would get on with this Teresa if they were her favourite bits too. The crust disappeared down the girl's gullet with a speed that startled Annie. She was reminded of a bird with a worm, an impression reinforced when her new friend put her head on one side and regarded her for a moment.

'How old are you then?'

'Thirteen this last week.' Thinking it was expected of her, she said, 'What about you?'

'Fourteen. I been here a year. You get faster, so you do. Don't go anywhere. I'm away to ask the doffing mistress something.' With a scatter of crumbs and a slap of bare feet on boards, Teresa tore off down the line of women chewing bread and drinking lemonade or cold tea. The space where she'd been suddenly felt cold to Annie.

In a flurry of skirts and the faint tang of sweat Teresa settled back beside her. 'I'm getting to run with you, so I am. I promised I'd make you faster, so I'd better.'

And it worked. Teresa taught Annie to look ahead, to scan the rows of bobbins to see which were getting full, in an elaborate game of juggling and timing. It became a competition with the machines to keep them running full pelt, to work the best way to eye the bobbins and calculate how many scurryings back and forth were needed with the empties and the ones already fully wound, how many could be carried in one go, whether it was worth waiting a few seconds more for another bobbin to be ready. The girls fell into a rhythm, in which they could call out as they passed on their run where to go to next.

'I think I might even get to like it,' Annie said to her mother, walking home that evening.

*

A year later it was Annie who got up with the knocker-up and prepared her own breakfast to take to the mill, leaving her mother to wheeze and cough and sweat in the room above. She glanced up as the back door opened and Mrs Doyle came in, bringing with her a familiar odour of musty clothes and boiled cabbage.

'What night did she have?' asked the old woman, as she always did.

'I was in to her three times with the coughing,' said Annie, remembering going outside in the black silence before dawn to sluice the blood-flecked phlegm out of the tin bowl. Back in bed Annie's feet never really recovered their warmth, and she achieved not much more than a doze. Regularly now, sitting by the fire mending of an evening, she would find herself nodding off like a woman of seventy, not a girl of fourteen.

'God love your poor mother,' said Mrs Doyle.

If he does, why can't he spare her? Annie grasped the knife tighter, her knuckles whitening.

'Have you the window open?' asked the woman.

'I have, the way the doctor said.'

Mrs Doyle grunted her disapproval. This was a bone of contention between the two. It was hard enough finding the money to pay the doctor, never mind not taking the advice he gave. 'Outside, preferably in sea air,' he'd said was best, 'and failing that, fresh air, whatever the time of year.' Annie wasn't sure if for him Strangford Lough counted or if she and her father were somehow expected to trundle the sick woman on a cart to Ardglass; for her mother's sake she hoped the lough was enough. She'd never seen the narrow channel joining it to the Irish Sea except on a school-room map but took comfort from the fact that it must exist – it shouldn't really be called a lough at all, then, should it?

'Will we need the sheets off her?' said Mrs Doyle.

'We will so,' said Annie, laying down the knife and rolling her hands in her apron. She followed the old woman's swaying bottom up the narrow staircase, holding her breath. In the room above, with the sash open and the tang of her mother's night sweat, Mrs Doyle's sour smell would be less noticeable.

Mary Maguire was almost upright in bed, propped against a bolster, three pillows and beneath them a rolled-up rug, all with the aim of making it easier for her to breathe. Her face was bluish-pale.

'You're awful good to me,' she said, her glittering eyes focusing on her neighbour. She'd stopped saying, 'I'm sorry for all the trouble I'm causing,' some weeks ago, when Annie had begged her not to: 'It's not that you can help it, can you?'

The nails in Mrs Doyle's boots scraped on the dark varnish of the floorboards as she went to the window and pulled down the sash.

'Just while we change her,' she said, not looking at Annie, who was already pulling back the bedclothes. Mary Maguire let out a whimper. 'No reason for us all to catch our deaths,' added Mrs Doyle.

Annie didn't even wince; she'd heard the woman's tactless comment too many times already. There was no sign in her mother's exhausted face that she'd registered it. Annie said nothing, knowing that none of them in that house could do without Mrs Doyle, and that Mrs Doyle herself knew it. She might be old and smelly, but she was cheap and strong with shoulders and arms that could lift the sick woman – even when she'd been heavier than she was now – and work the mangle. With the night sweats, there were sheets on the line in the yard all the time, not just on Mondays. Annie had marked the ones that belonged to her mother, remnants of not just Mrs Maguire's own bottom drawer but also of Annie's grandmother's. The others were loaned by the ladies of the St Vincent de Paul, and would go back to them when they were no longer needed. After Mrs Finucane, the solicitor's wife, had brought those sheets to the house, Annie had resisted using them as long as she could, haunted by the thought of who else might have died wrapped in the bleached poplin, but she'd accepted the kindness with the gratitude the woman expected. After a while she was too exhausted to think about whose sheets were continually stretched on the bed. All of them were quickly imbued with the earthy scent of peat, from being draped on the little wooden airer by the fire. Annie wondered if her mother loved that smell as much as she did. To her, it had come with them from the farm along with the furniture. She didn't ask though. She didn't want to know if having ravaged lungs meant more than not being able to breathe properly.

'Get along with you now, child,' said Mrs Doyle, not unkindly. Annie bent over the bed and kissed her mother's clammy forehead. She held her face stiffly immobile until she got downstairs and washed her mouth at the kitchen sink.

Annie had one more task before going to the mill. She'd brought the ewer and basin down with her mother's potty the moment she'd woken. The potty was back under the bed and the basin on the washstand. She now only had to bring up the ewer filled with warm water. Annie did not wash her mother. Mrs Doyle had made it quite clear from the start that she was not to.

'She wouldn't want it,' the woman said firmly. 'It's not right for a girl to do such things for them that has brought her into the world. She can do it for others. Honour your father and mother – don't see them as helpless as babes.'

Placing the ewer outside the bedroom door, Annie heard her mother's indistinct murmur and Mrs Doyle's cajoling response.

'Sure we'll get you to the window when the weather's warmer. Then you can have all the fresh air you want. I'll move you now and get some calamine on them sores, will I?'

Annie left the house in the half-light. She didn't look up to see if the window had been reopened; she knew it wouldn't have been. However, she fully expected that by the time she came home, the sash would be up as it always was, but it would only be because Mrs Doyle wanted to stop her complaining. The air of the room would be so close that Annie knew the window had only been opened minutes before.

By the time she reached the mill it was almost daylight, an oppressive, pearly-grey shimmer. Annie prayed to be so busy that she couldn't think about home.

At breakfast she and Teresa sat, as they usually did, not so far apart from the other women as to cause offence, but enough to give them some privacy.

'How is she the day?' murmured Teresa.

'Not so good.'

A quick touch on the arm, and the girls began to eat.

CHAPTER FIVE

Comber, 1899

'The boiler house is quite ready . . . We have engaged a manager for the mill at a high salary . . . We are most anxious to commence hackling in March . . .'

From the letter books of Andrews Flax Mill, Comber
(Public Record Office of Northern Ireland), 1864

Then warm days came, and with them the letters that had to be written to Canada, folded into a few black-barred envelopes bought singly from the stationer's so that their recipients could prepare themselves for the news inside. The sash was flung open and the last clammy sheets stripped from the bed, this time for burning, for they were pink-spotted with the last bloody spume from Mary's lungs.

In the twilight of the little front parlour, the curtains closed here as at all the other windows until after the funeral, Annie rolled away the mattress her father had slept on those last few months. She swept and dusted. The gateleg table was opened and covered with a white linen cloth pristine enough to grace an altar. Upstairs she heard the tread of the undertaker's men and their murmurings, interspersed with the higher tones of Teresa's mother Philomena and Mrs Doyle, now in her creaky best bombazine. Mary Maguire would not have the benefit of having her coffin hoisted on the shoulders of the men she'd made, the men bearing the name that had been her own for so much of her life that she'd sometimes had to think what she'd used to be called. She would, though, have someone with her every moment until the earth closed over her coffin. As Mary had told her wide-eyed daughter at least ten years earlier, no one knew the moment when the soul left its earthly temple, but keening and prayers kept the devil from snatching it before it safely reached Purgatory. The closed curtains and covered mirrors meant Satan could not even see in. Annie absorbed everything in silence pale and dry-eyed. She took her turn at the side of the coffin but was quite sure the devil had got bored and gone to peer through the cracks in other people's curtains.

'I know you're not there, Mammy,' she whispered at the dead woman's marble profile, at the bony fingers with their bloodless nails, cat's-cradling a rosary. 'I don't know where I'll ever find you again, so I don't.' Several times she nodded off in her chair, waking with a start and finding herself straining her ears for a cough, before she remembered.

Now Annie stood close to her father's shoulder, though not touching, at the lip of the grave. Behind them stood a damp little knot of people. Some of the Protestant hands from the mill had come to pay their respects too, though they didn't come into the burial ground, much less into the church itself, but huddled respectfully at the roadside. Thomas was crouching now; Annie distinctly heard the crack of his knee joint. A fistful of earth thudded damply onto the coffin. Straightening up, he nudged her elbow. Annie bent, gathered a clammy fistful, threw it.

Then quite suddenly it was all over: the priest was shaking her father's hand, inclining his head to her, saying the professional words of condolence. Annie tried to smile at the pinch-faced altar boy who accompanied him, but the child seemed not to notice. Annie thought he looked cold though the day was mild; she guessed he didn't get enough to eat and hoped the priest would bring him back to the house. Now the other people were coming up to them. More handshakings, more murmurings of 'Sorry for your trouble,' and then they melted away, stumping and swaying in Sunday shoes up the slope to the crouching church.

A small hand snaked round her forearm.

'Teresa!'

'I'll be back at your house. Mammy's gone with Mrs Doyle to make the tea.'

*

Later, after the Nolans had gone home, and Mrs Doyle had murmured with Thomas at the back door as he handed her a fistful of coins for the laying-out, Annie put away the tea things that Philomena Nolan had insisted on washing up herself. More than once she found herself putting things in the wrong place.

'Ah sure, what does it matter?' she said to herself. 'The right place was back on the farm.'

Her father came in then, his jacket over his arm, his free hand fiddling with his collar stud. He gave up, dropped the dark garment on a chair and put his arms around Annie.

'They've all gone. We can cry now.' Thomas dropped his head to her thin shoulder and sobbed. It was only the second time Annie had ever seen him weep; the first had been after Polly had been led away. Her own crying was almost silent, great gulping shudders, as far as they could be from the high-pitched keening that had come from Philomena Nolan and Mrs Doyle when the coffin still lay on the table in the parlour, a sound more to do with the driving away of some nameless evil than with the grief that would go on, day after day, a deep bruise that never quite faded.

*

'A lodger?' said Annie. 'Where would we put her?'

'Him,' said her father. Annie's shoulders relaxed as she realised she needn't have worried. *He wouldn't do it, sure he wouldn't. Not with her only three months in the ground.* Even if her father wasn't thinking of marrying again, she didn't want another woman under their roof. But any lodger would mean fewer walks with Teresa, and going to the vigil mass on Saturday evening where you saw nobody but homebodies like herself, so that she would be free to prepare the Sunday midday meal for her father and this stranger, the moment they got back from Our Lady of the Visitation. It was the only meal of the week where they were neither rushed nor tired. Her father slept upstairs again, in the room Annie and Mrs Doyle had swabbed down with vinegar and hot water. The curtains had been taken down and washed, the palliasse taken out and burned and a new one bought. She had scrubbed the floorboards on hands and knees, and with a handkerchief tied around her face and the window wide open she had painted them over with another layer of treacly varnish, working section by section.

'We need him,' said Thomas. 'With not having your mother's wages. I'm still paying the doctor – and Fitzsimons the undertaker.'

Annie knew this. She'd seen the accounts, and the scrap of paper her father kept with them, with each month's payment ruled through.

'Mr Crawford,' said her father. 'A respectable man, a widower. The people where he is just now are going to England.'

Correctly interpreting Annie's surprise, he added, 'It's a Protestant town, Comber, so we have to mix with them. And you'll know him when you see him. He's at Andrews' too. A hackler, combing the flax – so a skilled man. He was at the gates there at Our Lady of the Visitation when your mother was buried. A quiet sort of fellow. We can make over the parlour to him, so's he has his own front door. A bit more private that way.'

'His meals?'

'He'll have them with us, of course. It's no more work to make for three than for two, is it now?'

'I suppose.' Annie was wondering if the Protestant gentleman would be the kind who'd sit on the privy reading the newspaper, whether he'd get up from his meal and go straight to his room, or whether he'd expect to sit in the chair she usually sat in opposite her father as the evenings ebbed away. Still . . . the rent.

*

Reginald Crawford had brought with him only a grip. Annie thought this wasn't much to show for someone who had lived as long as her father. He'd shaken hands with her when her father brought him in: his grasp had been cool and soft, though she thought the man had held onto her hand a little longer than was necessary and she hadn't cared for the way his sandy-lashed eyes had travelled over her face, down the length of her body and then up again, *But sure, what would you know about it? Protestants are different, maybe.* She felt a little spark of resentment that the man seemed to know the house already. *Dadda musta shown him when I wasn't here.*

Annie prepared the deal table in the back room for their meal, an ear cocked to hear the furtive sounds that came from the front parlour. The gateleg table on which her mother's coffin had rested had been sold, an iron-framed bed bought to take its place. Her father got up from his chair by the hearth as Annie put down the dinner plates.

'You'll need to tell Mr Crawford his dinner's ready.'

'Could *you* not get him?' muttered Annie.

'Catch yourself on, child,' said Thomas quietly. 'There's no harm in him, so there isn't.'

Biting her lip, Annie went to knock softly on the door to what was now Crawford's room, stifling a yelp as the handle immediately turned to reveal the lodger in his shirtsleeves.

'Forgive me, my dear, I didn't mean to startle you.' Annie wished the man wouldn't smile so. She took a step back and nearly stumbled.

The awkwardness deepened when at the table Thomas cleared his throat and muttered grace, followed by Annie's echo.

Both of them rapidly, almost furtively, crossed themselves, as Crawford's hands lay palms down either side of his plate, and he murmured some words of his own.

Between the clicks of pewter on delph, Thomas kept the conversation going, for Annie's benefit asking things she knew he already knew the answer to.

'I was telling Annie you've been at Andrews' five years, is it?'

Crawford dabbed his moustache with his napkin. 'I have so, and a fine firm it is too. Mr Andrews is a good, God-fearing man and a friend to Comber.'

'You know him?'

Crawford hesitated. 'By repute.'

'Where was it you were before Andrews'?' asked Annie quietly.

Crawford turned to her with a slight laugh and raised eyebrows, as if surprised she'd spoken at all. 'Belfast,' he said. 'York Street Mill. The biggest in Ireland it must be.'

'Oh! Did you not want to stay there then?'

Annie caught the flash of anger in the man's eyes, quickly suppressed. Her father fidgeted; she heard his chair creak.

'It's our fortune Mr Crawford didn't,' said her father.

Crawford relaxed his grip on his fork. 'My dear wife died. Every corner of that building reminded me of her. She'd had family in Newtownards. I thought I might have happier memories of her down here.'

'I'm sorry for your loss,' said Annie, her eyes dropping to her plate.

That slight laugh, again.

'Have ye children, Mr Crawford?' asked Thomas.

A sigh Annie thought deliberate, then, 'My wife and I were not blessed with that heritage of the Lord,' he said. He took a swig of his tea.

Annie observed Reginald Crawford over the meat and potatoes, thinking he was the kind of man she could have passed in the street – in fact probably had – without noticing him. Then the lodger glanced up from his plate to meet her eyes and stretched his lips at her. To cover her confusion and the sudden heating of her face, Annie coughed and reached for her napkin, longing for the meal to be over.

As she took the dirty plates into the scullery she heard snatches of the conversation at the table; the timbre of her father's voice deepened when he spoke with other men. As she put the plates of rice pudding down in front of each man, the two fell silent. Though she didn't look at him again, Annie was aware of the lodger's eyes on her.

Ten minutes later Crawford pushed his chair back. 'I can see I will be very well cared for here, Miss Maguire. That was an excellent repast. I take it the water in my ewer is fresh?'

'It is so.'

'Then I will take my leave of you. I always read my Bible for an hour before retiring. I shall reflect on my good fortune in coming under your roof: "I was a stranger and you welcomed me."' Crawford stood, and Thomas followed. Annie wondered if they were meant to shake hands again. She reached instead for the empty plates.

'Goodnight, then,' added Crawford.

'There's a basket for your linen,' said Annie suddenly. 'If you'd put it out Monday morning before going to work then Mrs Doyle will have it laundered. Your sheets once a fortnight. If you'd put them out too.' Reddening, she turned to the scullery, the cutlery clinking on the plates in her hands.

'Ah, so you'll not be taking care of my things yourself?'

Annie paused in the doorway.

'If Mrs Doyle sees there's mending to do, she'll tell me. I can't be doing the washing as well; I'm at the mill six to six and Sundays aren't for working.'

'Right enough. But you'll be cleaning my room, will you not?'

'That would be me with Mrs Doyle, yes.'

'That sounds satisfactory. Goodnight, then.'

'Goodnight, Mr Crawford.'

*

'I don't like him!' hissed Annie, her eyes beyond her father to the two doors between them and Mr Crawford's Bible. 'I feel itchy, so I do. It's the way he looks at me.'

'Oh sure, there's no harm in him,' said her father, chinking the coins in his pocket as a reminder.

'The hacklers get good money – you know that yourself. And he's no weans. Sure could he not afford a house to himself?'

Thomas hesitated. 'What man can live on his own? He'd have to have a woman in to make his meals. He told me he does good works – sends money to the Proddy orphans at Ballygowan. You can't take agin a man for being lonely.'

Annie breathed in deeply. On the exhale, she said, 'Just don't leave me alone with him.'

Thomas studied her, his only girl, not quite fifteen and a woman's responsibilities thrust on her.

'I'll not. But what was that about Mrs Doyle and his cleaning?'

'Dadda, not so loud. I don't want to be touching his things. Not on my own, anyway.' She shivered.

Thomas patted her shoulder, then left his hand there. 'It'll be all right, so it will. I'll make sure.'

Annie turned from the sink. 'Oh Dadda,' she said, her head sinking onto his chest.

Thomas put his arms around her. 'My own darling girl. I'll see you come to no harm,' he whispered over her hair. 'Is there a wee treat you'd like for yourself – something out of this first week's rent?'

*

The following Sunday afternoon Annie joined Teresa on a bench by the Gillespie Memorial.

'So tell us about yer man,' said Teresa, 'now there's nobody earwigging us.'

Annie wrinkled her nose. 'Well, I don't like his eyes. They're as cold as a dead fish's, only they've them wee black points that bore through you.'

'Does he smell like a dead fish too?'

Annie shuddered. 'He smells, aye, but of that pomade he sticks on his hair and his moustache. I couldn't say what colour they are as they always look wet, so they do. Apart from the tash he's shaved within an inch of his life by the look of him – horrible flabby cheeks that'd make you think of a plucked chicken.'

'Ugh! So you don't like the rest of him either, so you don't?'

'I do not.' She hesitated.

'What is it?'

'I told my da I don't like the way he looks at me.'

'How *does* he look at you?'

'The way I should be ashamed of who I am.' Annie leaned forward a little, hunching her shoulders. 'Like this. That I shouldn't have my bust.'

'Ugh!'

'Only I can't quite catch him doing it. I'll turn round and he'll be behind his newspaper or moving his food about on his plate. He has the finickiest way with his knife and fork you ever saw. He must think Dadda and me a right pair of wee bogtrotters. He always says please and thank you and praises whatever I put in front of him but he eats in a way you'd think he couldn't be enjoying himself. As if mutton and tatties is sinful. Poor Dadda asked him one night would he share a bottle of pale with him and you should have seen the face of him. If he'd come out with some big oul' sermon it would have been better but he has this way of being that polite that cuts like a knife. Said he and his wife had signed the pledge, the both of 'em, and he couldn't in conscience besmirch her memory by contributing in any way to the cause of all the wickedness and misery around us. Poor Dadda put the bottle back in the pantry. I felt for him. I could see he'd been looking forward to it but hadn't wanted to drink it alone. Are all Protestants like that?'

'Not the ones my da has seen coming out of the Brownlow Arms,' said Teresa.

'I got this though,' said Annie, turning her head so her friend could see the pretty tartan ribbon holding back her hair.

'He gave you that?' said Teresa, dismayed.

'Not *him*. Dadda did. A wee present for me out of the rent.'

'So it did come from yer man, really.'

With a quick, irritated movement Annie went to pull out the ribbon. Teresa put her own hand over hers.

'No don't. It's a present from your da, so it is. Don't mind me – I was just being jealous. Where'd you get it?'

'Mickey White's.'

'Take me next time. I love going for messages,[1] even if I'm not getting anything for myself.'

---

[1] Going on an errand.

CHAPTER SIX

Killyleagh, July 1900

'Purify me with hyssop, Lord, and I shall be clean of
sin. Wash me, and I shall be whiter than snow.'

From 'The Order of Celebrating the Sacrament
of Extreme Unction' (pre Second Vatican Council)

From the doorway all Robert could see of the dying woman
was her feet, pale and helpless, sticking out from beneath
the folded-back sheet. He wondered if it was the priest or
the silent nurse who had removed her socks, despite the
fact that as her illness advanced Kathleen had struggled to
keep warm. Although he knew no Latin, Robert strained
all the same to make out the words murmured over the
white-shrouded form, competing with Kathleen's rasping
breath in the close air of the unventilated room.

The boy's fingers sought out the scratch on his chin where
he had cut himself that morning trying for a closer shave.
The little sting of pain distracted from what was happening
in front of him, though not from the distant rat-tat of the

drums and the spattering overlay of the fifes that reached him through the open window of the room behind him. Robert tore himself away from the scene in the bedroom to go and push down the sash, for the marchers of the True Blues Lodge were getting closer. He wondered if they would stop in front of the house, the only Catholic one in the street, to redouble their noise, as they had done in previous years. Surely not? Even a taig should be allowed to die in peace. Kathleen no longer spoke, but the nurse had told him that hearing was the last sense to leave.

He looked around for the cats, but they were nowhere to be seen. Did they know she was dying? He thought they must do. Then he remembered that they'd been wary of the nurse and probably hadn't cared for the clatter of the priest's bicycle in the yard either; the man had come round the back, of course, and by a circuitous route; better that way, given the neighbours were Protestants. Robert wondered what would become of the cats, along with what would become of himself. He felt a stranger in the place he'd thought of as home for five years, the only place he had ever really felt *was* home.

*

On the threshold of the bedroom he saw the priest anoint Kathleen's eyelids, her ears, her skeletal chest, her feet, to the drone of the Latin. The boy shivered; the ritual to him was incomprehensible, pagan – foreign. One mercy, though: the marchers this year had not come past Kathleen's door.

What was the point, Robert thought, *of trying to put fear into a poor woman who was leaving anyway, whether she wanted to or not?* He heard again her voice telling him that first Twelfth of July he'd been with her, with the cacophony of the Orangemen's drums and fifes and pipes and shoenails reverberating against the windows, that 'Sure, isn't it all for show? They know I'll not leave this street for all the noise they make, for it's Mr Cairncross keeps me here. And now I've a fine wee Protestant gentleman to look after so they'd hardly be putting *you* out, would they?'

The priest was putting away his oils in a little bag, snapping it closed. He looked up at Robert, as though surprised to see him still there.

'Has she grave clothes?' he asked.

Robert nodded. 'There's instructions for the undertaker, too.' He thought about his own words afterwards, identifying them as the first he'd spoken as a man.

'Right, so,' said the priest briskly. 'She'll go in with her husband, God rest him.'

Robert opened his mouth to say that Cairncross still lived – and Kathleen too, just about – but stopped himself in time. The land agent had muttered something to him one day about Kathleen being a widow, but he had never heard her speak of the man she'd married; there were no images of him about the place. *But maybe she put them away so the poor dead fella didn't see Mr Cairncross.*

After the priest had wobbled off, his bag in the basket on the handlebars of the bicycle, Robert took up his place by the side of the bed, opposite the nurse. He wanted to hold Kathleen's hand. He wanted to cry. Yet he was afraid to touch her, as if he would violate whatever the oils had done and make her journey the more difficult. Robert didn't believe in the Purgatory Kathleen had talked vaguely of, when she could still talk. That is, he didn't believe it for himself. Catholics went there, but he wouldn't, just as Kathleen cycled to mass in Crossgar and sat at the back (as she'd told him), sneaking in after the mass had started and sneaking out before it ended, while he similarly skulked at the back of the Presbyterian church on Plantation Street, though not regularly, since being asked once why he lodged with a taig. 'I was sent, so I was,' was all he could find to say. Presumably if God wanted the faithful separate in life he'd be keeping them apart in heaven as well.

'She's far from all harm,' said the nurse, breaking in on his reverie.

'How long?' he whispered.

'It'll be the night, so it will.'

Kathleen died at dusk. Robert thought there could be no silence as total as that in the little room when the death rattle ceased. The nurse waited a full minute before she rustled to her feet and laid two fingers against Kathleen's neck.

'I loved her,' said Robert. He was startled when the nurse answered, as he hadn't realised he'd spoken out loud.

'Sure you did. She was a good woman, no matter what folk say.'

Robert didn't know how to respond to this but was saved by a knock at the front door that made him jump.

Cairncross filled the doorframe. He looked bigger to Robert than he had the last time' he'd seen him, because Kathleen in dying looked so small, so frail. He brought in a miasma of beer and tobacco, the shreds of celebration of another Twelfth. Robert glimpsed the fringe of his sash poking out of a trouser pocket.

'She's gone, Mr Cairncross.'

The man's face sagged but all he did was squeeze the boy's shoulder.

'Here, Letty, something for your trouble.' The nurse murmured her thanks and then turning to Robert said more clearly, 'Goodbye, Mr McClure, and all luck to ye.'

Startled, for no one had ever called him 'Mister', Robert didn't manage a reply. The moment the door closed, Cairncross said, 'Would you leave me alone with her a moment?'

'I will so.'

Robert sat by the dead fire in the chair he'd occupied the day he was brought to the house. Through the closed door of the bedroom he heard muffled sounds he thought he never would: a man of Cairncross's bulk and confidence, weeping. Something brushed against his leg. He looked down. The cats had returned, were looking at him expectantly. He leaned forward, stroking the head of the nearest one.

'I don't know what'll become of us, so I don't.'

*

He didn't know how long it was that Cairncross sat with Kathleen's corpse. When the door finally opened, the man was blowing his nose into a vast handkerchief, the noise deafening in the silent house.

'Come away in, son,' he said. 'Someone should be sitting with her. It's what the papists do, only there's none of 'em here for her so she'll need to make do with a wee Presbyterian. They'll remove her to Crossgar in the morning. I'll not be let go to her funeral, so I won't. But you'll go for me.'

Robert stared at the man's flushed face. What power existed, he wondered, that would prevent the land agent going to a funeral? As if he'd read his thoughts, Cairncross added, 'Lodge members are forbidden from attending papist functions of any kind. You'll find that out yourself soon enough, when you join.'

*

Kathleen's coffin was lowered into her husband's grave in the presence of the priest, a puny altar boy and a little knot of people who had been her customers. With a small flush of pride Robert recognised them as 'the Quality', members of the Church of Ireland and not members of the Lodge. He was the only one who was nudged to pick up a damp clod of earth and throw it onto the lid.

*

Cairncross called to the little house two days later.

'You've to go to England.'

'Can't I stay here? She trained me up, so she did.'

'The house is needed.'

'Her things . . . She said I was to have the machine . . . the shears and all.'

'Where're you to put them? They can't go on the boat with ye.'

'They can't be sold, so they can't.'

Robert was on the verge of tears when Cairncross said: 'I'll see can they not go to the Offices at the Big House. Same as the cats. In case you come back for them – the machine and the shears and all, I mean, not the beasts. Go to England and you'll be able to save for to open your own shop. There's red gold in Cumberland, son. You've only to dig it out of the ground. I'll make the arrangements.'

*

Cleator Moor
4th April 1901

Dear Mammy,

I do not know did you get my other letters as you have not wrote back. I have changed the place I was living in as there was too many of us. I had to share a bed which I had not done since I went to Kathleen's but as we were grown I had the other fella's feet on the pillow by my face it was not good.

The place I am in now the landlord is English and he was hard for me to understand at first. All the other fellas in my room are from Antrim. We each have our own bed.

The pit is hard work but the foreman told me I would get used to it and I have a bit though the days get no shorter and I miss the daylight. I am only down there until I can get the money for to be a tailor.

Like Mr Cairncross told me would happen, I've been asked would I join the Lodge. There was a wee group of them come to the house and Mr Spedding showed them into the front room. Three gentlemen in new collars and watch-chains come to see me! Everyone tells me it is a great honour. I'll join as they said my job will be safer for it and I would get help if I had any trouble and also because if I do not I would be doing Mr Cairncross an insult because everything here he has got for me: the boat fare, the lodgings, my job in the pit. I did not want him to do them but I do not have a choice and will not until I have the money put by. Perhaps the Lodge will help me get my little shop one day. They knew everything about me, Mammy. They did not say but it could only have been Mr Cairncross told them. So I am making my way in the world.

Your loving son,
Robert

CHAPTER SEVEN

Comber, June 1901

'Linen that wears well and sells at the cheapest price is made in Belfast.'

Advertisement, Robinson & Cleaver, pre-1922

Annie didn't wear her best ribbon in Andrews' Mill. She kept it with what she thought of as her 'special things' in the warped drawer along with a few items of her mother's: worn linen handkerchiefs with her initials embroidered in the corners, a best blouse, the dead woman's baptism certificate and Annie's own.

That Sunday she'd gone upstairs to get the ribbon. Everything was ready for the meal her father would eat after coming back from mass, the stew simmering gently over the fire. Even the fact that Reginald Crawford would be present at that meal didn't damp her enthusiasm. She was alone in the house. Crawford had left after breakfast, wearing a clean collar and ostentatiously clutching his Bible. 'You'd think he was the only person that read it, the way he has about him,' she'd muttered to her father as she opened the back door to swill the tea leaves down the outside drain.

'That's not fair,' he'd said gently, pulling on his boots in readiness for going out to mass, 'and not a good thought for a Sunday.'

'You're right, so you are – and anyway, whatever keeps him out of the house of a Sunday is good for me,' she said, coming up to her father and standing on tiptoes to kiss his forehead. 'Will you light a candle for me, Dadda?'

'I will so.' He pushed his hand into his pocket; she could see the movement of his fingers through the serge as he checked the coins, knowing there'd be one for her, one for her mother, and one for each of her distant brothers.

That day, though, the drawer where the ribbon lay was more difficult to open; it had rained during the night. The effort Annie had to go to meant that when the drawer did eventually come out, it was with a scrape of sound that dragged the entire chest forward on the varnished floor, a noise loud enough to muffle the opening of the front door below. So when Annie trotted down the narrow staircase, humming at the thought of being out after the midday meal on a sunny spring day with Teresa, she could not stifle in time her cry at the sight of a strange man standing in the back room. For he was a strange man – the light from the window obliterated all detail. It was only the scent of his pomade and then the sound of his unctuous voice that revealed his identity.

'The last thing in the world I wanted to do,' he said, 'frightening my charming housekeeper.'

'I wasn't afeart, so I wasn't,' she said, in a voice she knew sounded quite the opposite. She cleared her throat, and in a more normal voice added, 'And I'm not your housekeeper.'

'Oh, fire in a woman, and such a young one. You're blushing with it too. Most becoming. Allow me . . .'

Annie stood open-mouthed, as Crawford came closer to her than he had ever been, to lift a tendril of her hair and tuck it behind her ear. She recoiled at the sheen on his jowly cheeks, the hairs in his nostrils, the wetness of his purplish lips. His pupils were not their usual pinheads but black, gleaming discs. His breathing was laboured.

Without thinking, Annie said, 'You've had drink taken.'

'Never a drop,' he said, grasping her shoulders.

*

Teresa stood up as Annie came hurrying up to their usual bench below Gillespie on his column.

'God love you, what's happened?'

Annie sank onto the bench.

'I'm all right,' she said, bursting into tears. About a hundred yards away a plump middle-aged woman in an old-fashioned bonnet and tartan shawl paused and peered in their direction.

'C'mon,' said Teresa. 'Let's move off before Ma Maxwell comes any closer. It'll not matter what you've done but she'll be putting about some tale all over the place.' She made to rise, but Annie held her wrist.

'Wait. I've done nothing, so I haven't.' She glanced at the woman, who was pretending to look for something in a pocket, then said more loudly, 'There are some men should be ashamed of themselves, so they should. Trying to take liberties with a motherless girl. If my da hadn't come in when he did, I'd've had to scrab him, so I would. Old enough to be my father himself, the Pharisee.' Annie raised her fingers before her face, noting that, had it come to that, her nails were cut too short to have done any real scrabbing. Through the spaces between them she saw her shot had gone home. Looking straight at Annie, the woman raised her chin once in acknowledgement and waddled off with greater speed than her bulk would have suggested possible.

'What did you just do that for?' stage-whispered Teresa.

'I'm going to tell Da what happened once I can get him alone,' Annie said. 'Then he'll have to send the oul' bastard away, right enough. But away wouldn't be far enough. If Ann Maxwell doesn't know me from Queen Alexandra she'll find out soon enough, and who that snake is who's lodging under our roof. Every delivery she makes with that poor donkey and cart of hers in the next fortnight she'll talk of nothing else.' Annie started to tremble. 'Dear God, what have I done?'

'You did right,' said her friend. 'If you'd not, your woman there would've put it about you were having a baby. You might even have ended up having to marry the oul' feller to stop the tongues wagging.'

Annie cried out.

'You're some girl, Annie Maguire!' went on Teresa. 'I wish I could think as quick as you. Now before anyone else turns up wanting to know your business, would you please tell me all what happened?'

Annie took a deep breath. 'I'd gone upstairs so I never heard him come in. I came down for to lay the table and there he was, looking really strange, coming up to me that close.' She held her hands up, the palms six inches apart. 'Dadda knew I didn't like him, but I don't know he took me seriously when I said never to leave me alone with him, though to be fair to him he never did, until today. And that's only because Dadda is always back from mass anyway before that man's back from Second Presbyterian or wherever it is he goes in his Sunday best. Honest to God, I thought he'd had drink taken, and said so. Ohh . . .' She pressed a hand protectively over her heart.

'What is it?'

'I hope he's away out again. He usually goes for what he calls his "constitutional" after Sunday dinner. Says that's allowed on the Sabbath, so's he can reflect on the minister's sermon.'

'Hope he falls in the Enler, so I do,' muttered Teresa. 'So you told him he'd drink taken, and then what?'

'That's when he tried to kiss me,' gasped Annie. 'I turned my face away and he was slobbering at my neck and pawing at me and calling me a sinful Jezebel though it was him doing them things, not me. I couldn't even cry out. My throat was all closed up, like, and it was hard to breathe. Then there was a noise out the back – Dadda's boots on the scraper – and he let go of me with a squeak like a rabbit in a trap – and there he was rubbing his big sausagey hands together and smiling at Dadda and saying something about what a fine morning it had been, and here he was getting in my way with me needing to prepare the dinner and all. I could barely eat a thing, Teresa. Dadda was looking at me but he never said anything. Probably just thought it was my monthlies come but knew he couldn't ask – not at the table and not in front of that man – or not anyway. Sure didn't Mr Crawford swallow down all I'd left on my plate himself. "Gather the pieces left over. Let nothing be wasted," he says, cool as anything, always coming out with his bits of scripture. I wanted him to choke, so I did.'

Teresa blew out her cheeks. 'I'd bet you anything he's done this before.' She patted Annie's hand. 'Will I come back with you?'

'Oh yes, please. Just in case Dadda's away out again.'

'If he's not, and that pig is gone out instead, I'll stop for a cup of tea and then leave yous to it. Tell your da all of it before any of it slips your mind.'

Annie shivered. 'No danger of that. I wish there was.'

'If Ma Maxwell does her work he'll be away before the week's out.'

*

'Hello, Teresa. So how's my second-favourite girl?' Thomas was standing on the back step smoking his pipe when the two girls came in through the gate into the back yard.

'I'm grand, Mr Maguire.'

Thomas took out his pipe, contemplated the contents of the bowl, then knocked it empty against the brickwork. 'Come away in till we see if Annie will get us another cup of tea.'

He stood back, so Annie went in first, darting her head into the back room. Empty. She breathed more freely.

'No more money for ribbons unless I find somebody else for the front there,' she heard her father say.

'*What?*'

'You mean pardon, don't you? Mr Crawford just told me there's a Presbyterian family has made him the offer of a room. He's been very happy here, he said, and wants to tell you himself that he's doubtful the lady of the house will be the cook that you are. Only he says he's sure I understand it's better he should live with them he worships with.'

'He's *going*?'

'He is so.'

Annie glanced over at her friend and both of them started to laugh. Thomas looked from one creased face to the other in astonishment. 'What's the matter with yous?'

'You're codding me?'

'I'm not. He's away out to see the people now.'

Annie jumped up and went to the foot of the staircase, tilting her head against the door into the front room.

'Annie?' said Thomas, watching her as she very slowly turned the handle and edged the door open. She glanced in, then swiftly closed it again. She walked slowly back and joined Teresa at the table, suddenly serious.

'His grip's in the middle of the floor. And he's stripped the bed, so he has.' She looked up at her father, and said in her usual voice, 'I'll make us tea, then. But Teresa and me'll go out again after.' Annie glanced at her friend. 'So's I don't have to see him.'

'Come on, now, Annie. He's going. Where's the harm in saying goodbye?'

The girl got up, shaking her head, and went out to the scullery. 'I'll tell you after, so I will.'

*

Robert edged into the empty dining room, turning up the gas. He'd already thought about what he was going to write, meaning to get it down quickly before the others came in from what was supposed to have been his celebration. Nor did he want to presume on his landlord's kindness, allowing him lighting in a room empty but for himself.

*

Cleator Moor
3rd July 1901

Dear Mammy,

    I hope you are well though I do not know as you have not wrote me. I was made today a member of the Unexpected Loyal Orange Lodge and we are getting ready for the Twelfth, my first march, though I will only be walking not knowing for how to play any music. I have sworn to be loyal to the King and to the memory of King William of Orange and his victory over papist domination. I am never to go in a papist church though what would I want to be doing that for the dear knows. Even Kathleen that Mr Cairncross put me with did not make go and she was a pape.

    Mammy, I know Mr Cairncross is my da. I have known a long while. He done right by me though he did not have to. If he was not my father then I woulda gone to the Olivet at Ballygowan with the other wee orphans and they woulda sent me to work by now on a farm in Canada as that is where the most of them misfortunates get sent. I woulda been in the fresh air right enough but I woulda missed you there. I miss

63

you now. I hope you are proud of me for what happened today. I would like it if you was.

Your loving son

Robert

*

Robert closed his pen carefully, weighing it in his hand. It was one of his treasured possessions, for it had been Kathleen's. He thought for a moment of Canada, and what his life might have been like there. He knew of boys who had gone, but of nobody who had come back. He knew that had he been sent inside Olivet's gaunt orphanage walls instead of to the Lamonts and the other farms before theirs, then that was almost certainly where he would have ended up. Instead he had a skill, the greatest gift Kathleen could have bestowed on him. He smiled, remembering that she decided to teach him to be a tailor that day he'd shown his deftness in making St Brigid crosses. A rare smile, as fragile and bright as a butterfly's wing, crossed his solemn face. Imagine how they'd have looked at him today, there in the Lodge, if they'd known about those little bundles of reeds. The smile vanished. They'd known about *her*, of course. That Mr Bawden had patted him on the shoulder and said, 'Our brother did wrong putting you in with that papist, but you've come out of it unharmed. You're one of us, now.' Robert knew why he'd failed to defend Kathleen. It was the 'one of us' that did it. The first time in his life he'd felt part of something. He folded up the letter. He wanted to get to the washstand and be in bed before the others came in. If he pretended to be asleep he'd not have to talk to them.

CHAPTER EIGHT

Upper Distillery, Killinchy Street, 1901

'The legendary Cummer Ann Maxwell, general haulier, described as a rather uncouth woman . . .'

Comber Historical Society Photographic Library

Scurrying from one machine to the other the following morning, neither Annie nor Teresa had much chance to speak. Then finally the handbell rang, and the girls huddled close over their breakfast in their usual place at the end of the hall.

'So, did you tell yer oul' fella?' said Teresa, glancing round to make sure the others weren't listening.

'I did. I thought he'd bring the house down over the both of us, he was that mad.'

'With *you*?'

'With him. Wants to kill him if he sets eyes on him again. I'd to tell him there were better men worth swinging for. Poor Dadda – he's heartsore for letting me down, he says. I've to choose the next lodger myself.'

'You could put out word here, so you could. Ask the doffing mistress does she know any new hands coming in.'

Annie was silent for a moment. 'Stay close to me, Teresa, will you? Crawford's still working here. I'll need to ask can I walk back with some of the other girls that go my way.'

'Of course I will. What's that wee frown for now?'

'I used to like walking home on my own. A bit of peace after the din in here.'

Teresa patted her knee. 'We've yet to see the work of Ma Maxwell's tongue.'

*

By Wednesday, they saw it. It was there in the muttered asides, the glances, the stares that weren't broken when Annie glared back, the complicit smiles. Evidently that redoubtable female haulier, in her greasy buttoned bodice of thirty years ago, had leaned down from her cart at every delivery she made and beckoned the recipient over, not relinquishing their bolt of cloth or bag of peat strips until she'd said, 'You'll have heard, won't you, about that misfortunate young woman in Brownlow Street?'

In the distillery yard Thomas's colleagues came separately up to the dray, putting a hand on the horse's bridle to ask him how 'that brave girl of yours does' and express their outrage – though more than one of them warned him 'The boss'll not like it. Seeing as he's in the same congregation as thon Crawford.' Thomas thanked them in a daze and let the horse set the pace while he thrashed over in his mind how it was possible that all these men knew the reasons for the lodger's swift departure. He vowed to have words with Teresa the moment he had a chance.

On Thursday the pay-clerk counted out Reginald Crawford's last wages, handing them over without meeting his eyes. To the foreman who asked him where he was going next, Crawford had said, 'Lurgan.' To the clerk he'd muttered something about Banbridge. An able young man in the flax-dressing hall was asked if he'd be interested in going from there to the drier, better-paid work of hackling.

*

But embroidered versions of Ma Maxwell's tale got about. 'What sort of girl was it that would make up a story about a grieving widower, a decent God-fearing man who read his Bible and never touched the drink?' 'Sure, didn't she lead him on? She'd've seen that he had money put aside – she'd'a gone ferreting in his room for it, for a man that wore a watch-chain as fine as anything in Barrett's window must surely have had plenty of tin? He'd refused the wee hoor and this was her taking her revenge, so it was.'

Then there was the evening that her companions had rushed off without her: Annie had seen them scurrying away. She told herself she didn't mind that; Crawford and his soft purple mouth and his waxed moustache had gone with his grip and his Bible to wherever it was in County Armagh, and so couldn't be following her home or waiting to ambush her from behind a lamppost. But Ma Maxwell and her spavined old jennet had passed that way with other deliveries, other gossip, and the animal had emptied its bowels while a docket was being signed. A carefully aimed clump of that ordure now spattered Annie's back, with the yelled epithet 'Papist hoor!' The voice was high-pitched with

67

hate, so the girl couldn't tell if it belonged to man or woman. Though Annie swung round at once, she was not quick enough to see her attacker either. She ran the rest of the way home and sank sobbing at her father's feet as he leaned over in his chair and stroked her hair and told her, 'Michael Nolan called round. They're leaving. They're going to England.' She'd looked up, shock drying her tears.

'But Teresa never said.'

'I think maybe she's getting told right now.'

*

When Thomas came into work the next day he went first into the foreman's cluttered little office to pick up the delivery manifest for the day. At first all he thought had changed was that the crepe-edged photograph of the old queen had been taken down from its hook behind the foreman's desk and replaced with a tinted image of King Edward and Queen Alexandra. Thomas nodded his good morning as he always did and turned to lift the chit from its hook. It was empty. He turned round, as the foreman's chair scraped back and the man got to his feet.

'How's it not there, Mr McKinley?' But he already knew.

'Joe's taken it. He's away out already. The manager said I was to give you this.' McKinley held out a little gummed-down packet, in which coins chinked. 'I'm sorry. It wasn't just me said it wasn't your fault. He'd not see reason.'

*

'I've never settled here anyway,' said her father that evening, over their tea and bread and butter. 'We could do as well over there as here.'

'I'm sorry, Dadda, so I am,' sobbed Annie.

'It's not your fault. You were right about thon Crawford, only I wouldn't listen to ye.'

'It is *so* my fault. Giving out loud enough for Ma Maxwell to hear me.'

'The problem is people'll believe what suits them, Annie. But there's nobody will give me a job in Comber now. I'm only sorry I'd never the chance to say goodbye to the horse. But honestly, Annie, if I can't be on the farm then it doesn't matter to me where I am. There's work over there at a mine.'

'A mine? But you've always wanted to be outdoors. You'd be underground.'

'No, they'd not want me underground. You need to start young for that – Michael Nolan said so. The money's good for them that do, though. But they've labouring jobs too at the sur-face. That's what Michael'll do – what I could do. There's a mill, same as here – work for Philomena and Teresa. Work for you as well if you want us to go too.'

Annie breathed deeply, looking round the shabby little room, wondering if she'd miss anything of it. 'It's always dark in here, so it is. Even if that window's bigger than the ones on the farm. And the walls are that thin. I'm forever tiptoeing about and trying not to sneeze.'

'You've heard them fighting through the wall, haven't ye?' said Thomas, tilting his head towards their neighbours.

'I have. At least Mrs Doyle's quiet on the other side.' *I've heard them making up too.* She looked down at her hands, feeling the flush creep up her neck.

'Are the houses different in England?' she asked.

'No. From what Michael's been told, they look like here, only without the half-doors. He said there are many gone from round here – but there are more Catholics in Cumberland than in Comber. He said the children have boots there, or clogs. They don't go barefoot outside.'

Annie flexed her own feet, remembering running on grass at the farm. In Comber she wore boots, but like the other spinners took them off at the mill. It was easier to move on bare feet, and with the floor in there perpetually wet leather was quickly ruined.

'If Teresa's going, and you want it too, then I'd go. But only if you tell me there's no way back to the farm.'

Thomas flinched. 'You know there's not,' he said gently. 'Unless you want to live with Patrick and Agnes.'

'Oh . . .'

Annie shook her head mutely, thinking of those fields, her eyes filling with tears. She could still walk them in her mind, remembering even the shape of a stone used to keep open a gate. She saw Mr Harris, and the walk up to Slievenalargy, him telling his stories. She'd felt part of them, for hadn't all the people who'd gone before her made her what she was?

'Mammy,' whispered Annie. 'Nobody'll visit her grave.'

'I was thinking. If I was able to put something by, over there, I'd have money for a stone for her at last. A proper, decent stone that'd be there long after me. Long after you, even. And when we've sold the few sticks we have in this house, I was thinking I'd leave something for masses for her.'

'I wonder is the mass different over there,' said Annie.

'Mass is the same wherever you go,' said Thomas. 'Mr Harris said so. For a Protestant gentleman he knew a lot, so he did. He said Catholic means universal. From here to Australia – in Canada too.'

'There's no reason not to go,' said Annie finally. And thinking of the clod of donkey droppings hitting her back, she added silently, '*And plenty reasons for to go.*'

CHAPTER NINE

Leaving Ireland, 1901

'Sweet Heart of my Jesus, make me love thee ever more
and more!'

Indulgence of Pope Pius XI, 26 November 1876

Annie saw the following weeks run through as inexorably as the
sand in the tiny egg timer on the scullery windowsill. Michael
Nolan wrote again to England with a description of Thomas
condensed into his height, his healthy colour and the assertion
that there was no whistle in his chest. A reply came back that if
Thomas Maguire's appearance in the flesh satisfied the foreman,
then there would be work for him too. Annie's possessions and
her father's were gradually reduced to what would go into one
trunk. The Nolans and the two Maguires would go into a lodging house to start with, the men in one room, the women in
another. 'Like the workhouse, only you're let out,' said Teresa,
her enthusiasm faltering for the first time, excited about sharing
with Annie but knowing they'd never be able to talk freely with
her mother there. Once both families could show their wages,

then they'd go looking for their own front doors. ('You'll choose this time,' said Thomas said to Annie, 'you being the woman of the house now.')

The Sacred Heart was lifted down, leaving a shadow of its outline on the wall. In her bedroom, Annie eased her Brigid Cross off the nail above her bed. The reeds were dry and starting to split, loosening the once tightly woven centre. She retied the embroidery threads that held together the ends of its four arms and folded a linen handkerchief reverently around it. Annie had plaited the cross herself, with reeds she'd plucked smooth and green from the bog the other side of the hill, while her mother sat opposite her by the farmhouse fireplace darning a pillowcase. That memory made the little reed cross as precious as a lock of her mother's hair.

Day by day the house emptied, its contents trundled away up the cobbled street bit by bit in Ma Maxwell's cart. And then came a morning when Thomas and Annie had breakfast in Mrs Doyle's dingy parlour and the girl hugged the old woman for the last time, thanking her again for her unflinching help in her mother's dwindling days.

That final morning Annie and her father stood outside alongside the beds they'd never sleep in again. The girl thought there was something indecent about those iron bedframes being out in the open air. The landlord's agent had taken the key with a muttered thanks, not looking at either of them, and disappeared up the street. Annie wondered who next would stand at the sink, or twist the stiff tap in the yard – someone who might never know that a mother had fought for breath in the upper front.

The last caller but one was Ma Maxwell. She and Thomas heaved the beds onto her cart. 'Good luck to yous both, so,' she said, and giving the donkey a pat on the flank strode off, the ribbons of her frowsty old bonnet flapping.

Thomas squeezed Annie's hand. 'Sit on the trunk, now, they'll be here any moment.'

Then the hired trap carrying the Nolans turned into the street, and Teresa twisted round and waved her arms, looking to Annie not like a mill girl but like Maeve in her chariot in a book Mr Harris had shown her, a marvellous volume with illustrations as colourful as stained glass. She thought, *I'll remember this moment all my life.*

*

Belfast terrified Annie. One hand behind her, she clung to the rail at the back of her seat, folding her other hand under her skirts so the others wouldn't see it was trembling. Teresa by contrast had to be made to sit down by her mother and keep still, after the driver had glanced round a second time.

'You'll have us over in the gutter, so you will!'

'Look at all them people away up there!' Teresa shouted at her wan friend, as a trolley-bus roared and sparked past them. Annie was sure the trolley-buses would tip over like shipwrecks, the people on the open top deck lose their hats and bowlers and brollies and cigars before their heads cracked on the cobbles. It wasn't just the traffic, through which the patient horse plodded as though on a country track; the people walking purposefully along the wide pavements intimidated her. They looked to her to be a different species, as remote from her as the men and women in ruffs and farthingales in Mr Harris's books. She thought their little huddle on the cart must look like the coarsest of bogtrotters to the Belfast people, until she realised that nobody was taking any notice of them at all. Those people were all much too busy. In the country everyone greeted each other, including the occasional stranger – and that same stranger was the subject of conversation over the meat and potatoes on Sundays, with the aim of establishing some sort of identity for them, something like, 'That'd be Mulligan the publican's brother-in-law from Carlingford.'

After the clang and crash of the streets gave way to the cranes and gantries of the shipyard, Annie was almost relieved to see the flat grey stretch of sea.

*

The placid chug of the little steamship did something to calm her nerves. It was carrying cargo but took a few foot passengers over without providing anything but a couple of hard benches from them to sit on. Teresa for once was subdued, standing at Annie's shoulder on the rail looking towards England. *White-haven's where we're going*, thought Annie. *Do they call it that because all you see is cloud?*

'Look!' she said, her hand on Teresa's sleeve. The weather was clearing, and what Annie had at first thought was the darkness of impending rain was resolving itself into a backdrop of mountains. She felt tears come. *They're not the Mournes, so they're not.* Nevertheless, she gazed on them with awe. They were remote, forbidding; she screwed up her eyes looking for signs of tillage on their lower slopes as there was at home – none. She remembered what Michael Nolan had said, that here men laboured below ground, in a network of tunnels so deep they ran even under the sea, that there'd always be work, for coal and iron would always be needed, sure wouldn't they? And here, he'd added, unlike at the Belfast yards whose hooters sounded only for Protestants, any man's hands were welcome.

Annie saw that the mountains circled Whitehaven protectively, the town huddled in a basin. She saw a pincer of a harbour, something that looked like a lighthouse, tall buildings on the harbour front – Annie counted four storeys, nearly as many as Belfast. Houses straggled upwards beyond the harbour. A squat, sturdy church tower looked over its shoulder at their approach. The chug of the boat slowed, and the gusting salty air took precedence. *The doctor said the seaside wudda helped Mammy.*

Teresa nudged her and bent her mouth close to her ear: 'We'll find husbands here, so we will!'

'Not here. Your da says we've another four miles to go.'

'You know what I mean.'

Annie didn't answer. Land stretched interminably away north and south.

CHAPTER TEN

Ainsworth's Mill, Cleator Moor, 1901

'Thomas Ainsworth was a Lancashire man of good family, means, and position, and settled early in life near Cleator. He became a large flax spinner there, his works at first being driven by the old and powerful waterwheel, and afterwards by new and splendid steam-driven machinery . . .'

Tom Duffy, *Cleator Moor Revealed,* 2019

Annie looked up at the towering mass of Ainsworth's Mill and shivered. Andrews' Mill in Comber had looked positively homely in comparison. Passing through the main gate, she and Teresa were directed into an inner courtyard and the door they were to knock on pointed out to them. The mill was as big as anything they'd glimpsed in Belfast, the sheer four-storeyed wall of the inner building dwarfing any other construction for miles around, even Leconfield's pitheads.

The courtyard was a terrifying crescendo of noise, women's laughter crashing off the enclosing walls, their clogs on the asphalt as deafening to Annie as the tumbling hammers of a beetling shed. It was eight o'clock in the morning, breakfast hour for those who'd been labouring since six, and as it was a dry day the spinners, rovers, reelers, hacklers, scutchers and beetlers had flowed out of the stairwells and sheds and congregated here; their shouts, Annie knew, were also a way of getting the 'stir', the flax dust, out of their lungs. The only quiet ones were the couples standing in corners, boys with their hands in their pockets, girls with theirs under their aprons, as if defying each other to touch. At sixteen years old, Annie felt her face grow hot looking at them. They stirred something in her she didn't understand, something she feared and envied. She knew that only 'bold' girls looked at boys. Then it occurred to her what this space really was. If Ainsworth's was anything like Andrews' Mill then the jobs people performed here separated men from women as surely as the workhouse. This courtyard was a vast dance floor where no music was played, but a girl and a boy might be drawn one to the other and never want to pull away.

But I've Dadda to look after, so I do. And I'm too young.

It was better once she was taken to what was to be her stand. Annie took off her shoes and rolled down her stockings, leaving them as instructed alongside the shawl she'd put folded on the windowsill. As Annie looked down at the diamond patterns of the quarry-tiled floor, the doffing mistress inspected her feet for 'toe rot'.

'Healthy.'

'I wash them at night with vinegar and baking soda, so I do,' said Annie.

Mrs Birkett nodded approvingly. 'So, show me what you can do, lass.'

It didn't take long for Annie to get the measure of the machines either side of her. She walked up and down, wheeling round at the right moment, making sure her 'ends' were up, getting into the swing of the timing of when a rove bobbin would need to be replaced, checking whether the yarn bobbins were filling smoothly, and shifting the drags, the weights, along the front rail so that the tension was just right on the bobbins, for Annie prided herself on keeping down the numbers of snapped threads. Her apron was only a bleached and remodelled flour sack but she'd sewn darts in it so it sat neatly on her; in Comber she had washed it every Sunday. On a cord tied around her waist were hackling pins and a penknife. Looking at these, Mrs Birkett said, 'You'd be able to do my job just about, wi' them,' though not unkindly. Annie had stammered in protest, saying that she'd never meant anything of the sort, but all the Englishwoman had said was, 'I like a girl that knows what she's about,' and then had shown Annie the best place on the trough to put her little kettle so the heat of the steam would run not just her machine but keep her tea warm.

'We clean Friday afternoons,' said Mrs Birkett. 'Every girl does her own stand.'

Annie cast an experienced eye over the machinery. Despite the cloying smell of the yarn, the grease and oil of the machine, the steaming water in the trough that meant the air was always warm and moist and the freshest clothes clammy, Annie could see it was kept as clean as a weekly blacked grate or whitened front step. Without thinking, she said, 'Who was the girl on here before me?'

Mrs Birkett hesitated. 'She'd to go, poor thing. They say she was having a baby. She got took up to Carlisle for it, to the nuns.'

Annie didn't dare ask if she'd be coming back.

'She'll be in a Belfast mill by now, I'd think,' added Mrs Birkett.

Poor wee baby, thought Annie, but she knew she'd also been given a warning.

*

Annie washed up the cups and plates, staring out at the brick wall of next door's scullery, thankful that she and her father had quickly found a little house to themselves, not like the poorer families with more children than they could count, crammed in with other lodgers whose extra rent was needed if there was to be enough food on the table. Being in that new home reminded her of Comber, before Mr Crawford came. So many things were the same here as there: the way the houses were built in a row, thin brick walls separating one family from the next, mothers and fathers calling to each other – or shouting – in accents often familiar, mixed in with the harder vowels of Belfast. But Cleator Moor wasn't clean like Comber. How could it be, with the pitheads, the shale heaps that hemmed the houses round, the iron ore that stained the country paths and men's faces? The first time she'd heard the distant roar of drilling beneath the scullery floor she'd gone stiff with fright but she'd quickly got used to it. Teresa's brother Frank was already underground; he'd told her there were some pits where you could hear the bells in the tower at the Montreal Schools.

St Mary's church, though, was a revelation. Annie thought she'd never seen such a beautiful place. On their first visit, sitting in the pew with her father on the aisle side, Teresa and the Nolans ranged to her right, Annie had had to make herself concentrate on the words of the readings. Oh, the colours, the gilding, the statues, the rich glass of the rose window, the altar of carved white marble as intricate as lace, with the saints peeping out of it. Built by Irish labour, Thomas had told her, but the architect had come up from London. *His* father had designed nothing less than the Houses of Parliament – think of that! And the things on sale in Cleator Moor were like nothing she could have imagined. Horizons that had been limited by the wares in Mickey White's little shop in Comber were broadened by the displays of impeccable linen blouses and buttoned gloves too slender for her mill-girl hands in the plate-glass windows of Frank Fowles's grand corner-site store. Right enough the little fountain in the main square with the stork on top wasn't as impressive as Gillespie up on his pillar back in Comber, but with that pink and grey marble it was a lot prettier, and sure where was the sense in putting Gillespie's statue so high up that nobody could see it? But best of all was the new library, built in dark red Cumberland stone, with the money of a man called Carnegie who'd never set foot in Cleator Moor, where you could take home the books you wanted for free. Dadda had said that the man must've been a Quaker, for in Ireland they were the only people who'd give you something you needed – food or clothes or coal – without wanting something back from you or asking you what religion you were.

The priest was a Munsterman; Annie thought that he had a voice like those tramp-hacklers, Corkmen mostly, that used to

in 1884 they shot her son, the Orange boys did,' she'd murmured. 'Seventeen years old, God love him. Just standing in a doorway with his hands in his pockets watching them with their big drums and fifes. The man they arrested was let off, so he was. And they're still marching, hell mend them.'

CHAPTER ELEVEN

Cleator Moor, 1901

'The wet spinning process, invented by James Kay of
Preston in 1825, involved a six-hour soaking of the linen
yarn in cold water which prevented it from snapping,
thus allowing mechanised spinning.'

Peter Collins, *The Making of Irish Linen*, 1994

Six months later Annie felt as though she'd never worked anywhere else. She liked and respected Mrs Birkett and was gratified
to hear the Englishwoman describe her as 'one of my best girls'.
Though the doffing mistress smiled at Teresa, Annie knew she
didn't rate her as highly. The new girls, whether straight from
the school or just off the ferry, were put with Annie and exhorted
to 'do like that lass' because she was patient and methodical.
To begin with Annie was embarrassed by this, because she'd
never forgotten that it was Teresa who had taken her, a country
child, under her wing, but Teresa herself had shrugged this off
when Annie broached the subject: 'Sure don't bother your head
about it. I helped you because I liked the look of you. I never put

myself out for any of them others, so I didn't. But you're like a wee teacher or a wee mother, so you are.'

It was when Annie stayed behind one dinner-time to show two new little girls the ins and outs of the machines that her friend was approached by Percy Bartwell. That evening Teresa had just about hopped from foot to foot with excitement all the walk home, until Annie begged her friend to 'Come out with it, for the love of God! Is it St Vitus's dance you have?'

'Come out with *him*, you mean,' said Teresa, her eyes sparkling. Suddenly Annie knew who her friend meant.

'It's that fair lad, isn't it – long legs and arms? I seen him looking at you, so I did. Only he never said a thing.'

'He did today!' cried Teresa, exultant.

'The one time I wasn't there,' said Annie.

'Don't you see? It's *because* you weren't there.'

Annie could see her friend was too happy to realise how much this hurt.

'First thing he said was, "Where's your friend?" I swear to God I thought it was you he was after.' Teresa tucked her arm under Annie's and pulled her closely. '*I* said, "You'll be meaning my *best* friend." He said he thought it'd be rude to come up and want to speak to me and leave you out of it, so he'd been waiting on his chance. And *I* told him I'd introduce yous both because if he didn't pass the test with you he'd never do for me.'

'Oh Teresa,' said Annie, moved.

'Well, it's true, so it is.'

*

'It's going to be easier to hide Percy from Mammy at work than it is outside,' grumbled Teresa two days later. 'She never comes down from Reeling if she can help it. Them up there think themselves better than us spinners.'

'Teresa!'

'She does *so*. The problem I have is trying to meet him anywhere else. It's not as if we can go about arm in arm in the market square.'

'If you're courting, can he not just come to the house?'

Teresa stared at Annie in amazement.

'It's not just that he's English, is it?' said Annie slowly.

'I asked him about that, so I did. He says he's Church of England according to where he was baptised – in thon wee mission chapel on Wath Brow – but that nobody in his family bothers their heads about it let alone going to church, and he can't understand why Irish people make such a fuss about it.'

'Not make a fuss about his eternal soul?' said Annie, wide-eyed.

'The problem is, everybody thinks they're right, don't they? The Orangemen as much as Father Hagerty. How do any of 'em *know*?'

'Well, at least we're not like the Orangemen. Marching down our streets and past our church, just like at home,' said Annie.

*

Annie got used to that particular spot on the stone wall where she left Teresa and Percy and walked back into the town. It was lonely, though, finding things to do with herself when Teresa and Percy went for their walks. She'd sometimes go part of the way on the fell road to Egremont with them, linked to Teresa's left arm while Percy linked her right. Percy was polite. It was right what they said about hacklers, Annie thought. The gentlemen of the mill – though Reginald Crawford had been a hackler and he'd merely pretended to be a gentleman. Percy even had an old watch on a chain, an inheritance. He would ask Annie questions, especially about life at Moneyscalp. 'My grandad was a hill farmer. He didn't last long once he'd to come down to the town,' he explained. Annie appreciated that Percy never failed to thank her for being there, but she felt like a gooseberry just the same.

Annie missed Saturday afternoons wandering around the town with her friend, looking in the shop windows. She tried not to think about what Teresa and Percy might be doing when they weren't with her, though she was sure kissing must be a grand thing. All the time she kept half an ear open for the bells on the tower at the Montreal Schools, letting her know when she'd need to start out on that path again to meet them coming back. She was sure the time passed much more slowly for her than it did for Teresa and Percy, because somehow admiring fine muslin and cambric wasn't very satisfactory if you'd no one to tell what you thought of them or what occasions you'd wear them at, given the chance.

Instead, Annie began to take refuge in the Carnegie Library. At least there it didn't look odd if you were on your own, because you weren't. You'd a book, hadn't you, same as everyone else in there? She just had to make sure she didn't get so lost in what she was reading that she'd forget to look at the clock.

One afternoon, though, she was so absorbed in *Jane Eyre* that she didn't immediately hear her own name being whispered.

'*Annie!*' The whisper was louder now, enough to get a 'Ssh!' from the librarian's desk and to turn two or three heads.

She looked up to see Teresa's brother Frank. Annie gathered up shawl and book, and went to hand over her ticket so she could take her heroine home with her. Frank waited for her by the entrance. She had no idea what she was going to say to him.

'Our Teresa's got a fella, hasn't she?' said Frank, as soon as they were outside.

Annie nodded mutely. She knew she was a terrible liar and that Frank must have already spotted the flush creeping up her neck.

'Mammy wouldn't want him, would she?'

A shake of the head, her cheeks flaming.

'Well, I'll not say, so I won't.'

Annie looked up at him in a surge of relief.

'You look awful nice when you smile like that, Annie.'

Annie didn't know what to say. As Frank was her best friend's brother he felt almost like her own brother; Frank with his serious brown eyes, plump cheeks and pomaded black hair, as far from a brooding Mr Rochester as it was possible to be. If it weren't for the russet tinge to his skin that marked him out for a miner, she thought, he'd look like a clerk. It suddenly occurred to Annie precisely why Frank had been in the library. He wasn't there to read stories about plucky lone women lovesick for men they couldn't have – he was there to better himself.

'Will you come for a cup of tea?' he said.

'Oh ... I'd better not. I'll be late. It's awful kind of you. Another time?'

'Anytime you'd like,' he said gently, but Annie could see he was disappointed. Disappointed, but not surprised.

'Goodbye, then,' she said, 'and thank you.' She walked off with shoulders bent, hugging her book to her chest. It was too early to meet the others, so she'd lied to Frank. Another sin to take to the confessional, though she wasn't quite sure that going to have a cup of tea with a man you weren't married to mightn't have been a greater one than her little fib. Now she'd to sit on that stone wall half an hour longer than was necessary. She'd wait for Teresa and Percy, warn the pair of them, and then go home and heat up water for her weekly hip bath. Then later Dadda would come in from wherever it was he went on a Saturday afternoon and she'd make tea and afterwards read her book.

Where does *Dadda go?*

CHAPTER TWELVE

Cleator Moor, 1902

Thou shalt not lie with thy neighbour's wife, nor be defiled with mingling of seed

Leviticus, 18:20

The two girls sat on the little bridge at Wath Brow, swinging their legs beneath their skirts. Annie liked the rush of air on the skin of her knees, above her gartered stockings. *How nice it might have been to have been a boy*, she thought, *to be able to run about freely and get heroically scabbed legs.*

'Penny for them,' said Teresa.

Annie didn't want to say how much she appreciated Teresa's time. It seemed unkind, both to Percy who was so considerate, and to Teresa who was clearly happy, exuding a calmness Annie had never before seen in her friend. The sweethearts had decided to meet less often, to give themselves greater cover. Annie privately thought this was hopeless, even if Frank had promised his silence. People were always found out in a wee place like this, weren't they?

Annie was indeed about to discover just how quickly people did find things out. And besides, there *was* something bothering her. *Tell her. It's probably nothing after all. Then you can stop worrying.*

She looked up the slope of the grass towards the houses. 'Do you remember when we thought everything in England was going to be big? Like Belfast, maybe. Here's not even as big as Comber – though the mill is.'

'You've said this was a toty wee place before, Annie. What are you wanting to tell me really?' said Teresa.

'Cross your heart and hope to die?'

Teresa sketched the sign of a cross. 'I'm your best friend, amn't I? Something's been at you for weeks.' In a stage whisper she added, 'You've a boy yourself, is it?'

Annie shook her head, half-smiling. 'I've not. I'd never'a been able to keep that from you.'

'So?'

'I hardly know. Well . . . it's Dadda.'

Teresa was silent. Annie glanced at her profile and realised her friend couldn't look at her. *So there is something.*

Teresa lifted her feet, contemplating the toes of her boots, polished to a Sunday shine.

'What about him?' she said, in a throttled little voice.

Annie spoke to the water. 'He goes to the public bath-house Saturday afternoon, to save me heating the water for him, but he can't be all afternoon getting clean. He comes in later some evenings. It's the same days every week. He tells me not to wait for him but to get my own tea, that he'll go to the pie shop instead. He says he's got extra work, but I . . . I seen his wage dockets when he wasn't looking. They're the same as always. And I can *see* he's lying, Teresa. He's so bad at it, so he is.'

'That's something, isn't it? That he's bad at it, I mean. And it could be they're paying him casual, right enough,' said Teresa, but from her tone Annie could tell she didn't believe it.

'He's never been for the drink, neither. Then this morning at mass he did it again . . .'

'Did what again?'

Annie sighed. 'I've never not seen him go up to communion. He always sits – well you've seen him – on the end of the pew if he can. I've not to. It's just this wee protective thing he's always done. Him on the end, me in the middle, Mammy on the other side. Only now there's no Mammy.' Annie realised her normally fidgety friend was listening intently, for she had stopped swinging her feet and was sitting absolutely still.

'He'd normally go up ahead of me, but he'd point me to a space at the rail before he looked for one for himself. Only today . . . well it's been the same for a few weeks now . . . he got out of the pew and waved for me to walk up.'

'I seen that. And so did Mammy.'

'He didn't follow me. He'd be standing at the end of the pew when I came back, to let me in. He must've let yous in as well.'

'He did.'

'Then once I was in he'd get down to his knees same as me.'

'You know why somebody wouldn't go to the sacraments, Annie,' said her friend quietly.

Annie hesitated. 'Because they were in a state of mortal sin. Something you'd not get let off for in the general confession. But Dadda's always gone up . . .'

'You really don't know, do you? It's been the talk of the place for ages.'

Annie turned a bewildered face to Teresa's incredulous one.

Teresa took her hands. 'I was waiting on you coming to talk to me, Annie. I never thought you didn't even know.'

*

That evening, quietly lighting the oil lamps, Annie wondered if she'd even get to stay in this house. *Where will I go?* Blinking back tears, she went over Teresa's revelation yet again. *Why did I have to be the last person to know?*

As if on cue, she heard the latch of the back gate and Thomas's reluctant tread. Often she'd open the back door and smile down at him on the bottom step. She heard him scraping his boots – dear familiar sounds – then clearing his throat as though he was about to speak. *Speak you will, Dadda.* The door rattled open, and a moment later he was standing in front of her pale, tear-tracked face holding his cap in his hand, and Annie did the last thing she'd been thinking of. She ran to him and, putting her arms around him, started to cry into his shirt.

'Could you not'a said?' she sobbed.

'I was afraid to. And I didn't know myself.'

'Know what?' she said, looking up.

'Sit down, Annie.'

93

'Will you have tea?'

'No . . . no thank you.'

'You'll have already had it, then,' said Annie.

'Yes.'

'At hers.'

'At Elsie's.'

'Elsie.' *An occasion of sin. It's her as is to blame. Poor lonely man.* 'Where did you find her, this Elsie?' She felt she was picking a scab, making herself bleed.

'I wasn't looking for her, so I wasn't. I'd gone to the Crown.'

'The Crown? You never go drinking.'

'I used to,' he said, with a brief smile. 'When I'd the farm. To Mulligan's. Better than the *Down Recorder* to know what's going on – better'n thon Ma Maxwell even. I only went this time for to please a workmate – he'd wanted to talk over some problem of his own. She was there – working there, I mean.'

Annie shivered, remembering an impressively corseted lady who had come to speak at the school. The nuns had introduced her as 'a lady auxiliary of the knights of Father Mathew' which had made Annie think that the woman's bombazine concealed a suit of armour, but to her disappointment the lady auxiliary had rustled rather than clanked. The picture the woman painted of the evils of drink was a terrifying one: babies abandoned in gutters and pigsties, neat homes transformed into damp, miserable dwellings where broken windows were stuffed with rags, where the fire had gone out for lack of fuel and there was no oil for the lamps. The gaudy pagan altar to which all domestic bliss was sacrificed was the public house, and all those who entered in were lost souls. 'Especially,' said the woman, her black glittering eye fixing that of every pinafored child in turn, 'if that person be a female. Our bodies are temples of our Blessed Lady and must be kept free of all defilement, be that the drink our beloved founder preached against, foul words in mouths made for prayer and praise, or loose living.' Annie then had had no idea what loose living meant, assuming it must be something to do with not having corsets.

Annie sank into her chair, unable to look at her father.

'You'd bring her here, would you, this Elsie?'

'I would not.'

'Ashamed of her, are you?' She startled herself at how cold her voice sounded.

'No. Sorry for her.'

Annie looked at him then and saw she had no weapons against the tenderness she found in his face.

'She has two weans. Six and four. She's in the pub to keep them.'

'A widow?' Not from what Teresa had said, but she wanted Thomas to tell her himself.

'There's a husband, only she doesn't know where. Liverpool, maybe, or Manchester. He'd beat her when he'd drink taken. She has scars—'

'I don't want to know about them!'

'No, well . . . you see, he's never sent money for to keep the children.'

'What are they?' said Annie dully.

'Wee boys. Joseph and Mark. Great wee lads.'

Annie felt the tension in her shoulders lessen. *At least they're not wee girls.* But she disliked herself for feeling jealous of mere children.

'Another man's wife. That's a mortal sin, so it is.'

'I know, Annie. But she done nothing wrong.' He sat down at last, looking at her stormy face across the tabletop. He lifted his hands as if pleading, then let them lie on the oilcloth.

'I'm forty-three years old, so I am. And I'm lonely. The wee boys – they remind me of when your brothers were that age.'

'My brothers. We'll never see them again this side of heaven.'

She saw her father look away and wished her words unsaid. He wiped the back of his hand across his eyes and suddenly she saw him as she never had, as a man, not her father. A handsome man – careworn, and grizzled, but yes, a fine-looking man. He'd always just been Dadda. Mammy's husband. Now he was the man this Elsie loved.

'I wish it hadna been Teresa to tell me.'

'I'm sorry. Would you meet her, Annie?'

'I don't know. Honest to God I don't. Not in that pub, anyway.'

CHAPTER THIRTEEN

Ainsworth's Mill, 1902

'Marriage is honourable in all, and the bed undefiled: for
fornicators and adulterers God will judge.'

Hebrews, 13:4

'I suppose working in the Crown is better than her working in
Ainsworth's where I'd be wondering which one of them is her,
or having to see her if I did know.'

Annie and Teresa were outside, eating their breakfast. Percy
and Teresa had exchanged fleeting glances in the big yard, but by
mutual agreement did not speak at work. You never knew what
might find its way up to Philomena in Reeling. As it was a fine
morning, the two girls had walked out of the main buildings of
the mill and towards the sawtoothed roofs of the single-storey
weaving sheds. Even from a distance they could hear the crash
of the looms within.

'Does he stay out the night?' whispered Teresa, though there
was nobody to hear them.

'No. He never has. He has his tea there maybe three times a
week and he's never late home. Pie shop indeed! I've never had

to wait up for him. It's maybe not because of me. She's the two wee boys, so she has. She'll have a bit of shame over them if not over herself, maybe. But when he's there, I can't help but think about what they're doing. Kissing, and that.' Annie shuddered. 'Dadda. I never saw him doing nothing like that with Mammy. He'd give her his arm. That's all.' She paused. 'I'm worried will he want to give up the house and me and go and live with her.'

'No! Father Hagerty would never stand for that! He'd have you packed off to the nuns for safekeeping.'

Annie laughed despite herself. She could see that her fears were preposterous though. For her father to live openly with a married woman in a village the size of Cleator Moor would be an impossibility, an occasion of sin flaunted in everyone's faces. And the ill-repute would extend to her.

'You're right. Dadda would never do that to me.'

*

Annie trudged home that evening, thinking about her own destiny. The little house she was going back to now – where she had been content taking care of her father, even if she couldn't say she'd been obviously happy – might not be her sanctuary for much longer. It crossed her mind that no one, apart from poor unwanted Frank of course, would want to walk out with her, precisely because she was her father's housekeeper – the assumption would be that she would have to stay and look after him, that she couldn't marry because of it. Yet she couldn't, just couldn't cede that place to the unseen Elsie.

If I was to go under the same roof as the woman, I might get gentleman callers, but they'd hardly be what you'd call gentlemen then, would they? They'd be calling at an infamous house.

Once home, Annie paused in the scullery and inspected her face in the little mirror her father used for shaving. Her hair was pinned up on her head, in the style she'd learned from the English girls, like a squashy cushion. It had to be worn up for work; long tresses could get caught in the machinery. She unpinned it now, letting it fall. Pulling a ribbon from her pocket, she took a wing of hair from each side and tied them together at the back, arranging the rest on her shoulders. Annie sighed. She looked at but did not see the dark lustre of her hair, black as a raven's wing – it looked sombre more than rich to her. She thought the eyes looking back at her were tired and anxious; she couldn't imagine that to others they might look as endlessly blue as the sky would to a man lying on his back in a field in drowsy August. She dismissed the sweet, pure oval of her face as being as dull as a spoon. Annie shrugged, reminding herself that she'd better get the tea made, even if it was only for herself.

*

As the weeks went by Annie noticed the change in her father. Never a talkative man, he seemed turned in on himself. She'd watch him, and see in his face and the movement of his eyes that he was reliving other conversations, ones she had not been a part of. But the edges of his face were softer, as if he smiled more often. His own smile, for her, was gentler. He had not looked like that to her, not since they'd lived on the farm. Not since she had been a child.

There were other things: little considerate acts, like finding he'd emptied out the ashes or taken away the rubbish, or a vivid splash of yellow on the mantelshelf provided by a small earthenware pot of primroses. Annie continued as she'd always done, to get the messages, though she bought less now, for her father ate fewer meals with her. As a pattern of his evenings out was established, Annie found herself invited to join the Nolans. She thanked Philomena every time, even if at the table Teresa's mother was polite but somehow distant. Annie wondered if there was more warmth shown when it was just the family.

'Oh no, I think in some ways she likes it when you're there,' Teresa said one Sunday afternoon when they were strolling past the safely locked shops. 'My brother's on his best behaviour. Frank's still soft on you, so he is.'

'Oh, get away with you! Isn't Frank always on his best behaviour?'

'Not when it's just us! But it wasn't him thought to ask you round. Mammy woulda had a fit if he had – you tempting her golden boy.'

'It was you, of course.'

'I wouldn't'a given her the satisfaction of telling me no. It was my father.'

'Your *father*?'

'With a bit of encouragement from myself. I can get him to do anything I want. Not her. I'd have to be a boy for that.'

'*She* has wee boys, so she has.'

'You ever seen them?'

'No, and I've not gone looking.'

*

Over the tea things that evening Annie asked her father as casually as she could the question she had been rehearsing in her mind ever since her walk with Teresa that afternoon.

'Them wee boys,' she said, 'do they like you?'

Thomas looked up and smiled.

'They do so,' he said. 'Wait now and I'll show you something.' He put down his bread and jam and got up from the table, something Annie never did; her mother had taught her and her brothers that interrupting a meal was 'corner boy' behaviour. She heard his feet thump up the narrow staircase, the click of his door opening, some rummaging. He came back down and handed her a framed photograph: a group of schoolchildren, flanked by their teachers.

'This here is Joe,' he said, pointing with the nail of his pinkie finger at one of the older boys, in a row of children who must have been standing on a trestle, as they were half a head higher than the teachers. Joe gazed out of the photograph suspiciously. Annie read him as a child who would not say much, who needed to trust first.

'And this wee man is Mark,' Thomas said, pointing at one of the smaller children in the cross-legged front row. But Annie had already noticed Mark; his sad little face had drawn her attention the moment she saw the photograph.

'He's not happy, sure he isn't,' she said softly.

'Not at St Patrick's, no. They tease him for not having a father.'

Annie scanned the solemn faces in this bleak anteroom to mill and pit. She felt suddenly older, weary, wishing she could remember her brothers like this. They had one photograph of them that her father kept on the chest of drawers in his room, of unsmiling young men standing against a studio backdrop, alongside a straggling potted plant. But this image of the Cleator Moor school Annie had never seen; she guessed Thomas kept it folded away amongst his clothes.

As if he read her thoughts, Thomas said, 'It's because of them in Canada, too, you know. Joe and Mark'll never be your brothers, but it's a way I have of remembering them. Is that nonsense, Annie?' She caught his earnest gaze, his eyes glistening in the light of the oil lamps.

'No, Dadda,' she said quietly. 'They're nice wee boys. And you'll never leave her as you'll never leave them.'

Thomas touched her hand so briefly it was over before she could respond. He took the photograph and went back upstairs. When he came down again he asked, 'Is there any more tay in that pot there?' as if nothing had happened. Yet Annie knew everything had.

*

After that, Annie felt able to ask her father about Joe and Mark, much as he would ask her about Teresa. *Though he must know,* she thought, *he's working with Michael every day at Crowgarth. That's unless they've stopped speaking.* Yet somehow she knew the friendship grown up between the two men through her meeting Teresa at Andrews' Mill would endure, though she was certain that her father would no longer be welcome at the Nolans' fireside – Philomena would see to that.

Gradually Annie ceased to think of what sinful things Thomas might be doing when she was alone in the house and he was at Elsie's. She imagined him instead with the two little boys, doing what he was good at, which was being a father. She got used to the evenings when she knew she'd be alone. After she'd done the chores she would sit by the hearth and read a novel from the Carnegie Library, wishing Mr Harris could see her. She was deep in poor Jane Eyre's account of her happiness being dashed at the altar – reading the book for the second time – when she heard the back yard gate open and heavy feet run up to the door. She glanced up at the clock – *Why's he early?* – then seeing her father's face in the shadows by the door she put the book down without noting the page number. He burst in without stopping to scrape his boots – something he'd always done automatically, no matter how clean and dry the weather.

'Whatever's wrong?'

'Hagerty,' he said, panting.

Annie put her knuckles to her mouth. She had never heard Thomas refer to a priest without calling him 'Father'. It was almost as if he'd blasphemed.

'He was there – in her house – calling her names – all got up in Bible words but names all the same.' Thomas's hands were on

103

Annie's shoulders, beating on them for emphasis. 'The weans came down crying he made that much noise. You could hear next door – not hear them, I mean. Holding their breath for to not miss a thing. Said he'd caught us in sin when all we were doing was drinking our tea.' Incoherent with rage, he grasped a chair and sat down. In seconds he deflated before her eyes, the fight going out of him with each panting breath. He wiped the back of his hand over his forehead and said in a changed voice, 'I'm sorry, Annie. I never even asked you how you are.'

'Me? Oh . . . What'll yous do now?'

'I'll tell you what I dream of, Annie. Sit down a wee minute, will ye? I'd like us to go away. Us . . .' He waved his hand expansively. 'You, me, her, Joe and Mark. Somewhere where we're not known. Somewhere where she could have my name.'

'Dadda . . .'

'She *is* my wife,' he said. 'No matter what the priest says. In heaven's eyes she's my wife.'

Annie crossed herself and burst into tears.

CHAPTER FOURTEEN

Birks Road, October 1902

> 'Barrow was an insignificant village at the tip of the Furness Peninsula until the early 1840s. The Industrial Revolution arrived quickly and it was the catalyst for a frenzy of work, population growth and development.'
>
> Gill Jepson, *Barrow-in-Furness at Work*, 2017

'Thank you for the tea,' said Michael Nolan, nursing his cup but not tasting it. Annie sat opposite, waiting to find out what he'd come round for.

'You're set on not going with them, then,' he said.

'I am so.'

'You'll not stop him, Annie, if that's what you're thinking,' he said gently.

'He'd not leave me alone here, so he wouldn't,' she said, but she was no longer sure. 'I can't believe he wants me to live under the same roof as him and thon . . . thon woman.'

Michael shifted his weight, making his chair creak. Looking away from her he said, 'I know Philomena wouldn't agree with me, and please never let on I said so, but Elsie Fagan is a decent wee woman.'

'*Decent?*'

'I mean . . . there's no harm in her, sure there isn't. She was bate bad by Fagan—'

'Maybe she gave him cause.' Annie surprised herself at the venom in her voice. She wiped her fingers across her eyes, angry with herself, angry that the woman made her feel so much hate.

'That's not like you, Annie,' said Michael quietly. 'He put her in Whitehaven Infirmary more than once. The neighbours had to take in the wee boys that time. She came back and tried to stay alive because, if she hadn't, they'd've been sent to a home, so they would. She's a grand wee mother.'

'She might be, but she's not *my* mother,' cried Annie. 'My mother's barely three years dead, and I'm supposed to go under the same roof as them and pretend? What did you come here for, Michael? Did he think you'd persuade me when he couldn't?'

'No, I'd another idea altogether. If you really don't want to go to Barrow—'

'Barrow? He never said it was Barrow they were away to.' Then she fell quiet, remembering that she'd stopped her ears and shouted at her father that she didn't want to hear any more of his foolishness, wishing he could see the pain she was in.

'There's labouring work in the shipyard,' Michael said. 'They'll want your father. Crowgarth'll give him a good character and the bosses in Barrow say they can't find an Englishman who'll carry a hod.'

'I can't ...' said Annie, but already she was wondering whether she *could* go to Barrow. *Could we not do the same as here in Cleator Moor, only he's living under her roof? I could look for work – there must be mills there as well, surely? If I'd a room of my own somewhere Dadda could come for his tea three times a week, maybe four ... You know that's pure foolishness, don't you? Whoever heard of a girl your age living on her own? You'd never have the money for it, never mind the wagging tongues.* Then she realised Michael had asked her a question.

'You'd like that, wouldn't you now? Can't keep you and Teresa apart as it is. Philomena took a bit of talking round to the idea, but I'd lie if I said a bit of rent money from you wouldn't be welcome. Maybe some help in the house just out of goodwill as Philomena always has her hands full and Teresa – well, you know how Teresa is.'

Annie pulled herself back into the present. 'You're asking me would I lodge with yous?'

'That's what I said, wasn't it?'

'Whose idea was it?'

'That would have been mine. Mind, we've said nothing to Teresa, in case you didn't like the idea and wanted to go to Barrow instead.'

Annie looked around the little room, at the fire-irons, the crocheted mat on the narrow mantelpiece where the two china dogs she'd bought in the market sat. One of them had been broken and mended, but you couldn't see that from the front and it had meant they were a bargain. She thought of the other poor furnishings of the place, the few bits of linen that had come in the trunk from

Ireland which graced the Sunday table, the way she had positioned both furniture and rag rugs over the worn or cracked places in the green and red leaves of the linoleum. *This was my home.* Then she thought of the bustle and noise of the Nolans' similar-sized dwelling. There was Philomena of course – but Teresa.

'Where would I sleep?'

'We'd put another wee bed up next to Teresa's. The one you've got here, maybe. You'll come then?'

*

'God help me, Annie,' said her father, 'not being with you'll be like losing the boys all over again.'

'It's like leaving Comber,' said Annie, her hands on the rim of a tea-chest that would be sent on ahead. This time there'd been a bit more to pack up; was it possible their lives were becoming less transient? She thought of the farm, though she knew she was forgetting details of it by the day. Maguires there as long as anyone could remember. Before Cromwell's time, according to Mr Harris.

'Yous are only going to Barrow,' said Annie, realising she was somehow taking all of this in her stride. That first sight of England, leaning on the rail of the boat with Teresa, had been like a great lumpy carpet, unrolled and stretching out into infinity. She wasn't exactly sure how far Barrow was, but somehow her horizons had shifted; that town was merely a stop on the train. It was moving from the farm into Comber that had been cataclysmic; she'd thought she'd never get over it. Everything else since then was merely a halt on the road to wherever she was going. *There's got to be somewhere, surely, that'll be my own one day?* Annie had always imagined she'd be the person to leave home, to go under her husband's roof. *That's what you did, wasn't it? Not your father going instead.*

'I wonder what Barrow's like?' she added.

'Bigger than here. Mills as well. Houses like this one, probably. You'll come and see us?'

'I'll come and see *you*, Dadda.' The fact was, she felt herself backed into a corner. Michael had called Elsie 'a decent wee woman'. Annie knew her continued obstinacy put her on the side of Father Hagerty, a man she had never warmed to and who had burst into a quiet tea and frightened two small children. Yet, by everything she had been brought up with, by mother *and* father, she knew the priest couldn't have done any different. She heard her father's sigh, saw him turn his face away.

'I'll see yous off, so I will,' she said.

*

What Annie took to the Nolans' in Birks Road was only a grip, some holy pictures – including the Sacred Heart, which she could now look at without a tremor – the repaired china dogs, her fragile but precious St Brigid cross and her own iron-framed bed, dismantled and clanked down the stairs. The landlord's agent gave her something for the remaining furniture; it would do the next tenants, he said, off the next Whitehaven ferry. Annie wondered if anyone ever took the ferry back again.

*

Looking down from the bridge onto the platform at Moor Row it was the little boys Annie saw first, not because they were tearing around the way most children of their age would have done, excited at the prospect of a train journey, but because they were still. The older boy guarded a pitifully small heap of luggage, while his younger brother sat on a cardboard suitcase, his little face as resigned as a thirty-year-old man's. Then she noticed a woman sitting on the bench nearby, almost as still as the children but for the twisting of her hands. Annie watched her, this woman with a husband, whom her father blasphemously claimed as his wife, plainly dressed as a mill girl on Sunday – *Maybe she was one once* – in a dark skirt, buttoned boots, a snowy white blouse poking out of the old-fashioned little jacket. Then the woman turned to look up at her and Annie realised she'd stared too long. She saw a pale oval, a compressed mouth, fine arched brows and streaks of grey in the soft brown hair tumbled on the top of her head. At that moment Annie's father came out from the ticket office and caught sight of her up on the bridge. Flushing, Annie saw the little group for what it was: a working man and his family, moving on to the next town, the next wage.

Catch yourself on, Annie told herself, hoping the woman would think her pink face was only because she'd been hurrying. *There's only ten minutes and they'll be away.*

As Annie came down the steps, the woman stood up, smoothing down her skirt and tucking a strand of blown hair behind her ear. Annie saw her father move to Elsie's shoulder, and prayed he wouldn't touch the woman in front of her, no, not even her arm. Instead it was Elsie who stepped forward, putting out a hand which after a moment's hesitation Annie took, good manners taking over. The woman's grip was firmer than the girl had expected, the palm warm and dry despite her hand-wringing.

'I'm Elsie Fagan. I can see you're Tom's child.'

Annie bridled a little; Tom had been the name her mother used. For everyone else he was Thomas, or occasionally Tommy.

'Them's your wee boys, then?' she said, fighting down her resentment. Children were safer ground.

'This is my son Joseph. Say hello, Joe.'

Joe stepped forward in a soldierly way and put out his hand too, murmuring something.

They're well-brung-up anyway, thought Annie. 'You'll be going to a new school, then?'

Joe nodded, and Annie saw him as good as shackled to a desk, his stylus scratching on a slate, afraid just as she had been to raise his hand off its surface when doing 'joined-up' words, for fear of a rap on the back of the knuckles. In a flash Annie could see Joe's life mapped out: an apprenticeship in the shipyard that everyone said was as big as Belfast's, rising every day for the hooter, one day being made foreman and having boys answer to him who were not much bigger than he was now. Then one day when he was older and his eyesight not so sharp, nor his movements so quick, his workmates would say goodbye to him and wish him luck and turn up the next day and not miss him for there was always someone to take his place.

Then her reverie was interrupted by a small hand pushing its way into hers. She looked down.

'You must be Mark.'

'I am so.'

Annie smiled: the child spoke with the flattened vowels of Cumberland but that turn of phrase was pure Ulster.

'Are you coming wi' us?' he asked.

'Not this time.'

The solemn little face frowned. 'When?'

'I couldn't say, Mark.' Annie was aware of her father's eyes on her, but she didn't dare look round.

'Who's going to watch Joe and me, then?' Sensing a movement, the child broke his gaze, turning to Thomas.

'Your mammy. She won't be working – at least not to start with,' said Thomas. 'It's me will be in the shipyard.'

A blast of a whistle came down the line and their five heads swivelled in its direction. The black barrelled shape of the train was coming into view, smoke and steam billowing around it like an old woman's frowsty skirts. Backbones stiffened, hands tightened on luggage. The station platform was wreathed in fumes like mist on the Cumberland hills. The doors of third class swung open and the three carriages sucked up the people on the platform like tacks to a magnet.

'Goodbye Miss Maguire,' Annie heard Elsie say. There were other words lost in the rapid-fire of slamming doors. Her father's arms were suddenly around her.

'Oh Annie—'

Someone shouted – the stationmaster, the girl thought – words he'd said so often that they took on a distorted shape of their own, but which nevertheless conveyed something like

'All aboard.' Thomas was gone, the last door closed, the engine hissed, pistons reared and the train moved.

Annie watched it out of sight, thinking, *I could have gone too*. She strained ears and eyes until there was nothing left down the line, not even a blur, and walked slowly to the steps, still feeling the pressure of Mark's small hand in her own. *I could have been his sister.* Then she remembered she needed to hurry. Her chit from Mrs Birkett was only for that hour.

*

'Ah, you're back quick, lass,' said the doffing mistress, glancing up at the clock on the end wall. 'Within your time. I put Kitty on your stand this morning so we'll leave her there till dinner-time. I've set you up over here.' Annie followed the woman down the spinning hall.

'Get away all right, did they?'

Annie nodded, digesting the 'they'. She'd only mentioned that her father was leaving. But they all knew. Of course they did.

The woman leaned in to her ear. 'I'll get you to work through two dinner-times. Save us the work of docking your pay.'

'Thank you.' Annie had already calculated that even with paying bed and board to Philomena Nolan she would be able to put something by, bit by bit. *But what for?* As her hands slipped unconsciously into the rhythm of the machine, she thought: *What have I to look forward to?*

*

That evening Annie stood in the Nolans' back room as Philomena ticked off on her fingers the rules her lodger would need to abide by. The way Philomena spoke, Annie could tell the woman had rehearsed everything. She was wondering how on earth she'd remember the entire litany, until she realised that all she needed to do was follow Teresa's lead in stripping her bed on the right day, not changing the tea leaves in the pot below a certain level, being there for meals at an allotted time and do her part in clearing up after them, washing her aprons herself (by now Annie had six, priding herself on going to the mill each day in a clean one). Finally Philomena said, 'And absolutely no callers,' to remind her that she was only a paying guest, not a member of the family.

*

It was better later, when she and Teresa were lying in their narrow beds, placed closely enough to each other in the little room that they could stretch out without having to straighten their elbows and clasp each other's hands. They whispered, even though two doors and the head of the staircase separated them from where Michael and Philomena slept. Frank was downstairs on a put-you-up.

'We're nearly eighteen, Annie. You'll only be leaving this house, same as me, the day you get wed. Mammy was already married by the time she was our age.'

'What about when you marry Percy?'

Annie heard Teresa shift in her bed.

'*If* I marry Percy. I've not said yes yet.'

Annie looked up at the shadowy ceiling, waiting. He'd asked, then. Teresa hadn't told her that.

'He's said he'd go and see Father Hagerty. He doesn't bother his head about things like that though. It must be on account of being English. It must be nice not having your life decided for you by priests and ministers. Not like at home.' Teresa turned on her side, facing her friend. Annie could sense her smile even in the dark.

'We should find an English boy for you too. That's unless you want our Frank or for the nuns to get ye.'

'Neither of them – with no offence to Frank. Anyway, who'd give me away, Teresa?'

There was the slightest pause, then Teresa said with conviction, 'Sure, Dadda would do that. He thinks the world of you.' She laughed. 'If Mammy wasn't there he'd come and ask you for himself, so he would. Only Frank'd knock him down.'

'Get away with you!' said Annie, though her youthful belief that falling in love wasn't for people in their forties had already been shaken.

'Ssh! Not so loud.'

*

Annie lay awake for an hour, listening to Teresa's regular breathing, thinking about her friend's words. Marriage? There had never been what she'd have thought of as followers to the little house in Bowthorn Road. True, Frank had been an occasional caller, but she'd made tea for him and her father while they'd talked about plans to regularise a football club in the town and whether, for rugby, the Wath Brow Hornets would ever re-form. Annie had marvelled at the capacity of men to talk for hours about sports they didn't actually play themselves. After his tea, Frank had always politely thanked her and put his cap back on.

Then she thought about her father, and what he might be doing now. She imagined him and Elsie settling the two little boys to sleep in a strange place, murmuring reassuring words to them, then looking across the children at each other, and smiling. They'd teach the boys to call Thomas 'Dadda', wouldn't they? And their mother would pass as Elsie Maguire. In a few weeks' time they'd be spending Christmas Day together, a family, while she, Thomas's own flesh and blood, would be a paying guest of the Nolans. In the morning – Annie could not allow herself to think of how they might pass their first night in Barrow together – her father would present himself at the shipyard in the hope that he'd get to see someone in charge and that there wouldn't be too many other men there with the same purpose, younger and fitter ones. He'd be wearing a clean collar and would have shaved himself to a rash. The testimonial from Crowgarth would be crinkling in a long envelope inside his jacket. Annie could see him so vividly in her mind's eye that she felt she could almost touch his arm as he stood there patiently.

What would he say if they asked him if he was a married man? Annie had some idea they'd want that – someone who was steady. Would he pretend to the world that Joe and Mark were his or would he tell everyone Elsie was Fagan's widow?

What if she is? Annie seized on this. *I could pray that she be one, for the sake of Dadda's immortal soul. But I'd be praying for the death of the other man. That's a sin too, so it is.* She went around in circles, until the thin dark figure of the other priest, the curate Father Clayton, entered her thoughts.

That's what I'll do. I'll go to confession. Just not to Father Hagerty.

*

Annie saw the priest's shadow shift again behind the grille. The tiniest sounds were amplified in that space. She could almost convince herself she could hear him blinking. A shift, and then a sigh.

'That's the problem with sin, my child. It is not just the harm the sinner does to himself and thus to God, but the way that sin causes others to stumble too. The first sin is that man Fagan's. Had he not gone from the family home, leaving his wife undefended, your father would not have seen her alone and felt pity for her – a beautiful, human, God-given emotion but one which Satan saw as his chance to exploit as a weakness. Your father saw those half-orphaned boys and felt the pressure of that little lad's hand, just as you did. He probably felt some pity for himself – vulnerable too, without your mother. Try not to blame him, child, but pray for him, and leave it in God's hands, for whom nothing is impossible.'

'But . . .'

'Go on, child.'

117

'Mr Fagan beat her and the boys, Dadda said. Is that not a sin too?'

Clayton hesitated. 'It is, of course. It's a sin against the married state, against the vows he made. Had the lady come to us, we might have been able to do something – given them permission to live separately. Well . . . that's what *I* would have done for her . . .' He tailed off, then said in a more confident voice, in which Annie sensed the priest taking over from the man, 'But she would not have been allowed to take another man instead. You see, what the word sin means is to shoot wide of the target, Annie. It distorts. Then everything else follows, down to you wishing ill on the head of a man you've never met, even if, from what you say, the world would say he deserves it.'

'What must I do?'

'Pray for your father, and everyone else caught up in this. I'm not going to give you ten Hail Marys and two Our Fathers to repeat. I want you to go to the statue of St Joseph and light candles for all of them. They mightn't ever know that you did, but God will see you do it and be merciful.' Annie heard him take a deep breath. 'It might even be the case, you know, that your father lives without sin with this woman, caring for her children just as St Joseph cared for his family.'

As Father Clayton pronounced the words of absolution Annie listened with head bowed, but remembered her father's cry, 'In heaven's eyes she's my wife.'

CHAPTER FIFTEEN

Twelfth of July 1903

'The Protestant Boys are loyal and true
Stout-hearted in battle and stout-handed too
The Protestant Boys are true to the last
And faithful and peaceful when danger has passed.'

Traditional, sung to the tune of 'Lillibullero'

Robert McClure's heart thrummed in his chest as he joined the crowd massing outside the doors of the Lodge. He was part of something at last, accepted as more than the fourth bed in the room in the house on Leconfield Street. A space was made for him now in the crush of the front bar of the Railway Hotel. But the speakers he'd heard in the Lodge had made him feel uneasy at first. He'd wanted to say to them, 'I knew a good taig, so I did,' in loyalty to Kathleen's memory, but even with her, even as a boy, he'd learned that she was *not* considered good by her fellow Catholics. She hadn't even lived where they did, had she? She'd preferred the cold disapproval of her Protestant neighbours every time Cairncross visited to taking a house in a Catholic street where they'd have told her to her face that she brought scandal and would be punished in some corner of hell reserved for women like her. She'd told Robert as much, and he'd tried to square his imperfect understanding of what she said with the pale faces with their liquid eyes in those religious images that adorned the walls of her cottage. He'd been too little then to really comprehend what it was Kathleen did wrong, though he understood now. *How many of them neighbour wummin knew I was Cairncross's bastard?* he'd asked himself later. No, Kathleen was a good soul not because she was a Catholic, but in spite of being one, was his reasoning.

The Catholic religion paid allegiance to a foreign power, the speakers informed him. Their loyalty lay with a bedizened old man enthroned in Rome waiting for people to come forward to kiss his ring or even his toe, a man enriched with alms extorted from the needy, running a network of men who debauched innocent young women lured from behind the grille of the confessional, men who had entered that unholy priesthood because it absolved them of the ties and responsibilities of hearth and home, allowing them every comfort – and vice – without having to pay for them.

No picture of Their Majesties the King and Queen would grace the walls of a Fenian home, one of the speakers had said. Standing on the podium in the main chamber of the Lodge, he'd gesticulated towards the large tinted photograph of a heavy-lidded bearded man in a dark suit and a lady with an impossibly narrow waist, her hair crimped on top of her head. Robert was privately disappointed in this image. He would have preferred a king to look like one, not like a respectable doctor living in one of the nice houses in Ennerdale Road, nor the queen to have had hair that reminded him of the curls between a heifer's horns.

And now the rat-tat-tat of the great Lambeg drums was starting, the fifes following, and outside the pub the procession swerved into place, office-bearers in their gloves and bowlers to the front, the banners held aloft behind them, their tassels dancing as they moved, the sunlight reflected off their brass pommels. Robert, in his usual cap but with a new collar, was happy to be one of the mass at the rear. He glanced down at his Lodge badge with pride.

He noticed though when the streets that had been lined with waving women and children gave way to those that were shuttered and silent. Here the drums sounded louder, the roar of their singing mightier, and the insults and catcalls began. The street looked to him as though it held its breath. Then somehow, amidst the din and the brightness, he had the sense he was being watched. Instinctively he glanced at an upper window, glimpsing a girl's pale face. Their eyes met and for the first time he thought, *What am I doing here? Frightening a lovely girl like that in her own home.* He wanted to break ranks and run to her door, apologise to her and tell her there was no harm in it really, just high spirits and a bit of tradition. He wanted to tell her about Kathleen. But the momentum of the march carried him forward. Some of his companions were indeed banging on doors, but not to reassure anyone. Out of the corner of his eye he saw a lace curtain shiver quickly into place.

*

'Come away from that window, Annie!' exclaimed Teresa, through the rattling tattoo of cane on taut goatskin. 'Do you want them to break it for us?'

Annie backed away from the window, her heart thumping. Meeting that young man's eyes had felt like touching his hand. There'd been something thrilling though about the march, vast drums carried by men bowed backwards, swinging them from side to side and occasionally birling right round. Annie wondered if they did this to distract themselves from the weight they carried before them like great tumescent extensions of their own bodies, bodies which the following day would bend forward in the pit, where in the darkness and dirt and toil the village's divisions might be forgotten. A phalanx of fifers had followed, and beyond them the tramp tramp of miners' and millhands' nailed boots and clogs, bearing faces raised triumphantly, the favoured men carrying banners showing images not of saints but of a bewigged and hatted man on a rearing white horse, holding a sword aloft. Annie had seen these faces in the market square and outside the pubs she'd never entered, but on this day only did they come down this street, reminding its inhabitants that here, just as back across the Irish Sea, their rule prevailed. Yet when that one face had turned to hers, she hadn't feared the man. *He looked lonely.*

'Cost us a day's work, so they did,' muttered Teresa. 'We don't make them celebrate our feast days but we're supposed to put up with theirs.'

The racket died away in the direction of Trumpet Street and the church. In the sudden quiet Annie heard a beer bottle roll from the cobbles into the gutter. Behind her, Philomena shifted on Teresa's bed. Annie couldn't understand why the woman hadn't gone into her own room at the back.

'Let's hope they leave the Priory House alone,' said Philomena.

'Let's hope we can go out now,' said Teresa, tapping her foot impatiently on the dark varnish of the floorboards.

'Go *out?* Why in the name of God would ye go out today of all days?' said her mother.

'They're going for their picnic on Wath Brow. So I'll not go to Wath Brow, obviously. You coming, Annie?'

Annie hesitated, but knew she couldn't refuse. She knew an enforced day's holiday was too good for Teresa to miss when it meant Percy too was free.

'Well, I'm off downstairs to wash the delph. Some help would be good, so it would,' said Philomena, back to her old self now the danger was past. She stomped out.

Annie's shoulders slumped. They'd moved all the crockery out of the parlour to the back room to enable Michael to push the dresser up against the front door. *I shoulda known she'd'a wanted it all washed before putting it back.* To cheer herself up she said, 'It's maybe gone off all right this year, Teresa.'

'If we coulda got her to go and lie down and have a fit of the vapours instead of sitting here with us we'd'a had all the oul' delph done ourselves quicker. I'm supposed to meet Percy in the square in an hour.'

*

The girls got to the square a quarter of an hour early. By force of old habit the two of them gravitated to look in the windows of Fowles. That it was closed was irrelevant; neither Annie nor

KATIE HUTTON

Teresa ever had enough money to buy anything there. It was a wonder to both that there were people who did. There was the prettiest hat perched roguishly on a stand, with a softly turned brim and a jaunty feather. Annie found herself exclaiming aloud at the sight of it, and pointing.

'You'd be a princess in that, so you would,' said Teresa.

'Not much call for princesses in Cleator Moor,' said Annie.

'If I'd the tin I'd come here for my wedding true-so,' said Teresa. At least that's what Annie thought Teresa had said. *Wedding and true should go together, right enough.* Blinking, she made herself look at a linen blouse, set far back in the window so as not to be spoiled by the sun. *I could wear that and nobody stare at me*, she thought, *but I'd feel a lady in it.* The blouse was plain except for the three lines of descending lengths of drawn thread work that ran down from each shoulder seam. Her experienced eye told her that this linen was the finest, and she knew all the ways that had made it so, from the choice of flax seed, the stripping out of the fibres, the scutching, the beetling . . .

'Percy!' she heard Teresa exclaim. Annie turned her head and nodded a quick smile at Percy, before looking back to the window. The reflection of their figures, merged into one as Percy dipped his head to kiss Teresa, superimposed itself on the pretty blouse.

'We'll have to take the long way round if we've to avoid Wath Brow,' said Percy. 'But they'll have drunk their way home by the time we get back.'

CHAPTER SIXTEEN

Wath Brow, Twelfth of July 1903

'The trouble in Ireland is water. There's Holy water and there's Boyne water. The two don't mix.'
Protestant woman trade-union organiser, b. 1906, Belfast.

From Betty Messenger, *Picking up the Linen Threads*

Where are they? Annie shifted on her usual place on the wall, straining her eyes up the path to see if she could see Teresa and Percy. She'd just heard the bells tolling five o'clock. *If we're not back to set the tea things I'm in deep trouble. Philomena'll scald the heart out of me.*

Just then she heard a scuffle of footsteps coming down the path, but from the wrong direction. There were several pairs, and joshing male voices with an unmistakable Ulster cadence, a cadence though that wasn't quite her own.

'Sure, we showed them Fenian bastards who's boss, so we did!'

Annie slipped off the wall and leaned against it, her back turned to the path, pretending to look at the sheep. She knew those words were a test. She was meant to turn around and congratulate the speaker, or at the very least smile her approval.

The feet had stumbled to a halt behind her. She could hear breathing, and caught a waft of stale beer and tobacco.

'Come on, lads, leave 'er be,' said a new voice.

'Not till I've seen the lass's face,' said the first man. There was some scuffling then, sniggering and whispering. Annie felt as though her heart rose in her chest, cramping her breathing.

'Leave her be, Willie!' said the second voice.

'No. We deserve some respect. And we'll have it.' Respect came out as 'reshpeck'.

'No, Willie!'

The sound of boots thudding on compacted earth, then hot breath on the back of her neck, and a hand gripped her shoulder, spinning her around.

'You'll look at me when I'm talking to you, so you will!'

Annie stared into a red, sweating face, bad teeth in a distorted mouth, hair and eyebrows like tow beneath a greasy cap.

'Like I thought. You can see it in her eyes!' The man's hand pushed her shoulder as if shaking apples from a tree. 'Pape hoor! You shoulda been hiding indoors like all the rest of yous. This is *our* day!'

There were four of them, she saw now. One stood slightly back from the others, twisting his cap in his hands. Still no sign of Teresa and Percy. Nothing for it but—

Her blouse tore as she pulled away from the man's grip. The air was suddenly cool on her shoulder. There was confused shouting, something like 'Now look what you've done,' and just as she was wondering what on earth she'd tell the Nolans her toe hit something and the ground came up to meet her with such speed she didn't even have time to put her hands out to protect herself. Something sharp dug into her cheek, and in seconds she was surrounded, as if by a pack of panting dogs. An arm pulled her roughly around. Tow-haired Willie leaned over her, spraying her face with beery spittle.

'Ye wee bitch. That'll learn you.'

She saw his eyes widen. A series of grunts, then a scuffle and Willie's face veered back and out of her line of vision, as though pulled by a string.

'Get *off* me!' he roared.

'Away home now. Yous go with him an' all.'

'Aye, come on, Willie. She's not worth it,' said a third voice. To her relief, they scuffled off.

Dazed, Annie propped herself on an elbow, wondering what she could have done to have made the day so bad. She put her hand to her face, then saw there was a smear of blood on her fingertip. *It's all right now. They've gone, so they have.*

'Are you hurt there?' said a voice.

Annie gasped, and looked up. 'It's you,' she said, gazing into the eyes of the man she'd seen from her window, seeing recognition dawn in his face also.

'It is so,' he said, with a shy smile. 'You've a bit of a graze there. If you've nothing broken come back down to the bridge and we'll wet my handkerchief.'

'My blouse . . .' She sat up.

'Here,' he said, putting his cap back on and reaching his hands to her.

'I'm all right, so I am,' she said, scrambling to her feet. Then, 'Sorry.'

'What for?'

Annie didn't answer. *Aye, what* am *I sorry for? Existing?* But she knew it wasn't that. It was refusing those outstretched hands. Hadn't the man rescued her? She glanced up. He was about a head taller than she was, sturdily built, strength in the broad hands now held tense by his sides. The reddish tinge to his face marked him as one of those who toiled underground in the haematite mines, as distinctive as the reddle on the wool of the sheep in that field. It emphasised the whites of his eyes and the warmth of their hazel irises.

She thought the young miner was dressed too warmly for that summer day, in a jacket and waistcoat and a new cellulose collar. A pin gleamed on his lapel: a bewigged and hatted man astride a rearing horse, his sword raised. She made out the words 'loyal brethren'. Annie dusted down her skirts. 'I'd best go. I'll be late for my tea.'

'Not alone you won't. Not looking like that,' the man said. He took hold of the torn cotton of her sleeve and tried ineffectually to lift it back to her shoulder. She felt his fingertips, calloused hard, brush the skin of her upper arm, yet gently.

'I've my pin,' he said. 'You'll maybe not like it but it'll hold you together.' Before she could say anything, he'd unhooked King Billy and was busy with the folds of cloth. Those broad fingers felt surprisingly deft.

'There,' he said, his head on one side as he appraised his work. 'It's not perfect but it'll keep out the draught.' For the first time he smiled. 'Now let's have a look at your face.' He studied it as carefully as if it was a map. 'Can you walk? You're not sprained, are you?'

Annie tested both ankles, shaking her head.

'Come away back then,' he said. 'The picnic's over, so it is.'

She followed him down the path, walking two feet to the side and looking back over her shoulder every few yards.

'Someone you're supposed to meet?' he said.

'Yes . . . my friends. I was waiting on them.'

'Strange friends to leave you alone. Especially today.'

They reached the little bridge at Wath Brow. Even from some distance away, the grass looked crushed. Several women were working over the slope, bent over and gathering up bottles and other flotsam into jute sacks. Annie saw one of them pick up a torn orange and purple sash, flapping it and shaking her head. Pigeons and sparrows were also diligently hunting for crumbs and scraps.

'Sit yourself here, so,' said her companion. 'Otherwise you might get your shoes muddy.'

Obediently Annie propped herself against the low parapet of the little bridge, while the man walked down to the reeds at the bank of the stream. Crouching to wet his handkerchief, he twisted his face up to her and said, 'Wouldn't you 'a done better to 'a stayed indoors the day?'

That angered her. *All I was doing was sitting on a wall minding my own business. I didn't ask yous all to come and bother me.* She said nothing, reminding herself that he was helping her. She fingered the little pin holding her sleeve in place but withdrew her hand quickly. It had pricked her.

He was standing in front of her now, the sodden handkerchief raised. 'Sit still now.'

As he dabbed at her face, not meeting her eyes, he said, 'You'd to get out of the house, right enough. A grand day like this one.'

She watched the compression of his mouth as he concentrated on his task, a frown between the dark brows. She saw the faint burn on his neck from too close a shave. The collar looked as though it chafed him too. He smelled of something clean – carbolic soap, she thought. There was no trace of the beer and tobacco stench of the man Willie.

'There,' he said when he'd finished. 'You'll live, so you will. Don't pick the scab when it forms and you'll be like new. I'll see you home now.'

'There's no need.'

'Sure there is. I hadn't the chance to see the number of your house when I went past earlier and I'll need to find where to come back for my pin. Unless you'll be wanting to keep it.'

She looked at him. Afterwards she couldn't remember which of them had started to laugh first.

*

'Where are you from, then?' he said as they reached the cobbled streets. She was looking sideways at him – anything but meet the eye of anyone they passed. Annie already knew from his accent that she could be precise. 'Moneyscalp Townland,' she said. 'Then we moved to Comber.'

'Get away! They said I was born in Crossgar . . . I lived all over when I was wee, but in Killyleagh the longest. Just you, is it?'

'It is now. Mammy's gone. My da's in Barrow with his new wife.' *There's other lies I'll be telling the day. Thon isn't going to be the weeest of them.* 'My brothers are in Canada. I was wondering shouldn't I join them.'

'Oh, don't go just yet,' he said.

'I haven't the fare anyway. And it's a long way to go alone. What about you?'

'Mammy's a cook in the Big House in Crossgar.'

'Your da?'

'Him?' There was a slight pause, and a hardness came into his voice. 'He's the land agent.'

'Oh.'

'I'm lucky. I coulda been in the Olivet at Ballygowan,' he said. 'The man that ran the place hanged himself to not stand his trial, they say, so the weans he'd harmed never got their day in court. My father got me my job here and paid my boat fare.'

'Which pit do you work then?' she asked, with the memory of his fingertips on her arm.

'Crowgarth – Leconfield's. You're in Ainsworth's, are you?'

'I am so.'

'I wonder why I never seen you until today.'

She smiled slightly. It could only be that he was polite, she thought. He knew all about Cleator Moor's demarcated streets, didn't he?

'What are you there?' he asked.

'Spinner. They learned me that in Comber, but here the money's better. What's the mining like?'

He smiled. 'What you'd expect. Dirty. Damp. The lads are good, mostly. Only not the ones I lodge with. I was thinking

131

should I not try to find a different place – after today I think I'd better. Only it's cheap.' He paused. 'I'm saving up, you see.'

'To emigrate?'

'I think we've already done that – emigrating, I mean. No. Mr Cairncross – my da, that is – said I'd never starve if I went underground. He never said nothing about black damp or falls, right enough. I'm really a tailor, though – at least I want to be – mind, you're the only person here to know that.' He looked suddenly shy, younger beneath the iron-ore weathering of his skin.

'I'll not tell, but why aren't ye?' she said, thinking about the displays in Fowles's window, the blouse she and Teresa had admired.

'That's what I'm saving up for, for to have my own shop. I've the machine and the shears and all back in Crossgar. Mammy has them stored in the Offices at the Big House. Mr Cairncross arranged that too. The last lady – where I used to live, I mean – she learned me. The tools were all hers. Only I've not the capital. Not yet. I've a wee account book with the bank on the square.'

'Wouldn't your da help?'

He gave a short laugh. 'He's a few others pulling on his pocket, so he has. I shouldn't complain.'

Stopping in front of the Nolans' house, Annie fumbled at the neck of her blouse, pulling out the key on its string. From the rumble of voices within she knew Michael and Frank were inside, so there'd be cladding between her and Philomena.

'What'll you tell them?'

'I'll tell them I slipped and fell. It's partly true. That's not the problem, though.'

'What is? Me?'

'No, covering for Teresa – the girl I was waiting for. Her and her man. I'll not be mentioning you. I'll wait for them, maybe.' She propped herself on the windowsill, wishing him away before all the neighbours saw him.

He glanced at the door, memorising the number. 'I don't even know your name.'

'Annie.'

'Annie . . . I'm Robert. I'm sorry again about the blouse.'

'It wasn't your fault. Thank you for bringing me home. '

There was a short silence. 'I'll go then, so I will.' He touched his cap. 'Goodbye, Annie.'

She watched him to the end of the street, willing him to turn round, but when he did, and waved, she didn't know what to do, settling for a timid smile she thought he probably couldn't see from that distance, and a barely raised hand. Then the moment he turned the corner, Teresa came hurtling around it.

'Oh, you'd the heart out of me!' she exclaimed, bent over, her hands on her knees. 'I've a stitch, so I have. Percy forgot to wind that watch of his. And there was Orangemen on that path – I heard them from the other side of the wall. Where were you?' Then Annie saw her friend's eyes widen. 'What happened to your face?'

Annie explained as quickly as she could. At the end, Teresa glanced up at the street mouth. 'Him? So I just missed him? Brown curly hair? I seen him, so I did. Fine-looking fella with a wee secret smile on his face.'

'We'd best decide what to tell them indoors.'

'They'll not notice when they've heard my news,' said Teresa, triumphant. 'Percy's been to see them at the Priory House. Says he'll agree to whatever Hagerty says, and we'll be wed.'

*

Michael and Frank were sitting at the table, playing rummy. They looked up as the two girls came in and, seeing Annie, their cards stilled in their hands. Philomena called out from the kitchen.

'Back are ye? Come and give me a hand then,' she said. The silence from the table made her turn round.

'Dear Lord, what's happened to *you?*'

CHAPTER SEVENTEEN

Birks Road, Twelfth of July 1903

'By its very nature, lying is to be condemned. It is a prof-
anation of speech, whereas the purpose of speech is to
communicate known truth to others.'

Catechism of the Catholic Church, 2485

Philomena heard Annie's stammering story in a hardening
silence. She tailed off in the face of the woman's implacable stare.
At her shoulder Teresa fidgeted. Annie could hear her breathing. Michael looked from Annie to his wife and back, perplexed.

'I think you need a wee drop of the hard tack, Annie,' he said.

'You'll give her nothing, Michael Nolan,' said his wife, without taking her eyes off Annie. 'She wants bate, so she does, her
and our girl. Bold liars, the both of 'em.'

Annie heard Teresa's sharp intake of breath, but Philomena
went on before her daughter could speak.

'I seen Father Hagerty an hour ago. Poor good man, told
me couldn't make himself heard at midday mass for all the row
them Orange Boys were making.'

'You never said you'd gone—' Michael tried to interject.

'He'd a visitor yesterday, so he did,' said Philomena, ignoring her husband.

'Percy!' said Teresa, delighted. 'See, Annie, didn't I tell ye?'

'Wanting instruction. He has it in his head to marry our girl, Michael. Only Father Hagerty says the boy has no religion. "Thought it was like going to the Post Office for a postal order, so he did," was his exact words.'

'That's unfair!' shouted Teresa.

'Don't you yell at me, my girl. Think you can tell the priest his business? After you've been seein' this fella and never a word to your father or myself?' Philomena rounded on Annie then. 'And as for *you* – it's you I blame. Took you in when you were as good as orphaned, against my better judgement only you did that moony face of yours at my husband—'

'Philomena—'

She went on as though Michael hadn't spoken. 'Butter wouldn't melt, would it? But if my daughter's been able to walk out with this English boy, bold as brass, then she could only do it with your help. That'll learn me to be kind, so it will. You'll pack your bags, milady.'

'No, Mammy—' cut in Frank, the first words he'd spoken since the two girls had come in.

'Stop it, Philomena,' said Michael, in a quieter voice.

His wife's eyebrows shot up, and her mouth opened, but before she could go on, Michael said, 'Who is this boy, Tessie? Will we get to meet him?'

At that, Philomena spun round, muttering something inaudible, and flounced off through the scullery, to rattle open the back door. The slam she gave it made the window panes quiver.

'Frank,' said his father. 'Away and get the hard tack from the front room, will you? And glasses for all of us.'

The two girls, still standing by the door, parted to let Frank through. He didn't look at either, though Annie offered him a timid smile in thanks for that '*No, Mammy.*'

'We'll have a wee toast, so we will,' said Michael. 'Then I think you'd best go up, Annie, and I'll fetch my wife back in from the wash-house. Don't pack your bag just yet. It's this Percy business has her through other, not yourself.'

*

Annie kicked off her shoes and lay on the bed, half-hazy with the finger of whiskey Michael had insisted she drink. It made the thought of having to pack and move on unreal, like the shreds of a dream. Unreal because she hadn't the faintest idea where she would go. Downstairs the voices murmured on. Every now and then she heard Teresa's higher tones raised in protest, but the most she could make out was a peevish 'It's not fair.' Then finally there was the sticky squeal of chair legs on lino, and the sounds split in different directions, with Teresa's lighter tread coming up the stairs. Her friend came in, and threw herself down on her bed with such force that the metal legs shifted on the varnished floorboards.

'Twenty-one! That's forever, so it is. I'll be an old woman.'

Annie heard tears in her friend's voice.

'They'll not give their permission,' Teresa went on. 'So I've to wait till I'm of age.'

'Percy'll wait, so he will,' said Annie, as confidently as she could manage. 'You could both put a bit by in the meantime.'

'I don't want to wait,' said Teresa, plucking at the counterpane. Then in a sudden change of mood, she added, 'Gretna's only a bit above Carlisle anyway.'

'*Gretna?* What class of marriage would that be? You're never thinking of that, are ye?'

'I threatened them with it unless you got to stay.'

Annie propped herself up on her elbow, suddenly sober. 'You never!'

'Cross my heart and hope to die,' said Teresa, her hand sketching up to down, left to right, above face and breast. 'That's the deal we have. I'll wait, but you'll wait with me. Dadda wants to meet Percy and we've to hope Mammy won't put senna powder in the soda farls. Dadda's a wee bit put out with you, by the way.'

'Of course he is.'

'It's not for you covering for me, so it isn't. It's for telling fibs about them marks on your face. He didn't believe a word of it but says it's to your credit that you're a terrible liar.'

'I only said it because I didn't want them knowing about Percy.'

'That's what I said. Then he told me I was lucky to have a friend who'd do anything for me. Poor Dadda. He hasn't that in Mammy, so he hasn't.'

'Ssh!'

'It's true, though.'

'No, I mean ssh because they're coming up.'

Both girls lay there holding their breath as they heard murmuring and footsteps on the stairs. There was some shuffling on the tiny landing, then silence. Annie wondered if they were listening. Then a door closed on a bedroom she had never seen.

A moment later she whispered the most daring thing she thought she'd said in her life. 'Do they even like each other, Teresa?'

'No,' her friend whispered back, so promptly that Annie knew Teresa had realised this long before. There was a pause, then, 'Can you keep a secret?'

'I never said about Percy, did I?'

'They don't know, but I seen their marriage lines. Our Frank came only six months after.'

'But she's so . . .'

'I know. Right on top of you if you put a foot wrong. I think she wanted better'n a poor working man, Annie. She was a wee bit happier when I said Percy was a hackler, though I'd bet my bloomers she wanted a clerk in an office for me.'

'I'm just glad we're not hiding anymore.'

'So'm I. You were class, though. But it wasn't fair on you, so it wasn't. Musta been boring, all that waiting about for Percy and me.'

'You couldn't call today boring, so you couldn't.'

Teresa giggled. 'Right enough. A Twelfth like no other. Will you see your man again, then?'

'Why would I? Well, I might. Only because he'll want his King Billy pin back.'

*

They were about to sit down to tea two days later when there was a tentative knock at the door. Though she was carrying a plate of bread and butter, Teresa nearly upended it nudging Annie's elbow, which in turn meant the delph on the tray she was carrying shivered. Annie looked round, to see Teresa mouth, 'Percy.' Frank Nolan went to answer, as he was nearest.

'It's someone for you, Annie,' he said, leading in Robert. The young man was carrying a flat brown paper parcel as if it was a plate. Annie put down the tray and wiped her hands on her apron, nervously remembering Philomena's veto on any callers. She felt four pairs of eyes on them both as she went forward, not knowing what she should do.

'There's a chair here, son,' said Michael Nolan, solving the problem but creating another. 'You'll have some tea, won't you now?'

'This is Robert,' said Annie, wanting to put things on the right footing. 'He brought me back when I had my fall.' She gave him a look, which with an almost imperceptible nod he showed he understood.

'I was worried she hadn't twisted her ankle,' he said, 'sliding like that.'

'It was a good deed you did,' said Michael. 'Especially on that day. There were men about who might've wanted to do her harm.'

Annie held her breath. Did Michael know what Robert was? Were his words a test?

'Annie,' said Philomena, the first time she'd spoken since Robert came in. 'Away and get your guest a cup.'

Heart thumping despite her relief, and straining not to miss a word, Annie backed into the front parlour to fetch an extra cup, saucer and plate from the cupboard beneath the dresser. Those sufficient for the family were in constant use between table and sink and so were never put away.

'I was farmed out a bit near there,' she heard Robert say, and knew that the ritual of placing the stranger in relation to everything else the Nolans knew had begun; she knew where it would lead. By some oblique or not so oblique way of questioning, Michael would get an answer to the unspoken question 'What are you, son?' and all the little imaginings of the past few nights, daydreams she hadn't wanted to share with Teresa, would be torn up and trampled in the dust.

At least Michael's natural tact would prevent him going the usual route of 'Where's your father from?' now he'd heard those words 'farmed out'.

Instead, to her surprise, she heard Robert talking about a woman in Killyleagh. 'Them cats had fish on Fridays, same as us,' he said, to general laughter. Annie saw that even Philomena started to relax. The discussion moved on to work.

'Good money underground, isn't it? You must have prospects,' said Philomena.

Annie's face burned. *Wedding me would be one way of her getting me out of the house.*

'I try to be a good worker, Mrs Nolan. That's all.'

'Where would you be living just now?'

'Lodgings. Not so good as here,' he said, looking around the room. 'There's me and three other lads in the one room. I've to get to bed first so's not to be climbing over the others' cots.'

'In whose house would that be then?'

Robert named a street. There was a short silence.

'I've not seen you at mass, have I, Robert? Which one is it you go to?' said Philomena.

'I don't, Mrs Nolan.'

Another pause.

'You were kind to bring our Annie back,' said Michael.

Though she knew it was a dismissal, Annie was grateful for the 'our'.

Robert knew what it was too. He pushed back his chair.

'Thank you for the tea, Mrs Nolan. I just wanted to know was Annie all right.'

'I'll see you out,' said Annie, wanting just that pitiful little moment with him on the doorstep, hoping too that he'd be seen with her, before her hopeless fantasy evaporated like smoke.

He turned on the doorstep, looking warily over her shoulder into the murmuring house.

'I nearly forgot,' she said, fumbling in her pocket. 'Your pin. I've fixed my blouse, even if one sleeve is a wee bit shorter than the other.'

Rather than put it back on his lapel, he stuffed it into his trouser pocket without looking at it.

'You'd not want to be keeping something like that, right enough.' He smiled. 'Maybe you'd like this better.' He handed her the parcel. 'One day, when I've Kathleen's tools, I could make you a better one.'

'That's the first time anybody's ever given me anything,' she murmured, forgetting her father's gift of the ribbon.

'*Annie!*' came from the far room.

'I'd give you more if you'd let me,' he whispered. 'Could I see you again?'

'*Annie!*'

'Yes,' she heard herself say.

*

'What was in that parcel?' said Philomena, handing Annie a plate to dry.

'I don't know. I'll open it after.'

'You should be more careful, so you should. Talking to fellows you don't know and accepting things off them. Forgot, did ye, what I said about no callers?'

Annie bit back a retort about what might have happened had Robert not been there, meekly saying, 'I never knew he was coming round, so I didn't.'

'Be kinder now, Phil,' rumbled Michael from the table. 'He helped her, didn't he? I thought he was decent.'

Annie shot a grateful look at Michael, but he wasn't looking her way, deliberately, she thought.

'Can we go up now, Mammy?' cut in Teresa. 'I don't know about Annie, but I'm a bit tired, so I am.' Annie could see from her friend's face that this was just an excuse to see what was in the parcel.

'Goodnight, so. God bless,' said Michael, looking up.

The two girls thumped upstairs as wound up with excitement as children going to a funfair. But sitting on her bed, the parcel in her hands, quite different thoughts caught up with Annie. *What am I going to tell the priest about what I feel about him, though? He's bound to tell me it's wrong.* The King Billy pin made that clear, that and the memory of Robert's fingertips on her shoulder. She racked her brains trying to think of a saint who'd intercede for her. *There's somebody for everything except this, isn't there now? St Anthony when you can't find your purse. St Brigid if you've only water and what you want is beer. St Margaret to see you through childbed.* There was St Valentine, of course, but Annie wasn't even sure he was a real saint or just somebody whose name got written on secret messages she'd never received. Certainly the priest never mentioned him at mass around the day that was supposed to be his. Two brothers called Cyril and Methodius had taken his place, it seemed, and Annie couldn't imagine praying to anyone with those names. Cyril sounded like the class of man who'd work in a solicitor's office and the other one had to be something to do with the Methodies, surely? Finally she settled on St Jude. *Patron saint of lost causes. It'll have to be him.*

'Hey! Are you there?' Teresa waved her hand in front of Annie's nose, bringing her reluctantly back to the present. She unpicked the knots in the string as Teresa fidgeted with impatience, but Annie had learned early in life that nothing should be wasted. In a flash of memory she recalled the drawer in the dresser in the farmhouse where her father kept lengths of twine, horseshoe nails and an old tin of bear's grease (though who used it Annie had no idea, as her father had always had a good head of hair). *I wonder has he a drawer like that in Barrow?* Finally she unwrapped the brown paper. She gasped, a hand to her mouth. There was the blouse she and Teresa had seen in Fowles's window. She remembered Robert talking about his bank book, the saving for the day he didn't know would come, and thought of him going to the bank and taking out the money that would push his dream just that bit further away. Doing it for her.

CHAPTER EIGHTEEN

Birks Road, July 1903

'It would be in the power of everyone conversant with the manners of the country [Ireland] to produce instances of the undoubting beliefs in these superstitions.'

Thomas Crofton Croker, *Fairy Legends and Traditions,* 1828

A week later Percy came to tea, his long body trussed up in his best clothes and with his floppy hair inexpertly pomaded into place. It was a stilted but polite occasion in which Annie felt for the young man, though Michael strenuously looked for common ground. Percy did his best by compliment-ing Philomena on her cooking, but Annie could see, though Teresa seemed oblivious, that he was so nervous he had to force himself to clear his plate. Everyone looked relieved when after the last cup of tea was drunk Teresa stood up and said he and she would go for a walk. Nothing was said about Annie tagging along, for now Percy was 'official'. She smiled and wished them fair weather and, unbidden, began to clear the table. Philomena didn't help; she wanted to talk to Michael about Percy, and because Annie didn't want to hear what was said as she'd have to recount everything to Teresa, she went out into the scullery and started to wash up as noisily as she could without breaking anything.

Shortly after she'd scraped the plates Frank came out to talk to her.

'I asked around a bit about thon Orange boy, so I did,' he said quietly.

'Frank, whatever for?'

'Don't take on so. I saw how you looked at him, that's all.'

'How I looked at him . . .' To her chagrin, Annie felt a flush creep up her neck.

'Annie,' he said, 'I know you don't want me that way—'

'I think of you as a brother,' she interrupted, half wishing him away but half wanting to know what he might have found out about Robert.

'I know. Even if you didn't, *she'd* never accept it,' he said, with a backward movement of his head. 'I don't know what she wants for me. Lord Leconfield's daughter if he has one, mebbe.'

They both laughed. 'Catch yourself on, Frank. Pit owners' daughters don't marry pitmen!' said Annie.

'Frank?' came his mother's voice.

'Coming!' Frank leaned forward, whispering. 'He's down Crowgarth, as he'll have told you, though I've never worked with him there. A decent enough fella, they say. Quiet. Came here on his own. But he's in the Lodge, Annie.'

'I know,' she said.

'Well, you'll know then there's no point in thinking of him.'
Annie couldn't help but notice the relief in Frank's face.

'*Frank!*'

*

'Have you seen Robert again?' asked Teresa a week later. They
were sitting by the hearth. Teresa was cutting worn out trousers
into strips, and Annie was doing the harder job of hooking and
knotting them through the loose weave of a jute sack to make a
rag rug. They were alone, for Michael and Frank had gone to the
Men's Club and Philomena had gone to pay the laundress and
listen to her gossip.

'You know I haven't. I'd'a told ye.'

'You'll see him again, so you will. I know the signs,' said Teresa,
with all the confidence engagement conferred on her.

'Frank warned me off, or as good as.'

'He would, wouldn't he?'

Annie's hands stilled on the rug. She was sick of the greasy
feel of the sacking and the musty smell of the rags. 'Let's not
talk about it, Teresa,' she said eventually, and took hold of her
hook again.

For some minutes the silence in the room was broken only by
the snip, snip of Teresa's shears and the rasping tug of the rug
hook. Then Teresa tumbled the mutilated trousers into the basket
on top of the strips she'd cut from it and threw down the scissors.

'*I* know! We'll do that freit[2] with the nuts, so we will!'

---

[2] Superstitious trick or observance

148

'What's that, Teresa?' said Annie wearily, wishing on this occasion that her friend would just leave her with her thoughts.

'We'll just do this and then honest to God I'll leave it alone, I promise. You get on with your rug if you want.' Teresa jumped up and went out through the scullery to the dank little larder where Annie could hear her rummaging around. She hoped her friend wouldn't leave too much of a mess, as doing so broke another of Philomena's rules.

Teresa came back and opened her fist to Annie. Four cobnuts lay in her palm.

'I got them all the same size. You've to choose. One is you, one is Robert, one is me and one is Percy.'

Annie picked out the one she thought had the most regular surface. 'Robert,' she said.

Teresa placed it carefully on the hearth in front of the smouldering fire.

'Now you.'

Annie pointed to one at random. It joined 'Robert' inside the fender.

'Now me.'

Out of love for her friend, Annie made a show of choosing carefully. Teresa placed her nut and the remaining Percy nut at a short distance from the other two.

'Now we've to heat them up,' Teresa said, picking up the little shovel with the polished brass handle from amongst the fire-irons. 'Best use this too, as I'll have to get it good and hot,' she added, wrapping the handle in what was left of the trousers. She squatted, holding the shovel to the flames. Eventually she tested it by spitting, watching the little ball of moisture fizzle into nothing.

'So here's Robert, and here's you,' she said, carefully placing the two nuts about two inches apart. She held the shovel above the flames, watching the nuts intently. Annie rested her hands, fascinated by the strange ritual playing out in front of her.

'What now?' she whispered.

With her free hand Teresa flapped her into silence. Both girls watched the nuts inert above the flames. Then so suddenly that Annie flinched, there was a popping sound and the nut that was Robert darted across to hit the nut that was Annie.

'You see?' cried Teresa, triumphant. 'I knew he was sweet on you!'

'You tipped the shovel, so you did.'

'Honest to God, I never. My turn now.' Teresa tipped the two nuts back within the hearth and replaced them with the others. Annie's eyes weren't on 'Teresa' and 'Percy' on the hot shovel, but on the two nuts cooling on the ground, her thoughts on Robert's fingertips on her shoulder. Teresa's cry of distress brought her back to the present. Only one nut remained on the shovel.

'Which? I didn't see.'

'Me . . . I've gone in the fire.' Teresa tossed the Percy nut into the flames and crashed the little shovel back in with the other fire-irons. 'Sure, it's all cod, so it is.'

'Percy loves you,' said Annie. 'You don't need an oul' freit to tell you so.' But she shivered, though the room was warm. 'We'd best start the tea.' She put her half-made rug into the basket on top of the scissors and bent to pick up her two nuts.

That night as Teresa slept, Annie whispered an extra Hail Mary into the darkness. 'Pray for us sinners, now and at the hour of our death.' She thought of the two nuts, her and Robert, hidden in the drawer where she kept her underthings.

CHAPTER NINETEEN

The Commercial Hotel, Cleator Moor, September 1903

'Satisfies your finer taste – Mazawattee Tea.'

Advert, early twentieth century

'Annie?'

The voice behind her made her jump. She turned round from her reverie looking in the window of Fowles to see Robert standing there.

'You gave me a fright, so you did,' she said, brushing a lock of hair from her face.

'I'm sorry. I shoulda seen you were miles away. Was there something else in there you were wantin'?'

Annie felt herself colouring and tried to cover it with a laugh. In truth she hadn't been looking for anything. She'd only been standing there trying to imagine Robert doing the same, choosing that beautiful blouse for her. Had he gone in first and asked them to wrap it for him before going out to the bank and withdrawing that money so carefully put aside?

'Would I have to fall over again first?' she asked.

'No. And anyway, I'd rather make something myself for you. Perhaps you'll let me, one day. Have you been wearing the blouse?'

'Not yet,' she said. 'It's too beautiful. Far more than anything I've ever had. I'm saving it for a special occasion.'

Oh, his face is something else altogether when he smiles.

'You could invite me then,' he said.

'I would ...' Then her face lit up. 'When my best friend weds,' she said. 'Only it'll be a wee while yet.' *Two years. But a lot can happen in two years.*

'Thon girl where you lodge?'

'Yes. Teresa.'

His face darkened with disappointment. 'I'm sorry, I'd not be let. I'd wait outside to see yous all come out though. I took my oath,' he added, seeing her puzzled face, touching the pin on his lapel.

'Oh ...'

'You musta known that? You've never seen any of us in one of your chapels, have ye?'

Annie shook her head. 'I never thought about it. I never even met an Orangeman before yourself.'

'Nor one so clean, I should think,' he said, smiling again. He took off his cap and she could see his curly hair was still damp. 'I've just been to the bath-house. This is the cleanest I am all week.'

'You'll catch your death, with your hair wet.'

'I should get indoors then. Would you ... shall we see can they give us a cup of tea in the Commercial Hotel?'

Annie hesitated, but not for long. She'd never been in the hotel and knew nobody who would go there. Somehow it sounded more respectable than going into a pub. *Go with him*, she told herself. *Don't pretend you hadn't been hoping you'd'a seen him. It'd be rude to say no after him buying you that lovely blouse too.* She thought of Teresa, halfway along a country path kissing Percy, as she was allowed to do, and wondered in a delirious moment what it would be like to be kissed by Robert.

'Yes. Thank you.'

She hadn't expected him to offer her his arm. Her heart thumped as she took it, yet her body felt as light as air, as if she walked on springy grass and not cobbles. She wished there was a mirror she could look in, for walking beside him she was convinced she was pretty.

There was initially an awkward silence over the teacups. He'd asked her if she wanted anything to eat and she'd shaken her head, concerned at the cost.

'Shall I pour?' she said, when the little jug and the pot were placed in front of her by a waitress whose starched cap and apron intimidated Annie, though the girl looked no older than fifteen. Annie, who had never been served by anyone in her life, didn't know quite what you were supposed to do. Put a coin in the girl's hand? She'd said, 'Thank you,' then worried she'd spoken too loudly. The waitress had chirped, 'You're welcome!' and flitted off.

'Oh . . . yes, please,' he said. 'You look more used to a place like this than me.' He was turning his cap in his hand and Annie realised he was as nervous as she was. She felt a little spurt of – oh, she didn't know what to call it. *He needs protecting, that's what it is.* Annie picked up the dainty crocheted pot holder and wrapped it around the handle of the teapot, but Robert's hand over hers stopped her.

'Put the milk in first,' he whispered. 'That's how I seen the Quality do it. Seeing as we are in here.'

'Oh!' she said, feeling her face heat up. She obediently poured a little milk into the two cups, then followed up with the tea. She eyed the tongs in the sugar bowl nervously, afraid of making another mistake. She'd never seen such an implement before.

'No sugar for me,' he said. 'They never gave it me when I was wee, and when I did get to try it, I didn't like it. Makes you thirstier, I think.'

'Yes,' said Annie, resolving to do without.

'Let me,' he said, deftly handling the tongs. 'One or two? I can see you wanted one.'

'One. Thank you.' Annie dipped her head in embarrassment. Her little triumph in speaking to the waitress had evaporated completely. Thankfully nobody else at the tables in the wood-panelled room seemed to be taking any notice. There was a man who looked to Annie like a prosperous farmer still deep in the *Whitehaven News*, his pipe clenched between his teeth though it gave out only fitful puffs of smoke. At another table two ladies in hats piled with what looked like bits of dead bird were busy with their own gossip. A moustached man in a bowler was jotting in a notebook.

'Kathleen learned me that,' said Robert. 'Them wee tongs. And the milk thing.'

'Kathleen?'

'The lady that learned me the sewing. I'd go with her to her customers' houses. She called me her assistant, so she did, so I got to take tea with the Quality. She put good clothes on me, and shoes. *They* took a bit of getting used to.'

'I go barefoot in the mill,' she said quietly. 'But I've never gone barefoot outside here in England. Not like in Ireland.'

'They're not as tough as us here,' he said, smiling.

'You must miss Kathleen.'

'I do. Loved her like my own mother.' He paused. 'Maybe more. I saw more of her. I've never lived with my mother.'

There was a short silence, in which both sipped their tea.

'Your da'll write, so?' he said.

'He does. He's maybe more to tell than I have.'

'Did you not want to go with him, Annie?'

'Yes, and no. I'm afraid I didn't tell you everything, Robert.'

'You don't like the new wife, is that it? But tell me if I'm too nosy.'

'I barely know her. I only met her when they were leaving. They tell me she's a decent wee woman.'

'She's not his wife, though, is she?'

Annie started. 'How did you know that?' She was realising that he missed nothing, even her hesitation over the sugar tongs. *Perhaps that's what you do when you're really alone. You notice things.*

'It was when you said "new wife" that time. Your eyes went sideways. I like it, you know, when a person doesn't know how to lie. You can trust them.'

'She's not, right enough,' she said, her eyes downcast. 'She's someone else's.' Quietly, she told him about her father and Elsie, about the school photograph, about Mark's small hand stealing into her own.

'Your da must be a good man,' he said. 'A true father. Them wee boys must think themselves lucky to have him.'

To her dismay, Annie felt her eyes brim, and fumbled for her napkin. To cover her embarrassment, Robert lifted the pot of hot water and refreshed the tea.

'He puts them in his letters. Mark's doing well at the school. Joe is keen to leave and go to work, but Dadda makes him keep to his books. And in Barrow they're a widow's sons with a respectable stepfather. A man who can go up to the school if there's any bother.'

'You could have gone with them,' he said softly.

'I . . .' She fiddled with her napkin. Force of habit made her feel the weave. *Fine yarn. Washed and ironed more times than it can remember, but quality lasts.*

'Not wanting to share with another woman?' he prompted.

'It wasn't that . . .'

He leaned forward, as Annie spoke so quietly.

'I mean, I've to do Philomena's bidding as it is,' she went on. 'I'm here now because if I'm not doing chores for her she wants me out of the road. It's that I can't . . . I can't live with them that's in a state of sin.' Hearing herself say those words, it was as if someone else said them. Words that Father Hagerty would use, frightening two little boys out of their sleep. She looked up at Robert's patient face, and remembered how she'd learned at school that bastard children were to be despised, conceived in sin and thus themselves sinful.

'It says in the Bible, so it does,' she went on. '"What therefore God hath joined together, let no man put asunder."'

'Matthew chapter nineteen verse six,' said Robert, 'but your way of saying it's a bit different from the way I know it.'

Annie's eyes widened.

'And in verse nine it says there's to be no putting aside except for . . . for fornication. So our Lord himself says you can divorce.'

'How do you know all that? Are you a preacher?'

His rare smile returned. 'No, but I've heard plenty of 'em. The ones that shout and thump the pulpit like they'd break it to bits are reckoned the best ones. They stop you falling asleep, anyway. Knowing your Bible is just what Presbyterians do. We don't need a man that's been shut away in a seminary for years to tell us what we should think. We can go and read it for ourselves, so we can. Annie – how do you know that wee woman wasn't what God intended for your father? Because the priest said so? And if I'd'a been one of them wee boys you can be sure I'd have wanted him to be mine.'

Annie was unable to meet his eyes. In the silence Robert lifted the teapot.

'Another one? Get our money's worth.'

Annie nodded, picking up the milk jug.

'I'm sorry,' he said. 'I didn't mean to shout you down.'

'You didn't. I'd better be going though.' She drank her tea down and got her purse out of her pocket.

'No, I asked you, so I did,' he said, waving the purse away. 'I've enjoyed your company.'

'I've enjoyed yours.'

'Here. Wait a wee minute.' His fingers explored an inside pocket, and eventually he pulled out a folded-up piece of paper. 'I'd meant to give you this before. When I brought you the blouse. It's just where I lodge,' he said. She saw his fingers tremble slightly. 'It's if you have any more trouble, you know, with them people you live with. I mean . . . I don't know what I could do to help, but I would all the same. The man that'll come to the door is Mr Spedding.'

'Thank you,' she said, putting away the paper without unfolding it.

*

Outside the Commercial, Robert became taciturn again, awkward. 'Well . . . thank you again,' he said, twisting his cap.

'Goodbye, Robert. Well, at least your hair's dry now.' Feeling exposed out on the street, Annie looked everywhere but at him. She dipped her head and walked away, cursing herself. *I never gave him the chance to ask if he wanted to see me again. I was rude, so I was. What am I thinking of? He's just kind. But I am going to go to Barrow.*

CHAPTER TWENTY

Cleator Moor, October 1903

'*Cavendo Tutus*'

> 'Safety through caution' – motto of the
> Furness Railway, 1846–1922

'Percy's been up to see the vicar at the mission church,' confided Teresa that night.

Annie shifted in bed to face her friend. 'Go on.'

'He went for his baptismal certificate, so he did. His mammy couldn't find it, so he'd to go for a copy.'

'Will he not be baptised as a Catholic, then?'

'No need. It's the same thing. Father Hagerty told him so, though you know *him*. He said it the way you'd talk about a workman you'd had to settle for because you couldn't afford the best one. But when he went to the vicar he got led a dance as well, with some story about how St Patrick was probably an Englishman.'

'Get away!'

'That wasn't the best bit. When Percy had the bit of paper he needed, he said to the fella that he was wanting it to get married and that the Church of England was only there because of that king wanting his divorce.'

'He never!'

'He said you should have seen the look on the man's face!' The two girls collapsed into giggles. Annie's subsided first.

'Teresa . . .'

'Yeah?'

'Does Percy believe it all? What Father Hagerty is telling him?'

'Oh, that? It's me he's wanting, not the religion. He's going along with it for that and that's good enough for me, so it is.'

'What do his old ones say?'

'They're fine, so they are. The only thing they said was maybe to take rooms in another part of the town. Maybe somewhere not so Irish. Oh, I've other news too. I'd clean forgot, though it'll help us get married, so it will. I'm to go to Weaving. My mother's got me an opening there, just as soon as the next weaver leaves.'

Annie swallowed her dismay, trying to be pleased for her friend. Amongst the women working at Ainsworth's, weavers, like reelers, thought themselves a bit of a cut above the rest; it was good news for Teresa. More money to marry on.

'I'll miss you,' said Annie. 'But at least you'll be able to wear shoes and stockings.'

'Mammy says I've to get a coat. You should hear her. "Weavers don't wear shawls. They work in the factory, not the mill."'

Annie fought down her envy. She loved her friend, and would never forget the way Teresa had taken her under her wing when she'd first gone to Andrews' Mill as a frightened child, how she'd been there for her when she'd fled Reginald Crawford. But Teresa had everything, thought Annie: she was lively and beautiful, with that dark red flame of her hair, her laughing eyes. She managed even to make what she saw as her faults into an occasion of fun, reducing those around her, Annie included, to helpless laughter with her descriptions of attempts to darken her sandy eyelashes with boot polish. *Well, she'll not be able to sing and laugh in the weavers' sheds*, thought Annie, but that was no consolation. She knew that getting a place as a weaver meant there had to be an experienced hand willing to train Teresa up. Someone Philomena knew, evidently.

*

Annie lay in bed, staring up into the darkness. Once things had been so certain, so preordained. Like lambing, or harvesting, long ago and in another country. You got in a boat thinking the world the other side would be a bit like the one you knew, but it wasn't, no matter how many of your own people you came with and stayed with. *Dadda living with Mrs Fagan. Teresa marrying thon English boy whether he's got religion or not. It doesn't matter who baptised you or where, so maybe we're all the same after all. And it's taken an Orangeman to show me my da's a good man. I'll write to Barrow tomorrow.*

The reply came by return. 'You've made me very happy, Annie,' her father wrote. 'There are no Sunday trains. See if you can get your Mrs Birkett to give you Saturday morning off and come on the last one Friday. I'll come to the station for you.'

*

'Coming back tomorrow?' said the man in the ticket office, looking at Annie doubtfully. She wondered if she'd done something odd, buying a return ticket. Perhaps when you left Cleator Moor it was like leaving Belfast. You never came back. Eventually, along with a rattle of coins as her change, he passed the rectangular piece of card through the little trough and said, 'Don't lose it.'

Annie tucked the ticket into the inner pocket of her purse and went out onto the platform. Five or six other people were peering up the line towards Whitehaven as if doing so would make the train come quicker. She was relieved that none of them seemed to be travelling alone. They'd be less likely to want to talk to her then.

The blackened engine as it approached looked to her like a creature from hell, hissing and panting. The carriages though shabby looked solid enough, a calming blue with gilt lettering, a roof grey as the slate on a house. Though she'd seen the train that took her father off it was quite another thing to move through the wreathing steam and smoke to open the door of the third-class carriage and get inside. She tried to close the door quietly behind her but it refused to click. She tugged at it, until the stationmaster appeared on the platform below her and said, 'You've to treat 'er rough, love,' seizing the door and giving it a great slam that sent Annie backwards in fright to sink onto one of the wooden seats. She looked round to see she was in a compartment, with another door at the far side, but alone. She didn't know whether to be comforted by that or not. What if someone got in and did her a mischief?

Too late now. A man's voice shouted something unintelligible, followed by a piercing whistle, much louder than the one that hung from the cord on Mrs Birkett's apron. The train groaned, lurched momentarily backwards, and then moved off at what for Annie was a frightening speed. Stone walls, farmhouses and sheep hurtled past. The sea came into view, and by contrast seemed not to move at all, though if she looked out of the windows opposite, everything else went by in a rush. She looked back at the flat water, whispering 'Ireland,' and it came to her in that moment that she was probably never going to go back.

Then with a shrieking of brakes the train came to a stop. Annie peered out at a country halt. From where she sat she couldn't see a sign. But it was too late to worry; the train was moving again. At the next station a ticket inspector appeared at the window. She fumbled in her bag. Where was the ticket? Heart hammering, she poked and poked. There it was, caught in a corner of the lining. She handed it over; a hole was punched in it, and it was handed back.

'Please, how far is it to Barrow?' she asked, but much of the answer was lost in the roar of the engine; all she heard was 'Train terminates there.' She sank back into her seat in relief. At least she couldn't be carried on to Liverpool, or Manchester. Annie closed her eyes. It wouldn't matter if she fell asleep then, would it? They'd find her at the station and wake her, surely. She didn't think she could sleep in all that row, but as she'd never had the experience of pushing a baby in a perambulator over cobbles, she didn't know how soothing the rocking and roaring of a train could be, or that relief of tension eased sleep.

She woke up at Foxfield, with no idea what time it was or how far the train had come. It was nearly dark, but there were dim lights in the compartment, and the signal box looming over the line was a bright beacon. She looked up to its windows, and a young man in shirtsleeves and braces waved down at her, smiling. Timidly, she smiled back, then remembered Robert. It occurred to her that she might have asked him to come with her, and thought how different this journey could have been. She as quickly rejected the idea for only a 'bold girl' would go knocking at a man's lodgings, and anyway, hadn't he said he was thinking of leaving that place?

Minutes later, the train screeched to a halt and a voice bellowed, 'Kerrby!' Annie peered out on a pretty cast-iron awning, and read in black on white on a sturdy sign that the place was called Kirkby-in-Furness. *We must be getting close, then.* Despite her sleep she realised she felt horribly tired. She wasn't used to sitting still for so long in one place, either. It occurred to her that the longest she ever sat down was when she had to listen to one of Father Hagerty's homilies.

Then there was a halt, in pitch darkness. Annie waited to hear the slam of doors, see figures moving across the platform in the gloom. There were none and the train picked up again.

'Askam!' Annie looked out again: this time there was a ricochet of doors and some figures tramped off into the shadows. She wondered then how many people had been on the train; she could remember only two carriages, but travellers were boxed into their compartments as surely as if they were in a terrace of houses. Askam-in-Furness, she read. The station was larger; in the gaslight she could make out a gable, built in the same red stone as St Mary's, and a long, low building under an awning, with a dimly lit empty waiting room. Unexpectedly she felt some longing for the place she'd left behind only a couple of hours ago.

The darkness lasted little longer. The lights of a town twinkled in the darkness and, as it approached, Annie made out ribbons of little houses, their chimneys puffing fitful smoke into the reddish air. Gantries reared up, then the terrifying bulk of a half-built ship. How was it possible that mere men could create such a thing? The vessel loomed as vast as the Tower of Babel 'with its top in the heavens' in the Bible. How could something that size not sink? Then houses, gantries, chimneys disappeared, as the train moved between long brick walls which amplified its roar. She saw porters' trollies leaning against cast-iron pillars, a news-stand festooned with newspapers and magazines.

We've stopped. Annie got up, clutching the little bag Teresa had lent her 'instead of that big oul' grip'. She fumbled at the catch of the door.

'Dadda!' she cried, and half-fell out of the train into his arms.

CHAPTER TWENTY-ONE

Barrow-in-Furness

'Kendall and Cooper – complete funeral furnishers – horse and motor funerals arranged.'

Advertisement, *Furness and District Year Book,* 1902

'Welcome to Hardwick Street. We're above that shop,' said her father. 'The rooms are cheaper because of it.'

Annie peered into the shadowy window. There were some flowers in a stone urn, around which some prospectuses were arranged. At the back were photographs pinned to a screen. She made out what looked like a horse and carriage. Above the screen was a glow of light: someone was still there, late into the evening. With a start, she realised it was an undertaker's.

Thomas had found the right key in the gloom and opened a door on a narrow hallway. A steep staircase went up to a glimmer of gaslight.

'I don't mind it, personally,' said Thomas. 'It means there's always someone there, looking out. I can't complain that it isn't quiet, though!'

A door opened on the landing, and a woman's voice said, 'Tom?' Annie was moved by Elsie's tone: it was both loving and anxious.

'I've got her!' said Thomas. The door must have opened wider then, for the light above strengthened.

'Come away in, Miss Maguire,' said the voice.

Annie heard her father laugh. 'Has anyone ever called you that before, Annie?'

'Annie, then,' said Elsie, smiling shyly and standing back to let the visitor in. The room that greeted Annie was cramped, dominated by a forbiddingly large black range which someone had tried to soften with the addition of a dark red fringed overmantel on which the treasures of the home stood: a willow-pattern transferware jug, old enough that its glaze was already crazed; a pair of miniature china cats; and two brass candlesticks, polished to a gleam. A jam-jar contained some sprigs of what looked like dried rosemary. Annie could not imagine where this could have come from: she hadn't seen a handkerchief's worth of earth since she'd arrived in Barrow. Either side of the range were two old wood-framed parlour chairs, which Annie noticed were both dented, brightened by the addition of embroidered cushions. *That's where they'll sit, them two, when the weans have gone to bed.* Hanging on the wall above the range was a framed chromolithograph of the Holy Family seated beneath a rose bower, with Joseph's carpenter's bench standing incongruously behind them. Her eyes sweeping over to the window, she saw that the Belfast sink beneath it had a tap. Following her eyes, her father said, 'We're lucky, aren't we? They always need water downstairs, so we benefit. We've even got a privy under the stairs that's just for us.'

Sitting patiently at a precisely laid table in the centre of the room were the two little boys, with an empty chair between them.

'It's them decided you'd to sit there,' said Elsie proudly. 'They've been that excited. You're the first visitor they've had – not counting the landlord.'

'I'm honoured,' said Annie, and took her seat. Joe, she could see now, looked more like his mother than she remembered. Mark had lost the frightened look she'd seen in that photograph and on the platform at Moor Row. He seemed peaceful – content. *He must look like his da*, thought Annie, *though it's my da has made him happy.*

'So you *have* come to stay with us,' said Mark.

'Only until tomorrow. And only if you'll have me.'

'Sure we will. Dadda Tom is our new father and you're his daughter so you have to be our sister. That means you'll be coming to see us more often, so you will.'

'I'll try.'

Elsie filled the teapot from the kettle on the hearth and joined the others at the table. 'Only if you let the poor girl eat. She's come an awful long way today.' She turned to Annie, offering her the plate of buttered bread.

'They've waited up for me, then?' said Annie. 'I'm sorry.'

'Ah, don't be,' said Elsie. 'I was going to get the wee gossuns their tea earlier but they wouldn't have it without you being here. I've put the camp bed in the room with them, if that's all right? They'll be asleep by the time we turn in.'

'Thank you for all your trouble.'

'It's none, so it isn't.' Elsie's eyes returned to her plate. Annie noticed that the woman seemed wary of speaking if it was not behind the shield of her children. What would she be like in the morning? Annie's father would be at the shipyard until midday and the children, doubtless, playing outside in the precious time they were freed from school.

'It does me good to see you,' said Thomas. 'It's all right then, is it, at Michael's house?'

'Actually, I don't know how long I can stay there.'

'Oh?'

'I mean, I can stay until Teresa's wed. She wants to go into lodgings with Percy after. But I won't want to stay with the Nolans after she's gone. I'll not be that welcome anyway.'

'Philomena?'

'Yes.'

Thomas exchanged looks with Elsie. 'Boys,' she said, 'time you was washed and in bed. Say goodnight to Annie.'

'Goodnight, Annie,' the boys chimed, then Mark added, 'Do you snore?'

'I do not,' she laughed.

'I'll come in to kiss you boys goodnight,' said Thomas.

'Come on, yous,' said Elsie, ushering them from the table and into an adjoining room. Through the open door, Annie could hear the murmur of their voices, the splashing of water in a china basin, the creak of a bed and the low drone of prayers.

Then Elsie came back into the room, pulling the door closed behind her. With much faltering, Annie got out the story of how

Robert had rescued her on the path and how he'd come back to see her, bringing the blouse. This got a reaction, a fleeting glance between the two, whereas to her astonishment neither blinked at the revelation of the King Billy pin. She went on to recount what had happened in the house in Birks Road in the aftermath of that momentous Twelfth, finding it easier to talk about Philomena's dislike of her than Robert's kindness.

'So I'm only there still because of Teresa,' she ended.

'You could come here,' said Thomas quietly. 'To Barrow, I mean.'

She knew what he meant. *Well, I could hardly live with them, could I?*

'We'd be a bit tight here, right enough, but we could look for somewhere else. We would have tried for something bigger, if you'd come before.'

'I don't know . . .'

'Nobody knows about us here,' he said. He put out a hand to Elsie, indicating a closer chair.

'It's not that,' said Annie. *It's really not. They're a great wee family.* She felt crushingly lonely, for the first time since she'd got off the train.

'So what keeps you there?'

Thinking of Robert, Annie couldn't meet her father's eyes. 'I'll think about it,' she said, sidestepping his question. 'There's no rush. Percy's his instruction to get through, though the meal Father Hagerty is making of it Teresa'll be thirty by the time he's done.'

'Poor Percy!' Thomas put his hand out to Elsie's shoulder, and squeezed it. Annie felt the scales drop from her eyes. She thought of Father Hagerty in the Priory House, him and nice but stiff Father Clayton, with Mrs Kennedy the cook and the two parlourmaids. She thought of Philomena's rules and her disapproving eye. *There's love and comfort here, so there is.*

'What about you, Annie? Anyone you're sweet on?' said her father.

Annie was about to deny it, but remembered Robert's words that day in the Commercial Hotel: '*I like it, you know, when a person doesn't know how to lie. You can trust them.*'

'Well, not what you'd call courting . . .' Annie's face started to heat up, aware of both her father and Elsie watching her. 'I seen that Robert in the town once. He got me a cup of tea, so he did.'

'So you're courting?' said her father, smiling.

'Sure it was only a cup of tea, and it was ages ago.'

'Annie, you mightn't think it's courting but I'd be pretty certain he thought he was courting *you*. Buying you that blouse, taking you to tea.'

'How could he, Dadda? He's in the Lodge. Anyway, I've not seen him since. I never gave him any encouragement, so I didn't.'

Her father's hand reached for Elsie's. 'Things change, so they do. But I wish you'd told me before about that business on the path. You've to be careful of them eejits, not your man Robert,' he said. Then, to Annie's immense gratitude, for she was on the edge of weeping, Thomas diverted the conversation to a row in the shipyard about tea-break times.

*

The train home to Moor Row seemed to take less time than the journey down. There was something marvellous, after all, about simply sitting in what was a very long and exceptionally fast cart, protected from wind and squalls, and being taken to another place altogether – a place where, it seemed, people could think and do things differently. Annie had woken just once the previous night, on the little truckle bed, to muffled noises downstairs. The two boys, tangled like kittens in sleep, hadn't stirred. In the sliver of gaslight through the curtains she'd seen their innocent faces, their soft open mouths, and heard their gentle breathing. Another bump then came from the floor below. A street door opened, some feet came out, without hurry, and the door closed softly. She'd heard the quiet nickering of a horse, some murmured words of reassurance, and thought of Polly. *I wonder is she even still alive?* The roll of wheels on cobbles followed, but the expected clip-clop was deadened, as though the horse wore something over its hooves. Then she remembered why. Death had come in the night for someone in those teeming streets. *It'll be a Protestant lying down there*, she'd thought. *We never leave a corpse alone.* She'd mouthed a quiet prayer into the darkness and fallen straight back into oblivion.

The following morning had been a revelation. Elsie had conquered some of her shyness; Annie wondered had she gained confidence from seeing how the two boys had immediately accepted and welcomed their visitor. Annie accompanied Elsie to 'get the messages', learning from her that it was only the Ulster people that said that: 'English people go on an errand.'

Annie thought errand an odd word, like error, and said so. Then she'd mentioned the sounds in the night.

'I don't fear the dead,' said Elsie. 'It's the living I'm feart of. And your man – or woman – down below – mightn't be a Protestant. It's only back in Ireland you've to keep company with a corpse. Here they'll take a coffin into St Mary in Furness the night before the requiem mass, but there'll not be anyone stays with it – besides God and all his angels, that is.'

'Where's back there – home, I mean – for you, Elsie?'

'Home? Home's where them wee boys are. And your dadda. Back there was Ardglass.'

'I wanted Mammy to go there. When she'd the consumption.' Annie could have bitten her tongue. It felt less like an offence to the dead woman to mention her to the woman her widower now loved, than a slight to the living one walking alongside her carrying her shopping basket.

'I know,' said Elsie. 'Tom told me. He told me lots about you, and your brothers.' She hesitated, looking at Annie. 'I hope you don't mind.'

'I don't. I'm glad he did.'

'He's awful proud of you, so he is. Told me about thon man with the books . . .'

'Mr Harris?'

'That's him. He told your da he thought you shoulda done more than the National School, a clever girl like you.'

'Never!'

'He did *so*. Only Tom said he never telt you.'

'He was right not to. The only way woulda been going with the nuns. I couldn't do that. I wanted a home and a hearth, same as we had. Same as you've got here in Hardwick Street, Elsie. It's lovely, so it is.'

'I thank God every day for my fortune, Annie. Even if I'm not meant to.'

There was a short silence, then Annie said, 'They're great boys, Joe and Mark. Wee dotes.'

'Thank you. They've a good father – the one they have now, I mean.'

'Do you . . . ?'

'Ever hear from Tim Fagan? No, and I pray to God I never will. Joe's asked me is he coming back – because he doesn't want him to – and I've telt him he doesn't know where we are. I hadn't the heart in me to say I didn't think he cared either. Such a tongue he had in his head, that man! You'd think he could charm the birds out of the trees, so you would, except he'd only do it so's he could wring their poor necks.'

'When did you realise?' asked Annie softly.

Elsie puffed out her breath. 'A week. Barely a week. I'd never dreamed marriage lines could change a man so fast. I learned the first time he came home late from the pub and took on at me for not having the tea ready. I'd had it mashed that many times you coulda stood your spoon in it, but he still hadn't come. I telt myself I'd not bring the boys up to be men like him. That's what troubled me the most. That whatever I did he'd make them like him. And then one day he saved me the bother, even if he went without a word with the rent money out of the jar. I thought we were for the workhouse, so I did, but the landlord was a publican. That's how I ended up behind the counter. They say it's not a decent woman will do that job, but a mother who needs to feed her weans won't think twice, I tell ye. I was grateful for it. And the very first time your father came to them rooms we were in he brought food – for me. He said, "You'll have fed the boys rather than yourself, Elsie." He was right.' Her gaze held Annie's, determination in the grey eyes.

'Anyway, that's all behind me, thanks be to God,' Elsie went on. 'You'll come and see us again, won't you? Your father's happiness would be complete if you did. And Barrow's a good place. It's been good to us. It could be good to you too.'

'I will. I'll come again.'

'Annie, what made you decide to come now?'

Annie hesitated. 'It was the Orange boy, so it was.'

'Bring him too, so.'

'Catch yourself on, Elsie!' said Annie, in astonishment. 'How could I do that?'

Elsie held her arm, stopping their progress. They were nearly at the corner of Hardwick Street, where eddies of small boys, Joe and Mark amongst them, were chasing a football.

'You have a wee think about yourself, and what you want,' said Elsie. 'I'd hate for a lovely girl like you to make the same mistake as I did, because of people who think they know better than you. People like Father Hagerty, who might be a man of God but has no idea how some of God's poor crayturs have to live. I'll never forgive him for making my wee boys cry. The names he gave me don't matter, but that does. You mark my words, Annie. We don't choose how we're born, so we don't. We all come naked into the world but that's the only thing that's equal about us. Thon Orange boy is what he is because his dadda was, because his workmates are. You don't know who learned you to say the Hail Mary, so you don't – though it musta been your mother – but you'd never be able to unlearn it, would ye?'

'No, but . . .'

'Well, maybe he's the same in his own way. Sure, the Orangemen put the fear of God into us on the Twelfth but I've known them – taken one by one, I mean – as would help a Catholic neighbour in need and not make any noise about it either.'

'He was farmed out,' said Annie stiffly.

'God love him, Annie. He'll have joined out of loneliness, so he will. Or because the ganger in the pit telt him to. Far beyond me to defend an Orangeman, but this one stopped them others when he coulda joined in with them. He went and got you that blouse. He took you across thon square in public view of all them oul' gossips and gave you your tea. Tell me what would be wrong with a man like that?'

'His religion.'

Elsie pressed her hand to her forehead. 'Look at the *man*, would ye, and stop pretending.'

'*Pretending?*'

'You've the kind of face can't keep secrets, Annie, though you're doing your best to keep them from yourself. What reason else have ye to be going back to Cleator?'

Before Annie could think of what to say, Mark ran up and grabbed her hand. 'Did yous remember the sass?'

'We did so,' said his mother. 'But you'll have it with your dinner, not now.'

177

'Marsh's Sass, a penny a glass. When you drink it, it goes splash,' sang out the boy, skipping in excited anticipation. There wasn't an opportunity to continue the conversation, and after the midday meal the whole family accompanied Annie to the train.

Her tears only stopped at Ulverston, but Annie didn't smile for the rest of the journey. She was thinking about the prospect of Christmas at Philomena Nolan's table, contrasting that image with the family in Hardwick Street 'If it wasn't for Teresa,' she told herself, but it wasn't Teresa she had in mind.

CHAPTER TWENTY-TWO

Cleator Moor, October 1903

'. . . liveried Irish damask became the standard in luxury
hotels, railways and ocean liners, the world over.'

Peter Collins, *The Making of Irish Linen*, 1994

By the time Annie arrived back at the house in Birks Road, she
felt she had been away for far longer than a mere day or two,
yet in the Nolans' home, and indeed in Cleator Moor itself, it
was as if she'd never been gone. Philomena's chilly welcome
was thawed only momentarily when her lodger handed over the
week's rent. Annie tried to press home this advantage by picking
up the brush to tidy the backroom hearth, only for Philomena
to stop her. 'I can do that myself, so I can,' she'd said, and Annie
had murmured sorry, though in truth she was only sorry that her
desire to help had been taken as a criticism.

Over the tea-table no questions were asked about her excur-
sion, apart from Frank showing an interest in the train journey
itself. Only later, when she was at the outside tap getting the
washing-up water, did Michael come out to smoke his pipe and
to murmur, 'How's Tommy, then?'

Annie straightened up and looked him in the eye. 'Dadda's happy, so he is.'

'You tell him I was asking after him, so.'

'I will. Mrs Fagan and the wee boys were grand too, so they were.'

Michael raised his eyebrows, his glance flicking towards the back door. 'Don't say that in there, now.'

'I know better than that,' she said, stretching her lips in a mirthless smile. 'They've made a lovely home, so they have.'

'Lucky them,' whispered Michael, then in a louder voice, 'Can I help you in with that pail?'

*

The envelope Annie posted to Hardwick Street that evening was addressed to her father, but for the first time the letter it contained mentioned each member of the little family in turn.

On Sunday afternoon she walked around the square peering into the windows of the closed shops without really seeing their wares, glancing back over her shoulder periodically to see if anyone might be behind her. Robert never was. Teresa would be somewhere with Percy; now that he went conscientiously once a week to see Father Hagerty in the Priory House, it was felt that he and Teresa could be trusted unchaperoned, and Annie had no reason to go and sit on her old perch on the wall.

Teresa herself had been subdued by her first days beneath the sawtoothed roof of the weaving shed.

'It's desperate, Annie,' she said, when they were in their beds that evening, the prospect of the knocker-up and the tramp to the mill looming up in a few hours. 'The whirling of them power belts, the shuttles tearing back and forth as if the devil was after them. The awful crashing of them looms. Like they could pick you up and fling you as high as the ceiling. It's not the machines doing what you tell them. It's them commanding you. My head's singing, so it is, even when I'm not there. I feel sick half the time.'

'I thought that as soon as I saw you today. You're pale even now.'

'I can't keep my breakfast down. And the smell in there! I know it's all grease and oil in the spinning room as well, only there's more air back there and you're not so crowded. In the weaving shed you don't see daylight hardly. Just them wee sideways strips of glass in the roof, but you can't be looking at them or you'd miss a mistake and the tenter – oul' bastard that he is – he'd be down on you for idleness. My stand's so narrow I think sometimes the looms'll move in closer and I'll be crushed in the middle. I miss you, Annie, and I miss Mrs Birkett – tell her, will you?'

'Could you not come back?'

Teresa shook her head.

'I can't wait to get out of this house, so I can't. I'd marry Percy now if I was let, but we've not enough for to get our own place. Money's better in weaving, so it is. And when I'm good – I'm going to get good, if it kills me – they'll pay me for what comes off my loom, so they will. The jacquards are the best, they say, so I want them to learn me them too. I'll get used to the banging. Either that or I'll get so deaf if me and Percy have rows I'll never hear what bad names he's calling me . . .'

*

CHAPTER TWENTY-THREE

Ainsworth's Mill, November 1903

'Well, that first day I went to the weavin'... was desperate ... It's what you call the fever you take. Well, it's the awful blunderin' of the looms ... You only have to be in a weavin' shed to understand ... it's sort of fear on you ... I was very sick.'

Female weaver, born 1891, began work 1904, Protestant, Belfast. From Betty Messenger, *Picking Up the Linen Threads*

Annie moved back and forth on her stand, judging the timings as though engaged in a stately dance with the machines. Mrs Birkett had already hinted at the possibility of promotion, but Annie had softly rebuffed the suggestion, not believing that being good at something meant you'd be able to get anyone else to be good at it too. In the rhythm of her work she was able to think of other things: the dear faces of the little Fagan brothers at the tea-table, the murmuring of their mother over their bed, her father sitting at the hearth with his stockinged feet on the fender, twisting old newspaper into firelighters. She tried to see herself at such a fireside. Conscientiously she strove to put Frank in the chair opposite, but his image wouldn't stay. It was Robert she saw and Elsie's emphatic words she heard: '*What reason else have ye to be going back to Cleator?*'

She spun round, knowing where there was a bobbin that would be about ready for doffing, only to see to her surprise her machine was whirring softly to a halt. Glancing across at the stand opposite Annie saw it was running normally but the girl who worked there met her eyes, her mouth parted as though about to say something. A hand went up to push a lock of hair behind her ear and then the girl turned back to her machine. Then Annie realised that her other machine was also slowing. There was Mrs Birkett with her hand on the lever.

'Coom wi' me, Annie love,' she said. 'Bring your shoes and shawl. There's been an accident.'

Annie gathered her things in a daze. 'Which one of them is it?' she managed, as the doffing mistress guided her down the aisle and out into the empty stairwell. The air was immediately drier and cooler. 'Is it one of them wee boys?'

'What wee boys? Put your things on. Wrap up well. We're going outside.'

Annie obeyed, but her movements felt sluggish as sitting on the stairs she struggled to get her stockings to roll out straight.

'I don't understand . . .'

'I'm sorry, Annie. Such a bonny lass too. They'll be asking how she was on the loom by herself – tenter says she weren't ready, poor lass.'

'Teresa!'

'Ssh, Annie love. She's beyond hearing you.'

'What?'

'Her mother'll need comforting.'

Huddled in her shawl, Annie hung on Mrs Birkett's arm across the yard. *Teresa can't be dead. It must be someone else.*

'Percy,' she muttered.

'Her young man? Manager's gone for him.'

*

There was a knot of people outside one of the weaving sheds, where two policemen impassively stood guard. Some of the women were crying: the capped, shirtsleeved men were pale. There were strangers amongst them, with moustaches and wearing bowler hats, waistcoats and watch-chains, conferring with each other; one of them was writing in a notebook. A patient horse attached to a cart stood by, the reins held by a boy of about twelve. Beyond them, on the bleaching green, Annie saw lengths of newly woven linen stretched out. *Winding sheets*, she thought, as the reality of what was happening hit her and she began at last to cry. Someone asked, 'Have they gone for Mr Ainsworth?' Mrs Birkett's arm was around Annie's shoulder. With her free hand, she offered her a clean handkerchief.

From inside the shed came an unearthly cry, half-shriek, half-wail. As Annie watched, holding on to Mrs Birkett, the crowd fell silent and eddied out, making way for two men carrying a stretcher. Several people crossed themselves; Annie followed their example, though she couldn't quite believe what she was seeing. Beneath a length of freshly woven linen, unbleached brown, something or someone lay motionless. As the stretcher was loaded onto the cart, Annie caught sight of the splayed shoes extended beyond the improvised shroud. She staggered; Mrs Birkett caught her.

'Whatever happened, she wouldn't have known owt, poor lass,' she murmured.

'How can you know that?' cried Annie.

Mrs Birkett swallowed audibly. 'No blood,' she muttered. Her hand tightened on Annie's shoulder. 'Oh the poor soul . . .' Annie followed the doffing mistress's gaze. In the doorway to the weaving shed stood Philomena, deathly pale, supported by two women.

'Where are they taking her? Where're they going with my wee girl?' she shrieked.

'I should go to her,' said Annie. 'I should try.'

'I'll coom with you.'

They moved forward, but hesitated at the tumult around the cart. One of the bowler-hatted men was quietly remonstrating with Philomena, blocking her view of the stretcher being loaded, four men ensuring it was held up high so that its pitiful burden didn't slip. Once it was safely stowed, one of the men pushed up the tailboard and clipped it closed.

'They're taking her to Carlisle for the post-mortem,' Annie heard someone say. 'The coroner'll have to sit.'

'Mrs Nolan . . . Philomena,' said Annie, venturing closer. It was the first time she'd used Teresa's mother's Christian name; the 'Mrs Nolan' had sounded too distant in her ears.

Philomena's head swivelled, bewildered. When her eyes met Annie's, her face went as stiff as a mask. 'Get that wee hussy away from me!' she hissed.

'Coom away, love,' said Mrs Birkett in Annie's ear. 'She don't mean anything by it. The poor thing int herself.'

'Teresa . . .'

'Mind, love, let the horse by.' Annie turned at Mrs Birkett's gentle tug on her arm and stood back. She was a foot from the wheel when the cart rumbled by; looking up, she saw a blur of the linen covering the corpse, a bareheaded man sitting alongside the stretcher. The small crowd evaporated. To Annie's astonishment, she saw the tenters ushering most of the people back into the weaving shed, though the way they moved, with heads bowed, it looked as though they were going to a funeral. Philomena was now nowhere to be seen, but one person detached himself and came forward to where she and Mrs Birkett stood.

'Percy,' she said, looking up at him and mechanically uttering the formula, 'I'm sorry for your trouble.' He looked like a man of thirty, his skin dry and his eyes dull.

'They say she went back in alone. Wanted to show them she was good enough to go on piecework sooner. We were going to be married, Annie. Not when she was of age. In the next few weeks if Hagerty would have let us. Scotland if he didn't. Teresa was going to have a baby.'

CHAPTER TWENTY-FOUR

Birks Road, November 1903

'Such infants as quit the body without being baptised will be involved in the mildest condemnation of all . . .'

St Augustine of Hippo

Annie stood at the back door, fearing Philomena's grief and rage. She wished she'd had the presence of mind to ask Mrs Birkett if she knew anywhere, anyone, who would take her in, and had not done so only because her absence too would have been an offence in Philomena's eyes. As she hesitated on the back step, the door opened, and Frank stood there. He looked shrunken, unkempt, in a way she had never seen him.

'Come away in, Annie.' He stood back to let her pass, but she hesitated on the threshold.

'Frank . . . I don't know what to say. I can't believe it yet.'

'Nor can we,' said a man's voice from the back room. Michael's, but older. As Annie walked up to him where he stood before the fireplace, she heard the murmur of women's voices from the front room, in their midst a low keening sound. Michael reached both hands out to her.

'You have her home?' she whispered.

'No.' Michael inclined his head in the direction of the voices. 'Them's the neighbours. Philomena's in a terror that we won't be let to wake our poor girl. She's in Whitehaven till they see what happened. She should be in her shroud, not under their knives.' His face creased and sagged. 'If they'd'a brought my poor child home and I seen her lying in her coffin sure I'd'a believed her gone. Phil was full of the devil carrying off the poor blameless soul the minute they'd'a left the body alone but that Father Hagerty has got word to St Begh's so's she'll be watched – one of the nuns will be with her.'

Annie's stomach twisted. *Please God them doctors don't find out about the baby – or if they do that they keep it to themselves.*

'I should go through, so I should.'

'Don't, Annie. Phil's not herself, so she's not. Give her time.' Michael took a deep breath. 'She said to Father Hagerty why was it Teresa was took and not yourself and Father said that even if we don't understand it or think it just, we've to put our faith in God's plan all the same.'

'Would you make us tea, Annie?' said Frank behind her. 'Just a pot, I mean, but get some bread for yourself. I don't want to go in there and ask any o' them.'

*

When Annie went up that night it was to find that Teresa's bed had already been stripped, the things her friend had left strewn around the room gone. She sat on the bare mattress and cried with great gulping sobs until her throat ached and her eyes stung. Several times during the restless night she could have sworn she heard Teresa moving close by. She didn't realise she had slept at all until the knocker-up tapped the window and she had a fleeting moment of normality before in a rush the memory of the previous day's events overwhelmed her. Twitching the curtain and looking out on the awakening street, she was convinced that she saw Ma Maxwell pass by in the shadows, leading her horse, the cart's burden covered by an unbleached length of linen. Annie rested her forehead against the cold glass and shut her eyes. When she opened them again there was nothing there.

*

The whole mill buzzed with the news that the coroner would be hearing the witnesses in an upper room of the Commercial Hotel. Nellie Birkett insisted on working Annie's stand with her, but instead of going down to breakfast in the yard the spinning mistress ushered Annie into her cubbyhole, a place dreaded by most of the mill girls. Nobody went in there usually unless it was for a telling-off – or to get their cards.

'Have they called you for evidence, lass?'

Annie shook her head, thinking of Percy's revelation. 'I don't know what I'd tell them if they asked. That Teresa was as white as milk and said she couldn't hold her breakfast? She thought it was the noise in there – all the banging she said she'd never get used to.'

'There were a baby on the way, weren't there?' said Mrs Birkett.

Annie nodded, knowing it was both useless and wrong to lie to the woman.

'But it weren't the noise that killed her, nor the feeling sick, was it?' said Mrs Birkett. 'If you went and told them all that it would only add to the poor mother's tears, wouldn't it? I'm not going to say about the baby, and you'd best not either.' She took Annie's hands. 'I'm going to tell you, lass, what the tenter told me, if you think you can bear it. But you've to keep it to yerself until it's in the newspaper, a' right?'

'I will. I want to know. To stop me imagining it.'

'The tenter found her on the floor. He only realised when he saw the cloth was rising up without the weft. A shuttle had flew off and got her in the eye. I don't know if she wouldn't have lost it altogether, and now we'll never know. But it looks like wi' blunderin' about an' all, she fell against the machine at her back, hit her head and down she went. Tenter was away fixing a tearing and the loom the other side of the aisle was idle so nobody saw her in time and with the racket in there nobody would hear. She was gone by the time he got to her. The manager'll be called as a witness. Mr Ainsworth's a decent old stick and he'll want action taken – but you must see, Annie, if you go and say what you've said to me the whole world will know Teresa was in the family way and not wed, and the mill's lawyers will argue that she weren't herself because of it, weren't running her loom right and fell down in a faint. There should've been guards on them machines long before now. Don't let Teresa be dead for nowt, because they won't fit 'em even now if they say it were her made the mistake.'

*

Annie hung back by the dark silhouette of a yew tree, struggling to hold back tears. She was not family, yet not a mere neighbour. The Nolans were clumped around the open grave. There'd been a good turnout, final handshakings and the oft-murmured words 'Sorry for your trouble,' and then those who'd followed the coffin out of the church melted out into the street. Beyond the diminished family group, by the side of a bleached white praying angel, Annie saw Duffy the sexton and his son leaning on their spades, waiting in the soft drizzle to move forward and shovel the earth over Teresa.

Annie resolved then to stay, at a distance, until they had finished. Only then would she go and stand above what had been her friend. Philomena, with her muttered, 'She wasn't your child, wasn't your sister,' that morning as they huddled into coats and shawls, had made it quite clear that Annie's sympathy, Annie's tears, were the last things the bereaved mother wanted. The girl saw the woman's resentment in every buttoning of her black coat.

'I wanted my poor child closer to the church,' came the mother's wail, followed by her husband's indistinct murmurs. Michael Nolan hadn't wept, but though he was a sturdily built man he'd looked to Annie since the death the previous Thursday as though he had shrunk. His face was pinched, his cheeks sunken, his eyes smaller. Finally the little group stumbled off, the mother hidden by the dark phalanx of her husband and son, but her keening like the cry of an animal in a trap soaked into the damp air. Annie longed for one of them to look around for her, but knew they wouldn't.

Where's Percy? I never seen him.

Duffy and his boy straightened up and lifted their spades.

*

Annie stared down at the neat camber of earth. She knew that six months from now the ground would be flat, or even gently concave. Her mother's grave had been like that. She'd had bad dreams about it: the thin coffin lid giving way in the darkness as what had once been warm, living flesh with a familiar dear scent was lost forever. 'Earth to earth,' she murmured.

'And dust to dust,' whispered a voice at her shoulder. Annie jumped.

'I'm sorry, child, I didn't mean to frighten you.'

She turned, looking up at Father Clayton, the curate.

'I've just been to the house,' he said, opening his hands apologetically. She caught the faintest scent of whiskey on his breath. Annie remembered that Father Hagerty quite often smelled of it, but not his curate. She could see him now in the cramped front room, accepting a glass from Michael, fearing refusal might offend.

'I looked for you there,' he said. 'After seeing you at the back of the church.'

At that, Annie crumpled. Her head butted the priest's chest like a bullock at a gate. He patted her shoulder, awkwardly at first, then placed both hands more confidently on the caps of her arms. Afterwards she'd wondered, with a rush of blood to her face, if he'd done it so as to keep her at a physical distance. She'd encountered a young priest in Comber who'd looked at her with a mixture of longing and resentment, doubtless a country boy who'd gone south to the seminary in Maynooth only because he knew there was no living for him on a farm destined for an older brother and because he hadn't had the strength to withstand a mother's pride: 'My son the priest!' This austere Englishman was different, with his granite-hewn face, his close-cropped curling hair. She wanted to tell him that she'd always liked his homilies, that she could tell he prepared them for that day, that moment, whereas Father Hagerty's she was pretty sure came out of a carefully docketed drawer, and were recycled, more or less, every three years.

'When they brought her home, Philomena wouldn't let me in to see her, so she wouldn't,' she sobbed into her already sodden handkerchief. 'Not even to say goodbye to her. I'd to wait in the kitchen. Then Mr Nolan came for me. He . . .' She paused, remembering.

'What is it, Annie?'

'He was kind, so he was. He said, "I'm sorry, Annie. You can go in now." Only there was the strangest look on his face. He said, "You'd not know her." He was right, too. The surgeons had taken off all her hair. She'd this white cap on, you know, like a nun's coif. And that wee pinched face looked like it had never been alive.'

He looked down at the grave. 'Teresa is far from all harm.'

Her eyes followed his. 'Is she now? I think she'd'a wanted a bit more harm in her life before she left it, so I do. I can't think what life'll be like without her. I mean . . . if I ever wed, she'll not be there for me, nor me for her. I'd have wanted her as godmother for my child, if I ever had one.'

'She will be there. And waiting for you when all this is over.'

Annie looked at the dark earth and was pricked with doubt.

'You'll know what to call a daughter, too.'

Annie said nothing. She was wondering what the little crea-ture curled dead inside Teresa's body would have been. *Known only to God.*

'I'd better go back to the house,' she said eventually.

'I suppose you should. Mrs Nolan mightn't want you there, but she is sure to remark on your absence.'

'I'm useful in the kitchen.'

'What a dull thought, even if out of Martha and Mary I've always thought Martha a bit hard done by,' he said, smiling gently.

'I don't like to leave her here,' said Annie, looking down at the grave. 'She never liked to be alone.'

'Michael has said he wants a nice stone for her,' said the priest. 'And he wanted me to tell you that you're to choose something of hers.'

'He did?' Annie struggled not to cry again.

'He's asked my help to give away her things. I shall send them to a dealer in Whitehaven, probably. Her mother'll not want to see them on anyone here.'

'I'll choose something she won't see on me either,' said Annie, wondering. She knew what it would be. An embroidered needlebook – something she could use.

'She gave me courage. Teresa wasn't feart of anything,' Annie went on. 'Not like me. I'm feart to go home, even.'

'Well, don't go just yet, then. There's someone over there looks as if he's wanting to talk to you.'

Annie's heart fluttered. *Robert!* Then she felt a surge of guilt, chiding herself for thinking of him on this day of all days. Nevertheless, she turned in the direction of Father Clayton's gaze to see the man standing by the dark bulk of the yew.

'Oh . . .'

Poor Percy. And I feel awful altogether for wanting you to be somebody else.

'I'll go back to the Priory House,' she heard Father Clayton say. 'You know where I am should you need me.'

'Yes, Father . . . thank you.' As he walked off, Annie suppressed an irrational urge to run after him and beg him to find her somewhere to live. There'd be space in the Priory House surely, just for a few days . . . *Don't be an eejit. The scandal'd be nothing to the looks on the faces of them parlourmaids.*

CHAPTER TWENTY-FIVE

St Mary's Churchyard, Cleator Moor

'There are a good many pious people who are as careful of their religion as of their best service of china, only using it on holy occasions, for fear it should get chipped or flawed in working-day wear.'

Douglas William Jerrold (1803–1857)

Percy looked as though he hadn't slept.

'I missed you in the church,' said Annie.

'I wasn't welcome,' he said bitterly. 'I came – early. I know what you're supposed to do now. Wet your fingers in the stoup at the door, drop your knee before getting in the pew. I was going to be a Catholic, remember? Well, Father Hagerty won't see me for dust now. I was only doing it for her. It was Frank noticed me and said he was sorry but it was better his mother and father didn't see me there today. He wouldn't look me in the eye and I could see he was all red round his collar, but he did shake my hand. They know, Annie, that's the only explanation I have. It mightn't have been in the papers but the surgeons must've told them. You were the only person I said anything to.'

'I said nothing. But the doffing mistress had guessed.'

Percy sighed. 'I keep thinking – by now the storm might've been over. We'd have told them. The wedding would've been brought forward and them flowers wouldn't have been wreaths . . . I've been walking about out here all this time, not daring to go near that hole they'd dug for her, talking to her, telling her I loved her and the baby. I couldn't not do it.' He started to cry. Annie laid a hand on his arm.

'Percy . . .'

His arms went around her and his head rested on her shoulder. His hair against her neck was damp with drizzle; she remembered now that inside the church she'd heard the patter of rain on the windows and Father Hagerty saying something about heaven's tears of joy at receiving Teresa into paradise. Annie put her arms cautiously around Percy; he felt very large, very tense, and smelled of the mill: oil and grease and the musty smell of flax. His sobs were great juddering spasms, but almost silent – so different from the keening sounds coming from the women who had sat with Philomena. She was sure holding him was sinful, *But what else can I do?*

At last Percy stood back, but grasped both her hands. His palms felt rough, from all the linen fibres that passed through them daily in his hackling berth.

'Thank you, Annie. Thank you for all the times you covered for us. We couldn't have had what we had without you. I'll never forget your kindness.'

He pushed his cap onto his damp hair and, as he did so, Annie caught sight of another figure standing under the yew tree. Their eyes met, but Robert gave no sign. His face taut, he held her gaze for a moment, then turned and walked briskly away.

Percy bent and kissed her cheek. 'Goodbye.'

'Goodbye, Percy.' *Goodbye, Robert.*

*

Approaching the back door of the house in Birks Road, Annie saw the curtains, which had all been closed since the death, had now been drawn back. Forcing herself not to peer in the window first, she took a deep breath and went into the scullery.

'It's yourself,' said Michael, filling the doorway into the back room. Beyond him, the doors were open to the front parlour. She could hear the murmur of women's voices and the chink of china.

'How are you, so?' he went on.

At that, the floodgates opened again. He was the first in the family to ask her that. Michael stepped down into the scullery and embraced her. 'You poor wee girl.' Grief was a strange thing, Annie thought. *He's the second man to do that today. Sure why does someone have to die for us to show each other that we care?* But Michael let go of her more quickly than Percy, glancing over his shoulder. The murmuring over the teacups continued uninterrupted. Annie saw relief flit over his face.

'I'd best tidy up,' she said, looking through at the detritus of dirty cups and plates on the table, Philomena's good delph that should have been taken out and washed for Teresa's wedding, or the baby's baptism.

Michael said, 'We'd a good number come, so we did. Both the priests.'

'I know. I seen Father Clayton.'

Michael raised his eyebrows.

'I was still at the grave. He came there.'

'That was good of you. To stay a bit with my girl.'

Annie wanted to say that it was the most she could do, because she'd not been welcome with the other mourners at the vigil at the coffin.

'I loved her too,' she said quietly.

'I know.' Michael stood back as she started to gather up the crockery, as quietly as she could.

Michael said, 'Let me help you.'

'You don't have to . . .'

'I need something to do, so I do. It's as well I'm back at work tomorrow.'

Annie shivered, remembering how close Crowgarth pit was to the Church of England cemetery at St John's. *What if the ground gave way and all them Protestants tumbled into a seam thinking it was the Last Judgement already? They'd have to dig through the bodies to get the miners out.* She opened the back door, tipping the crumbs off the plates for the sparrows, who swooped down immediately.

'"Are not five sparrows sold for two farthings, and not one of them is forgotten before God?"' quoted Michael, watching her.

'The poor wee sparrows,' said Annie. 'What would they be selling them for? They musta ate them, so they musta.'

'Oh, the Orange boy came to pay his respects, so he did.'

Annie saw him studying her expression.

'That was kind of him.'

'It was. He was awful polite. He said he'd only had the pleasure of meeting Teresa the once but you'd spoken of her often enough that he thought he knew her more.'

Annie couldn't hide her fluster in the face of his intent gaze.

'Sure, I only seen him the once or twice.' She swallowed. It was easier to brazen it out. 'I seen him just now at the burial ground.'

'And . . . ?'

'I never spoke to him, so I didn't. Percy was there—'

Michael flinched, his eyes flickering sideways. 'For the love of God don't name him here, Annie,' he whispered. 'Herself won't stand for it.'

'I won't.'

'You knew, didn't ye?'

Annie nodded, looking down. 'Only afterwards. *He* telt me.'

'I'd'a not minded a rushed marriage, so I wouldn't. Just as long as she was still with us.' He wiped his eyes with both hands. 'I liked Percy. I've lost a grandchild, not only my daughter. Phil doesn't see it that way. Only you wouldn't add to a mother's pain, would ye?'

'No, I wouldn't,' said Annie, picking up a teatowel to stop herself putting her arms around him. 'I was thinking, Mr Nolan . . . yous'll not want me here – not now. I should look for somewhere else maybe. Or Barrow . . .'

'Frank and me'll want you here. You've brought a bit of calm to this house.'

'*Me?*'

'Ssh. You.' He glanced over his shoulder. 'You take it in the neck for us, so you do. If Phil can give out to you, there's less trouble for us. But go to your father again if you can. There's no love like a parent for a child, so there isn't, though none of us know how much we're loved until we've our own children.'

*

The atmosphere in the little house chilled over the following days. It was more than Philomena's stony grief or Michael's abstracted look when he sat by the fire of an evening. The Sunday after the funeral the two women moved between the scullery and the table in a practised dance in which they would never touch. If Annie wanted something from the scullery or the larder beyond and Philomena stood in her way, she hung back, until the older woman came up the step into the room and went past her as if she wasn't there. A memory returned from long-ago Moneyscalp: Agnes from the neighbouring farm reminiscing with Annie's mother about her youngest days as a servant at Lord Roden's. '*You were never to look them in the face. If you saw them in the corridors and galleries of thon place, you weren't just to stand aside. You were to stand facing the wall so his lord-ship didn't have to see the eyes and nose God gave ye. They'd never speak to you but to bark at ye to do something for them. Some of what her ladyship wanted woulda cost her less bother to do herself than ringing her wee bell for to get ye to do it for her.*' Annie wouldn't have been surprised if Philomena had told her to eat like a servant, away from the table where Teresa's chair was already missing, standing up in the scullery instead of sitting down with the family. But that Sunday as usual Annie brought the dinner to the table, grace was said, and then she stood up to apportion out the chops and potatoes, a task she had always shared with her dead friend.

'Sit down,' she heard Philomena say curtly. Annie did so, glancing beneath lowered lids at her landlady, but the woman's face was impassive. Philomena started doling out the food herself, Michael first, then Frank, then her own plate, then Annie's. The chops were small and fatty, but there were two for each of them – though only one for the lodger. Likewise the dole of potatoes was stinting. No one said anything, and Annie's embarrassment was only increased when silently Michael dissected one of his own chops and, wordlessly holding half of it between his knife and fork, deposited it on the side of Annie's plate.

Afterwards, Annie took the plates outside and rinsed them under the tap, trying to remove the worst of the grease. She'd have to boil the dishrag later. She hated the way the fat stuck to her fingers. Her hands either smelled of food or when at work of the waxy residue of the linen thread. At least the beeswax for polishing the furniture had a nice scent and softened her fingers. The girls she read about in books never had these problems. Their hands were white and smooth and perfumed with rosewater. The books never mentioned the broken nails and chapped knuckles of those who served their heroines. *But sure, who'd want to read about their own lives?*

The two men came out for a smoke. Annie went in before they passed down the yard to the privy.

To get everything properly clean, the kettle was bubbling over the fire. Annie wrapped the handle in a teatowel and emptied it into the two inches of cold water she'd poured first into the Belfast sink, to ensure the plates wouldn't crack. It was a brief relief for Annie to plunge her hands into the hot water, to seize the fissured block of soap on the windowsill and rub it against the delph until it squeaked, and into the tines of the forks. In the other well of the sink she dunked the plates in fresh cold water and put them to drain.

'You've chipped this one,' said Philomena, coming up alongside her with a teatowel.

Annie looked. 'It was like that, so it was. I know because it was mine. Look – you can see the chip's not new.'

'Are you calling me a liar?'

'No . . . but—'

'You are so.'

'I'm not. But I didn't chip the plate, so I didn't.'

Frank came in, glanced from one woman to the other, and went to find his newspaper. There was a click of the back gate, so both women knew Michael had gone for a walk. Annie was aware Frank could do no wrong in his mother's eyes, but that he would not intervene; he was too afraid of Philomena for that.

'Them plates were a wedding present. Good quality.'

To Annie they looked no different from the transferware to be found on any farmhouse dresser. Her shoulders sagged.

'Look – I don't know what I should do,' said Annie. 'I never chipped the plate. I'd'a telt you if I done it. I can't do right by you however I try. I'm all right for the skivvying and the cleaning and the mending, though I've seen you – I have so – looking for faults. I swear to God you're happier when you find them, so you are.'

'You little vixen! The pure cheek of you!'

'I can't help that I'm not Teresa. *I'm* mourning her too, but you'd never notice it or you ignore it if you do,' said Annie, starting to cry.

'Too right you're not my daughter,' hissed Philomena. 'It shoulda been you, not her!'

Annie gasped as though she'd been struck. She took her hands out of the sink, rolled them in her apron, and fled to get her shawl.

CHAPTER TWENTY-SIX

Carnegie Library, November 1903

'This only is the witchcraft I have us'd.'

Othello, used in an advertisement for
Pears soap, 1890s

Annie walked fast to reach the corner, tears filming her eyes. She turned towards the high street, almost deserted in its Sunday afternoon way. There were a few strolling courting couples and some little boys playing tig. The further she got from the Nolans, the more her present predicament overwhelmed her. *I can't stay there. But where'll I go?*

She knew though she had to go back and face Philomena. But if she stayed out longer, perhaps Michael would be back from the Wheatsheaf or wherever he'd gone; she'd feel safer if he were there. It occurred to her that he was staying out because he didn't want a reckoning over the piece of chop he'd cut for her.

The door of the Wheatsheaf opened and she caught a glimpse of cloth-capped men in a world as closed to her as the door of the Orange Lodge, along with a whiff of beer, smoke and sweat. She couldn't possibly go in and look for Michael. *He'd be mortified, so he would.* She dawdled back, willing Nolan to come up behind her and walk home with her.

'Miss Maguire?'

Afterwards, she wondered how long Robert had been standing there, if he'd been watching her hesitating outside the door of the pub.

'I'm sorry for your trouble,' he said.

'Mr Nolan said you came to the house. That was a good thing you did.'

An awkward silence followed.

'I'll not disturb you,' he said. 'You'll be waiting on someone maybe.'

'I'm waiting on nobody.' She felt the blood rise to her face. *He'll think you're a bold girl, so he will.* 'I'm just not wanting to go back there just yet.'

She saw him glance round, as though checking that they were truly alone.

'That was Teresa's intended,' she heard herself say. 'In the cemetery.' With soaring hope she saw relief wash over his face.

'I'm not sure I shoulda been there,' he said. 'We're not let inside Catholic chapels and I shouldn't'a been in the burial ground either.'

Annie couldn't help but smile gently at the serious look on his face.

'Miss Maguire – Annie – would we go for a walk, do you think?'

'We could. I can tell you then about when I went to Barrow. It was what you said made me go.'

'Me?' he said. She could see he was pleased.

'I'm glad I did. I'm thinking now that I might join them there after all,' and from the crestfallen look on his face she could see that what Elsie had said about him was right.

*

Half an hour later Robert stood with her at the mouth of the street. 'You're good company, Annie,' he said. 'You'll have found me a bit boring though. I don't have much to say for myself, so I don't.'

'That's not true ... I mean you're not boring. You listen. There's nobody really ever listens to me at home. The men because they daren't, and I daren't say anything with Philomena there anyway.' Annie hung her head. 'I shouldn't say wicked things like that of a house in mourning, sure I shouldn't. Only I was only let to stay on there because Teresa bargained for me, against her own happiness.' Despite her resolve, she felt her chin wobble.

'Don't let them see you cry, Annie,' he murmured. He glanced past her down the street. Now that the afternoon had worn on, and the weather was fine, a number of women were out on their doorsteps, ostensibly to watch their children but really more to gossip with their neighbours. As he eyed them, a distant memory flickered: Cairncross swinging him down from a cart as scowling neighbours looked on. Cairncross, unperturbed, muttering, 'Oul' bitch.' He wondered what his father would make of Annie, and with a little spasm of anger imagined how he'd look at her. Appraising her, fancying his chances. *Just as he musta done with my mother.*

'Robert?'

'Sorry. I was away with the fairies there. Will yer man be back by now, do you think?'

'Mr Nolan? I've to go whether he is or no.'

'Would you walk with me again, Annie?'

'I would.' She couldn't stop herself smiling.

'Saturday at three? Outside the Carnegie?'

*

Crossfield Road
Cleator Moor
26th November 1903

Dear Mammy,

I wonder do you get my letters seeing as you don't write back. I am sorry I haven't written for a while but I have thought a long time about what to tell you. I have met a young woman here and I want to ask her would she marry me though she has no idea of it I am sure. Only I don't know is it possible and I don't mean whether she would have me or not. This place is too much like home for it. Also I have nothing to offer her.

I just wanted to tell somebody and you are the best person. Please do not say anything to Mr Cairncross.

Your loving son,
Robert

*

Positioning the tin bowl carefully beneath the mouth of the pump, Annie heaved the handle up and down until she had filled three-quarters of it, then carefully carried it towards the out-house. She put it down on the scrubbed wooden surface where on Monday, a neighbour, too old to work in the mill, would come to sort the laundry, and went to wedge the door closed with the chair with the broken seat. With half an eye on the cloudy-paned window, she stripped off her blouse and chemise and, dampen-ing a cloth in the icy water and greasing it with the bar of soap from her tin, she washed first her face and neck, then shoulders, breasts and underarms, gasping at the cold. Patting and rubbing herself dry, she put on a clean chemise and the blouse Robert had bought her, then washed her knees and thighs and the secret places beneath her skirts. On went a clean pair of bloomers, crackling agreeably with starch. Then her stomach contracted with a whisper of cramp, her usual early-warning sign.

Tomorrow, then, she thought. *I'll be all right this afternoon, so I will.* She dreaded the week that was coming, and the back-ache that came with her monthlies, standing there feeding her machines. She'd bring a candle to the washhouse each night while the curse lasted, to covertly wash those cloths in this same bowl, with copious quantities of salt. They were yellowed with use, but who would use blue bag laundry whitener on things no one else should see? Tears came to her eyes. This was once a chore she'd performed with Teresa, for little by little, sleeping side by side in their iron-framed beds, the two girls' cycles had synchronised. She could hear Teresa's laughing voice as though she stood at her shoulder. *We've the curse, Mammy, so we have!*

The both of us! Philomena had shushed her for a bold-mouthed hallion. Annie glanced down at the other zinc bowl sitting dustily on the shelf below the worktop. At night sometimes she would wake and stretch a hand out to the bare ticking mattress on the narrow bed that still stood alongside her own.

Teresa, I need your advice. She stared at the bricks as though expecting an answer. *He's an Orange boy. But he has the kindest eyes . . .*

Back in the house, Annie lifted her shawl from its hook. It was a warm day, but the winds from those mountains could whip round you once you were beyond the shelter of the streets. Philomena was sitting by the back parlour window to get the light. Annie saw her take another sock out of the basket by the chair and pull it onto the wooden egg darner with a force that made her wince. On the far side of the fireplace Michael glanced up from his newspaper.

'Away out, are ye?' said Philomena, peering up at the girl.

'A walk only,' stammered Annie.

'You've a fine day for it, so you have,' said Michael, folding his newspaper noisily. 'Would you be wanting company?'

Annie blushed. 'I . . . oh . . . I'd be fine . . . you know, just to clear my head.'

Michael regarded her silently for a moment. She couldn't meet his eyes.

'I'll see you to the corner, mebbe. Arthur's got new pigeons he wants to show me.' He put down his newspaper. Annie tried desperately not to fidget as he tied his bootlaces. She might have to run to be in time if he didn't hurry up. What was the point then of scrubbing herself clean in that cold outhouse and dabbing precious oil of roses behind her ears?

Philomena said nothing but stabbed her needle through the wool of the sock so energetically that Annie hear it scratch the darner.

*

Neither Annie nor Michael spoke a word until they reached the end of the terrace.

'Where is it you'll meet him?' asked Michael quietly. Annie ducked her head and pulled the shawl tighter.

'At the Carnegie Library,' she murmured.

'Thank you for not lying, Annie. But you'll not be able to bring him back here,' he added. 'Herself'd have a fit, so she would. It was all Frank and me could do to make the peace the last time.'

'I . . . it's only a walk, so it is.'

'It was good of him to come and condole. But don't forget what he is.'

'I've not.'

'It'd best only be this walk, then. They'd make life hard for Robert too, you know.'

'He'll mebbe not be there anyway. He'll mebbe have forgot.'

'He'll not.'

'You'll not say?'

'I won't. But it's not me you've to worry about.'

CHAPTER TWENTY-SEVEN

'If a Dress should wear badly, or be in any respect faulty,
LEWIS'S will give a New Dress for Nothing at all, and pay
for the full cost of making and trimming.'

Advertisement for Lewis's, Manchester, 1902

Annie saw Robert sitting on the steps of the fountain before he
noticed her. Her first thought was, *I only ever see him alone. He's
like myself.*

'I'm sorry I'm late,' she said, as he scrambled to his feet,
brushing the seat of his trousers.

'You aren't. I'm not long from the baths myself.'

Annie knew this was a white lie. He smelled of tar soap, but
his hair was bone dry.

'Where would you like to go?'

Annie hesitated, although she'd thought about this a lot. 'If
it's not too far for you, maybe the way Teresa and Percy used to
go. I'd like to do a wee pilgrimage for her, only I've not wanted
to go alone.'

'You mean the place I saw you first? Right enough you
wouldn't want to go there by yourself. Not after what happened

with them eejits.' He offered her his arm. Annie adjusted her shawl before taking it, revealing the blouse underneath.

'Oh! You're wearing it!' He looked to her as delighted as a child at Christmas.

'The first time.'

'Let me see properly. Just for a minute, so's you don't catch cold.' Looking at her, with his head slightly on one side, he tweaked the blouse at the shoulders. 'It drapes right, so it does. It's properly cut. A good fit – if I say it myself. I'd to go on memory to get the right size, after seeing you only the once.'

Annie pinked. With his tailor's eye, he'd assessed her accurately that time, even with her face scratched, her sleeve torn, her hair bedraggled.

'But you said you were going to keep it for a special occasion,' he went on, with that shy smile that melted her heart. 'This'll be the first time in my life I've been a special occasion for anyone.' He helped her arrange her shawl, and in the way he did it Annie could see him, a boy, with that lady Kathleen he'd told her about, watching her adjusting a garment on a dressmaker's dummy. His fingers were deft.

'You deserve a good paisley shawl, so you do,' he said. 'And a nice cameo to pin it together.'

'A mill girl?'

'Why shouldn't a mill girl have them things?' he said, suddenly serious. 'I seen fine ladies – the ones Kathleen sewed for – but you move like a princess, so you do, without even trying. An' your hair – it's like the best black silk. What them ladies woulda given for them gifts you have, Annie.'

Annie's eyes flared in surprise and delight. 'Nobody's ever said anything like that to me, so they haven't!'

'Well, they've no eyes in their heads, is all I can say.' He offered his arm again.

'What made you come to England?' she asked, as they fell into step.

'You'd have to ask Mr Cairncross that. I didn't know a soul, but he gave me the address of a boarding house and a man to ask for at the pit – when I got there he acted as if he'd been expecting me. It was all so laid down for me that I thought maybe Cairncross had sent others before me.' He gave an uncertain laugh. 'I even wondered was I not going to meet brothers and sisters here – other by-blows. I wasn't really given a choice, anyway. He'd another family wanting the house Kathleen and me were in, the moment she died. Her cats got took up to the Offices at the Big House because of the rats. So they had to work for their living too. Mammy complained about "that woman's leavings" but not to his face. She cried plenty when I said goodbye to her, though my father insisted with her that I should seek my fortune somewhere where I could be the same as any man. One like my brothers – the ones called Cairncross, I mean.'

'Have you met them?'

'Never. I don't suppose they even know about me. He knows full well I can't be like them, anyway. They'll end up like him: a fella who can write a good hand, drive a pony and trap, and make decisions about how others have to live their lives without bothering his head if he's the right to it or not. All I ever wanted was thon wee tailor's shop. A job where I can wear a clean shirt and see daylight.'

'My father always said working indoors was what everyone wanted. Except he didn't want that for himself. He'd hoped working at the surface would give him something of the farm back after the mill, only the sound of the pithead drowned out the birds. He likes the yard better. He's a foreman now – in charge of labourers, not shipwrights, but even so.'

Beyond the streets the mountains reasserted themselves, and as the asphalt ended and the surface of the path became uneven, by tacit agreement she let go of his arm. Nevertheless, they walked closely together, and when her hand brushed his, he took it and held it. As they passed the spot where she used to sit on the wall, she felt his eyes on her, and looked up to see his shy smile. However, when Robert spoke again, it was to the landscape. The girl thought for a moment he was simply thinking aloud.

'To be fair, Cairncross always provided for me in his own way. As I said to Mr Nolan, I coulda been sent to Olivet's.'

He turned to her, with a smile that forced down the corners of his mouth. 'So I'm not just a Proddy bastard, Annie. I'm a bastard bastard.'

'It's not your fault,' she said.

'Nobody's child,' he said, averting his face. 'Other people brought me up.'

'Kindly?'

'Not all – they weren't all like Kathleen, God rest her. Where there was other weans, they'd make it weigh on me, some of them, tell me to walk behind them on the way to school and that. But Cairncross'd come from time to time, and if I told him I wasn't happy, he'd move me.'

'Well that's something . . .'

'Is it?' he said, turning back to her, eyes dark with pain. 'It might have been better than what other wee nameless ones got. I shouldn't complain, but it wasn't a family life I had. It was like spying through a window into somebody's kitchen, and seeing Dadda and Mammy and weans there, but not being part of it, even while I was in the room with them. Kathleen was the last of them and the best by a country mile. A saint of a woman no matter how badly the neighbours looked at her. Only she was Cairncross's skirt, and when I realised that I thought perhaps did she not take me in just to please him. If she did, she loved me anyway after a bit. Then I started to worry he'd get tired of her same as he musta got tired of my mother, and then where would I be? I heard him, you know . . . them . . . in the night, I mean. He had this laugh.'

Annie flushed and, to deflect the conversation, said, 'Do you laugh like him?'

He smiled wryly. 'You know, I've no idea! You'd have to make me laugh and then I'd maybe be able to tell you. It's not something I get to do that often, so I don't.' He stopped then, and faced her. 'Come to think of it, I don't even *talk* that much. I didn't even with Kathleen. Probably because she was a powerful talker herself. I'll have a sore face tonight from talking to you, so I will, for I'm not used to it.'

He ran the fingers of both hands through his hair. 'It was all right, though, him and her and me, even if I didn't know he was my da then. It was like a family, in a way. It wasn't Cairncross told me he was my da. She did – Kathleen McCann – when she was dying. For once there wasn't a rush to get grave clothes made. I thought I'd be making my own to be following her coffin, and I wouldn't have minded, so I wouldn't.'

'Robert—'

'I'm all right, so I am. Don't mind me.' He wiped the back of his hand across his eyes. 'The poor wee woman had thought of everything. The clothes was all ready in the press, along of a shroud for her. Cairncross paid the undertaker, though he never went to the graveside, and it was strangers, hired men, that carried her. I went, and saw her put in atop her husband. That's what you do, isn't it, you Catholics? Return you to the first one even if you're years and years married to the second?'

'That's right . . .' Annie thought of the little family in Barrow and her mother's lonely grave. *He and Elsie'll not be let to lie together in that cold bed.*

'But of course Kathleen and Cairncross never were wed, though he said to me before I left that he'd've married her if he coulda done, only the wife wouldn't see her way to it, even if she'd gone back to her father's house years before, and Kathleen wouldn't'a done it even if he'd got his freedom. I never told my mother that, right enough. Especially as she looks set to marry her ostler.

'We'd lived in that house off funerals, Kathleen and me – she learned me everything. I did the finest bound buttonholes in all of the County Down, she said.'

He glanced round, checking there was no one on the path. Then he lifted the hand he held, his broad, blunt fingers engulfing Annie's, and with his thumb drew circles in her palm.

'Can I do that?'

'Yes,' she said, startled at how good it felt.

'With Kathleen that was the last time – the only time – I was part of a family, even if that wasn't what most people would call it.'

'They made me feel like a family in Barrow, so they did,' said Annie. 'That's not a proper family either. But look at the Nolans – they're a family – and not a one of them is happy, so they're not – not even when Teresa was alive. She couldn't wait to get away from them, but she stayed for my sake.'

A lock of hair had blown over Annie's shoulder. Robert went to lift it back, pausing with the glossy skein in his hand.

'Will you go too, Annie?' he asked softly.

She nodded. 'I will. There is no one for me to look after here now.' She began to cry, in an unselfconscious way, like a child. Robert brushed back her hair; both hands came to rest on her shoulders.

'The world's full of people would need you, Annie.'

Her head tilted up, sniffing the tears. 'I should be a nun, is it?'

'I'd hardly be telling you that, no. That's not what I mean at all, so it isn't.'

He imagined himself beside this girl, leaning on the rail of the Whitehaven ferry, taking her back home to the Offices at the back of the Big House, to wait for his mother to come out and tend to the hens. He watched himself signalling Annie to silence, then stepping out into his mother's path and, after her embrace, her face strokings, taking her hands and saying, 'That girl I wrote to you about . . .'

'Robert?'

'Sorry?'

'You're miles away.'

'Oh . . . I was just thinking. *I'd* need you, Annie. That's all. But if you're spoken for . . .'

'I'm not.' She made herself meet the troubled hazel eyes.

'It just about killed me to see thon man in the burial ground with his arms around ye,' he said.

'I wanted to explain. Only you'd disappeared.'

He was smiling then. 'Annie . . .' he said. His face came closer and she saw his eyelids come down as she tilted her own face towards his, knowing exactly what he was going to do. A kiss, her first kiss, that she never wanted to end, but which somehow did end at exactly the moment it should have.

'You're lovely,' he murmured, his breath warm against her cheek.

CHAPTER TWENTY-EIGHT

Crossfield Road, Cleator Moor

'. . . every nun is bound to the will of the Priests; she is to
live for their own use, whenever they choose.'

H.M. Hatch, *Popery Unmasked, Showing the
Depravity of the Priesthood and Immorality of
the Confessional, Being the Questions Put to Females
in Confession,* 1854

Robert lay on his bed that Sunday evening wishing he was alone.
The other three were sitting on theirs smoking – they'd given up
ribbing him for not doing so when it got too repetitive to be
fun, though sometimes they'd call him 'our Methody' though
they knew he was as Presbyterian as themselves. None of the
three had come home the night before – they'd been 'on the
blatter' in Whitehaven. In their absence, Robert had thrown up
the window sash and swept the varnished boards, shaken the
rag rugs out of the window. He'd wanted to keep the memory
of the scent of oil of roses, to not suffocate it in the reek of stale
sweat, unwashed clothes and tobacco. If the others had noticed
the room was cleaner, they'd said nothing.

'Took our turn up the ginnel so we did.'

The others cackled and tow-haired Willie made a lewd gesture. Robert turned his face towards the window, thinking of Annie's face on their walk, the breeze blowing a strand of hair across her cheek.

'You'd've thought the hoor coulda given us a shilling off for a bulk order, wouldn't ye?' said Ernie, cueing more hoots of laughter and a thump on the wall from the adjoining house.

'Yous are disgusting,' muttered Robert.

'Disgusting yourself. One o' them sodomites, you must be,' snarled Willie.

'I am not!' shouted Robert, his head turning, his hands beating on the bed. Another thump came through the wall, and a muffled yell.

'Lads, lads . . .' said George, a hand raised for silence. 'Leave the feller alone, won't yous? Can't you see he's sweet on someone?'

Robert pushed himself up on his elbows, wary. 'Get away!' he said.

All three faces swivelled towards him, scenting their prey.

'Who is she, then, Robbie? Sure we've done you a favour then, leaving the place clear for you on a Saturday night?' said Ernie, leering.

'Which of our beds did you have her on?' said Willie, pretending to examine the cover of his own.

'All of 'em, wasn't it?' cried Ernie.

Feet came thumping up the stairs then, and the door opened without warning. Their landlord put his head round the jamb. 'Any more of this and you'll be out on your ears in the morning.'

The door slammed before anyone could respond. Ernie suppressed a snigger, which set off Willie. But George, his face stiff with hate, said, 'It'd better not be thon wee taig.'

'*What* wee taig?' said Robert.

'The one that was disrespectful to us.'

'She wasn't,' said Robert, without thinking. All three faces swivelled back towards him.

'Them priests teach them,' said George with quiet menace. 'They think they're the Lord Jesus Christ himself, so they do. And them wee girls delivered up to them in their wee white wedding dresses. That's what their "First Holy Communion"' – his fingers danced apostrophes – 'is all about, so it is.'

'Catch yourself on!' exclaimed Robert.

'I'm just warning ye, that's all. If it's her, it's not the Lodge you'll need to worry about. You'd do well to come with us next time, so you would.'

'I'll not.'

'Too good for us, are ye?' said Willie.

Robert swallowed. 'I never said that. I'm putting everything by, so I am. For to get out of the pit.'

'See, he *is* too good for us,' said Willie, appealing to the others.

'Aw, leave him be,' said George, pulling off his boots. 'Sure, there'd be no fun in a night in Whitehaven with *his* sour face, so there wouldn't. Even Sadie there couldn't put a smile on it for him.'

Robert said nothing, and in the morning it was as if the argument had never happened. They were as indifferent to him as always.

*

On Monday morning Annie moved back and forth on her stand between the two machines as though she danced, imagining herself like one of the heroines of the books she borrowed from the Carnegie Library, Robert holding the tips of her fingers as he led her down a glittering ballroom. With no musical accompaniment but the whirr of the machinery, she sang. Passing each other down the centre aisle of the spinning hall, the doffing mistress and the foreman exchanged glances, smiling and nodding. When six o'clock came at last, Mrs Birkett came up to Annie as she was cleaning her now silent machine.

'It's good to see you looking happy at last, lass. Is it because of who I think it is?'

Annie said nothing, but her smile gave her away.

'Suits you, a bit of a blush like that. You have a good evening, love.'

As she walked home, Annie felt impregnable even against Philomena's scowls.

CHAPTER TWENTY-NINE

Cleator Moor to Egremont, November 1903

'One side may well drop the use of such words as "Romanist", "Popery", "Papists", because objectionable to neighbours. On the other side it should be borne in mind that such designations as the bald term "Anglican", but especially the word "Non-Catholic", are peculiarly offensive and repellent as applied to English Churchmen.'

Caesar Caine, *Cleator and Cleator Moor,*
Past and Present, 1916

'The way I see it is this,' said Robert, once they were out in open country. 'You can't be loyal to two masters. Your master is the pope of Rome or the king, not both.'

'The Holy Father has his authority from God, handed down from Peter himself. The nuns learned us that, so they did,' said Annie.

Robert's experience of nuns was non-existent, beyond the sight of a high convent wall near a farm he'd been sent to. The fact that the nuns were never seen outside the place but priests had been seen going in, according to the farmer, was evidence that — well, Robert didn't get to hear what it was evidence of, as the farmer's wife had spotted him sitting silently on his chair in the corner of the room and had hushed her husband: 'Not in front of the boy.' It was a tirade delivered from the rostrum in the Lodge that had finally confirmed what as an adolescent he had begun to suspect. All he said to Annie was, 'What are nuns like?'

'Same as anyone else. Good ones and bad ones. And some of them no holier than anyone else.'

'And the priests?'

'Them too, maybe. I think Father Clayton – that's the curate – is kind. Father Hagerty I'm afraid of. I only go to confession when it's Father Clayton.'

'I can't understand why you do that, so I can't. You believe God knows everything you do, say or think, do you?'

'I do. That's in the catechism.'

'It was in mine too,' said Robert, thinking of the faded pink pamphlet the missionary lady had given him. It was still in his grip, under his bed in that crowded room. The bird skull and the stone he'd thrown overboard when he had sailed from Ireland, seeing them as childish things and wanting to make a fresh start. He'd regretted doing so the moment they left his hands.

'So he's looking down at us now,' Robert went on.

'Ye-es,' said Annie, pulling her shawl closer, feeling that the sun had gone out of the afternoon and that the delicious thoughts she'd been having all that week while she'd been waiting to see him again were disappearing like smoke. How was it that they'd got to talking about the one thing that divided them?

'Then why tell it to a priest? God knows what you've done already.'

'That's true. But he needs to know you're sorry for having offended him.'

'So just tell him yourself. Not give a man in a dog collar in a dark box something to get excited about.' Robert nearly said 'with his hands' but bit that back. *She'd not know what I meant – or if she did I'd not like it.*

'The priest acts for God on earth,' Annie said. 'If he gives me penance now I can do it and be washed clean and there'll be less time to do when I get to Purgatory. Why are you looking at me like that?'

'It sounds like an account book at the Co-operative, so it does. How much you've got on tick and how much you're able to pay off this month.'

She turned away, offended, but also knowing she would think of confession like that from this day onward: a list of her sins in flowing copperplate, with totals carried forward, and intermittently 'paid in full' written at the foot of the page. Her face still averted, she said, 'I like it, so I do. It makes me new – afterwards. To know I'm forgiven. And Father Clayton makes me feel better. He says things that make me think he understands me completely.'

'How can he?' said Robert, but more gently now. He wondered if this priest Annie obviously liked had been inside the church that last Twelfth of July – the day they'd met. The march had paused outside and redoubled its noise to cause the maximum disturbance to whoever was within. It struck him now as not the fun it had been at the time but something as childish as ringing someone's doorbell and running away.

'He knows human souls. You've to study years before you can be a priest.'

'Studying with other priests, Annie. Not out in the world where people can't pay the rent if they hurt themselves at work through no fault of their own and end up in the Union work-house. They'll be comfortable and warm in them clergy houses with three meals put in front of them a day, coal on the fire whenever they want, all paid out of the collections. They've maybe brandy after they've eaten. They've not even families of their own so how can they know what it's like for anyone else? It's not natural, Annie, so it isn't. "And the Lord God said, It is not good that the man should be alone; I will make him an help meet for him." Yous read the Bible, don't yous? It's right there at the start, so it is.'

'But it doesn't say there that Our Lord had a wife!'

'Thon priest isn't Jesus, Annie. And St Peter had a wife.'

Annie was about to say that the priests weren't alone any-way. They'd the cook and the two parlourmaids in the Priory House, hadn't they? Then she realised that wasn't what he meant, and mentioning those three women would probably only be more grist to his mill. Adam and Eve had been naked in that garden. The thought of Father Hagerty and the Priory House cook unclothed amongst the apple trees made her widen her eyes with disgust. Would she need to confess that thought too? This conversation? It was not as if she could argue that she and Robert were there for the purposes of bringing him 'back' to the true religion. That would be another lie, even if told only to herself. She knew full well they weren't. And he was getting the upper hand of the argument so far anyway. Annie let out a little cry of frustration, looking over a drystone wall at some equally perplexed sheep.

'How old are you anyway, Robert McClure, if you've no helpmate for yourself either?' she flung back.

He flushed as though she had struck him.

'I don't know how old I am. Not exactly. My birth isn't written down anywhere. Mammy didn't know she was supposed to and Cairncross wasn't right keen to go and see the clerk himself.'

'I'm sorry—'

'And as for a helpmate, who'd want me? Maybe one day when I've my own little shop I could look for a girl to help me with it. A wee girl from the workhouse who has nobody herself and isn't too proud. Not that it's her I want. But I'd better get you home. Before them good Christians in your road give out to you for walking out with a Proddy by-blow.'

'I said I'm sorry,' said Annie again, and burst into tears. Without hesitation, Robert did what he'd been wanting to do all afternoon – what he'd intended to do if they hadn't got into this stupid argument – and put his arms around her. Her head on his shoulder and one of his hands in the small of her back, the other on her hair, he said, 'It's not the wee workhouse girl I want, God love her. It's you, Annie.'

She lifted her head then, and Robert bent his face to hers. He found he was more nervous about kissing her than he had been the previous Sunday, but that somehow it came right. It was amazing, really, that noses didn't get in the way. What if you turned your head one way and hers followed you? When did you stop? And now he was again doing something he'd had no instruction in and all of those fears evaporated.

*

'There's rocks in that field we could sit on,' said Robert. 'Sure the sheep won't mind.'

'All right,' Annie said, and put a foot on the lowest rung of the gate.

'I was going to untie it for you,' he said.

'You'd be forever with that knot,' she said over her shoulder, 'and the farmer would know.'

He watched her in admiration as she swung over the gate, catching a flash of pale calves above her short black socks. Landing on the other side, she put her hand through the slats to take the cloth bag containing their bread and cheese and ginger beer. The stoneware bottles chinked against each other. Robert followed her over less nimbly and they stood smiling at each other in the tussocky field.

'If we sit along there nobody'll be able to see us, so they won't.' He took her hand, leading her to an outcrop of lichened rock close to the drystone wall.

'*They* will,' she laughed, gesturing at the little group of sheep that had stopped what they were doing to stare fixedly at them out of black-blotched faces. The only sound in the field was the cry of a lone yellowhammer. Annie settled on the rock, tucking her skirts around her bent knees.

'I've not heard that wee bird since I was on the farm,' she said.

He settled beside her, deliberately not close enough for their bodies to touch. '"A little bit of bread and *no* cheese",' he said. 'That's what it's singing. I was on a farm too. The wee girl there said that's what they were singing. I don't know its name.'

'If I half shut my eyes so's I don't see thon big mountain I could nearly be back home. Thon wee bird's call, the bleat of the sheep, the whin bush in the corner there . . . I wonder if I stay longer will I talk like they do here. Them wee boys – the ones Dadda is fathering – they do.'

'You'll go and see them again, won't you?'

Annie sighed. 'I've wished that many times I'd gone with them to start with. I'll see can I not get there for Christmas.' She lifted her head. 'I've thought about *her* many times – Elsie Fagan. She spoke to me like a mother; I was able to say things to her I don't know if I'd'a been able to say to my own mother, if she was still with us.'

'If she was, your da wouldn't be with Elsie, would he?'

'No, he wouldn't. Da keeps his promises – strike me down for saying it, though, I never saw him and Mammy look at each other the way them two do. Elsie *is* a decent wee woman, even if Father Hagerty told her to her face otherwise. And Dadda was lonely without her; I could keep house for him but it's not the same thing. What choices did Mrs Fagan have? The St Vincent de Paul would've helped her out, right enough, but sometimes the people who give you charity make it weigh on you, you know?'

'I do,' Robert said, looking at the purplish hills on the horizon. 'They did that where I was sent. Even though they were getting money for my keep. There was one place they had me doing jobs while their own weans got to play: cutting up newspaper for to hang on a string in the outhouse. Giving me the scrag end of what they were eating, or a potato less. I was always hungry. They let on to me it was punishment.'

'What had you done?'

'Got myself born,' he said.

Annie put her hand on his. 'Oh, Robbie.'

'I like it when you call me that,' he said, edging closer to her, propping himself up on his right hand on the rock behind her, while with his left he gently turned her shoulder towards him. He saw her look down, a flush creeping up her neck, and the rise and fall of her breathing against the little buttons of her jacket. His kiss landed softly on her mouth. He knew he'd remember the moment forever, his eyes closed, the insistent verse of the yellowhammer and the patient munching of the by now indifferent sheep in his ears, the November breeze tickling his cheek with strands of her hair. He broke away at last, reminded by his quickening heartbeat and the deepening of his breathing that he was already wanting to go 'too far' and didn't want her to know it. Annie was smiling at him, her face flushed and her lips moist, and, to his eyes, slightly swollen. He took a deep breath, trying to master himself.

'We should eat,' he said, 'before it comes on to rain.'

She looked towards the mountains, where indeed clouds were gathering. Robert loosened the strings of the little cloth bag and handed her a hefty sandwich wrapped in greaseproof paper.

'I might be good with a tailor's scissors, but I'm not very straight with a breadknife.'

Annie opened the paper and smiled. 'You've not held back with the cheese is the main thing.'

'Here's to wash it down.' With his thumb he eased out the stoppers on the ginger beer bottles. 'Our first meal.'

Annie crossed herself rapidly, almost furtively, mouthing something silently. She put the bottle to her lips and tipped it up, widening her eyes as the tart, fizzy liquid met her tongue. Stoppering it again, she put the back of her hand over her mouth, stifling a tiny belch. Robert was utterly charmed by her startled expression.

They ate in companionable silence, afterwards putting the empty bottles in the bag so that Robert could take them back for the deposit. Their hands free again, Robert nudged closer to her, so that his thigh edged into the folds of her skirt, and put his arm around her shoulder. Annie took his free hand in her own, pressing it, and looked up at him as he turned to her and their lips met.

Afterwards he said, 'You taste of ginger.'

'So do you.'

Then without realising he had spoken aloud, he said, 'Marry me, Annie.'

Seeing her utter astonishment, he said, 'I'm sorry. I didn't mean it to come out like that. Though to be honest, it's what I thought the moment I saw you at the window. So I'll not take it back.' He glanced away, mortified, to where the sheep were standing stock-still. He remembered what that meant. It was about to rain. He looked down to where her hand lay in his. He heard her sniff and realised she was weeping.

'Annie!'

'It's all right,' she stammered, taking her hand away to rummage in her sleeve for her handkerchief. She turned away to blow her nose.

'I never wanted for to make you cry.'

'Why did you say it, then? You know full well we can't get married.' Annie stood up, brushing down her skirt. 'I'd best get home. Philomena will want help with the tea, so she will.'

'Annie, wait!'

But she was running over the tussocky grass, holding fistfuls of her skirts, and was over the gate before he could gather up the bag and take off after her.

CHAPTER THIRTY

Birks Road, November 1903

> 'Shines like a sunbeam. Durable – waterproof – preserves
> the leather – economical and cleanly in use. Black and
> Tan. In Tins, at 3d., 4d. and 6d.'

Advertisement for Day & Martin boot polish, 1907

Annie paused at the far end of the yard, trying to catch her breath. She brushed down her skirt nervously, twitched the bodice jacket into position, and retied the ribbon in her hair. Then she took her shawl from where it was tied around her waist and drew it protectively around her shoulders, before forcing herself to walk slowly up to the back door. Glancing in through the window, the room appeared empty, though the table was already partly laid for tea. Her heart sank. Michael and Frank hadn't come back from fishing then, or were in the Wheatsheaf. From the scullery she could hear the soft sawing of bread on the scarred wooden board, accompanied by some low muttering – she couldn't make out the words but didn't need to. Philomena was angry, and without the men there there was nothing to absorb her rage. Her heart pounding, Annie lifted the latch.

'Where've you been?' Philomena waved the breadknife. Annie flinched, eyelids fluttering.

'What—'

'A walk in the town with girls from the mill, was it?'

Annie flushed, knowing she wasn't a good liar, didn't want to be a liar, and resented that Philomena made her into one. The woman's eyes swept her from head to toe and flashed in triumph.

'Forgot your shoes, didn't ye?'

Annie's eyes dropped without thinking. Her good shoes were no longer the gleaming black they'd been when she'd polished them to a shine on the back step before going to mass that morning. They were splashed with pale, dried mud, dulled with a patina of dust.

'Hoor!' hissed Philomena. 'Hoor and liar! You've been with that Proddy bastard.'

Annie backed off, bumping into one of the chairs.

'He's not—'

'Not a Proddy?' jeered Philomena. 'Dropped him and got yourself somebody else? I pity the man'll be your husband one day. And to think that my Frank—'

Philomena's head flicked to the window, for there was a murmur of voices out in the yard, and the scraping of boots. Frank himself opened the door, glancing from his mother's heated face to Annie's panicked one. 'Give me that,' he said quietly, and his mother handed him the breadknife without argument.

'Here, son,' she said in a conciliatory tone, 'you're a good boy, so you are, helping your mother.'

Frank ignored this, turning to Annie. 'Are you all right there?' His father appeared at his shoulder, in his stockinged feet, frowning as he saw their faces.

'I'd forgot to clean my shoes,' babbled Annie. 'I'll away out and do it now.' Michael stood aside to let her past, barring the disarmed Philomena. Outside, working at the footscraper, Annie heard scraps of their conversation through the window. Philomena was doing nothing to keep her voice down, and it occurred to Annie that the woman wanted the neighbours to hear. Michael's voice rumbled beneath; Annie could detect the note of weariness and disappointment. Then she heard Frank's clear tones. 'I don't believe it of her. She's a good girl and our Teresa loved her.'

Hearing him, Annie's eyes were hot with tears. She stood wavering with indecision and shivering, for she'd left her shawl inside, but she didn't know how she could walk back into that terrible atmosphere. Then loud as shotgun pellets against the window came the rain, driving sideways, and Frank opened the back door.

'Come away in, Annie.'

*

The meal was tense, passed in near silence. Annie could barely eat, though Frank was solicitous: 'Wouldn't you be wanting some jam on that?'

Eventually Philomena snapped: 'She's a mill girl, remember, not the Lady Mayoress.'

'Who's she? The cat's mother?' said Frank coldly.

'Don't speak to your mammy like that,' said Michael.

Annie could stand it no longer. She stood up, gathering the dirty crockery onto the tray. Philomena lifted the lid of the teapot and silently poured herself another cup. Annie was glad of it, for that meant she would be doing the washing-up alone. In the scullery her hands trembled; she was afraid she would drop something on the merciless quarry-tiled floor. Frank came through, going out to the yard, and she shot him a grateful look. He returned it with a tight little smile, frowning at the same time. Annie escaped upstairs as soon as she could, got ready for bed, but lay sleepless for what felt like hours, two thoughts chasing each other through the dark woods of her mind. *He wants to marry me. I can't stay here. Because he wants to marry me I can't stay here. I can't stay here but where can I go?*

When the knocker-up passed by she was surprised she'd been asleep at all. She went to the window and waved her hand between the net and the glass to let the man know he could move on. Her next conscious thought was, *I love him.*

*

The whirr of machinery at work eclipsed all other noise, but not what Annie heard in her head: the bleat of sheep, the call of the yellowhammer, so like the sounds of home. Voices came and went like shreds of smoke on the wind, intuited more than heard. Mrs Birkett smiled and nodded. In the damp steam and the relentless movement of the spinner she heard the refrain *I can't stay there . . . he wants to marry me* so clearly it was hard to believe the machines hadn't always been saying it and she just hadn't known.

As she put her hand on the latch of the back-yard gate, Annie remembered that Monday was parish men's night, so Michael and Frank would be late. *That's the reason they have all them clubs*, she thought. *Married Catholics have to stay together.* The sacrament of marriage was indissoluble; it couldn't be repeated when needed like confession. It was for forever, but to help it be forever there were all these activities that took people *away* from the domestic hearth, and, if that hearth were cold, made going back to it more bearable. The Church, in her wisdom, understood that for a marriage to last the pace those who entered into it also needed a place to escape to that wasn't the pub. Annie's heart lurched with pity for decent, quiet Michael Nolan. Then she thought of Robert, and couldn't imagine that she'd ever want to be part of those groups of ladies who polished the candlesticks, arranged the flowers, cleared away the stubs of candles from the row of spikes beneath the benignly smiling saints, when instead she could be with him.

An Orange boy. But he'll have them meetings in the Lodge. That's groups of men same as where Michael and Frank have gone.

Annie passed through the Monday wash-day sheets strung across the yard to get to the back door. It would be her job to get them down before tea. She took a deep breath.

No Philomena. Not in the scullery, not in the back room. Annie didn't try the front parlour as it doubled as Frank's bedroom; the last time it had been a public room had been for Teresa's funeral. Going upstairs, she heard movement and paused, holding her breath. The noises, shuffling and banging, were coming from her own room. Annie remembered distinctly bringing down her sheets for washing. All Philomena did was to dart in and leave the clean ones on her mattress for her to make up. It sounded as if the place was being ransacked.

Annie stood in the doorway. Philomena was working with such speed and concentration that Annie realised she couldn't have heard her approach. Furthermore, the woman was muttering a litany of insults just under her breath. Annie's grip stood in the centre of the room, and Philomena had every drawer in the chest pulled out, so that she could sweep its contents into her arms and straight into the bag, willy-nilly. Nearly finished, she banged the upper drawers closed, a noise as sharp as gunfire, and yanked open the bottom one. Hands working like great pincers, she shoved the contents of the drawer together and swung upright. A lavender bag fell to the floor with a soft puffing sound. Annie saw a blouse of her mother's, something she touched as little as possible to preserve what remained of the dead woman's scent, crumpled up with everything else, a sleeve hanging piteously. Philomena started on seeing Annie, but recovered quickly.

'You can do this yourself, so you can, seeing as you're here,' said Philomena, throwing the garments into the mouth of the grip. 'Then you've to get out. Before the men are back.'

'Why? Where—'

'You know full well why! You were seen, lyin' hoor that you are! Going off into the fields with thon Orangeman. Coming back hours later like the hounds of hell were on your heels, with your sin written in your face and your clothes upside down like you'd buttoned yourself in a hurry. And coming in here with that look of yours like butter wouldn't melt and making eyes at my decent son and husband when you thought I wasn't looking. *Where* you go I don't care as long as I don't have to see ye. Swallow your pride and go to your father and his woman in Barrow. Or you can work your passage with the sailors on the boat back to Ireland and earn your living in Belfast docks for all I care! So finish your own packing, milady. You'll find this week's rent money in the bottom, so you will, though it's me you've put out as I don't know when I'll get another lodger, only I'll make sure this time it's a fella.'

Annie shrank against the narrow doorframe as Philomena pushed past, catching a whiff of the woman's bitter sweat.

Crying, Annie dragged the grip over to the stripped mattress and lifted its contents out onto the bed. Her few clothes were tumbled together, letters and keepsakes thrown amongst them. She repacked everything as best she could, wrapping the pair of china dogs in her underclothes and the image of the Sacred Heart in a worn shawl of her mother's. Last of all she lifted down her St Brigid cross from its nail. She looked under the bed, ran her hands into the corners of the drawers of the chest, checked the hook behind the door.

'Goodbye, Teresa,' she said to the empty room. Minutes later, she bumped the grip down the stairs. The door to the back room was closed, but in the stillness beyond it Annie could sense Philomena listening. She turned left instead into the front parlour, averting her eyes from Frank's bed, Frank's things, and in seconds was out on the street. Only then did she face her immediate problem.

I can't go to the Priory House. If Philomena heard about me running back into town then certain sure so will the cook and them maids. I can't lose a week's lying time at the mill even if there is a train to Barrow at this time.

She closed her eyes, picturing the table in the room above the undertaker's – the children's contented faces, her father in his chair at the hearth – and cursed herself for a fool. Opening them, Annie looked up, and saw the familiar street as though it was for the first time. The closed doors and windows looked to her like dead sightless eyes. She opened her little reticule and drew out the piece of paper. She knew what was written there but wanted to be sure of the house number: she'd gazed on the careful loops of the handwriting many times, recognising that they'd been battered into the young Robert with a cane – a stroke across the knuckles should the small hand lift from the page in the midst of a word. She folded up the paper carefully and picked up her grip.

CHAPTER THIRTY-ONE

Crossfield Road, November 1903

'The present housing conditions in our district are deplorable. Houses are constantly being immorally over-crowded.'

Caesar Caine, *Cleator and Cleator Moor,*
Past and Present, 1916

To reach the road where Robert lodged, Annie had to cross one of the unmarked borders of the town, borders that were very real to the Irish population though a source of headshaking to the Cumberland people. Borders where there were no customs men or checking of documents but everyone knew the point at which you crossed. If a look in the eyes didn't confirm which side you were on, then the question 'Which school did you go to?' might suffice in place of a blunt 'What are you?' *If I do marry Robert,* she wondered, the mere thought making her heart beat faster at her audacity, *will I start to look more like him or will he start to look more like me?*

She thought it was quiet, for a road where hundreds of people must live, then remembered that it was tea-time. Families would be huddled around back-room tables. In lodging houses the inmates would be served orange tea in big tin pots in front parlours that would never be used for funerals or baptisms, the population of those houses being too transient for such solemn rites of passage.

Annie looked up at the house. It was even less cared for than its neighbours. The paint of the front door was faded and cracked, the net at the window dingy. A dormer, she'd noticed, had been let into the roof. Human beings were stacked in there, then, one above the other, like the bales of linen she'd seen in the mill store. The brass doorknocker however was dainty, though much in need of a polish, a lady's slender hand in a frilled sleeve holding a ball. Annie put her hand over the lady's, and knocked. Something inside the house changed; she realised that what she'd taken for the murmur of the wind had been voices. They'd stopped. She heard a door open, and someone apparently in bedroom slippers shuffled to the door, clearing his throat. A bolt was drawn, a key rattled.

A middle-aged man in shirtsleeves and no collar, with a half-eaten piece of bread and butter in one hand, stared down at her. The hallway smelled of boiled cabbage and tobacco.

'Wh'ista?' he said, masticating.

'Beg pardon?'

The man swallowed, then enunciated carefully, dropping his dialect. 'Who are you, lass?'

An Englishman then. The landlord?

'My name's Annie Maguire. I'm sorry to trouble you. Would you be Mr Spedding? I'm looking for Robert McClure.'

The man turned. '*Robert!*' Then he looked her up and down, raising his eyebrows at the sight of the grip. 'Yes, I'm Jem Spedding. Got you in trouble, has he?'

Annie gasped, but seized on the hint of kindness in his voice. Her face flaming, she heard herself say, 'No. But I need a room, if you'd have anything. I've the rent ready, so I have.'

The man took another bite of his bread and butter and stared at her. She could see he was thinking, the cogs of his brain turning as surely as the machinery moving at the mill. Eventually he said, 'I would have something – a port in a storm, you might say. But nowt permanent, mind, and you'd be sharing with a lot of lumber. We're a bit rough and ready here. All men. All miners. You'd best come in, then.' When he stood to one side to let her past, Annie saw an astonished Robert blocking the narrow hallway.

'Oh, there you are, lad. We've got what you might call a damsel in distress and she thinks you're her knight in shining armour.'

'Annie . . . what's happened?'

The landlord glanced from one to the other. 'You'll maybe want to talk about it in private, like. Later. Only I'm sure the lady could use a cup of tea and some snap, couldn't you, love?'

'Oh yes, thank you.'

'Through here then, Miss Maguire. Leave your bag. Robert'll take it up for you after.' Spedding guided her through to the front room, Robert looking helplessly on. Five faces turned towards her, all of them with the unmistakable tinge of iron ore in their skin. Three she recognised, and they, recognising her, exchanged gleeful glances. Panicked, her eyes darted around the room, taking in the porridgy woodchip wallpaper, the varnished dado panelling, the spotted engraving of a mountainous scene above the mantelshelf where two impassive china dogs sandwiched some dusty envelopes and almanacs. Her eyes came to rest on the mismatched cups and plates on the oil-clothed tabletop. Spedding had told her there were only men here, but looking round Annie thought he needn't have done so. The house had that sort of neglect.

'Right, lads, no need to get up.' One older man had risen anyway. The three Orange boys sniggered. 'This young lady here,' began the landlord.

'Annie,' said Robert clearly. 'My intended.'

'Annie is just passing through while arrangements are made for her future,' said the landlord. 'What's that you said, Willie McKeown?' he added, staring at one of the sniggering trio.

Passing round, that's what it was, thought Annie. She recognised the mutterer's tow hair, his leer. She wanted to cross her hands over her breasts.

'I'd like to be the first here to offer my congratulations,' said the one man who had got to his feet, putting out his hand. He spoke English as Annie had never heard it before. 'I'm John Trescatherick.' The man's warm calloused fingers enveloped hers. 'I'm your young man's partner in Crowgarth. You've got yourself a good worker in your Robert. I hope you'll both be very happy.'

'Thank you, sir.' She felt her eyes prickle, wondering why it was that kindness could make her cry.

'Sit here,' said the man, 'by Robert's place. I'll fetch another chair.' He followed the landlord out of the room. Annie sat, and when Robert joined her, put her hand in his. She looked up into his face for reassurance, and saw pride there. And relief. One after the other the men at the table introduced themselves, the three from the path last. Annie felt their eyes upon her still; they reminded her of hounds slavering at a rabbit hole. Thankfully John Trescatherick returned directly and placed his chair on her other side. She felt his sturdy presence there as a bulwark against the Orangemen. Later she learned that the Cornishman was a Wesleyan, a widower. The landlord placed crockery and cutlery in front of her: they were smeary from hasty washing and imperfect drying. 'The tea's the second brewing. Do you mind?'

'No, not at all.'

Trescatherick passed her the sugar bowl. 'You look like you need a bit of energy too,' he said.

*

The attic was reached by another narrower set of stairs after the wider one died on the first-floor landing.

'I've been meaning to do something about it for years,' said the landlord. 'It's dry, at least, and you'll be on your own.'

Annie wondered if she was hallucinating, but her dismay felt real enough. The scene with Philomena, and finding herself suddenly out on the street – could that really only have been an hour ago? Now, in this strange house that looked as if it had once been almost elegant but was now shabby and greasy, she had found both menace and friendship. But here, in this attic turned lumber room, was only melancholy. She saw the cobwebby remains of what must once have been the contents of a family home: a dismantled iron bedframe; a child's perambulator, the cloth of its hood rust-spotted and torn, reminding her of the limp wings of dead crows tied to farm gates; rolled carpets; a stuffed heron in a glass case; a heap of mildewed books, their fine bindings nibbled – by mice or insects? Seeing her eyes on them, her landlord said, 'Millie comes up here, so there shouldn't be mice.'

'Millie?'

'The only female under this roof besides yourself. My cat. There's a mattress in here somewhere – the one from that bed. Robert'll help you dig it out. I'll be back with some sheets. Mebbe on Saturday afternoon when there's a bit more time we can have a look at doing something with that bedframe. Well . . . I'll leave you to sort yourself out – you and your young man will want to have a bit of a heart-to-heart about how you got here, without me earwigging.'

'Thank you, Mr Spedding.'

'Think nowt of it, lass.' He hesitated. 'I'd've liked a daughter like you.'

Annie didn't know what to say, struck again by the kindness of strangers. With a pulling back of his shoulders Spedding said, 'Well, can't be maundering on here. Best get on.'

Robert and Annie stood facing each other as they heard the man's footsteps descend. When they heard his pace change as he reached the landing, Robert put his arms around her and she silently went into his embrace.

'She put me out. We were seen going up that path, then I was seen running down it after. I was called names, Robert, and never given a chance to say anything to defend myself.'

'But you came to me,' he said, and kissed her. In his encircling arms, somehow everything seemed simpler to her. It was the outside world that complicated things. Hearing rumblings and voices deep in the house, they separated, but by now Annie was smiling.

'We'd better find that mattress, before Jem comes up with the bedding,' he said. Only then did Annie remember that the bed she'd left behind in Birks Road was her own property.

CHAPTER THIRTY-TWO

Ainsworth's Mill, November 1903

'For the Irish in Britain . . . the sectarianism of the cemetery was exceeded by the realities of everyday life.'

Donald MacRaild, *Culture, Conflict and Migration: The Irish in Victorian Cumbria*, 1998

At breakfast-time at the mill Annie went outside, hoping the gusting air would put some life into her. The time wasn't passing that morning so much as shuffling along, like a dawdling person she was trying to get around on a busy pavement. Facing the hills beyond the mill chimneys, she closed her eyes to feel the tepid warmth on her lids, only to find herself staggering. All she wanted to do was lie down and sleep.

'Annie?' said a quiet voice at her elbow. She'd heard clogs approach, but the yard was full of their clacking sounds. She turned to see Mrs Birkett.

'Hoo'doo, love?'

'I'm all right . . .'

'Eaten your bait, have you?'

'Oh – yes.' Annie held up the little bag that had held the bread and butter she and Robert had shyly prepared that morning.

'Come inside a minute, will you? Have a cuppa with me?'

'Gladly,' said Annie. A fresh cup of tea was an unexpected boon, instead of the brew in the stoneware jar she brought to work. Annie followed the woman inside, then upstairs into the warm fug of the cubbyhole.

'Sit down, love,' said Mrs Birkett, indicating a bentwood chair. She leaned against the desk and studied Annie's face.

'You look as if you've the weight of the world on your shoulders today. I know you got yourself together like a little soldier after we lost our Teresa. It's the quiet ones you've to worry about, I told myself. I can see summat else has happened. So if there's anything Nellie Birkett can help you with, you've only to say.'

'I got thrown out yesterday,' blurted Annie.

'You did? Were you still lodging with that tornface up in Reeling? Poor Teresa's mother?'

Annie nodded.

'She's always been in a right bad mood, that one. Even before she lost the poor lass, I mean.'

Hearing this, Annie plucked up some confidence and started to talk, knowing also she had to make Mrs Birkett understand that she needed this job. As the words tumbled out, Mrs Birkett listened, her head on one side, reminding Annie of an intelligent hen. At last she said, 'Thank you for telling me this, love. I've an eye on that clock there, so I'll just say this for now. I'll never understand you Irish making life difficult for yourselves – though you're great workers. You love this lad, and he loves you.

Never mind running off to Barrow or back to the boat. Marry him, Annie. You'll be sorry for the rest of your life if you don't. Not least because nosy beggars'll talk. They've nowt else to do. You'd nowhere to go but to him I know, except others won't see it that way.'

*

With no key, Annie went round the back of Robert's lodgings and peered in. She could see Mr Spedding with his feet on the fender, his head hidden behind the *Westmorland Gazette*. She tapped timidly on the window. Spedding jumped as if he'd been shot. He dropped the newspaper and went to open the door.

'Coom in, lass. We don't stand on ceremony here. There's tea in that pot. Get yourself a brew and I'll call up the stairs for that man of yours.' Spedding went out to the hallway and shouted. Then she heard him go into the front room.

Before long she heard Robert's lighter tread. He stood in the doorway, collarless but with his jacket on, turning his cap in his hands and smiling.

I could do it. I could come back to that smile every day of my life.

'Will you come out, Annie? That's if you're not too tired. Just up and down the back lane?'

She was tired, but she wanted to talk. They could hear Mr Spedding in the next room moving things on the table; Annie thought he was being deliberately noisy to give them privacy. But outside would be better. They could hardly go up to the attic, after all. What if Willie McKeown or the others saw them, or saw

Robert coming down again? He'd be ribbed at the very least – she'd be stared at unashamedly.

'I'll just drink this tea then,' she said. She held the cup with both hands, like a child, but she did it for tiredness, liking its steady warmth against her palms. She drank the tea down, then stood up. Robert opened the back door, letting her pass through first. They went down the yard and out into the narrow lane behind the houses. Annie turned to him, putting her hand in his. He closed both his around it.

'When I told Mrs Birkett I'd been thrown out, and that I'd come here, she warned me against losing my good name,' said Annie.

'What did she say, exactly?'

Annie sighed. 'She said she knew I was a good girl, but the way people talk, the ones that have nothing better to do – and that's most of them, she said – I could end up being of bad fame even though I'd done nothing to deserve it.'

'The witches.'

'Robert – did you mean it, what you said on Sunday?'

'Mean it? I've never meant anything as much as I meant that. I don't think I ever will. I should beg your pardon, though. The way I spoke last night was as if you'd given me an answer, but you haven't. Marry me, Annie. And this time don't run away just because I've asked you.'

'I will. I don't know how, but I will.'

'Annie, Annie.' He bent his head and kissed her.

When at last they turned to go in, Annie held his arm and said, 'Just a minute. I want to remember this place, this time.' She looked round at the dusty little lane, the brick privy and wash-house walls backing onto it, Millie and a battered-looking tabby sizing each other up six houses along. She heard the throaty cooing of caged pigeons in a neighbour's back yard, the cackling of hens in another. She thought of those young ladies in gauzy dresses in the books she borrowed from the Carnegie Library and the dashing men who went before them on one knee in elegant drawing rooms or rolling parkland, places imagined for her in the tinted illustrations. 'I like this better,' she murmured aloud.

'I'll find better,' he said, not hearing her properly. 'A room of our own.'

*

When Annie and Robert walked in the back door, Spedding beckoned them closer. 'Them others are through there and I don't want them hearing me,' he whispered. 'I just want you to know that John Trescatherick told me about them that shares with Robert not treating you like the lady you are. So I just want you to know that John and me have just had a word with them. If there's any hint – any at all – of a repeat of it, then they'll be given notice and John told them he'd go and see the Master of the Lodge an' all. I think they were more bothered about that than about being out on their ears.'

But what'll they say when them in the Lodge hear Robert's walking out with a Catholic girl? That's if they don't know already.

'Now, would you give us a hand with the tea things? I've a suggestion I'd like to make to you.'

'Yes, of course.' Annie started to gather things onto a tray. *It's so nice when someone asks. All Philomena did was order me about.*

Spedding said, 'I can't charge you a proper rent for a mattress in a lumber room. What if we make it half of what Robert pays and you give me a bit of help in the house? There's Mrs Driscoll comes for the laundry and Mrs Pascoe comes in once a week and mops a bit and that but otherwise we make shift ourselves.'

'I'd be glad to.'

*

The three Orangemen ate in near silence, gruffly and resentfully polite when they were handed things, but Annie felt safe, sitting between Robert and John Trescatherick.

That night she took a long time to get to sleep. What sounded like a large bird cawed and scratched on the roof near the skylight. She could hear the metallic patter of its feet, then rustling pauses. She remembered Teresa's freit with the cobnuts, and wondered if the presence of the bird also meant something. She relit the oil lamp, which threw long shadows, so that the heaps of furniture, boxes and carpets loomed over her like a mountain range. Earlier, she'd carried the cat unprotesting up from the kitchen, talking to her as she climbed the stairs, rather hoping that Millie's presence wouldn't just discourage the mice but that the creature might want to stay and sleep on her feet. But the moment she'd put Millie down on the end of her makeshift bed, the cat had turned and padded off down the stairs without a backwards glance. *I can't blame her. She has her own wee cushion by the fender.*

255

Now, lying in the dark in sheets that though clean smelled musty from lack of use, Annie faced the twin unseen terrors that glowered at her from the corners of the attic: Mrs Birkett's warning about a reputation too easily lost, and what they'd say in the Priory House. The nuns had told her that Protestants were in danger of losing their immortal souls. Could that be catching? Yet if she did marry Robert all the mutterings about her living as a friendless girl in a house full of men would be as good as silenced. *But how can I marry out? Or how could he marry in?*

Exhausted but unable to sleep, Annie pulled on some socks and wrapped her shawl over her nightgown, and set off downstairs for a glass of water. She held the banister tightly, trying to transfer what weight to it she could, for she was convinced that the stairs creaked at night in a way that they never did in daytime. On the landing she paused, listening to the rhythm of snores that came from behind closed doors. The air was close and sour with the sleep of seven men.

She found the water jug by the sink in the little scullery, a plate over it to keep its contents fresh. Tiptoeing back through the kitchen she heard Millie wheezing softly in her sleep, and stopped to stroke her. The cat stretched, conceding a sleepy purr and flexing her paws.

Though she was aware out of the corner of her eyes of the flickering of the shadows on the bare walls as she made her way upstairs again, Annie kept her attention on the little lamp. But on the landing she saw something – someone – move, and nearly dropped it.

The shadow shifted again, whispering, 'Annie.' Relief washed over her. She hadn't immediately recognised him. Robert stood there in wrinkled long johns, socks and an old vest.

'You frightened me near to death, so you did,' she whispered back. 'What are you doing up?'

'I've barely slept. Then I heard you coming down and thought I was dreaming.'

'I think I must be. You asked me to marry you.'

She saw his smile, and thought, not for the first time, how it transformed his face. He normally looked so serious, a man who appeared to her to be most at ease not with companions of his own age, but with older men, men who had lived and suffered. She had seen that Mr Spedding liked him, and because of it things had been made easier for her. And the Cornishman – Trescatherick – he seemed to be an uncle as much as a workmate. With tender intuition Annie realised that as a boy Robert had probably rarely smiled – from what he'd told her he'd been given neither encouragement nor reason. She saw in her mind's eye the child he'd been talking more readily to an animal than to a fellow human being. The man, she had seen, was gentle and considerate with Millie, something which pleased Spedding. She'd noticed the cat was a bit warier of some of the other lodgers.

'I meant—' Robert stopped, as there was a pause in the rhythm of one of the soft snores coming from the shared bedroom. He put a finger to his lips, then pointed to the attic stair, raising his eyebrows in a question. Annie nodded and went first, thinking about all the days of her life when he would follow her up to bed. But she didn't fear him.

Once at the door of the room, he hung back, looking at the little cleared space where Annie's mattress lay.

'You deserve better than this,' he said, in not much above a whisper. 'And you'll have it, so you will.'

She crossed back to the door and went into his arms. They held each other, her head on his chest, listening to his heart thudding.

'You're as light as a wee bird,' he said, his voice hoarse. 'I'm afraid I'll break you.'

Annie made a small contented noise.

'We'd best marry soon,' he said. 'To stop their mouths.' He sounded suddenly weary. 'But mainly because I want to,' he said in a brighter voice, kissing the top of her head. 'In case you change your mind.'

She twisted her head up to look at him. 'I'll not, Robert.' Their lips met, and stayed.

Eventually he said, 'Lie down, and I'll tuck you in.'

She folded her shawl and left it on a trunk that doubled as an extemporised dressing-table, and got under the covers, pulling them up to her chin. Robert crouched beside her, trying to tuck the blanket edges under the mattress. She smiled up at him, though she couldn't see his face, just the outline of his shoulders and his curly hair haloed in the light of the oil lamp behind him.

'It's all right. I'm not going to fall out of bed, so I'm not. Not when I'm already on the floor.'

His lips brushed hers, but without intent, and Annie realised he was in danger of nodding off. As her own eyes closed, the tucked-in blankets felt comfortingly tight around her.

CHAPTER THIRTY-THREE

Crossfield Road, November 1903

'Despite poverty and hardship, the lure of non-religious affiliations . . . and the more secular nature of urban life, there is much evidence to suggest the continued piety and devotion of Irish migrants in Britain.'

Donald MacRaild, *Irish Migrants in Modern Britain, 1750–1922*, 1999

The knocker-up couldn't reach the dormer window, so there never was a tap on those dingy panes. It was the sound of male voices, boots thumping down the stairs and out to the privy, that woke Annie usually. But this morning was different. For a confused moment she thought Teresa was with her before she came fully awake, realising that the arm across her was not a hallucination. She was warm, from neck to foot, swaddled in the blankets, but Robert lay on top of them, embracing her, his face in her hair. All she remembered was his last sleepy kiss, followed by the deepest slumber she thought she'd had since childhood. She wriggled around under his arm until her nose was an inch from his.

'Robert,' she whispered.

His eyes opened. What a fine colour they were, she thought, gazing into his hazel irises. In that instinctive moment before full consciousness arrived, he smiled at her. Then his expression changed and he sat up suddenly.

'Oh Lord – I'm sorry, Annie!'

'It's all right. You never did nothing, so you didn't.'

'There'll be trouble,' he said, scrambling to his feet. Infected by his distress, her heart sank. *He's right*, she thought. *It's not just us in this house*, realising how their tender, private moment was going to be seen by others.

'I'll go down first. I'll be walking with you today.'

'Robert?'

'This'll be round Crowgarth like the measles, so it will. The hoors've got to see I'm standing by you.'

Annie flinched at the profanity. She had never heard him speak like that before, but Robert later told her why he'd used that word. He'd needed some of that fearlessness James Cairncross took for granted.

*

Annie could barely raise her head as they walked up the road, her arm under his. After a while she realised that all eyes were not in fact on them, as for everyone else it was a morning much like all the others. The whole street was emptying, leaving behind only the smallest children in the care of women too old to work outside the home, as a stream of people moved as one, miners and mill girls, the men walking singly for the most part, the women sometimes in pairs, huddled in shawls. The street rang with the thock-thock of clogs and the rasp of hobnailed boots.

Robert felt solid and warm beside her but his breathing was loud, agitated. All too quickly they reached the point when he would walk on in the direction of Crowgarth and she would take the path towards the smoking chimneys of the mill and the mountains. He turned to face her, letting go her arm.

'So,' he said, smiling gently, 'I'll see you at tea-time.' Then he bent his head and kissed her lips, so quickly that, walking on alone, Annie wasn't sure she hadn't imagined it. All that secrecy, and now he wanted to tell the world.

Breakfast-time was long in arriving. Mrs Birkett came up to her in the big yard, where Annie leaned against a wall wolfing her breakfast.

'Awright, our Annie? You've been away in a dream all morning.'

Annie nodded, swallowing down her bread and jam.

'What is it, love?'

'You're not to tell anyone.'

'You can trust Nellie Birkett.'

'Robert's asked me to marry him.'

Mrs Birkett smiled. 'And you've said yes – and mebbe some, by the looks of you. You've a nice little face, Annie Maguire, but a guilty one.'

Annie started. 'It's not like that, only . . .' She told the spinning mistress bit by bit about the encounter on the landing, being tucked into her makeshift bed, and then, flushing, waking to find Robert lying beside her.

'Well, I believe you, if thousands wouldn't,' said Nellie Birkett. 'But either way, you've got yourself a good 'un. Walking up the road wi' you and kissing you like that – you didn't dream it, girl, or you wouldn't be wondering if you had, if you get my meaning. He's protecting you, Annie. Letting the world know he'll not abandon you. But if I were you, I'd get yourselves married quick all the same.'

*

Every movement that morning was automatic. Annie worked as if she was an extension of the machine itself, keeping time with it. By now she had several years' experience; the frightened child who hadn't realised how much she would miss school until she was no longer there, who thought she could never get used to the noise, the scurrying, the relentless whirr of the bobbins, had come to Cleator as an experienced hand. She'd kept house for her father and soon – her heart leaped at the thought – she would do the same for Robert. She thought of him now, his quiet, reserved face with its rare and beautiful smile, his way of speaking that meant every word was significant because anything else would be a waste of breath. She wondered if he was thinking of her, as he toiled deep below the earth. Had he too spoken to anyone about the events of last night?

A frown puckered her brow as she deftly pulled off a full bobbin and dropped it into the bin with the others and replaced it with an empty. She birled round to pluck out the next one, thinking, *I'll have to confess it. They'll know by now in the Priory*

House. Philomena will have told the cook – told her whatever story she wants them to know. Sunday loomed up on the horizon. Annie shivered at the thought of going to St Mary's and not taking her place with the Nolans. Besides anything else, she did not want to cause kind Michael any embarrassment. *I'll walk to Frizington to mass instead, so I will. Maybe Robert'll come with me and wait in the porch if it's raining.*

*

Going back to Spedding's house at dusk, problems crowded in on Annie, chief of which was facing the other lodgers. She found herself walking more slowly, looking at the ground. *I just hope Robert will be back, or that Mr Spedding will be in the kitchen. Or if not him, John Trescatherick.* Even if Willie McKeown and the others had had a warning, there was menace even in their silence.

'Annie!'

She turned, looking up into Robert's concerned face.

'You're walking along there as if you're away in a dream.'

'Aye, amn't I,' she said, looking around. She'd already reached the row of houses without knowing quite how she'd got there.

Robert pulled off his cap and turned it in his hands. 'I wanted to come and meet you. So's you wouldn't be going in there alone. And, to be honest,' he added, smiling shyly, 'so's I wouldn't have to either.'

'Oh Robert!' Annie lifted her face and did what she never had before, and kissed him on the cheek.

263

'Do you love me, Annie?' he murmured.

'I do.'

'It's great – to be loved by you.' He looked around, as though he had forgotten they were outside. 'Come on, then,' he said, tucking her arm under his. Walking along the row of houses, he greeted the people they passed with 'Good evening,' whereas the most Annie had ever seen him do was nod or at most put his fingers to his cap. As they turned into the entry between the houses he said, 'I feel taller when I'm with you,' and looking up into his smiling face she thought indeed that he was.

Annie helped Spedding with setting out the tea. Moving familiarly from scullery to kitchen to the front room she felt put her on a different footing from the men around the table. She was aware of McKeown and the others watching her every move, but did no more than nod to acknowledge their muttered thanks as she put things in front of them. Out of the corner of her eye, at the other end of the table, she saw Robert and John Trescatherick watching the Orangemen watch her. The meal again passed off in a polite but tense silence and Annie was glad when she was able to occupy herself with clearing away and washing up. Robert and Trescatherick came through to the scullery as she stood at the sink, the seamed block of soap in her hand, on their way to the back yard where Trescatherick wanted a smoke and Robert wanted to keep him company rather than remain at the table. 'My one small sin,' said the Cornishman, waving his clay pipe at her as he opened the back door. Later she learned that the sin was small indeed. It wasn't that he smoked, but that he smoked merely once a day, and always did so outside, whatever the weather.

There wasn't much more to the evening after that. There never was, for everyone was bone-tired from their dawn-to-dusk shifts. The men went to the outhouse one after another for a rudimentary wash, as Robert said, 'making do' until they were able to sink into the abundant hot water in the cubicles of the public baths on Saturday afternoon. Millie watched them pass in front of her between intermittently wiping a paw over her own face. As the last of them trooped out, Annie went upstairs to fetch her own ewer, grateful she had the privacy of the attic.

She stopped on the threshold, her eyes pricking with gratitude. She wasn't sure if the lumber was any less, but it was better organised. Someone, Mr Spedding presumably, had pushed it together and draped an old sheet over the top. In the space made, the iron bedframe had been assembled, and her mattress and bedding arranged on top. A rag rug lay alongside. Annie looked round for the ewer and basin, for nothing was as she'd left it. A folding screen, the fabric of the middle panel torn, now stood at the far side of the bed. Annie looked around it, to find what she was looking for sitting on a trunk. She stood still, her hand on the screen, as a little vision of married life came to her. She decided then and there to fix the old screen, to rub beeswax into the dry wood of the frame, to go to Fowles and buy enough cloth to replace what was faded and torn, for in a little rush of heat to her forehead she knew she would never want to wash in front of her husband, and some instinct about the reserved Robert told her he would be the same. Before Annie's vision a pretty apparition of a furnished room that was all their own blurred her eyes, until a soft knock at the door brought her back to the present.

Robert was standing on the threshold. His arms were full of bedding. Annie looked from it to his troubled face. Was this something Protestants did? Once you'd promised to marry someone you were as good as married? She'd heard the Gypsies did things like that, so perhaps the Prods were the same, not needing a priest to join their hands if they could do it themselves before God without involving a third party.

'I'm not ready,' she blurted.

'They stripped my bed, so they did. Told me I'd made my decision when I stayed here last night. I tried to explain I'd only fallen asleep but they laughed in my face and said if I didn't go it wouldn't be the bed they'd strip next and was I bored of you already?'

Annie could see from the look in his eyes that they'd said worse than this. *Bad words and insults.*

'I coulda had it out with them and got Spedding involved, only I don't want to stay in the same room as them now and if Spedding throws them out, which he said he would if there's trouble, the poor man'll be short of the rent till he finds other lodgers. I'll not harm you, so I won't,' he said. He glanced around the room. 'Did you do all this? It's fine, so it is.'

'No. I came up and found it that way.'

'Mr Spedding musta had a wife. I've never heard him talk of her, but he wears a ring. Some of this musta been hers. Annie,' he said, dropping the bedding on the end of the mattress and taking her shoulders, 'I'll not make you my wife in here, so I won't. I want better for you.'

She looked up at him. 'I love you, Robert.'

He pulled her close, his head resting on her shoulder. 'Tell me you always will. I couldn't bear it otherwise.'

'I'll love you forever,' she said. She felt the shape of his smile as his lips met hers.

*

Later, he said, 'We'll lie like this, so. You'll be under the sheet and I'll be alongside you but on top of it. We'll both be under the blanket. Will you mind that?'

'No,' she whispered.

'Will I turn down the lamp?'

She nodded. He turned away from her and twisted the little lever to extinguish the flame. He could feel her tense warmth through the sheet and badly wanted to put his arm over her, but didn't dare. He was pretty sure that was where it would go, once he slept, but was afraid of making any deliberate move. There was a little gasp in the breathing darkness.

'What did I do?' he said, anxiously.

'I've forgot my prayers,' she said, in real distress.

'Can't you say them now?' he asked, imagining clacking beads and droning.

'All right, so.'

Instead he found himself murmuring the Lord's Prayer with her, except that she stopped at 'deliver us from evil' leaving him to continue with 'for thine is the kingdom' into her puzzled silence. There was a little pause and then she said some words to Our Lady that to Robert emphasised what he'd been taught – that the papists idolised the Virgin Mary rather than worshipping Our Lord Jesus Christ. Yet the words made some vague visceral sense. He'd been told a story by John Trescatherick who back in Cornwall had survived a collapse in a tin mine. His workmate had died in front of him, crushed below a weight of stone, but he had just had time to croak out one word: 'Mother!' And now Annie was asking a mother – 'Mother of God' – to pray for her 'now and at the hour of our death'. There was something short then about glory and a world without end and a furtive rustling, which he guessed was her crossing herself. Then from a subtle change in the sound of her voice he realised she'd turned her head in his direction.

'Have you no more prayers you say yourself, Robert?'

He hesitated, wondering if she might think him foolish. He saw his young self, in the little room with Kathleen's sewing machine beneath the window, while Kathleen knelt by his bed teaching him a child's prayer. Could he remember the words? Yes, perhaps he could. Would God be offended if you started a prayer and couldn't finish it?

'Now I lay me down to sleep . . .' he began, when to his surprise and delight Annie chimed in on the second line and they finished the little prayer together.

'. . . I pray the Lord my Soul to keep
If I should die before I wake
I pray the Lord my Soul to take.'

'Don't ever die on me, Annie,' Robert said, and without thinking put his arm around her. There was no response. From her even breathing, he realised she already slept.

*

When Annie opened her eyes the following morning, the first thing she said was, 'I won't be going to Barrow for Christmas.'

'But you wanted to!'

'I don't want to leave you alone. You've been alone too much, so you have.'

'No, you should go. We'll have Christmas together for the rest of our lives.'

'If you're sure.'

'I am so. Will you tell them?'

Annie hesitated, thinking of Teresa's freit. 'Maybe when we've decided when. So as not to tempt fate.'

CHAPTER THIRTY-FOUR

Frizington, January 1904

'. . . orare pro me ad Dominum Deum nostrum.'

> The Confiteor – '. . . to pray for me to
> the Lord our God'

That first Sunday of the new year, Annie tramped the two miles to Frizington alone. Robert had looked troubled when she'd suggested he came too.

'It's not that I mind waiting – I'd like to see you come out and you find me waiting on you there. I'd like the walk with you and all. It's just that I've my own . . . you know, I'm Presbyterian.'

'Right enough,' she'd said, after a moment. Somehow his insistence, she felt, made them closer. Missing mass was a sin that had to be confessed. Was it not good that the Presbyterians felt the same about their own Sundays?

'Will I meet you after, on the square?' he'd added.

'In front of the library,' she'd said, smiling. 'I'll pray for you, so I will.'

He could see from her face she was expecting him to say he'd do the same, but he couldn't. He'd a vague idea that direct personal requests of the Almighty should not be made, that somehow they were attempts to bargain with God. You'd to find out what He intended more than seek to influence Him, hadn't you? And didn't the papists make you pay for things like that? Robert wanted to tell her not to spend her wages that way, in his practical way thinking about the entries in his little bank book, those tiny increments that might one day allow him to send for Kathleen's sewing machine. Perhaps Annie could help him? If she didn't want to learn the Frister and Rossmann once he'd got it back, there would be buttons to sew on, wouldn't there? Or the bills to make out in what he was sure was a neat hand.

'Robert? You're miles away so you are.'

'Thank you for thinking of me,' he'd said eventually. 'I can't help but think of you.'

*

When they met three hours later, Annie saw in Robert's troubled expression a reflection of her own feelings. He had that closed-in look she'd come to recognise and knew she couldn't ask him what was wrong. He had to offer it.

Instead he said, 'Did you remember and pray for me then?' with a slight smile.

'I did so. For you, and Dadda, and for Mammy's soul and Teresa's. For the Nolans—'

'Even Philomena?'

'Especially Philomena. She's maybe the one who needs it most. For Mrs Fagan and her two wee boys. For John Trescatherick. And Mr Spedding.'

'You've been busy, so you have. So what's the matter?'

Annie wiped her eye. 'I thought it'd be a different priest. He must be away. It was Father Hagerty.'

'And?'

'It's a lovely wee church, so it is. Friendly people, but not sticking their noses in. I'd never been to a mass where I didn't know anybody – well, there was always Dadda and Mammy if there wasn't anyone else. Then *he* came out onto the altar and we all got to our feet. It was fine until I went up for communion. I knelt down at the rail with the other people and along he came but when I looked up and opened my mouth he stared at me fierce, as if he was angry with me. Honest to God I thought he was going to pass me by and he did pause, I'm sure of it, but in the end he put the host on my tongue and carried on to the next person, leaving me with my heart banging on my ribs.

'Afterwards I was wondering was there another way out so's I wouldn't have to pass him at the main door. The church is smaller than St Mary's though. So all I could think of to do was to stay inside and kneel at one of the altars so he'd think I was praying – as sure a priest wouldn't disturb a person when she's praying, would he now? But I didn't, because that would have been wrong – I would only have been pretending to pray.'

She looked up at him, and Robert thought he'd never seen an expression as lovely as her anxious innocence.

'So in the end I had to go to the door, but of course most of the people were away out by then. He was talking to an oul' lady but I could see he wasn't giving her his full attention as he'd half an eye on me. I tried to get past them just by nodding politely but his hand shot out and grabbed my arm – like this,' she said, grasping Robert's forearm just above the wrist. 'Without letting go of me he gave this big smile to the poor oul' soul as if to say he was sorry, and cut across whatever she was telling him, saying he'd urgent business to attend to. "Go and sit down," he says to me, as if I'm a dog or his servant, with that smile wiped off his face.'

'Annie . . .' Robert said softly, for she'd started to cry.

'Well, I'd to wait for him. He leaned over me when I was sitting there, close enough to me that I could smell the communion wine off him, and wanted to know what I thought I was doing there in Frizington, coming to pass myself off as a good girl where they wouldn't be bad-mouthing me the way they were in Cleator Moor. Somewhere where nobody would know I wasn't in a state of grace.'

She paused, pulling out a clean, pressed handkerchief, and turned her face away to dry her eyes and blow her nose.

'A state of grace?'

'That I hadn't sins on my conscience – not big ones. Not the ones he was thinking of, anyway. I swore I was in a state of grace, that I'd never have come to the rail if I hadn't been, and just for a moment I thought he was going to leave off, but then he came back. Honest to God it was like having a big crow coming and pecking at you, wanting to take the eyes out of your head.'

'Annie . . .' Robert wished for her sake they hadn't agreed to meet in such a public place. He was aware out of the corner of his eye that a couple of boys – twelve years old or so – had stopped bickering with each other and were watching them with merciless interest. Just beyond them was a knot of women murmuring and glancing in their direction, though when he glared at them they as quickly pretended they weren't.

'He said was it true that I was under the same roof as a crew of Protestants? I said yes, but – only he wouldn't let me go on. "Are you sleeping alone?" he roars. I could see the spittle in the corners of his mouth, so I could. Robert, I had to lie to him. Yes, I said, it was a Protestant house but in it I'd a room to myself. He asked me how long I thought I'd be let to keep myself pure in a lodging house full of men and that what I'd done was a source of scandal when I'd lived in a good Catholic home with a woman there that loved me like a mother!'

'Ssh, Annie, not so loud.'

'Sorry . . . but it's a big lie, so it is. Loving me like a mother! What has Philomena told them about me? She must've given out to Father Hagerty that it was me packed my bags, not her that threw me out so I'd nowhere to go but for a kind English Proddy like Mr Spedding to take me in. Sure there wouldn't be any scandal, would there now, if she'd not made me go?'

Robert shook his head. 'Let's get away from here, Annie.'

'I'm embarrassing you, aren't I?'

'No, but it's none of their business, so it isn't,' he said, a little more loudly, looking pointedly again at the group of women.

Annie couldn't help but smile as this time they moved away. 'I'm proud of you, Robert McClure.'

'Are you?' He was delighted.

She took his arm, leaning her head against his shoulder.

'I'm proud to be seen with you, no matter what Father Hagerty says about you.' She sensed his body tense.

'What is it he says? I'm sure the man doesn't know me.'

Annie was silent, not meeting his eyes.

'Look,' he said, 'let's go back to Spedding's and tell him we'll not be in for Sunday dinner. I'm not sure I could face them at the table, but they'll not complain if they get to eat our share. I've some ginger beer and a bit of bread and cheese in the pantry for us to make another wee picnic if that'll do ye and we wrap up well, and you can tell me everything you want to or nothing if you want. I've had a bit of a set-to myself this morning if the truth be known.'

'Oh Robert! And here's me talking for Ireland.'

'I asked you, didn't I?'

'So what happened to *you*, then?'

'Well, there was fellas waiting for me at the door too – not the minister – a couple of the committee from the Lodge, with faces that long on them I don't know how they didn't trip themselves up. I've to go and see the Master, they said.'

'What about?' said Annie, feeling her skin prickle with fear.

'I asked them that and they said that was for the Master to tell me.' He smiled unhappily. 'They'll not be wanting me for an office-bearer, I shouldn't think.'

*

Robert and Annie sat on the little bridge at Wath Brow as the gathering clouds over the mountains threatened rain, eating in near silence. They were alone, for just about everyone else in the town was at table for the most important meal of the week.

'So what did yer man Hagerty say about me?'

'I'm not bothering my head about what he said,' muttered Annie.

'*I* am.'

There was a short silence as Annie contemplated the water of the beck.

'He said you'd never marry me. And nor would anybody else – or not the kind of man a decent girl would want – only some corner boy. He said that even if you did want to, you'd not turn for me—'

'I'd do anything for you, Annie, only . . .'

'And if I was thinking about turning for you I was to remember my immortal soul and the only thing to be grateful for was my poor mother wouldn't be there for to see it. He added – as if he was the most generous man in the world – that I couldn't be all to blame for hadn't my own father set the example to follow?'

Robert loosened his muffler and ran his fingertips under his collar as though it was too tight.

'He told me then there was a way out for me if I'd the sense to take it.'

'Oh?'

'He said there was a place for girls like me. Somewhere for me to start again – "in fasting and repentance and honest labour", he said. I guessed what he meant but let him say it. The nuns in Carlisle would take care of me. Or if I wanted, a place could be got for me in a convent back in Ireland, with my boat fare found. He said it would be a sanctuary. I told him I gave honest labour in Ainsworth's six days a week, observed fast days and was sure I didn't know what I'd done to have to repent in a convent. He shouted at me then, Robert, inside that wee church. Called me a bold girl and an ungrateful liar. He said my face should be hidden away behind a convent wall because I looked like an innocent but I couldn't be one. He was a priest of God and so even if I looked him in the eyes the way I was doing – honest to God, I don't know what way he meant, so I don't – he was armed against me but other good men mightn't be and he was praying for the souls of Michael and Frank Nolan that they might put Satan behind them.' Annie took a great gulp of air as though she was struggling to breathe, and burst into tears again.

Robert's arms came around her then and he kissed her hair, her forehead, her damp eyelids and lastly her trembling mouth, but gently, until her sobs subsided. Annie leaned against him, her forehead resting on his coat buttons.

'I wish you could stay there like that always,' she heard and felt him say, the words reverberating in his chest. 'I want never to let you go. Look at me, Annie,' he said, his finger under her chin to lift her face. 'I don't know how, but I'll do what they say if you want me to. Anything to be able to tell this Hagerty to his face that you're not what he's making you out to be. Don't go into their convents. I never seen anyone let out of them, so I've not.'

'How would you know?' she said, puzzled.

'I seen them when I was a boy. Big walls and gates and nobody came out. Wee windows high up. They might've had bars for all I can remember. The missionaries told us what they really were. So what do I have to do? Go round to the priests' house and see will Hagerty speak to me?'

'Don't go to Father Hagerty. Go to the Englishman – the curate. You'd do that for me?'

'I'd do anything for you.'

She hesitated. 'What'll they say in the Lodge?'

He took a deep breath, and blew out. 'They'll be kicking me out, right enough. Perhaps I should tell them I'm leaving and not give them the chance. You remember the day I met you?'

'I'll not be forgetting it,' she said, nestling against him.

'We'd made all that din in front of the church – your church, I mean. Well, today the preacher was on that gospel about how you'd wash the dust from your feet if you went a place and they didn't make you welcome. He can't ever have been a miner, him. We're washing dust off our selves all of the time. He was saying it was about how we'd to mind how we spent our time. That there was people would waste it for us – publicans, gamblers . . .' He hesitated. 'Women. Maybe the class of women your Father Hagerty really meant.'

'He's not my Father Hagerty. But I know that story.'

'Well, you'll know what he meant. There's no point in working a seam where there's not much ore to be found when you could be filling your cart down one that's richer. If nobody'll heed you, go somewhere where they will. So why, for the love of heaven, does the Lodge march past houses where they're hiding out the back till we've gone by? Why do we stop and bang drums and sing them songs in front of a church where we *know* they're not wanting to hear us? But to hear some of the boys in the Lodge you'd think marching was the religion itself, so you would. They've been good to me in the Lodge, most of them, honest they have. They're not all eejits like McKeown. Nobody in my life had ever asked me to join them. When I was wee people were forever telling me to go away and not bother them. But what they say in the Lodge sometimes makes no sense to me. The problem is though – listen to me, Annie – it's that when you tell me how Hagerty was with you I can't say that makes any sense to me either.'

'I've not told you all of it, so I haven't,' said Annie. 'My feet were dusty enough by the time I got home, sure enough. Father Hagerty rushed off into the sacristy after he'd said that about saving Michael and Frank from Satan. There was nobody left in the church then but me, so I got outside somehow though I was shaking so much I could barely put one foot in front of the other. It was raining a bit.'

'I remember.'

'But I'd to get home. So I started walking, and that made me feel a wee bit better. Only a mile down the road I heard a trap coming up behind me. It was slowing up, so I stood to the side to see were they going to stop. I thought maybe I'd be offered a lift. Then I saw that coachman they have – at the Priory House. Father Hagerty was sitting behind. But they went past me, with Father Hagerty looking straight ahead, like he was made of stone. Anything but look at me.'

CHAPTER THIRTY-FIVE

The Priory House

'. . . [for] the reception and reformation of fallen women.'

St Mary's Home for Penitents, Coal Fell,
Carlisle, opened 1872

Monday morning reality reasserted itself with the thunder of boots on the stairs. One set detached themselves from the ruckus below and stopped outside the attic door. Robert sat up in the bed, motioning Annie to silence. There was some shuffling, a tobacco-stained cough and the sound of something being pushed under the door. The footsteps receded. Robert got up on stockinged feet and went to pick up the folded piece of paper. He read it in silence. 'Oh well,' he said, 'that's it, so.'

'Robert?'

'Here.' He passed her the paper and went behind the screen to wash and put on his outer clothes.

*

To Brother Robert McClure,

You are required to appear before the committee with regard to a matter that is bringing the good name of the Lodge into disrepute. We will expect you this evening after you have finished your shift.

Brother Bawden

*

'It's not as if they're asking you, is it?' she said. 'It's more like an order.'

*

'She's a bold girl, so she is,' said Father Hagerty to his curate. 'Took communion from me before I realised who she was. I'd put my last shilling on her going out to Frizington thinking she'd be seeing a priest who didn't know her. Then when I confronted her after, she looked me in the eye with that innocent face she has on her, and said she was in a state of grace, if you please.'

'Perhaps she was,' said Father Clayton.

Hagerty went on as though his fellow priest hadn't spoken. 'I can see why Michael Nolan was taken in, and why Philomena never trusted her. And now we know the cut of her, all right, going straight to him.'

Hagerty reached across the table and poured himself a second Bushmills. He glanced at his colleague, frowning. 'Don't look at me like that, Father. I'm only calming my nerves.'

Father Clayton made some indistinct apology. 'I meant nothing by it. I'm as concerned as you are.'

'I'd rather drink in a man's company even if he doesn't join me than drink alone,' said Hagerty.

With a little stab of pity, Clayton reached for the bottle and put a second half-measure in his own glass.

'Good man yourself, Father,' said Hagerty.

'I cannot help but feel that the girl wouldn't have gone to him had Philomena Nolan been kinder,' said the younger priest.

'Philomena's suffered, Clayton. But you think she took it out on the girl?'

'Yes. She'd threatened a scene at Teresa's burial.'

'Oh yes, you did tell me,' muttered Hagerty.

'Nolan would have let her stay, for Teresa's sake. He told me he thought there'd been words, only that Philomena was wise enough not to use them when he could hear. The boy, Frank, was sweet on her, too.'

'Sure, it'd have been simpler if she'd liked the lad too. As it is, we've to do all we can for the avoidance of scandal.'

'I could go and see her,' said Clayton.

Hagerty raised his eyebrows. 'Go to that street? Well, perhaps you could. You're an Englishman. You could probably get away with it.'

'Whatever they do, the pair of them are going to live their entire lives wondering who is coming to the door,' said Clayton. 'Neither side will want them.'

'I'd be satisfied if we could get either of them sent back on the ferry,' said Hagerty. 'Her if it turns out she's going to have a baby. We've less control over him, though a bribe might answer.' He unstoppered the bottle again and sent his whiskey down neat. Clayton was sure he'd be able to warm his hands before his colleague's face.

'Perhaps it's not her fault, the poor child. How else was she going to turn out, with the example her father set,' said Hagerty, made briefly magnanimous by the whiskey. 'The Orange fella took advantage of her – her having no place to go. Well, if not Ireland, there's always Carlisle. I told her as much.'

'You're not still thinking of St Mary's Penitents?' said Clayton. 'It's not as if she works the streets.'

Hagerty eyed him coldly. 'I believe the women there are wronged servants, most of them.' Clayton wanted to ask what penance their seducers had been made to do, but he was interrupted by the clatter of the doorbell before he could frame his words. He pushed back his chair.

'I'll go, Father,' said Hagerty, dabbing his mouth with his napkin. 'I told old Mrs Condon you'd call round to her after tea. Get the girls to give you something for her out of the pantry, would you?' He patted his pockets. 'Now, where did I put the clove sweets?'

*

'We expected better of you, McClure,' said Bawden.

Robert faced the Master and his three colleagues from the other side of the table. Standing there while they were seated, he felt the years roll back, a child before an irate teacher once more. He couldn't even remember what he'd been guilty of back then. He just remembered that he'd been crying. Bawden's next words pulled him back into the present, while reminding him painfully that the past was never far away.

'A quiet young man, we were told, a good worker and a faithful Christian. Vouched for. Rose above his misfortunate birth.'

'She'd nowhere to go, so she hadn't,' he murmured.

'Which makes your conduct all the worse,' said the man on Bawden's right. 'According to what we've been told, you left your own bed for hers the very first night.'

'It wasn't like that,' said Robert.

'*She* set out to seduce *you*, was it?'

'No. I mean I never touched her, so I didn't. Not like that.'

Bawden leaned forward, his hands clasped before him. 'I'm not going to say I don't believe you, McClure. But you're young. You've been a loyal attender at the Lodge meetings, and in the Presbyterian church. Tell the girl she's to go, and that'll be the end of it.'

'They put me out of my bed, so they did.'

'Who?'

'McKeown and the others.'

Bawden waved a dismissive hand. 'What nonsense. Brother McKeown—'

'I only met Annie at all because McKeown tried to take a liberty with her. If I hadn't helped her—'

'I'll not permit you to interrupt me!' Bawden was on his feet now. Robert saw a vein in his forehead pulsing. 'I'm giving you a chance. With us, you'd an opportunity to be somebody in this town – you, a nobody. A no name.'

Robert balled his hands into fists, feeling his nails dig into his palms. Anything but let the man see he was trembling.

Robert heard himself say, 'I'm going to marry her, so I am.' He saw the sheen of sweat on Bawden's face. A whiff of sour perspiration reached him across the table.

'Paul,' murmured the third man behind the table, reaching a hand to Bawden's elbow. 'Sit down a wee minute. I remember the lad's face when he took his oath. He means she'll turn.' The man's face swivelled to Robert's. 'That's it, isn't it?'

Robert's shoulders sagged. 'I don't know, so I don't. All I know is that I'm going to marry her. If I have to, how she wants it.'

Bawden's eyes bulged at him. Robert wondered if an apoplexy was a way God had of telling men their anger had gone too far.

'I'm sorry.' He knew he meant it. He wanted to say to the four of them that they'd been kind, that never before had he been made to feel that he counted, that he belonged. He fumbled with his lapel, unclipping the little pin he had used to reattach Annie's torn sleeve. He could hear Bawden panting like an exhausted dog, his colleague murmuring and patting his sleeve. He half-expected the man's tongue to loll from his gaping mouth. Robert placed the little pin on the oak surface. The tiny click it made set his teeth on edge. Bawden's head swivelled dangerously – to Robert's eyes it looked as though it would shake loose – until his eyes focused on the pin as though he didn't know what it was.

'I'll go now,' said Robert, backing towards the door.

'Yes, go,' said Bawden hoarsely. 'Go to your taig hoor.'

The words rose up at Robert like a slapping hand. He closed the door in a daze, moving through the narrow hallway to the entrance as if he had been plunged into deep water and had to reach the surface before his lungs burst for lack of air. He went off through the dusk not thinking only of the men at the committee table behind him but of Cairncross. Why was it that big, confident men, men with his father's loud voice and easy manner, Bawden with his red face and his broad hands, could use words like that with impunity when he, Robert McClure, had known since he was five years old that 'bad words' only got you caned?

The clock on the Montreal Schools chimed the hour, bringing him back to the present. He'd missed tea, then. The interview had taken longer than he'd thought. Then he remembered that they'd made him wait, something else that powerful men could do to smaller ones. *Annie will have saved me something, so she will*, he thought with a tenderness that brought tears to his eyes. Someone who thought of him, who, God willing, always would. He thought of Bawden going home now to beeswaxed furniture and antimacassars, and Mrs Bawden with her formidable buttoned chest and upswept grey hair not saying anything but fixing him with a cold glare while without looking she reached for the little brass bell that would summon the parlourmaid. Robert had never seen inside Bawden's house, but he had encountered Mrs Bawden and imagined their home being something like a cross between the dwellings of Kathleen's better-off clients and the Big House – only smaller but equally forbidding to live in.

Scraping his boots at the door, he glanced up at the window of the back room. A small oil lamp burned in the window; without it the room would have been in darkness. *She's already upstairs, then.*

As he went to go up, the door of the front parlour opened and he heard Spedding's voice. 'Is that you, Robert?'

'Aye.'

'Annie's gone out.'

'At this time?'

'One of them parlourmaids from the Priory House come for her. Said Father Clayton wanted a quick word.'

Robert paused, his hand on the banister rail, trying to convince himself that if it was Clayton Annie had gone to see, it couldn't be a bad thing.

'I'll go myself, then. For to walk her home when she comes out.'

*

'Ah, Miss Maguire,' said Hagerty in avuncular tones as Annie was shown into the chilly parlour.

'Good evening, Father,' she said, looking not at him but at the two nuns sitting majestically in their voluminous habits at opposite ends of the divan, their hands hidden. They observed her unsmilingly, their foreheads eclipsed by square white coifs, the guimpes below their chins so starched she was sure they made movement difficult. Annie remained standing, for no one asked her to sit down.

'Sister Euphrasia and Sister Joseph – Sisters of Mercy,' said Hagerty. The two women nodded in turn, though Annie noticed the younger of the two wouldn't meet her eye. Sister Euphrasia held her gaze, however.

'They've been kind enough to call at this late hour to help you in your predicament,' said Father Hagerty.

'My predicament?' said Annie faintly.

'I owe you an apology,' said the priest. 'I was a bit hard on you back there in Frizington, so I was. Overzealous, perhaps. And then leaving you to tramp all the way home. But I intend to make up for that. Galvin will be accompanying the Sisters on their train back to Carlisle in a wee while and you'll be with them.'

'You'll be coming to us for a little rest, Annie,' said Sister Euphrasia – Irish, but with an accent Annie couldn't place. 'Just till everything blows over. Peace and prayer and reflection. A bit of work just to keep you occupied.'

'I've the mill,' said Annie, backing towards the door.

'You'd be helping our mission,' said the nun.

'Where's Father Clayton?' said Annie. 'I was to see *him.*'

'On a sick call,' said Hagerty. 'Be a good girl, now.'

'I've nothing with me,' said Annie, her voice rising.

'You'll not need anything,' said Sister Euphrasia, rustling to her feet.

'*No!*' screamed Annie, fumbling at the doorknob.

'Bold hussy!' shouted Hagerty.

Behind her the door opened. Aware only of two dark figures in the gloom of the gaslit hall, one tall, the other stocky, Annie screamed again.

CHAPTER THIRTY-SIX

Crossfield Road

'The first step of humility is unhesitating obedience, which comes naturally to those who cherish Christ above all ... they carry out the superior's order as promptly as if the command came from God himself.'

Rule of St Benedict

'I'll be writing to the abbot in the morning to have you moved!' shouted Hagerty. 'What were you thinking of, showing me up in front of the Sisters? You – a priest – a Benedictine monk and a priest of God – in cahoots with an Orangeman to commission a mortal sin!'

'I'd no intention of showing you up. I found McClure outside,' said Clayton again. 'He wanted only to walk Miss Maguire home.'

'Walking her home indeed! She went straight into his arms, so she did, right there in front of those holy nuns. You're a pure innocent, so you are, Father. You've wasted the time and goodwill of the Sisters thanks to your meddling and disobedience.'

'I never knew they were coming,' said Clayton quietly, wondering just what would have happened had he and Robert not come in when they did. Would the nuns, the priest and Galvin have bundled the girl onto the trap and then into a train by force? And surely the spectacle of a screaming Annie being carried off to Whitehaven against her will would have been a 'showing up' such as Cleator Moor had never before witnessed?

'Sit down, Father,' said Hagerty, suddenly deflated. 'You'll have a whiskey with me.'

'Thank you, yes.' *Obedience in all things*, he thought.

Hagerty spoke with his back turned, getting glasses from the dresser. 'I'd other visitors a couple of nights ago, you see.' He poured out measures that made Father Clayton suppress a wince.

'Mr Bawden was one of them,' he said, handing Clayton his tumbler. The curate nearly dropped it.

'*That* Bawden? From the Lodge?'

'How many Bawdens are there, Father?' Hagerty sat down heavily, putting the back of his free hand over his mouth to stifle a belch. 'I oughtn't to have expected you to understand, you not being Irish, I mean.'

'Oh?'

'We've what you might call an uneasy truce here. Since the Tumelty lad was murdered. They know they did it and got away with it, and we know they know it and that they know we do. But you'll never get them to lose face. So we've to put up with the marching and the noise and all, but it is really only noise.'

'Broken windows.'

'Who do you think pays for them, Father? It always looks as if it's parish funds but there's a wee brown envelope comes two days after, so there is. Every year if it's needed. Now, the McClure boy. He's a by-blow of one of them back in Ireland. Has his job here thanks to them. They're after expelling him now but if they can welcome him back like the prodigal son they'll do it in the blink of an eye.'

'He told me he loves her,' murmured Clayton.

Hagerty eyed him coldly over his glass.

'He'll get over it. Haven't you ever had to?'

Startled, Clayton stared back. This was the closest his superior had ever come to divulging anything personal about himself, going perilously close to matters they both knew they had undertaken with their vows never to dwell on again.

Hagerty cleared his throat and spoke in a firmer voice. 'So, they wanted my help to separate the two. If there's a child, of course—'

'I don't believe there's a child. I don't believe it of them.'

'An expert, are you?'

'Hardly, but—'

'Anyway, that's all gone by the board, so it has. One or other of 'em'll need to turn and I don't give much for his chances here if it's him.'

'So he'll have to go away from here?'

'Don't you see? That's what I was after doing with the Sisters – trying to keep the boy's job for him, and keep him safe. Go and see him, seeing as you're so thick with the pair of 'em now, and get them to see sense.'

*

'You've a visitor.' Spedding stood on the back doorstep as Robert scraped his boots. 'He's already seen Annie. He's in front. I'll bring more tea, though by the look of your face you could use summat stronger. Mebbe the reverend could too.'

The reverend? Robert sighed. Was this Bawden's last-ditch attempt to save him from popery – sending the Presbyterian minister round as a rearguard action? What on earth could the man have said to Annie?

It was Father Clayton instead who got to his feet, offering a long knuckly hand to Robert. Out of instinctive politeness Robert shook it. When he'd been called before his brethren in the Lodge that night nobody had offered him that courtesy.

'I was hoping we might talk,' said Clayton, sitting back down. Robert pulled up a chair. 'Properly, I mean.'

'I've never spoken to a priest before yourself, so I haven't,' he blurted.

In answer, Clayton twitched up his trouser legs and moved his feet forward. Robert glanced down at an old-fashioned pair of black leather laced shoes, glossily polished. The last time he'd seen such fine footwear had been on the undertaker who brought Kathleen her funeral commissions. Then, as now, they made him feel that perhaps people were even born with different kinds of feet. He pushed his own in their workman's boots further under his chair.

'You see,' said Clayton, 'no devil's hooves.' He turned his noble head from side to side. 'And no horns either.'

'I didn't mean—'

'I know. *I've* never spoken to an Orangeman before. I've *heard* the men of the Lodge, of course. And fine singers you are too, I'll admit, even if I don't care for the words.'

'I'm not one,' said Robert. 'Not now.' He wanted to shift the conversation. 'Thank you for what you did last night, sir. I thought yer man was going to have a fit, so I did. He was in a right tear.'

'Your man?' said Father Clayton, perplexed. 'Oh, you mean Father Hagerty?'

'Yes. Your boss, isn't he? The way you stood there cool as anything and said I was come to take Annie home. The oul' nun looked like she was set on tying her up with them beads or something. The wee one mightn't have – she looked a bit fearty to me. Will you be in trouble for it?'

'Oh, probably. I'd do the same again, though.'

'We'd not have got her back, sure we wouldn't?'

Clayton hesitated. 'It might have been difficult, yes.'

'Annie's spoke about you, so she has.'

'A motherless girl, and to all intents and purposes a father-less one. In need of someone to guide her.'

Stung, Robert said, 'She mightn't be of age, but she knows her own mind, sir. And so do I, though I think she'd have the guiding of me. I've asked her to marry me and she's said yes.'

'I'm glad to hear it. I really think it's the only way forward now.'

'It's the one we want.'

'She'll need her father's permission, however.'

'She will so, but nobody else's. If she doesn't get it there's Glasgow.'

Clayton raised his eyebrows. 'Glasgow?'

'Not Glasgow. I meant Gretna. It's closer. She could be married in Scotland without her father's say-so, I've heard.'

'I'm sure that won't be necessary. But tell me, Mr McClure, what are you proposing to live on?'

'I've my wages, and a wee bit put by. There's plenty marry on less. I save. I don't drink or smoke.'

'Commendable. You've taken the pledge?'

'I've taken no pledge nor need to, save to myself and to her. And there's her wages too, so there is.'

'What if there's a child?'

Robert tilted his chin, mulishly. 'There's no child, so there isn't. And I'll knock down the next man that says there is, honest to God, I will. Even if he's wearing a collar. I've never touched her.' At this last his eyes slid away. He had the uncomfortable feeling this priest could see into his soul. They had ways of doing that, hadn't they? *Kissing her and putting my arm about her and thinking about her when she's sleeping in ways I'll never say* is *touching.*

'I admire your courage, Mr McClure, and I'm inclined to believe what you say though I suspect you don't tell me the entire truth.' Seeing Robert's mouth open, Clayton held up a hand. 'Only, as the poet Donne once wrote, "No man is an island," much less a woman. And least of all in Cleator Moor.'

'I wouldn't know. I only had the National School until I was eleven,' said Robert. 'And we didn't do pomes. Annie's more the reader.'

'I'd maybe not recommend that poet to her anyway. Not always suitable for a lady, or for a priest, for that matter. All I meant is that none of us exist without other people.'

There was a scuffling at the door then, and Spedding came in with a tray bearing a fresh pot of tea, the best crockery, and a plate of bread and butter underneath a piece of muslin. He turned to the priest. 'I know Mr McClure won't, but will you have a glass of Scotch?'

'Thank you, I will. The smallest,' said Clayton, making a half-inch space between finger and thumb, 'and well drowned.'

'Right you are.'

Spedding came back with the Scotch and water, but neither of the men at the table spoke until the landlord's footsteps receded back to the kitchen. Clayton took a sip as Robert watched, expecting a grimace. *They'll have better stuff in the clergy house.* No grimace came.

'Cleator Moor is a small place, Mr McClure.'

'I've never known different than small places. I only passed through Belfast for to get the ferry.'

'I have. I come from Nottingham. Do you know where that is?'

Robert shook his head.

'It's probably not as big as your Belfast, but it's a city. You've more privacy when you're with many people than when you're with few, Robert.' The priest leaned forward. 'Here everyone knows that Annie is living under this roof with you, as the only female in a house full of men. I believe you when you say you respect her. But your landlord has told me that there are other fellows living here who tried to insult her after that Orange march. He told me he sent one of them on his way today for a comment he didn't care for.'

'Oh?'

'I think from what he said he'd been pleased to see the back of the man. But what I mean, Mr McClure, is that idle gossips need little encouragement to claim that there'd been no insult to her at all. How could there have been if the girl has now chosen to eat at the same table with her tormentors?'

'She'd nowhere else to go,' Robert heard himself telling Clayton, just as he'd told them in the Lodge.

'She has now. I have arranged it. That in itself mightn't stop tongues wagging altogether, but it may damp their ardour if they know it's the Priory House's doing.' He got up.

Robert looked at him wildly. 'Not them nuns after all?' He stood up as well, his fists clenching. 'You'll do it over my dead body, so you will.'

'No, not the nuns, Mr McClure. Please don't get agitated. She'll still be in Cleator – in the big corner house on Dawson Street to be precise. If we had sent her to Carlisle it would have been tantamount to saying that she was guilty in some way. This is the price of peace with Father Hagerty, if I'm honest. It's not easy to live under the same roof with a man you've had that kind of difference with.'

'I know that well enough,' said Robert, thinking of the men he shared his room with.

'So I have told Annie to come to the Priory House with her things when she finishes work tomorrow.'

'She's agreed to that, has she?'

'She has, because I told her you can come with her to see where she goes. Then I'd like you to call on me the day after that. Now, do thank your Mr Spedding for me. No – I shall see myself out. Annie will want to know about the outcome of our meeting, I should think.'

After the priest had left Robert took the tea things out to the scullery and washed them up, trying to master his breathing before he went upstairs. There was no sign of either Spedding or Trescatherick or any of the others. *If McKeown has gone I should be grateful for small mercies*, he thought, as he dried Clayton's glass and then wondered where to put it.

He tramped upstairs.

Annie was sitting on the bed facing him. She was still and pale, but he saw straightaway that she'd been crying.

He sat down beside her and took her hand. 'We'll get married, Annie. Whichever way you want. Whatever anybody says. I just wish it could be nobody's business but ours.'

Annie leaned against his shoulder. She looked around the attic at the shrouded lumber, the flimsy screen around the washstand. 'I'll miss this room, so I will.' She dropped her head. 'I'll miss you being there at night most of all.'

Robert stroked her cheek. 'Our last night here,' he said. 'The next time we'll be together is when we're wed.'

She lifted her head from his shoulder and looked at him, her eyes huge and dark in the thin yellow light of the oil lamp.

'Everything will be all right then, so it will,' he said.

'Will it?'

'We'll make it so. Oh Annie, I can hardly believe you want me. Your wee Proddy bastard.'

Her eyes filled with tears. He bent his head, kissing one eyelid after another, and then her mouth. Her arms went around him, and they subsided back onto the bed. His head lay on her breast, rising and falling with her breathing. Her heart thumped against his ear and he thought with a kind of astonishment that for the rest of his life he would be able to hear that sound, as though her blood pulsed for him, and nobody else would hear it except for the babbies they'd have. He was almost overwhelmed at what they were taking on, but knew that without her he might as well walk up to Whitehaven and off the edge of the harbour into the Irish Sea. He wanted her too, with an urgency that terrified him.

Cairncross came into his mind, Cairncross who had always taken what he wanted, whenever he wanted, and who only fitfully had attacks of conscience about the consequences of what he had done. Robert resolved in that moment, as he held himself in an immense effort of will clear of Annie's lower body, that whatever else he did, he would be a better father than the land agent had been. Not a richer one in the world's sense, but a loving one. And his children would have a name. They wouldn't be farmed out to strangers who would stint their food and never let them forget that they were only welcome so long as there was money to pay for their keep. He breathed in deeply and propped himself on an elbow, forcing himself to draw away the hand that cupped Annie's right breast. As he did so, Annie grasped it and put it back.

'My husband,' she said, wonderingly.

'My wife,' he said, exulting. 'Will you write to your father?'

'I will. I've to get his permission.'

Robert hesitated. 'He'll give it, won't he?'

She answered so quickly he realised that she and the priest must have talked of it. 'Oh yes. He'll not be able not to. He'll be telt by Father Clayton if he doesn't. It'll be no surprise to him either. I could see from their faces in Barrow at Christmas that they knew something was up, only they were waiting for me to tell them.'

'He'll give you away, then.'

He heard her breath catch. 'It won't be like that, Robert. It'll only be a side-altar marriage. Father Clayton explained. He's only the curate so he's to do what Hagerty tells him. It's just to be us and two witnesses to make it all legal. He said Father Hagerty thinks anything different would be . . . like showing off.'

'Is that how you want it, Annie?'

He watched a little girl's disappointment flit across her face. Then it was gone, as her eyes turned to meet his and she said, 'All I want is you. You – and me wearing my best blouse you gave me and some wee bits that were Mammy's.'

CHAPTER THIRTY-SEVEN

The Priory House

> 'During marriage ceremonies priests exerted consider-
> able pressure upon any non-Catholic partners in mixed
> marriages to become Catholic and to raise their children
> in accordance with Catholic doctrine. Thus, at the same
> time as a priest might turn a sympathetic ear, he could
> also wave a big stick.'
>
> Donald MacRaild, *Irish Migrants in*
> *Modern Britain, 1750–1922*, 1999

'Thank you, Miss Dillane. Tell Mrs Kennedy that was grand,' said Father Hagerty, handing up his plate to the parlourmaid. He pressed his napkin to his mouth, stifling a belch. Father Clayton barely noticed, listening to the retreating footsteps, the squeal of the scullery door. He refilled his teacup, though he feared the tawny strength of the brew would keep him awake, and swilled away the greasy residue of the stew.

Deep in the back of the house, the scullery door protested again, followed by the unmistakable tap-tap of the cook's shoes.

It was her habit to bring through the last course, 'to see are the Fathers happy', as she always said to the parlourmaids, now unpinning their starched cuffs in the cold scullery and preparing to tackle the dirty crockery. The door opened.

'Apple crumble,' announced Mrs Kennedy.

'My favourite,' said Father Hagerty, as he did about most things put in front of him. Father Clayton had long since recognised that his fellow priest was afraid of the woman.

'I'll leave yous to it, so,' said Mrs Kennedy, this time closing the door. Hagerty reached for the custard jug then, remembering his manners, pushed it towards Clayton. The curate shook his head. Just thinking about the texture of the stuff made his gorge rise. Hagerty took the jug back and emptied it.

'So the date is fixed, is it?'

'Yes. After Easter, of course.'

'I'd give them their train fare instead if it was up to me. The Lodge'll crucify him. An accident down the pit wouldn't surprise me.'

The curate's skin prickled. He thought, *He likes this tribal nonsense. He likes his theology adversarial, just as much as the Orangemen.* Clayton remembered the priest's dismissive words about the mild-mannered Reverend Caine at St John's; it was the *closeness* of the vicar's brand of Anglicanism to Catholicism that annoyed him.

'Well, we'll see will the fella turn up as he's promised,' added the priest, tipping his bowl to get the last of the custard and crumble onto his spoon. Clayton looked away. Instinct told him that it was early poverty, not greed, that made the older man always scrape his plate clean.

Wiping his mouth, Hagerty said in a brighter tone, 'You'll have a nightcap with me, Father?' dismissing Annie and Robert. Without waiting for an answer he was on his feet, but when he was halfway to the corner cabinet there was a knock at the door. 'What the divil . . . at this hour? It'll be a death, so it will.'

Clayton's hand was already on the doorknob, though he could hear Mrs Kennedy muttering her way along the passage.

'I'll go,' he said, intercepting her. 'Father Hagerty and I are finished if you want to clear away.'

A moment later he called into the open doorway to Hagerty and the cook. 'I'll see our guest in the parlour.' As he ushered Robert into the room opposite, he heard the pop of the stopper on Father Hagerty's Bushmills.

'I'm sorry, you'll find it a bit cold in here, so I'd keep that muffler on if I were you,' he said to his visitor. 'You'd have to be a bishop for Mrs Kennedy to light that fire. Give me a minute to get the gas lit. Thank you for coming, Robert.'

He surveyed the young man in the light of the gas, taking in the obstinate line of the jaw, the hazel eyes, the stubbornly curly brown hair. The only betrayal of emotion was the whitening of the knuckles clutching his cap.

'I said I would. I'd'a come earlier only I didn't want half the Moor seeing me at your door.'

'We're getting used to visitors at odd hours.'

*

Half an hour later Clayton saw his visitor out.

'It's finding the right balance between silencing the gossipers and not doing things in such a rush that everybody thinks you're having to make amends,' he said.

'They can think what they like, so they can,' said Robert, his sober expression unchanged. 'But if wicked tongues mean she marries me quicker I'll not bother my head about them. Goodnight, Father, and thank you.'

Father Clayton watched his visitor trudge off into the darkness, with his cap pulled on, indistinguishable from any other working man finding his way home from the pub. Yet Clayton knew quiet heroism when he saw it.

'Come away in, Father,' said Hagerty at his shoulder. 'We'll catch our death if you leave that door open any longer.'

CHAPTER THIRTY-EIGHT

Hardwick Street, Barrow-in-Furness

'*Semper Sursum*'

'Always Rising', motto of Barrow-in-Furness

It was a Monday, a fine blowy early spring day, and Elsie Fagan was getting the laundry in. The boys sat at the kitchen table doing their homework. Elsie had put the felt protector over it so that no harm would come to the polished oak surface. Mark had protested briefly, but his brother reminded him that it all had to be done before the table was needed for tea and, if he hurried, they'd still have a chance to play at marbles in the back yard, before being called to eat.

Elsie was humming to herself as she unpegged the sheets from the line in the yard and tested them for dampness. The folding airer Thomas had made for her of wooden batons and canvas webbing waited inside, before the fireplace. He'd told her it was a comfort to come in on a Monday evening to the scent of warm washed cotton. He'd said more than once, 'You've made a lovely wee nest for me, so you have.'

'Not near as much as you've made for me, Tom,' she murmured to herself.

The latch of the door from the back lane clicked then, and Thomas's boots grated on the flagstones. Elsie clipped off the last sheet unveiling her to the man she could only think of as her husband.

'Elsie,' he said, catching her around the waist and kissing her. Elsie dropped the sheet she would normally have carefully folded into the straw wash-basket and turned into his embrace. He smelled of oil and dust and iron-filings.

'I'll take that in for you,' he said, lifting the basket and carrying it through the back door and on up the steep stairs. Elsie scuttled after him. She didn't want him putting the washing on the airer. She wouldn't ever say, but she wasn't sure he'd do it just the way she wanted, and besides, he needed to get that dirty jacket off.

'Sit down and take your boots off till I get you your cup of tea.'

'How are my wee men?'

On cue, there was a scraping of chairs, homework forgotten, as little Mark scrambled onto Thomas's lap, laying his head against his stepfather's heart, and Joe perched on the flock arm of the chair to show him his new marbles, traded for that morning in the school-yard at the Sacred Heart.

'Careful, boys, don't scald yourselves on Dadda's tea,' said Elsie, standing in front of Thomas holding a cup and saucer.

'Ah, just the cup, Elsie, I've only the one hand free,' he said; the other was wrapped around Mark.

'There's a letter come,' said Elsie, nodding towards the mantelpiece. 'Annie's writing.'

'Oh good. It's been a wee while, so it has.' He swallowed his tea down in two great gulps and gave the cup back to Elsie. 'Thank you, love. Now, Joe, would you be a good wee man and fetch that letter down for me?

'Hmm, it's fatter than usual. She's maybe been saving up her news.' Thomas opened the flimsy envelope almost at arm's length, for Mark showed no sign of budging.

'Three sheets, there is,' he said. 'I only ever manage the one.'

Elsie arranged the washing on the airer with half an eye on the man in the chair. Joe slid off the armrest muttering something about finishing his sums, but Mark, oblivious to the sudden tension in the man's face and breathing, stayed where he was. Elsie stopped what she was doing to watch Thomas's eyes moving over the pages. As he finished, he said quietly, 'Mark, wee man. I've to talk to your mother. Away and get Joe and play outside.'

The child unfurled with sleepy reluctance but without argument and slid off Thomas's lap. The two adults stared at each other in silence until the small hurricane of boys had passed out of the room.

'You'd better read it yourself,' said Thomas, holding out the pages. 'But Philomena's put her out, and she's marrying.'

'That's what she was keeping to herself, then, when she came at Christmas.'

'She wuddna been marrying at all if Hagerty had got his way. He tried to get her to go to the nuns instead. But it has to be soon – only not during Lent.'

306

'A baby?' She took the letter.

'She doesn't say that. Unless she's wrote it in a way I don't understand.'

Elsie went to the window where the light was better.

'It's the Proddy boy,' she said. 'I thought it would go that way.'

'He can be a Turk or a Zulu if he wants, as long as he loves my girl.'

'He's in the Lodge – no, *was* in the Lodge.'

'Well, they'll not like that. They'll have cast him out for this, with a gnashing of teeth and all the works. I wonder do they have a ceremony for it, like a dishonourable discharge.'

'Annie says she'll need your consent.'

'She'll have it.' He rested his head on the back of the arm-chair. 'Come here a wee minute, would ye, Elsie?'

She caught the catch in his voice and rustled over to kneel by the side of his chair. His hand caressed her hair.

'I'd dreamed of it, you know. My wee girl's wedding. But not like that. Not as if it's something to be ashamed of.'

'It's not her that says that, though. It's the priests she's talking about when she uses them words: "occasion of sin", "avoidance of scandal".'

'Jesus, mercy! For they've surely none of it, some of them. Come up here, will you, Elsie, and not be kneeling at my feet. I'm a foreman at the shipyard, not the Holy Father, so I'm not ... oh ... but you're heavier than wee Mark, so you are.'

Elsie came into his arms, resting her face against the scratch of his stubble.

'At least they can be married,' she said quietly. 'Even if it's just at a side-altar.'

'You *are* my wife,' said Thomas, pulling her closer. 'Even if we've always to sit in the back pew and never go up to the rail. You being here and them wee boys calling me Dadda is everything to me.'

'Because you're more of a father to them than Tim ever was.'

'Ssh. Don't name him even. He's the only man in the world I'm afraid of. That he might come back, I mean.'

'He doesn't know where we are. When he did it he never bothered his head about us.' She shifted in his embrace. 'I'd better get the tea.'

'And I'd better get thon letter wrote. Will we go up, Elsie? She's not said anything about me giving her away.'

Elsie paused. 'She maybe doesn't need that for a side-altar. See if she asks you to come – ask her when it'll be. But if you go, I'll not come with you.'

'Elsie!'

'It's her I'm thinking of. Her wedding day is her own and it's her mother should be in her thoughts, not me getting in the way.' She got up, smoothing down her apron. 'Instead of posting the letter, take it up with you. You could go Saturday morning if you can get the cover, and be back at night.'

'I'd promised the boys Barrow Park.'

'Tell them Saturday after. And the Saturday after that if it doesn't rain, Piel Island. You need to meet the man, Tom.'

'Help me with the letter then.'

'After tea.' She started putting things on the table. He got up and went over to the window. Down in the back yard he saw the boys squatting over their marbles, completely absorbed.

*

Spedding answered the door, taking in Thomas Maguire at a glance. The face told him Irish, the hands that he was used to hard work. The pale skin, though – *He works at the surface.*

'I'm sorry, sir, I've no rooms free.'

'I've not come about a room. I'm looking for Miss Annie Maguire.'

Spedding's eyes widened. He looked searchingly at Thomas's face, and his visitor saw recognition dawn. The landlord stood back from the door. 'Come from Barrow, 'ave yer?' You'd best step in a minute. Annie's not living here now, but there's someone can tell you where to find her. Mr McClure. Have a seat through here and I'll go get him.'

In the dining room Thomas didn't sit, but stood staring at the porridge-coloured walls, the spotty print above the mantelshelf and the oil-cloth on the table. He thought the place clean enough – the window panes looked as if they'd recently had a proper newsprint polish and he wondered if that was Annie's work – but at the same time the room had an unloved air. If Annie had been there, she would have lifted the sash, he was sure, to let out the lingering smells of food.

The doorknob rattled. A young man with the miner's ruddy glaze on his skin stood there in Saturday evening shirtsleeves and no collar. He was unsmiling and a little wary, but Thomas saw there was no hostility in the hazel eyes.

'You're Annie's father,' said Robert.

'And you're her intended.' Thomas put out a hand. He felt the callouses on Robert's palm rasp against his own.

'I am so. I love her,' said Robert, quite loudly, and Thomas realised the boy was nervous.

'And does she love you?'

'She does.'

Thomas smiled. 'And what's she told you about me? Her prodigal father?'

Robert flushed. 'Well, she talks about you a fair wee bit. She misses you. She telt me about the wee boys too – and—' he hesitated, 'your Elsie.'

'The weans call me Dadda now, so they do,' said Thomas softly.

'Sure they do. Why wouldn't they? Weans should have a father, so they should,' said Robert with a force that startled Thomas. 'And man wasn't made to be alone, sure he wasn't. We've talked about that, her and me. About you. I said the poor lady shouldn't be punished for what her husband has done. I couldn't see why she shouldn't be happy if there's another man to love her.' He smiled fleetingly. 'Gives me something to argue about with thon priest, anyway.'

'Instructing you, is he?' said Thomas.

'I don't know about that. I like the man, though – Clayton, that is,' said Robert. 'So I said I'd go. To him, not to the other old scunner. Not after he tried to get Annie taken away. I don't need instruction, though,' he continued. 'No man needs another to come between him and scripture. I'd say that about some of the preachers I've heard too, not just the papists. And I'd tell Father Clayton himself that even the pope of Rome would be better at his job if he had a wife alongside him. Being alone makes you think too much of your own affairs, Mr Maguire.'

'Well, that's true, right enough. And what do your own family say about your plans?'

'There's none of them in England, so there isn't.' Robert looked towards the window. 'Didn't Annie tell you any of that?'

'No.'

'I've no name, Mr Maguire. Only my mother's.'

'God bless and keep you, Mr McClure. That makes no difference to me.'

'You'll give her your consent, then?'

'When I've seen her. But where *is* Annie?'

Robert stood up. 'She's not living here now. Father Clayton found her new lodgings – somewhere Hagerty's happier about, as there's other women there – Catholic people, of course. It's in Dawson Street.'

'Off Birks Road?'

'Yes, Annie's forever on the lookout for Philomena, right enough. I'll take you round. I was going to see would they let me visit her anyway; since she went I've only been let to meet her on the street. It's a good enough place and she's even a wee room to herself, she says. If Philomena hadn't thrown her out like that sure there'd not have been any of this trouble. But then maybe we wouldn't be getting married so fast so in a way I'm not sorry.' He smiled again. Thomas thought it a boy's smile. A frank smile.

'Let you visit her? Have you to ask permission?'

'It's that I'm not let to see her alone. Father Clayton's instructions – to stop the gossip. It'll be different with you there – being her father and all.'

*

Annie's new lodgings weren't with nuns, but, as Robert waited for her to be fetched in the austere dining room beneath a tinted engraving of the Last Supper, he felt they might as well have been. He'd noticed the wordless look of recognition the woman who had opened the door had given Thomas.

'I know her,' whispered Thomas, the moment the woman had bustled out. 'Not her name, but she's one of them women does everything in the church. Organises the flowers, polishes the brassware, picks the drips of wax off of the votive candles. Everybody'd call her a good woman, but she'll be Hagerty's spy right enough. You'd think there wouldn't be a problem, would ye, a father calling on his daughter along with her intended?'

'Depends on who the intended is,' said Robert.

'*And* the father.'

'He doesn't want you coming,' muttered Robert, not meeting Thomas's eye.

'What's that?'

'Hagerty. Clayton said so. You've not to come and give her away, so you've not.'

Thomas cried out, clamping a hand over his mouth.

'Jaysus, they're cruel.'

'There'll be no giving away anyway. We've to meet at a side-altar. No nup . . . what is it?'

'Nuptial mass.'

'No incense, no communion, he said, and just witnesses. I've asked John Trescatherick and Annie's asked her doffing mistress. Mr Spedding wants to come too. No throwing rice. You'd think we were Presbyterians, so you would,' said Robert, with half a smile, 'not being let hae any show.'

'You'll not turn?'

'I will not. I said to her I'd do anything she wanted, and I would if it hadn't been for them nuns trying to take her away. . . That's her coming now, maybe.'

CHAPTER THIRTY-NINE

The Priory House

'[An Orangeman] . . . should strenuously oppose the fatal errors and doctrines of the Church of Rome and other Non-Reformed faiths, and scrupulously avoid countenancing (by his presence or otherwise) any act or ceremony of Roman Catholic or other Non-Reformed Worship . . .'

Qualifications of an Orangeman,
Royal York Loyal Orange Lodge no. 145, Belfast

Two evenings later Clayton steepled his long fingers, thinking about how to respond to the earnest young face opposite. Robert was leaning forward, his hands clasped between his knees.

'We cannot be literal about what we read in the scriptures, Robert. We can only seek to understand.' He saw his listener's brows pull together. 'Even the book of Genesis contradicts itself, in the very first chapter. Men can use the Bible to find an argument for and against everything, and they do – often for some pretty ungodly reasons. But as Corinthians has it, "We see now through a glass in a dark manner but then face to face. Now I know in part, but then shall I know even as I am known." Don't look so surprised, Robert. Believe it or not, we do read the same book – even if not in the same translation.'

'But who are *we* to decide what we believe or don't? If it's in there, should we not do what scripture tell us?'

'If we did that, Robert, then there'd be weekly stonings for adultery in every public square from here to Penzance.'

Robert winced.

'We all follow some of it, of course, whatever our denomination. It's right that there should be a day of rest, that you shouldn't be forced down the pit on a Sunday because it would suit your employer that you were. But not that you couldn't light a candle or ride your bicycle because it's the Sabbath. The Jews can't do those things, I believe, or not the Orthodox ones at least.'

'There's plenty *yous* are not let to do,' said Robert. 'Even if St Peter had a wife.'

'Is what you mean by that, why do priests not marry?'

'Aye.'

'It's a good question, Robert. I expect it's to do with property. The Church has enough mouths to feed without adding more of its own.'

'So what made *you* do it?'

'When I could have been running a greengrocer's shop in Nottingham, with a kind wife preparing my evening meal instead of me being at the mercy of Mrs Kennedy?'

Robert laughed, and the atmosphere in the parlour lightened.

'I felt it was part of God's plan for me – I still do. As there must be a plan for you, and Annie, and any children you may have.'

'It mightn't be a Catholic plan.'

'Perhaps not,' said Clayton mildly. 'But there's a plan nevertheless. This is what men in their arrogance forget. There's a nun in America, a very good woman no doubt, who works tirelessly to educate orphans and the children of the poor. But she lets no illegitimate children into her school, they say, because she doesn't want to encourage people to have them in the first place.'

'So she punishes the children,' said Robert hoarsely.

'My point. What she does in my view thwarts God's plan – *He intended those children to be born*. As you say, Robert, there mightn't be a Catholic plan for you. My colleagues would take issue with me for that, and want me to hustle you into the Church at all costs, with threats and promises. I'd rather you walked in because you wanted to, whether that's next week or when you're a seasoned man of fifty, though I'm quite sure that if my superiors knew it I'd never be made a bishop. You can talk to me about any of this. But Father Hagerty has to think I am instructing you.'

'And if I won't be instructed? Can I not marry Annie?'

'You can, but it would be quietly, without fuss. As I said before, at a side-altar, without candles or incense or an organ. I'd be wearing a plain white tunic.'

There was a pause before Robert said seriously, 'That's how I'd like it, so I would. A bit more Protestant.' To his surprise, Clayton threw his head back and laughed, and went on laughing until he had to pull out a handkerchief and wipe his eyes. Robert stared at him in astonishment.

'Oh . . . dear . . . oh! Forgive me. That is marvellous, Robert. All those restrictions are designed as a sort of punishment, you know. Yet here they are having quite the opposite effect. Whatever we talk about within these four walls, I would be honoured to marry you and Annie.'

*

'I tried to see would she take soup,' began Robert, sitting in the same chair, in the same room a week later.

'Take soup? I'm not with you,' said Clayton.

'Would she turn, I mean. It's from the Famine time. There was soup kitchens organised, only you'd to become a Protestant to get any.'

'Good God!'

'I thought when they told me that – I was in the school, so I was – that there'd got to be something wrong with you if you'd refuse. I was always hungry, you see . . . until the last place I was in. I thought how feart them starving people musta been, about hellfire and all. Even at the cost of your life. I mean, you've that oath you've to swear to the pope of Rome—'

'What oath?'

'The one that puts the pope above all things. Above the King and Queen even. Above country. So that the Church of Rome will work to dominate the world . . .' He tailed off. '*You* know.'

'I took a vow of obedience, to my abbot, my bishop, and yes, ultimately to the Holy Father. Along with others. To not have worldly goods – in effect to have to eat whatever Mrs Kennedy puts in front of me and be grateful for it. To not have a family as I'd put those children above the people who call me Father.'

'You've the nuns, haven't you?' said Robert, without thinking.

'*What?*'

Robert shifted in his chair. 'I didn't mean to say it like that, so I didn't. Only they've them tract things – I found them in the Lodge and took them for to have something to read. They said that the nuns in the convents were there – you know . . .'

'I do *not* know,' said Clayton, aghast.

'Well, for to do the bidding of the priests.' His face was aflame.

'I really . . . oh dear God! The ones I see the most of are the Selly Park nuns in Whitehaven – all I can tell you is that they are teachers. The idea that any of those women were . . . a harem for myself and Father Hagerty is . . . well, it's preposterous. You can't believe that, surely?'

Robert looked at the thin, upright figure, his austere face pale with shock.

'No,' he said slowly. 'No, I can't believe it.' He saw the priest exhale, his shoulders relax.

'I think,' said Clayton at last, 'that we have strayed a little from our argument. You said you tried to get Annie to "take soup". Did she pick up her spoon?'

Robert laughed then. Clayton thought it an attractive sound, unexpected in one so serious, but the young man's good humour was gone as quickly as it came.

'She did not, no.'

'As a priest I ought to be pleased. But this narrows your choices. I should not say this, but you could go to Whitehaven, of course, and marry before the registrar. You are of age, are you not?'

'I believe I am. Annie isn't. But she's her da's permission whatever she wants to do, he says.'

'She'd need it however or wherever she weds in England. And for us, I'm afraid, the Whitehaven registrar would be as bad as if she'd "taken soup" and been married before a Protestant minister. The Holy Father is very clear about this – some would say inflexible. Either way, Annie ceases to be a Catholic. She is barred from the sacraments – meaning she cannot go to communion, or to confession—'

'Would yous come to her if she was dying?' interrupted Robert.

Clayton paused. '*I* would. I would go to any soul in their hour of need, if they wanted me. I wouldn't care what flag they marched behind.' He leaned forward. 'Robert – may I call you Robert?'

Robert nodded.

'I won't talk to you about her immortal soul, mainly because I don't believe that heaven contains only Catholics. I can only tell you that you would be separating Annie from everything she has known since she was a little girl. Her mother died. She believed her father let her down, even if that particular bridge has been repaired. She lost her best friend not long ago and was unkindly treated by that friend's mother – motivated by jealousy, perhaps. You know all this, I'm sure. Can you not see that her unchanging faith in an unpredictable world might give her comfort?'

'I . . .' Robert cleared his throat. '*I can give her comfort too,* so I can.'

'Yet she won't pick up her soup spoon for you.' Clayton regretted those words as soon as he'd said them. The young man looked to him as winded as if he'd just punched him in the gut.

'I'm sorry, I—'

'No. No you're not. You've got to say them things. You swore thon oath. And I know what you're not telling me – or not yet. If we have babbies they've to be taigs too.'

'I—'

'Wait, now.' Robert's voice rose, but Clayton had the distinct impression he was fighting tears. 'None o' them that come to mass ever talk back to you, do they? But *I* can. I'm not bound by your rules even if I do what you tell me I've to do and stand and swear by your idolatrous altars for to have by me *my* wife.'

'Mr McClure – Robert—'

But Robert was already standing, pulling on his cap.

'Good evening, Father.'

Clayton followed him to the door, but Robert didn't turn round.

'I can let myself out, so I can.'

The priest watched the obstinate hunch of the boy's shoulders as he marched off into the near dark. *That's the loneliest soul I've ever met – or he was until he met her.* Only when Robert was out of sight did Clayton close the door and lean on it. *That ordure he's been reading.* He remembered the last mass he'd said for the nuns in Whitehaven, and the tea and scones they'd laid on for him afterwards. *The idea that those women could be my personal*

seraglio – it would be laughable if it were not so tragic. Nevertheless, when he listed the Sisters in his prayers that night he was
momentarily distracted by the question of whether any one of
those pale wimpled faces had ever betrayed any interest in him as
a man, not as a priest. He put the notion hurriedly by. *Sins beget
sins*, he thought, wondering what other poison that young man
had taken only because he'd wanted something to read.

*

Annie was a mere hundred yards away from her new lodgings when she heard her name called. She turned round to see
a girl she was pretty sure she'd never clapped eyes on before,
but Annie wasn't surprised the stranger knew her name. *Sure,
doesn't everyone know everyone else in this place?* The young
woman was dressed pretty much as herself, shawled like most of
the mill girls, brown hair piled in an untidy bun atop her head.
Ainsworth's was a big enough place so Annie assumed the girl
was new.

'I'm Annie Maguire, yes.' The faint narrowing of the stranger's eyes and her humourless smile disconcerted her.

'You'll be the one that's wanting to marry Robert McClure?'

Annie hesitated. 'We *are* going to be married, yes, but who's
yourself?'

'Call me a well-wisher, Annie. I've known Robbie for years,
so I have. Met him on the boat over.'

Annie frowned. *How've I never seen you, and you here all
this time?*

'Had relations, have yous?'

Annie gasped. 'That's nobody's business, so it isn't,' she retorted.

'By the look of you, I'd say not,' said the girl insolently. Then she slowly unfolded her shawl and, without taking her eyes from Annie's face, turned sideways, revealing the swell of her stomach.

Annie felt a tightening in the hollow of her neck and a sensation of dizziness, as though the ground beneath her feet was shifting.

'No . . .'

'Wee Robbie McClure from Crossgar. Mammy in the kitchens at the Big House. His da the land agent. Told you they'd put him out of the Lodge for you, did he?'

Annie tried to speak but her lips felt stiff and cold.

'Made you feel sorry for him, didn't he? It's the quiet ones you've to watch, Annie. Like father, like son.'

Annie turned and fled, her mouth opening in a terrible silent rictus of pain. She fumbled at the lock of the house in Dawson Street, got inside at last and tore up the stairs to her room, pulling her grip out from under the bed to stuff it with her belongings, this time with as little care as Philomena had shown that day she'd thrown Annie out. Great sobs escaped her as she worked. With the remnants of self-control she had left, she forced herself not to look around the room, the one she had been going to share with Robert once they were married. At last she was done, and wrapping her shawl high around her, so that her face was partially concealed, she bumped her grip down the stairs. Lucy Concannon, the landlady's daughter, appeared from the back kitchen, wiping her hands on her apron.

'Annie?'

Annie didn't look round. All Lucy heard was a thin wail like a child's, the word 'Sorry,' and the newest lodger shut the front door behind her.

*

Mrs Kennedy grumbled as she went to answer the knock at the Priory House door. *They always turn up when I'm trying to get Father his tea.*

Her eyes narrowed as she looked at the girl trembling on the doorstep. *It's all ended in tears, I see. I coulda told her it would.*

'Father Clayton?' was all the visitor could get out.

'Come away in,' said Mrs Kennedy, standing to one side. 'But it's Father Hagerty you'll have to make do with. Father Clayton's in Whitehaven, so he is.'

CHAPTER FORTY

St Mary's Penitents, Carlisle, March 1904

'Mercy is more than Charity, for it not only bestows benefits, but it receives and pardons again and again, even the ungrateful.'

Catherine McAulay (1778–1841),
foundress of the Sisters of Mercy

'I don't believe it,' repeated Father Clayton over the breakfast clutter.

'If you'd'a seen the girl last night, after streeling over here with all her worldly goods in a bag, crying out for sanctuary, you'd'a believed it all right,' said Hagerty.

'So she's gone to the nuns after all?'

'Begged to go. Said she couldn't face Barrow or anyone she knew. Her father's fancy piece encouraged her over the Proddy, apparently. I sent Galvin with her on the last train.'

'I'll go and see McClure,' said Clayton.

'Have sense, man! The only thing you could do is convince him to marry the girl he's got into trouble, but him and that one are none of our business. We'll not hear of Annie Maguire again. She wrote a wee note to go to the mill, that's all.'

*

Clayton refused Mr Spedding's offer of tea. 'I only need a brief word with Mr McClure, that's all.'

'Is Annie all right?' asked Robert the moment he came into the room.

Clayton felt like retorting, 'Not from what I hear, McClure,' but bit back his words at the look on Robert's face. *He's either an accomplished actor, or I was right.*

'Sit down, Robert,' he said gently.

'Is she ill?'

'I don't believe so. Unhappy, but not ill. Do please sit down.' As calmly as he could, the priest recounted to Robert as accurately as he could what he had been told of the events of the previous evening, though he had to remind the young man repeatedly to let him finish the whole story 'or I might miss some details. I am only sorry I was not there myself.'

'I swear on whatever Bible you put under my hand, sir, that I have no idea who that woman is. This is . . . unbelievable.' Robert swallowed, his fingers entangled so tightly that Clayton saw the gleam of knuckle-bone even through the miner's reddened skin. 'Her child can't be mine . . . you see, I've never had a woman.' Then to Clayton's consternation, Robert covered his face with his hands and sobbed.

'Robert,' whispered the priest. 'Robert, listen to me. I have an idea. It has some risks – more perhaps to myself than to you.

But please understand that I want to help you. You will need to be patient. A few more days. Perhaps the biggest challenge will be yours. When you see Annie you must convince her as you have just convinced me.' He reached over and squeezed the young man's shoulder.

*

Ten days later, on a Saturday evening, Robert paced outside the address he'd been given. It had taken him a while to find, for he'd never been anywhere so big as Carlisle, and had got himself an odd look from one of the people he'd asked directions of. Someone else had said, 'You mean the old workhouse.' St Mary's Penitents was at the edge of the town, as though it wanted to hide from respectable people. The place looked nothing like the convents he'd seen in Ireland. There was no high wall, though there was a locked gate giving onto a courtyard. As he'd been instructed, he walked round the corner into Burgh Road. Here the walls were high, with broken glass atop. He found a door, as he had been told he would, and gently rattled the handle, though he knew already it would be locked. He counted the chimes of a distant church bell. Eight o'clock and almost dark. He was on time then. He shivered, and turned up his collar. As he did so the door opened and a surprisingly strong hand grasped his upper arm – and pulled.

'Quiet, so!' whispered a woman's voice, though he'd said nothing.

In the dusk, he made out a pale oval of a face, beneath the gleam of a white coif. The remainder of her was eclipsed by a dark veil and habit; she stood out in the shadows against a backdrop of bedsheets hanging on rows of lines, blocking most of the yellow light from the upper windows of the convent. It occurred to Robert that he had never been this close to a nun before. *But you've hardly been near many women, so you haven't.*

The grip on his arm tightened for a moment as the nun hissed: 'What name is it you have?'

'Robert McClure.'

The nun peered at him for a moment. 'Hard to see you in this light. Ah yes, it's yourself. I only had a glimpse of you that time.' His arm was released. 'Right, so. I wasn't wanting to give Annie to the wrong fella. Her things are in that outhouse there. She doesn't know I've put them there, mind. She doesn't know you're here, even. My word, if I'd'a known this was what I was in for, I'd'a gone for to be a wardress in Dundalk Gaol, so I would.'

'What'll I do, miss?' he whispered.

He saw her eyes glitter. '*Do*, is it? You've to take her out that back door and then run, the pair of yous. That's if she'll come with you. I've been warning 'em in there that the lock was dicky, so I have. They don't know it's because I made it so.'

'*You* did?'

'There's no wonder in that, so there's not. I grew up on a farm. I can fix a plough and shoe a horse, so an oul' door's no problem.'

And with a flap of a sheet, she was gone.

In a dream, Robert moved behind the lines of sheets to the outhouse, looked inside, and found Annie's grip. He had to stop himself opening it and burying his face in the scent of her clothes.

A door opened and shut somewhere the other side of the washing lines. Robert stood absolutely still, almost afraid to breathe, listening to the flap of sheets, the clop-clop of wooden clothes pegs being pulled off and thrown into a basket.

The footsteps came closer, and fingers groped for pegs above the sheet he stood behind.

'Annie,' he whispered. The fingers stilled. He heard what sounded like a stifled scream, and pushed aside the sheet.

'Honest to God, Annie, it's not true. None of it's true!'

She was his Annie, but also not. Even in the gloom he could see that she was thinner, her face older, though not even two weeks had passed since he'd seen her last. The dull dress he didn't recognise, but its shapeless form recalled to him the man who'd spoken of the old workhouse and the nun's mutterings that she might as well have gone to be a prison wardress.

'How could you, Robbie?' she said, before her face crumpled.

'I didn't. I didn't . . . the first I knew of that girl was when Father Clayton came to tell me. Annie . . . we'll need to go or that nun'll be in trouble, never mind us. I'll not say I can explain everything because I can't explain none of it, so I can't.'

A door opened then and a shaft of yellow light streamed across the yard. 'Maguire? Haven't you those sheets down? *Maguire!*'

'*Now!*'

Robert grabbed her hand and lifted the grip.

*

They were winded by the time they reached the Carr's factory on Caldewgate. Annie said, gasping for breath, 'We'd best walk now. We don't want to be drawing attention to ourselves.'

Robert's heart leaped at that word 'ourselves.' She wasn't just running away from the nuns, then, she wanted to run away with him. As soon as his lungs calmed down, he began pleading his case, until at last she put a hand on his arm to stop him.

'I believe you, Robbie. I'm only sorry I didn't before.'

'I was afraid you wouldn't come away with me. Why did you, Annie?'

She looked down. 'Because I kept asking myself how it was I coulda been so wrong about you. I remembered what Elsie said about you – even though she's never met you. How you were with my da too . . . And because when I was in that place, all of us in that long room with just curtains between the beds, listening to them poor girls crying in the dark, I just couldn't imagine what life would be like without you. I'd run off to the nuns without giving you a chance to speak for yourself.'

'I swear to you again that I've no idea who the girl is,' he said. 'I don't know who'd have thought to send her.'

'Whoever it was, thought he'd right on his side,' she said. 'Whether he was in the Lodge or was Father Hagerty himself.'

'Not Hagerty,' said Robert slowly. 'From what Clayton told me you'd said about her, she knew too much about me, things Hagerty didn't know. But never mind me, Annie – what was it like back there with them nuns?'

'Oh ... it could have been worse. It was somewhere when I thought I'd nowhere to go. Sister Joseph was kinder than the others – but I never knew she was going to help me, and I couldna understand why she was sending me out for to get the sheets when it was another girl's turn.'

'It was all Father Clayton's doing.'

'God bless him.'

'But we're not to mention it. Not ever.'

'All right.' She took his arm and nestled into his side. He felt proud, now wanting the people in the streets to notice her with him. There were some glances, until he realised that it was her uniform-like dress they were staring at.

'Let's see is your shawl in that bag,' he said. It was; he wrapped it around her shoulders. 'That's better. You look more like you now.'

'I feel more like me too,' she said.

'They weren't trying to make a nun of you in there, were they?'

'They weren't, no, but there was some comfort in going to mass every day,' Annie said, 'only that when the priest put the host away in the tabernacle and turned the key I thought, "I'm locked in too."'

Not knowing what she'd meant by the tabernacle, Robert imagined some kind of punishment cell and shivered.

'It was work, though. I've muscles already from pounding away at that dolly-tub. But it was the sadness of the place,

Robbie. One girl said she'd been in service until the master forced himself on her and the mistress turned her out without a character. Others just had broken hearts. Some were going to have babies.'

*

By the time they reached the station there were no more trains to Moor Row. Robert's heart sank when peering at the timetable he saw there'd be none on Sunday either. They collapsed onto a bench outside the locked waiting room. He wanted to sit closer to her but didn't know if he dared.

'I could see about a room somewhere round here,' he said tentatively. 'At least for yourself.'

'No.' She put her hand over his. 'We can sit it out here and at first light see can we not get a lift on the road.'

*

The night grew progressively colder. Annie slept fitfully, her head on Robert's lap while he kept a protective arm around her. At first light they unfurled themselves, Robert stamping his feet to restore his circulation. The journey home took ten hours, but they were grateful for the three carts that stopped for them.

'Farmers don't have a day off,' said Robert, as he helped Annie down from their first lift. 'There's no Sunday for them.'

'I remember,' said Annie.

CHAPTER FORTY-ONE

'And there was a man of the Pharisees, named Nicodemus,
a ruler of the Jews. This man came to Jesus by night . . .'

John, 3: 1–2

To Robert's relief, Father Clayton answered the door of the
Priory House himself.

'Let's go in the kitchen this evening,' said Clayton, opening a
door at the end of the dark hall. 'Mrs Kennedy is at her sister's in
Frizington and Father Hagerty has a meeting in Lancaster. It'll
be a sight warmer in there too.'

Robert glanced around the room, taking in the range, the
chromolithograph of a square-faced, unsmiling Pius X, Mrs
Kennedy's polished copper pots and a row of six bells fixed
above the door into the scullery. Apart from the coloured print,
the kitchen was a smaller version of the one his mother laboured
in at the Big House and Robert felt a faint pull of what he recognised as homesickness, something he'd only ever felt before for
Kathleen's little house.

Clayton pulled out a chair and indicated the one opposite.

'I just wanted to thank you, Father, and ask you would you
marry us as soon as you can, the way you said, the simple way.

I can't turn, you see. I've thought long and hard about it, and I respect Annie – and you – too much to just go along pretending I believe in what you believe in, when I can't. You see, I know it because I'll be breaking a solemn oath as it is.' Robert opened his hands. 'To the Lodge, I mean. There was men there would help you in times of trouble – though not the trouble I've got myself into. I'm saying that even though I'm nearly certain sure it's one of them put that girl up to speaking to Annie.'

'After you're married would you be happy lodging at the Concannons, though? They're all Catholics there, you know.'

'It's a better house for the little I've seen of it than Mr Spedding's, with all due respect to a fine man and all we had there was the attic. Wherever we live we're going to be neither one thing nor the other. So I'd thole it, so I would. Annie says they're good people and were pleased to have her back. But won't Father Hagerty have something to say about it?'

'He already has, believe me – mainly telling me off for interfering. But I'm forgetting the rules of hospitality. I've not even put the water to boil.'

*

Crossfield Road
Cleator Moor
23rd March 1904

Dear Mammy,

I am to be married the first Saturday after Easter. I hope this is not too much of a surprise as I wrote you to say I wanted to ask the girl I love would she marry me and there are all manner of reasons why we are doing this quickly but not the one you might think.

Robert nearly wrote 'She's a decent girl and I swear I've never taken liberties with her' then remembered who he was writing to.

My intended's name, or my wife if you get this after 9th April, is Annie Maguire who works in the flax mill and she's from Moneyscalp Townland, her da was a farmer there only now he is in the shipyard in Barrow. It will just be a quiet ceremony with only the witnesses.

Robert paused, rereading those last words. There was enough there, he knew, for his mother to realise what Annie was, but she'd see that he wasn't 'turning' even if he was marrying out.

I hope I will be able to bring her to see you one day. I am not sure will we stay in Cleator Moor as we have both had some trouble. I have not wrote Mr Cairncross but I am sure he will know soon enough even if you do not say to him yourself.

I hope you will be pleased for me. I never thought I could be so fortunate.

Your loving son,

Robert

*

'Are you ready, me 'andsome?' said Trescatherick, and Robert realised from his slip into a Cornish way of speaking that his friend was nervous too. He found this oddly reassuring.

'Ready,' he said, and Trescatherick pushed open the door of the church. By the holy water stoup they paused.

'They said a side-altar,' whispered Robert, scanning the church. It was a shock to see so much colour and grandeur, used as he was to the stripped-bare Presbyterian interiors where no distractions to the minister's words were permitted. He had to admit that the marble altar where a little red light trembled was pretty, but the plaster statues with their bland faces made his skin creep.

'You look as if you've never been in here before,' said Trescatherick.

'I haven't.'

Before the Cornishman could reply, a figure emerged from behind one of the sturdy columns. Clayton, in his long, plain alb, shook hands first with Robert and then with his witness. 'Mrs Birkett is already here,' he said, smiling. 'All we need now is a bride.'

All three turned when the door swung open, but it was Mr Spedding who came in.

'Hoo'doo, Reverend?' he said to Clayton, and nodded at his two tenants.

Then at last Annie was there, right on the moment the clock struck the hour she was to be married. Robert guessed she must have been hiding amongst the yews in the burial ground rather than come in too early. He felt a great surge of tenderness for her, seeing her walk in alone. He recognised the blouse he'd given her but she wore a brooch he hadn't seen before and had her hair piled up and pinned high on her head. He wasn't going to tell her he preferred its glossy blackness when it hung down her back, with two sidewings tied behind with a ribbon. Then the thought that come the night he could ask her, as her husband, to unpin it and let it fall, that he could put his hands and face into it as he lay on a pillow beside her, made him nearly tremble.

He felt anger too. Of the little group who awaited her, not one, besides the priest, was a Catholic. On the Sundays on which the banns had been called in the building they now stood in, he knew she had trudged instead to Frizington again rather than face stares and gossip – and Philomena. Robert checked again the small roll of notes in his inside pocket. This was her day and his; he intended to ask all of this little party to tea and cakes in the Commercial Hotel afterwards.

'Well, if everyone's ready,' said Clayton, rubbing his hands together. 'It'll just take a few minutes, then some signatures in the sacristy, and you'll be man and wife.'

Obediently, the little group followed him to the side-altar. Clayton turned towards their mute faces. 'Before we celebrate this marriage, I would just like to impress on all present that though this is a quiet occasion, it is as valid as any celebrated with the mass and music before two hundred witnesses. The promises they are about to make to each other, before God and yourselves, will bind Robert and Annie together for life and—' He stopped, as someone else had come in and was moving swiftly towards them on squeaking Sunday shoes.

'Mr Nolan!' cried Annie.

'Am I too late?' said Michael breathlessly, looking from Annie to the priest, and brandishing a small posy.

'No—' said Clayton.

'Well, would you come with me back to the door a wee minute, Annie?'

'I—'

'Please. It's what I'd'a wanted for Teresa. Just to walk you up. I've brought her mantilla, so I have. With that over your hair and them wee flowers . . .'

Annie looked at Father Clayton, who nodded his acceptance.

'It's an honour you'd do me.' She followed Michael down the nave to the entrance, where both of them blessed themselves from the stoup. The others watched them in silence, but as Michael and Annie stood to attention and he murmured something to her, patting the hand she'd put through his arm, the priest muttered, 'They deserved an organ voluntary.' What Father Hagerty had called a 'hole-in-corner' marriage, with no music, no hymns, no flowers, no communion and himself in a plain white alb instead of the usual priestly splendour – all designed to reinforce the message of the Church's disapproval – was before Clayton's eyes turning into a union truly blessed. Against all that his upbringing and formation had taught him, he felt that this young man and woman, who the world said should not be together, were made for each other. All those people who on Sundays entered St Mary's, St John's, the Presbyterian church on the high street, the ugly little Primitive Methodist chapel – were all one, with the dogma, the hate, the divisions, the 'I can see it in your eyes' stripped away.

Michael and Annie were proceeding up the nave as proudly as though the church was filled with well-wishers. Now they turned into the gap between the pews, towards the little group waiting at the side-altar. Father Clayton took hold of the end of the silk marker in the book in his hand and the thin pages sighed softly open.

Robert kept his eyes on Annie's face throughout, though she didn't return his gaze. A tendril of black hair had unlooped from the knot on the top of her head; he loved its dark contrast with the edge of the frail white lace of Teresa's mantilla and longed to touch it, reminding himself that this and all of her, and all of him, would in a few short hours from now be given to each other. He knew in that moment exactly what Clayton had meant when he said they would be marrying each other. This was no longer about Bawden's red face or Hagerty's trap leaving Annie in the drizzle. He heard his own voice as though from a distance, promising to forsake all others; the idea struck him as absurd. *Who'd be wanting anyone else if they could have Annie?*

Then he heard Clayton giving him an instruction. He bent his head obediently and kissed Annie's soft closed mouth. Without thinking he pulled her into his arms. Someone in the little group sniffed tears – he thought it must be Mrs Birkett. A male voice let out a soft 'Oh . . .' And then the others were around them, patting his shoulder, reaching to shake his hand. Annie was engulfed in Mrs Birkett's maternal hug.

'I just need you two and the witnesses in the sacristy for a moment,' said Father Clayton.

A book was pushed towards him across a polished tabletop, a pen held out to him. He heard Annie ask, 'Which name shall I put?' and thought, *I am a husband. My children will have my name.*

'One more thing,' said Clayton. 'Come and find me some quiet Saturday afternoon. I should like to give you both a blessing at the high altar. Only I'd appreciate it if you didn't say anything to Father Hagerty.'

*

Outside the Commercial Hotel an hour later Robert wrung Jem Spedding's hand. 'I cannot thank you enough, sir.'

'I'm only sorry I hadn't a room free for you both,' he said. 'But your wife deserves better than a lumber room.'

'The lumber room was a roof over my head when I had none,' said Annie. 'For that I'll be grateful to you forever.'

*

Robert followed Annie up the stairs of the house in Dawson Street with his heart thudding. It was hard for him to believe he was in the same house where he and Thomas had had to sit in the dining room while Annie was fetched, as though she was a nun conceded an annual visit from her male relatives. Now he was to live here in a strange symmetry of Annie's arrival at Spedding's house. She'd been the only Catholic in a Protestant household. Now he was the only Protestant in a Catholic one.

He felt as though he had eyes boring into his back even though they were now alone. Mrs Concannon had been nothing but polite and had served him the fourth cup of tea of his day at the kitchen table. One by one the other lodgers had come in to congratulate Annie and to openly inspect her new husband. Robert had read in the newspaper about a freak-show booth at Carlisle Easter Fair and shuddered at the thought of the poor creatures having their oddities real or feigned exhibited to gawpers for a halfpenny. Did they see him, he wondered, as Annie's pet Protestant – or their own? Having spent most of his life either being ignored by others or doing his best to be ignored, the sensation of being the object of someone's curious attention wasn't pleasant to him. *Hetty Concannon's a nice enough woman though, even if she is the Priory House's spy.*

Now, as Robert stood at Annie's shoulder at the door of the room where their sacrament of marriage would be consummated, he felt a shiver of anxiety. He recalled to mind John Trescatherick's wise counsel, when he'd gone to him timorously and asked his advice, relieved for once that the reddish tinge to his skin from the iron ore disguised his blushing. The Cornishman had smiled kindly and told him not to worry: 'Just be kind and patient with each other and you'll both of you be fine. If it wasn't so, none of us would ever be born.' John had also gone on as plainly as he could to explain some of the mechanics.

'Kind and patient,' mouthed Robert, as Annie opened the door and he was confronted with a high iron-framed bed, with two pillows propped against the bolster.

*

The morning after when Robert came back from the privy, it was to find Annie sitting on the bed in a white crackle of starched chemise and drawers, holding a wet cloth, rubbing salt into a mark on the sheet. He sat down beside her and put his arm around her.

'Will you go to Frizington again today?'

'Yes,' she said, hesitating. 'If that's all right?'

'You don't have to ask my permission, you know. I'll walk with you. I'll wait for you.'

'Robbie . . .'

'You see, neither of us has to be alone now. That's what this means too.'

She rested her head against his shoulder.

'I thought there'd be the makings of breakfast downstairs, but there's nobody in.'

'They'll have gone to early mass, so they will. You can't eat before the sacrament, you know.'

'I *didn't*. We'll be as hungry as wolves after Frizington, then.'

'*You* can eat, Robbie.'

'No. We're husband and wife. We'll eat together afterwards.'

*

On Monday morning, Robert trudged with the other men in the early light to Crowgarth pit. His English workmates came quietly to congratulate him. The men he had known in the Lodge turned away, a shunning which made him feel as he had when the other children in the National School had not wanted to play with him, the nameless, farmed-out child. Their rejection chilled him, but he dismissed it, warming himself on the thought of Annie, feeling her presence still, all the length of his body, as he replayed in his thoughts the events of the last two nights.

He wielded his pick and filled his cart in a daze, his calloused fingertips marvelling at the memory of the silky skin below the slim cage of Annie's ribs. There'd been that difficult moment when he'd felt her tense and he was afraid to go on, though he so desperately, urgently wanted to do so. He'd opened his eyes to look down on her, afraid despite John's reassurance that he was doing something wrong. The pain in her eyes had been unmistakable, but she'd smiled up at him and said, 'It's all right, Robbie, honest to God,' and he'd felt the gentle pressure of the pads of her fingers on the skin of his back so he'd tried again; she gave a tiny sharp cry, and something gave. It was marvellous, what he felt, but it was over so quickly, his face buried in her shoulder.

'My husband,' he heard her murmur. He'd lifted his head then to kiss her and to his surprise and delight found his body prompting him to repeat what he had thought was finished. He was afraid of hurting her, though, afraid of what that wet was, for there seemed to be so much of it, as if he'd torn her apart, but then she murmured, 'Robbie, Robbie.' One hand came to rest on his buttocks, the fingertips of the other traced the links of his spine.

'I love you,' he said afterwards. 'I never dreamed I'd get you, so I didn't. I never thought I'd get to tell any girl I loved her, let alone one like you.'

*

It was three months later when Robert awoke to the gulping, anguished sounds of Annie being sick into the basin they washed in. He scrambled out of bed, and held back her hair as she grasped the edges of the washstand. It was early, with all the bright promise of a summer day to come, though the best of it would have gone by the time he came back up to the surface that evening. He put his jacket over his shoulders and pushed his bare feet into his boots, and took the basin downstairs to the outside tap. Mrs Concannon was already up. She opened the back door for him with no more than a knowing smile, but when he came back in said, 'Congratulations, Mr McClure. I was wondering when you'd find out.'

'You *knew?*'

'Sure I did. Maybe before she did. Her face is all soft round the edges. It'll be grand to have a babby in the house, so it will. I know just the midwife. I've helped her often enough.' The woman beamed at him indulgently, but all he could manage was a stammered 'Thank you.'

That was the day the foreman told him as he came off his shift that his services would probably not be required beyond the end of the year. The man, an Englishman, wouldn't look him in the eyes.

'I just don't want trouble, lad. Tek it as a warning, like. Give you time to find summat else.'

Robert tramped home looking at the ground. This was something else he wouldn't tell Annie, same as he hadn't told her when he'd found the sandwiches she had made for him strewn on the ground that time, or when he'd gone for his pick and it had been moved. Only John Trescatherick knew those things, and he'd counselled patience. But the foreman's words meant patience wasn't enough.

CHAPTER FORTY-TWO

Crowgarth Pit, 11th July 1904

'... for seck a stiff-necked generation o' vipers as theer is on Cleator Moor it wadden't be possable to fin' any spot else.'

Thomas Thompson, *The Hidden Witness: a Tale of Cleator Moor*, 1872

Annie looked up at the clock again. Half an hour late. Everyone else had eaten and left, not wanting to meet her eye. She'd helped Mrs Concannon wash up, performing familiar tasks automatically.

'We'll have another brew, so,' said Mrs Concannon. 'He'll be back in a minute saying he's sorry only the foreman had to have a word. It'll be a promotion, most likely.'

Annie shook her head. She had heard all the stories, though nothing had happened (she crossed herself again) in the time she had been in Cleator Moor. Choke damp. The gas that crept in silently and scentless, overwhelming the strongest men without warning, before they were even able to call for help or utter a prayer. The bodies were brought out unmarked, for wives and mothers to wash and weep over for the last time, perfect in everything but life. Then new tunnels were dug too close to old workings, their location inadequately recorded, to fulfil the insatiable demand for iron ore. Annie barely noticed now the subterranean sounds of drilling below every house she had lived in since coming to England. Forgotten passages beneath linoleum-floored kitchens filled inexorably with icy water, soaking into the shale, pushing against the too thin divisions until stones and props creaked and shifted and the dam burst. Annie's early visions of hell, planted in her young brain by a visiting priest who had flecked the cowering congregation with spittle in his enthusiasm, was one of a fiery furnace, stoked not with coal but with the writhing bodies of wretched sinners. Every time she heard bacon fat hissing and crackling in the pan she thought of that preacher's sweating contorted face, shouting about the splitting of skin and the melting of eyeballs in that lake of fire and sulphur. Could there not be another hell, though, one of an implacable rush of water in the darkness, with nowhere else for it to go but to fill the last space where thrashing men fought for air? With a cry, Annie sat down, clutching at her heart, feeling the breath leave her own lungs.

'Oh God love you!' muttered Mrs Concannon. 'Have a care for your child!' She went to replenish the water bubbling in the kettle above the fire, averting her face from the hiss of steam. It was then that the two women heard the first shout. Annie got up, unable to keep still. More cries, closer now, and running feet.

'Mother of God,' she whispered. She heard the click of the back gate, and nailed boots heavy on the paving. Annie rushed to the scullery door, opening it before Michael Nolan could knock.

'No!' she cried at the sight of his white face.

Michael grasped her shoulders. 'He's alive, Annie, but he's bad.'

She made as if to get past him. 'Where?'

'They've taken him to the infirmary in Whitehaven. He's breathing, but he's not conscious. His legs ... they're a bit smashed, they said. The other man got the worst of it. I've got Brennan coming with his cart.'

'Go through the front so's you'll see Brennan coming,' Mrs Concannon told them. Annie was already wrapping herself in her shawl. Then she instinctively put a hand out to Michael. He took it; it was numbly cold. He chafed it in his own large hands, and then did the same to the other.

'Are you well enough for the journey?' he asked gently.

'I am so.'

*

The street was murmuring, the neighbours out on their doorsteps. Annie saw them fall silent one by one, their faces turned towards her and Michael. With a shiver she was reminded of people gathered around a church door at a funeral, and the way voices were extinguished the moment the coffin was carried out.

The rattle of Brennan's approaching cart reminded her of where she was and why.

'Heard any more?' asked Michael.

'No more than yourself,' said Brennan. 'We'll take Mr Ainsworth's carriage path, so we will, for to be quicker.'

'Isn't that trespassing?' said Annie.

Brennan shrugged. 'If we meet the bailiff, we'll tell him why.'

Sitting opposite Michael, the brass rail of the cart cold against her back, Annie's hands grasped the edge of the studded leather seat until her knuckles whitened.

'Robert's tough, so he is,' he said. 'The foreman thinks he must have seen there was a stone loose, in the roof of the tunnel. He'd a prop lying by him when they got him out from under the shale, a fresh cut one. They think he must have gone for it, and not made it back in time. But if he'd'a been a moment earlier, then the whole lot woulda come down on his head and he'd be as lost as the other man. The size of the thing was that you'd not survive it. The poor fellow was with him woulda been gone in a moment – no time to cry out to his God. They'll be breaking that rock now for to bring him out.'

'Who was it?' whispered Annie, though she knew.

'The witness when you were wed. The Cornishman.'

'John Trescatherick,' murmured Annie.

'God rest him.'

'Poor John,' said Annie, at last starting to cry. 'He'd 'a sent Robert for the prop. Could he have not gone with him?'

'It musta happened too quickly.'

'Of course,' Annie said bitterly. *You know not the day nor the hour.*

'Them other stones woulda come after the big one, not big enough to kill except if they got you on the head, but big enough to break bones. Robert woulda hit his head on one when he went down, or it hit him, and that was him out cold. I don't suppose he'll remember to be able to tell us.'

'Who told you all this?'

'I was at the surface when the cry went up.' Michael paused. 'I was there when they brought him out. You could see he was pale even under the reddening, and blood on his forehead, but breathing. They kept shouting, "He's alive, he's alive," maybe so as he'd hear them though he was out cold, and take courage from it. I thought somebody'd thrown water over him to bring him round, for he was all wet, but there was water down there too, came in after the ceiling fell. That'd be what made the roof shift, right enough.' He paused. 'They said if it hadn't'a been that the tunnel was on a slope, he coulda drowned where he lay, so he could.'

'His poor head,' cried Annie.

'A dead man can't bleed. That's how you've to see it. The blood was coming fresh.' Michael decided to say nothing about the leg he'd seen on the stretcher, lying at an unnatural angle, cloth and flesh compounded. He was just hoping that by the time the two of them got to the ward that all of that would somehow be made decent. Michael had only been to the hospital in Howgill Street once, but thought of it as an anteroom to heaven – it was clean, and everyone wore white, as though they were angels in training. He was wondering though, if you lost some part of you but you survived, did they put it back on you when you finally did die, before St Peter let you in?

Annie whimpered, starting to shake spasmodically.

Shock, thought Michael. It was cold on the cart now they were into open country, so he took his jacket off and moved over to put it around her shoulders.

'Yous'll have the cart over,' warned Brennan, without turning round.

'Right you are,' said Michael, sitting back in his place opposite. Annie shrank into his jacket. It smelled to her of a mix of tobacco, mud and darkness.

'You said about his leg.'

'They'll have the splints on him by now, so they will. He's young . . . but how good he'll be for work after . . .' He tailed off.

*

The stiff blue-white of the nurse's apron and buttoned-on oversleeves impressed Annie nearly as much as the woman's thin, austere face. It reminded her of a nun's, a stripped, ascetic oval beneath a swathe of pale brown hair that was not so much greying as fading, topped off by an incongruously frilly cap that made Annie think of folded table napkins she and Teresa had admired in Fowles's window. She couldn't tell if the woman was thirty-five or fifty-five. A glance from the nurse's grey eyes made her realise that this was someone who did not act in a hurry and was in utter control of whatever she was doing. Standing before her, Annie felt crumpled, a slattern.

The nurse's voice, accompanied by the lightest touch on Annie's sleeve, told her that none of that mattered.

'I am Sister Rawlins.'

For a moment Annie envisaged the nurse standing in the path of an Orange march, and the Lambeg drums, the fifes, the resolute tread of the men from the Lodge faltering into silence before her cool glare.

'Mr McClure is young, and strong. He is also conscious—'

Annie could not suppress a gasp of relief. At her shoulder Michael muttered, 'Thanks be to God,' and both made the sign of the cross.

'It will be a long journey though, and by no means a certain one. Both legs are broken but had he taken the blow further up, then his organs would not have stood for it. We think he will learn to walk again, but I very much doubt he will be able to return to the mine.'

*

In a daze, Annie followed the swish of Sister Rawlins's skirt into the long whitewashed room. Though aware of eyes on her, and of lumpy shapes beneath grey blankets, Annie could not bring herself to turn her head, but looked straight ahead up the aisle between the rows of cast-iron beds. The strong smell of carbolic and disinfectant that had assailed her the moment Sister Rawlins had pushed open the door was less evident now; she guessed she was getting used to it. She wondered what it would be like to work always in an atmosphere where one's lungs were scoured out by the very air, so different from the cloying dust and dampness and fibres of the mill.

Sister Rawlins was bending over one of the beds. One of the occupant's legs was raised, immobilised in gleaming plaster. The other was covered with a sheet but Robert's toes protruded, blue with bruising. Annie wanted to fall on his foot and kiss it, but Sister Rawlins turned and twitched the poplin into place.

'Your wife and Mr Nolan have come to see you, Mr McClure,' she said, 'though I cannot allow them to stay long.' Sister Rawlins looked round. 'He has been given morphine for the pain but it may mean he won't understand all you say to him. He got quite confused when his other visitors were here.'

His other visitors?

Sister Rawlins stood back then, and Annie forgot all about whoever else had been there. Michael could not restrain his 'Oh!' He moved to the other side of the bed, standing by Robert's raised leg.

Robert's face was as puffy and bloody as though he had received a beating. But though they were mere slits within his swollen flesh his eyes were bright – too bright, thought Annie in the midst of her relief. He was looking at her and trying to smile, or trying not to for the pain; she couldn't tell which. His lips moved, but only a sound between a whisper and a groan came out.

'We came on Brennan's cart,' said Annie, wishing she could come up with something less inane, but conscious of the eyes and ears in a ward where there could be no privacy except perhaps when it was thronged at visiting times and everyone was distracted.

Annie saw Robert's mouth try to form a word. She came closer, bending her face over his, but she didn't dare touch him, afraid she would hurt him. His voice was little more than a whisper: 'Puh bee. Puh bee.' Then she understood.

'The baby's fine. My things are getting tighter every day.'

There was movement beneath the sheet, and Robert's hand emerged, fluttering towards her. Annie grasped it, and placed it over the gentle curve of her belly. A sigh escaped the man in the bed.

'Father Clayton's putting you on the sick list, so he is,' said Michael with forced cheerfulness. 'All them oul' biddies'll have to pray for you then, so they will. First time in their lives they'll have prayed for a Prod!'

There was a twitch in the shoulders in the hospital nightshirt and Robert's eyes narrowed and blinked. Sister Rawlins rustled forward, putting a hand on Annie's arm to displace her gently but firmly. Then she made some deft adjustment of Robert's head on the pillow.

'It might be true that "a merry heart doeth good like a medicine",' she said, 'but my patient shouldn't exert himself just yet. Your husband was laughing, or trying to. It's a good sign, but I think that's enough for today.'

'Can I kiss him?'

'I think you should. Here, perhaps,' said Sister Rawlins, indicating the least damaged portion of his cheek.

Annie bent over. Beneath her lips Robert's skin was warm with life and she silently mouthed, 'God bless and keep you.' Michael patted the hand nearest him.

*

'I'll come and see you in the morning, Annie,' said Michael, as he helped Annie down from Brennan's trap.

'But you'll be at work.'

'Pit's closed tomorrow. It's the Twelfth.'

'Right enough. I'd forgot.'

'If only the fall coulda happened tomorrow – nobody woulda been there.'

Annie walked slowly through to the kitchen, puzzling over Michael's expression as he'd said that about the misfortune of the accident happening when it did, to find Mrs Concannon waiting for her with a strong brew of tea and bright-eyed sympathy.

CHAPTER FORTY-THREE

Whitehaven

'But a certain Samaritan, being on his journey, came near him, and seeing him, was moved by compassion, and going up to him, bound up his wounds, pouring in oil and wine, and setting him upon his own beast, brought him to an inn, and took care of him.'

Luke, 10: 33–34

Outside the ward Sister Rawlins said, 'You will see a change in him each time you come, Mrs McClure. Gradual, perhaps, just the yellowing of his bruises to start with.'

'He'll get better though, will he?'

Looking at Annie's expression, the nurse hesitated. 'Better, if not best. It depends how well his fractures mend. But he will certainly live.' She smiled. 'He is young, and strong, and has reason to.'

'Thank you,' said Annie.

'I am afraid I have to ask you, though I'm sure it's not the moment . . . but the administrator will want to know . . .'

'Of course,' said Annie, fumbling in her bag. 'He paid up regularly ...' She found the envelope with the Providential Society certificate. Sister Rawlins brushed it away.

'That's all right. As long as you have it.'

Walking away, Annie said to Michael, 'I wonder what would have happened without it?'

'The Poor Ward,' said Michael, shuddering. 'If it wasn't for the pit and the mill, we'd all be days from the Union.'

*

As she had got into the habit of doing, Annie waited until right upon the hour before entering St Mary's, hoping there would still be a place for her on one of the pews at the back. She had abandoned the tramp to Frizington some weeks before, at Robert's insistence, but she always left straight after the final blessing, while everyone else was singing the closing hymn.

There wasn't really a space, but a woman Annie didn't know, she thought perhaps a new arrival, nudged her family to move up and Annie wedged into the space.

Annie wasn't going up to communion. She'd had a glass of milk that morning, the only thing that gave her relief from heartburn. Annie slid forward, her hands joined on the hymn book shelf in front, and prayed for Robert's recovery, for Michael Nolan to bear the resentment that came at him like a wave whenever he entered his own kitchen, for the nun who had helped her escape St Mary's Penitents and for Sister Rawlins, in gratitude for her austere efficiency and human kindness.

A bell tinkled, the organ swelled into life and the congregation scrambled to its feet to sing 'Soul of My Saviour'. This was a moment Annie loved, a sense that the glory and majesty contained in this beautiful little church, built by Irish hands alongside what had been a modest mission hall, was offered to all those huddled beneath its roof: millworkers and miners welcomed into the kingdom of heaven. Annie looked up past the bared and shawled heads to the sanctuary to see which priest progressed to the altar and was grateful it was Father Clayton. His homilies were longer than Father Hagerty's, it was true, but she felt he had crafted them always to the moment.

None more so than today.

The mass rolled on in its reassuring familiarity: Kyrie, Gloria, the readings, the response to the psalm, everyone scrambling to their feet to greet the gospel with the rapid thumb-crossing of forehead, lips and heart. Then as the congregation subsided back into their pews, Clayton cleared his throat. He started gently enough with a familiar exhortation to love one's neighbour as oneself. Listening, Annie thought again that she knew nobody who spoke as beautifully as the priest did. She was used to the flat pure vowels of Cumberland by now, but the same words in Father Clayton's mouth were tuned differently. She'd asked him once was he a southerner, having nothing to judge him against. The big bony face had broken into a huge smile. 'Nottingham? Well, it all depends what direction you're looking from.'

'Though it was not in the readings for today,' began the priest, 'I want to talk to you about the parable familiar to you ever since you were catechised: the Good Samaritan. A simple enough story, of the beaten and bleeding man ignored by the priest and the Levite, precisely those who should have helped him, and then aided instead by a Samaritan, of a tribe disdained by the Jews though they occupied the same land and worshipped the same God, only in different ways. Try to imagine being set upon and left for dead on the road between here and Whitehaven. First my abbot passes on the far side of the road, looking away. Then Bishop Whiteside comes by, and he too looks away. Instead this nameless Samaritan was the true answer to that question posed to Our Lord: "Who is my neighbour?" He alone practised the charity we'd recognise now as one of the seven Acts of Mercy. He is not the only one of his people to be found in the Gospels. Luke recounts to us Our Lord's meeting the woman at the well, revealing his divinity to her though he knew she was what we might now call "No better than she should be."'

A small frisson ran through the congregation at these words. The priest paused. Annie saw his eyes scan the pews. 'Brothers and sisters, Our Lord spoke through parables to help his listeners understand his message with stories that would make sense to their lives. I, his unworthy servant, will attempt to do the same. We too live and work alongside others who also worship the same God; perhaps they too are gathered together as we are at this very moment to declare the kingdom of heaven, "for where there are two or three gathered together in my name, there am I in the midst of them". On a recent Twelfth of July a young woman was attacked on a path just outside our town . . .'

Annie dipped her head, the blood pounding in her ears. Father Clayton continued.

'. . . her rescuer saw her home and called the following day to ask after her well-being.'

Annie heard her neighbour whisper to her husband, 'Who was that then?' and saw out of the corner of her eye the man's hand raised a moment, to quiet his wife.

'Had that young man been one of this congregation he would regularly have had his hand shaken and his back patted, but decent and hard-working though he is, that is not what he got, because he, God's child also, is not considered "one of us". He has been sent to Coventry by his erstwhile companions for having had the cheek to marry that young woman, so they too no longer consider him "one of them" either. He could have joined us, but he has chosen not to do so though he has come to see me often, just as Nicodemus visited Our Lord by night. That fine young man, a loving husband and soon-to-be father, God willing, now lies in the infirmary in Whitehaven, victim of that accident at Crowgarth Pit a week ago.'

I never said about the baby, thought Annie. *I suppose Hetty Concannon meant well, telling him.*

'He will live, thanks be to God, but will be unable to go underground again,' said Clayton. 'Yet I know of few of you who have reached out a hand to help his wife who is expecting their first child. I am not here to goad you into charity. I ask merely that you examine your consciences and remember him, his wife and the baby that is yet to be born in your prayers.'

Standing at the lectern, Father Clayton subsided into silence. The congregation seemed to Annie to be utterly still, the tension interrupted only by a child whining about being hungry. At an upward movement of the priest's hands, the people scrambled to their feet to recite the Credo. Her face flaming, Annie gathered up her bag. Her neighbour looked at her curiously for the first time, and Annie could see she was being assessed – a woman, alone. Was she a widow? Was her husband still abed after Owen Flynn had served him too many pints in the Railway Tavern? Or was he not a Catholic?

Her hand on the end of the pew, Annie dipped her knee towards the altar and turned to the door.

'*Et incarnatus est de Spiritu Sancto ex Maria Virgine, et homo factus est . . .*'[4] continued the ragged drone of the congregation.

Twenty minutes later Annie was sitting in an old rocking chair Robert had brought home and revarnished ('Somewhere for you to sit when you're feeding the baby'), trying to calm her breathing. She was wondering how grave a sin it was to go to mass and leave early, to turn her back on the sacrament and the final blessing. Was it as grave a sin as not going at all? Annie felt both moved and mortified by Father Clayton's public declaration. There was nobody in the kitchen; she thought everybody must either be out at that same mass, or behind closed doors upstairs. She intended to go for a lie-down herself before they came back. *My back hurts.* Her thoughts were interrupted by a tap on the window. She looked up.

---

[4] 'And by the Holy Spirit was incarnate of the Virgin Mary, and became man . . .'

'Come away in, Michael!'

Nolan came in, stamping his feet on the mat, bringing with him a miasma of incense and the mothballs of his Sunday best. He pulled off his cap.

'They've put Robert on the sick list for prayers, so they have,' he said, smiling at this small triumph. 'I wasn't having you on.'

'I'm sorry I didn't stay. I just didn't know where to put my face, so I didn't.' She put her hands on the arms of the chair and tipped it forward.

'No, don't get up,' he said. 'I'll get us some tea.'

'Thank you . . . won't you need to be home?'

He frowned momentarily. 'I said I wanted a walk. It's true – a bit. Let me bank up that fire for you.'

'Michael, you're awful good to me.'

Annie watched him crouch on the hearth and felt the tears come to her eyes, remembering her own father doing the same. Without looking at her he said, 'Shall I get Brennan this afternoon?'

'Oh . . .' Her heart surged but as quickly her spirits sank. 'I can't go that often,' she said, with tears in her voice. 'Not and pay the rent.'

'You can so.'

'You can't pay for me—'

'I won't be. Father Clayton says he'll deal with the rent until . . . until yous know what you're going to do. And thon homily worked. There's been a wee collection.'

Annie gasped.

'Don't get your hopes up, but I think there'll be another at the mill.'

'Oh they shouldn't—'

'They want to, Annie. Your Mrs Birkett is behind it, but you've to promise me you don't know that. There might even be a wee consideration from The Flosh,' he said, naming the fine house Ainsworth's father had built. 'The old man was generous when we lost Teresa. Sent a manservant round with something that made the funeral easier to pay for. The only one you'll not hear from is Lord Leconfield himself. That'd be too like accepting responsibility,' Michael added bitterly. 'But even if there wasn't all this kindness, Annie, I'd be grateful I could do something for you, so I would. I'd be doing it for Teresa.' He smiled up at her. 'Will I top up that kettle?'

She nodded. 'Philomena . . .'

'Philomena is after writing to the bishop to complain about Father Clayton,' he said shortly.

'All this trouble . . .' faltered Annie, and burst into tears.

*

Robert's colour was better and his voice stronger, but under the effects of the morphine he kept nodding off. At Annie's shoulder, Sister Rawlins sought to reassure.

'Rest is the best medicine. It'll take time for the bones to set. It's a delicate balance, too. We have to judge when to get him up and about. Not too early, but not too late. We have to keep his blood moving, you see.'

Robert opened his eyes then and focusing on Annie said clearly, 'It was no accident,' before subsiding into sleep.

'Robbie?'

'Don't worry, Mrs McClure,' came Sister Rawlins's soothing voice. 'As I said, morphine can disorientate sometimes.'

Annie saw Michael frown. He wouldn't meet her eyes. On the return journey she tried to draw him out, but all he would say was, 'Sure, the nurse must know what she's talking about.'

Annie was relieved to get home. All she wanted to do was have her tea, and clear up if the others would let her, especially now, as she believed she was living there on charity, and go to lie down. Except for that final outburst of Robert's, she felt calmer. He looked better. He looked as though he would live. She'd cross the bridge of *how* they would live, the three of them, depending on how good a job the surgeons' skills and his youth had managed between them. Tomorrow her stand at Ainsworth's awaited her, and Mrs Birkett's oft-repeated reassuring words: 'A spinner has a better confinement than any fine lady, take it from me. All that moving around you do makes it easier.'

The baby was due in six months. Sister Rawlins had said she thought Robert would be discharged well before then, but would need to convalesce. Annie closed her eyes. Mrs Concannon was kind, but she wanted someone by her she felt was her own. *Elsie. I'd want Elsie. But she can't come to a place the priests found for me. And what did Robert mean, 'It was no accident'?*

*

'There was a gentleman called for you,' said the landlady, putting down the milk jug. 'A Mr Lavery.'

'I don't know anyone of that name,' said Annie. 'Unless he's someone from the Providential Society.'

'I asked did he have a *carte de visite*,' said Mrs Concannon, pronouncing the final word 'visit'. 'Most of them professional men do, but he said no, it was a private matter and he'd call again.'

*

The week was long and Annie worked sluggishly, turning regularly to see Mrs Birkett working the other side of her stand just when she felt she had lost her rhythm, and vanishing with a brisk smile once she had caught up. She dismissed the thought of the mysterious Mr Lavery. *He'd probably only wanted to sell me something*, she thought, and went back to counting the hours until Saturday afternoon. On Wednesday a letter from Robert came, in which she wished he'd said more about himself and asked less about her. She took comfort though from the fact that his hand looked no different from that first note he'd given her with his address on it, and from the fact he wrote, 'Sister Rawlins says I'm doing grand.'

*

Annie's next journey to Whitehaven was in the company of Father Clayton and the Priory House coachman. If Galvin had any thoughts about being told to call round for the same girl he'd been made to pass by on the road from Frizington, he wasn't letting on.

Sister Rawlins stopped Annie and Father Clayton at the entrance to the ward. 'My apologies, but Mr McClure has two visitors with him already and we don't allow more than that at any one time. I am sure though they will leave once I tell them who else wishes to see him. Please just take a seat out here for a moment.'

*

When Sister Rawlins came back, only one of the visitors came with her, a florid, sweating man in a too-tight collar whose eyes swept Annie from head to foot, unsmiling. Then as Father Clayton rose to his feet the man's eyes flicked to him and to Annie's bewilderment the two of them stared at each other as if their eyes had been turned to glass. She heard Sister Rawlins say, 'The other gentleman would like a brief word with you, Mrs McClure, and then he will gladly make way for the reverend.'

*

Robert was sitting up. As he caught sight of her, Annie saw a longing smile break across his face, only for his expression to subside back into anxiety. The middle-aged man standing by the bed turned to face Annie, frankly appraising her. *His* smile was as confident as his dark eyes, the astrakhan collar of his broad-shouldered coat and the strong hands on the pommel of his walking stick. Annie recognised the shape of his mouth, though what was gentle on Robert was sensual on this man.

'There had to be a good reason for all the row I've been hearing about,' said Cairncross, 'and I'm looking at her.'

'Mister Cuh—'

'You can call me Da, Robert, now you've got me a daughter-in-law as pretty as this one,' said Cairncross, without taking his eyes off Annie's face.

'I don't know how,' said Robert.

At that, Cairncross turned back to his son, grasping the hand lying on the bedcover. 'I'm proud of you, so I am,' he said in a quieter voice. 'And Kathleen, God rest her, she'd be as well. I'll need to ask Albert at the Big House for five minutes alone till I tell his lady-wife what a lovely girl her son has wed.'

'Mammy's married at last?'

'She is so, but only just. Thon Albert went on at her till she said yes just to keep him quiet. But you should see them now. They look as though they've been married for the past fifteen years.'

'According unto the multitude of thy tender mercies blot out my transgressions,' muttered Robert.

Cairncross smiled – Annie recognised the smile too.

'You're not a complete taig yet, son, if you can still quote scripture!' Sensing Annie's flinch at the insult, he turned back to her saying, 'Sorry, daughter. The old ways, you know . . .'

Annie nodded, not knowing what to say. Being called daughter by this man in almost the same breath was as startling as being called a taig.

'I'm honoured to meet you is what I shoulda said,' added Cairncross and, taking her hand, brushed her knuckles with his lips. Annie felt herself flush scarlet. *He's like the men in them books.*

'What'll you be calling my grandchild?'

'If it's a boy, he'll be John James, but if it's a girl, Kathleen Teresa,' said Robert.

Cairncross bellowed with laughter, causing the occupants of the other beds to turn their faces in their direction and the nurse at her station at the end of the ward to look up and give him an admonitory stare.

'Oh you're a lost cause, so you are, Robbie,' he said, wiping tears from his eyes. 'It's time I took myself off, so it is, before I cause any more trouble. Take care of yourself, son, and remember what I said. You've not to bother your head about money. Bother your head about that wife of yours instead, so's no other man gets the chance to.'

Before Annie could say anything, her father-in-law had grasped her shoulders and kissed her cheek. 'Till the next time, then.' He strode off, not out of the ward but up to the nurses' station. He leaned over the desk and murmured something. The woman cried 'Oh!' and Annie saw her eyes widen and her hand cover her mouth. As Cairncross walked off, she was still smiling. He waved to Robert and Annie. Moments later, Father Clayton quietly joined them.

'He gave me this for you,' he said. 'He didn't want you to thank him, you see. He says to let him know when you've a place to ship the goods to.' Clayton held out an envelope. 'He said you'd understand what he meant.'

*

That evening the identity of the mysterious Mr Lavery was revealed. Annie came into the parlour to find the florid-faced man who had followed Sister Rawlins out of the ward.

'I've this to give you, Mrs McClure,' and again an envelope was passed to the speechless Annie. Her eyes were fixed on the man's lapel pin, exactly like the one Robbie had used to pin together her torn blouse.

'The Lodge helps them as is in need,' explained Lavery, 'regardless of persuasion. Not because your man was one of our own, and we had rather hoped . . .' He tailed off before clearing his throat and saying more confidently, 'We would like you to bear that in mind, you know? That we help the needy. And that we do not tolerate them that bear false witness. And not to say any more about it.'

Annie worried over these words for some time after he'd gone, taking the man's comment about not tolerating liars to be the closest he would come to admitting he knew something about that pregnant stranger. Eventually, though, she put the visit and the contents of the envelope down to something she remembered from school religious instruction about the need to do good, not to please the people who saw you do it, but because you were doing the will of God. Father Clayton would know more about that, but the look on Lavery's face when he'd said '*not to say any more about it*' she remembered as stern, even as she felt the thickness of the notes through the envelope.

There were notes sufficient to cover three months' rent, though Father Clayton had told her that was already taken care of. So this would pay the midwife and something for the baby until she could make arrangements with a neighbour or with Mrs Concannon and go back to work. Annie exhaled. With the priest present, Robbie hadn't opened that other envelope, so she had no idea how generous Cairncross had been, but at least this gift meant their child would not be born on the Poor Ward. With that immediate problem solved, Annie tried not to think about what they'd live on going into the future. So much would depend on what state Robert would be in. *I'll not be able to stay away from the mill long, that's for sure.* She remembered her reaction to learning that Elsie worked as a barmaid, and shut her eyes for shame. *I know now I'd do anything for my baby.*

CHAPTER FORTY-FOUR

Dawson Street, Cleator Moor, November 1904

'FRISTER & ROSSMANN'S IMPROVED SINGER SEW-
ING MACHINES with all the Latest Improvements are of
the very best quality & workmanship that can possibly be
produced and are THE MOST POPULAR MACHINES
IN THE MARKET.'

Advertisement, 1892

It was already Advent by the time, Robert came home. Little
boys clustered around the horse-drawn ambulance, but the
adults came forward to fuss the pale young man who grimaced
as he manipulated his crutches.

'We've made up everything for you down here,' said Mrs
Concannon solicitously, as Robert looked up at the impossibly
steep incline of the stairs.

A truckle bed was in the front parlour; the table had been
folded away.

'But how will yous manage?' protested Robert.

Mrs Concannon raised a hand to silence him. 'For as long as
you need to be downstairs, we'll all be taking our meals in the

back kitchen in shifts. Sure it's warmer there anyway and none of us stand on formality.'

Then one by one all the members of the household came in to shake his hand and wish him well.

'They've washed the ore out of you by the look of your face,' said Malachy Concannon. Then he glanced down at Robert's legs. Annie could see what the man was thinking, what they all were, but which nobody voiced.

'They're forever scrubbing you in hospital, even if you don't need it,' said Robert.

Then tea was brought, neighbours came, and another half an hour passed before Annie and Robert were alone.

'Annie ... oh Annie.' From his chair, he laid his cheek against the swell of her pregnancy, his arms around her as she looked down at him, stroking his hair. It was softer and cleaner, like his face, free of the miner's dust and grime that despite his best efforts with cold water, clogged it all week until Saturday afternoon when he paid for a tub at the public bath-house.

'Thinking about lying upstairs with you is what'll get me well, so it will.'

Annie blushed, glancing round at the door. Even in its temporary disguise as a bedchamber, the front room felt too much like a public place. She kissed his hair, held him to her.

'Oh Robbie,' she cried. 'You coulda been killed.'

'That was the idea.'

'*What?*'

She released him. He turned his face up to her.

'I didn't remember straightaway, so I didn't. With the shock, and then all the morphine.'

'Robbie?'

'They know in the Lodge. I don't mean they ordered it, but it's one of their own. They mighta given you that money out of the goodness of their hearts – I'd like to think that's what it was. But I think it was to keep us quiet.'

'How—'

'It was the way the prop sheared. You've to wedge a prop well so it takes the weight. So's it won't fall – or won't unless the roof is coming in. This one – I don't know rightly how to describe it – it was all in the blink of an eye. It went sideways, that's how I remember it. As if it'd been sliced through. Oh Lord, I should never have told you . . . here, sit down.'

He reached for his crutches.

'Robbie . . . no . . . I'll get another chair.'

Annie sat facing him, flushed and trembling, her back straight, knees slightly apart, her hands on her stomach.

'It was only the latest thing, and the worst.' He told her about the sandwiches, the missing pick, another occasion when the little store of candle stubs he kept had been plundered. All things honourable miners did not do.

'Why didn't you say anything before?' she cried.

'I didn't want you worrying, so I didn't.'

'So now you're herpling and poor John is dead,' she said. 'The coroner's already sat on him. Found for accident. But you're telling me it's murder.'

'The coroner's man came to see me in Whitehaven, but I couldn't tell him anything. I'd not got my memory back.'

'Who did it?'

'Willie McKeown,' he said, without hesitation.

'Then they musta known, in the Lodge, I mean. Why else would thon Lavery've come here with the money?'

'McKeown is loose-mouthed, especially when he's had drink taken. He'll have blabbed something about making a better job of it next time, if I know him.'

'So you get put out of the Lodge for marrying me, John Trescatherick dies, and they give us money,' she said slowly. 'And nothing happens to McKeown.'

'He'll be made to go. I'm sure of it. The Lodge mightn't want a bad seed like him, but they'll protect their own up to a point. They'll not want another trial like the one after Tumelty's murder, whether McKeown would get off or not. And people talk, same as at home. There'll be no one will pull a pint for him in Cleator Moor. They'll not keep him at Crowgarth, so they won't. He'll go to Workington, or Maryport, and try to get taken on there, but they'll not have him there either if the Lodge puts word out. I'd put money on him being away out of it already. After that it'll be the boat for him, and not back to Ireland, either. Australia, probably. Him and his girl, or wife she might be by now. The one he got into trouble. If he hadn't wanted to wed her, the Lodge wudda seen to it that he did.'

'That poor babby,' said Annie, as everything fell into place. 'But how do you know all this?'

'Because they've bought my silence, Annie.' Robert looked away, but not before she could see the tears shining in his eyes.

'I took their blood money,' he said. 'Because of you and our babby. Because of me and Kathleen's oul' sewing machine and all the things I hoped for in life.'

'Who knows?' she whispered.

'That I took their thirty pieces of silver instead of getting justice for John Trescatherick? Bawden, Lavery . . . all them others that drummed me out. My da. I'd plenty of time to think on it up there in Whitehaven. Annie, I can't go underground again. Even if my legs mended enough I'd feel I was going into my grave, so I would. I kept waking up in the hospital in a sweat about it but I don't know if that's because of what's in my head or if the morphine was to blame. If I opened my mouth and spoke now, what work would I get here anyway? Them that should know better would put it about that I was spinning a yarn. I'd already been told I'd not be wanted after the end of the year. It's not that I wanted to make trouble – you know I didn't. Only I'm tainted with it. Even if I'd'a had the money to set up as a tailor – which I have now, between the Lodge and Mr Cairncross – there'd be plenty *wouldn't* buy from me and might break the windows of my shop into the bargain.'

'We have to go, don't we?' said Annie softly.

'We do. And look, I seen you, Annie. When you think I'm not looking putting a hand to your back. I don't want you going back to Ainsworth's. On your feet all day, you are.'

'Nellie Birkett says the babies come out easier for it.'

'She's right, I dare say, but you'd end up having the baby on the spinning-room floor the way you are going.'

She nodded.

'Do you like Cleator Moor, Annie?'

'Not now.'

'Me neither. To stay in a place where just about everybody knows they've tried to kill you and got away with it and you've taken their tin to keep quiet about it – thon's not much good for a man's pride, so it isn't. Even if McKeown is out of the picture. Now, I've to write to Mr Cairncross – to my da, I should say. I've to tell him where Kathleen's treadle is to be sent. You and me could get on a train and leave here with our lives in a couple of bags.'

'To Barrow?'

Grimacing with pain, he leaned forward to take her hands. 'Where else, Annie? The ones you love are there. Even Elsie.'

'Especially Elsie.'

His fingers traced the tight drum of her stomach. 'Before – or after? You decide.'

She thought for a few moments, weighing up the memory of the train journey against the image of Mr Spedding's Millie, of all things. It was the way the cat turned round and round on the cushion in the kitchen of that house where she and Annie had been the only females, settling herself as though making a nest. Annie saw herself being helped groaning from the train, a trestle being brought into a cold waiting room and a doctor looking down on her.

'It's not long now, so it isn't,' she said hesitantly.

'After, then. But straight after.'

'There's nothing more they could do to us, Robbie, sure there isn't.'

*

Two weeks later Annie took her place in the queue in the Co-op, trying to ignore the murmurings behind her.

'Half a pound of the sliced ham, please.'

'Very good,' said Mr Slater, as he always did, laying a leaf of greaseproof paper on the worktop.

'Hoor,' Annie heard, spoken low but distinctly over her left shoulder. 'Orange hoor.' Her insides turned cold, and feeling the baby agitate she laid a hand protectively over the swell of her skirts. She saw first Mr Slater's raised eyebrows and then his gaze going beyond her, though his hands went on wrapping her parcel as deftly as before.

'I won't have that language in here,' he said.

'You should be ashamed,' muttered another voice. Annie turned, into the hard face of Philomena Nolan and Norah Tumelty's distressed one.

'Seventeen years old, my Henry. Never got to marry and give me grandchildren.'

Annie couldn't hold the woman's gaze. For more than twenty years she'd mourned her child, a pistol fired and the boy dropping to his knees, dead before he stretched on the pavement, a trial directed to acquit for lack of proof, and only the meagre comfort of a coroner's declaration that Henry had done nothing to contribute to his own death.

Philomena pushed Annie's shoulder.

'And you go with one o' them, shameless hoor that you are!' hissed her former landlady, her face twitching. 'Wasn't enough for you, sure it wasn't, to come between a husband and father and his own family.'

Annie wanted to walk out then and there, leaving her little purchases on Slater's counter, only it would have meant nudging past them and she no more wanted to touch Norah's blacks nor Philomena's crumpled sleeve than put her hand to a fire.

They had an audience. What had been the queue had fanned out into a semicircle, all women but for Slater's aproned assistant, and all as intent on the spectacle as men who'd placed bets on a dog fight.

Slater spread his hands on the counter. 'Sidney,' he said to his assistant, 'take Mrs McClure into the back shop and make her a cup of tea. You can have one yourself for your trouble. In fact, I'm telling you to.'

'Sir.' Sidney came forward, the two women separating wordlessly to let him pass. His shoulder towards them as a bulwark, he held Annie's unresisting elbow and led her to the end of the counter and through a door. Slater went on talking; Annie knew she too was meant to hear him.

'With respect, Mrs Tumelty, yours is a terrible loss but Robert McClure was maybe not even born when it happened. And to talk like that, Mrs Nolan, of a man that's had an accident that might've killed him does you no honour.'

'It was a judgement, so it was!'

'Judgement my you-know-what, Mrs Nolan. If it was that, then why spare him and take John Trescatherick? If you come in here again talking like that to any of my customers, you'll have to go to Whitehaven for your dividend as you'll not be served here. I'm past understanding you Irish, really I am. I thought you were all supposed to be Christians.'

*

Clutching the bag containing the small purchases that Slater had refused payment for, Annie slipped into the quiet gloom of St Mary's, hoping to find some peace and tranquillity before making her way home and having Robert read the distress in her face. Two shawled women sat separately near the front, one of them clicking her beads. Neither looked round at Annie, for which she was grateful.

Standing at the tray of candles next to the altar she had been married at, Annie dropped in the coins that she would have spent on the ham. The metal box must have just been cleared, for they clanged in the empty space. Annie lit candles for the souls of Henry Tumelty and John Trescatherick as well as for Robert, for her unborn child, and finally for the family in Barrow. With difficulty, she eased her bulk down onto the kneeler, but sat back on her heels, unable to lean forward for the swell of her belly. Her lips moved soundlessly through the prayers, the last, she knew, she would ever say in that church. It was in the midst of a Hail Mary that it happened: a tiny pop deep in her body, and her drawers were drenched. In horror, she saw the warm wet spread across the tiles.

CHAPTER FORTY-FIVE

Dawson Street, November 1904

'From and after the first day of April, one thousand nine hundred and ten, no woman shall habitually and for gain attend women in childbirth other than under the direction of a qualified medical practitioner, unless she be certified under this Act . . .'

The Midwives Act, 1902

'Stay right where you are,' said Kelly, laying his hand on Robert's shoulder. 'Is there more in thon bottle?' he said to the third man in the room.

'There is so.' Malachy Concannon splashed another finger into Kelly's glass and reached for Robert's.

'No . . . no, thank you,' muttered Robert, splaying his fingers over the top.

'Right you are, sticking fast to your pledge,' said Malachy, not unkindly.

'I'm stiff enough getting up them stairs as it is. I'd only fall down them if I'd drink taken.'

'You're a marvel, so you are,' said Kelly. 'You coulda stayed down here longer. I seen you going up. You're getting better all the time.'

'Thank you,' said Robert. 'It's the banister takes the weight. I made myself a wee promise when I was in Whitehaven – to Annie, really – that I'd be walking up them stairs the night I was made a father.' He didn't tell them of the pain he still felt, especially in the morning, and when it rained, or how he had to grip the banister until his knuckles went white. Kelly was right, though. Little by little, it got easier.

Someone was coming down – one of the women, for Robert's straining ears caught the swish of skirts against the banisters. Malachy's daughter Lucy came in, her arms full of crumpled sheets. Robert was transfixed by these, expecting to see blood or worse, but she held them close to her chest. The three men's faces swivelled to follow the girl's progress to the scullery. Kelly jumped up to open the back door.

'How is she?' he said, just loud enough for the others to hear.

'She's doin' grand, so she is,' said Lucy, going out to the wash-house. Kelly went back to his chair, opening his mouth to say something about that 'doin' grand' when another cry, clearer this time, reached them from above.

'Lucy'll have left the door open,' said Kelly, adding, 'when the cries are closer to each other, so is she.'

Robert felt he didn't know Kelly well. He was just a quiet man who lodged alone in a room on the first floor, but he now saw that the hand nursing the whiskey glass wore a ring. Until this vigil they were men he met only at the dinner table, too

380

tired out by work to ask more than for someone to pass the jam. Annie had known Kelly by sight though, had said she thought he was one of the hacklers at the mill.

'Have you children yourself, sir?' Robert asked, realising he couldn't remember the man's first name.

'I do so,' said Kelly. 'Seven that live. In Barrow, Liverpool, Maryport, Workington. The one that didn't is here, alongside of her mother.' Kelly inhaled sharply, crossed himself and finished his whiskey. 'Me name's Brendan. I've never had a man call me sir, let alone one as young as yourself.'

'Brendan.'

'I can see from your face what you're wondering. It's the cough took the wee girl and the consumption her mother. She'd never any problem with the birthing, so she never.' He nodded towards the ceiling. 'Nor will your wife. A good strong girl like her, with a fine pair of lungs.'

'I'm sorry for your loss,' said Robert.

Lucy came in then, rolling damp hands reddened with cold water in her apron, and made her way back to the stairs.

'Mindful of others, your wife,' said Malachy. 'Starting at tea-time and not in the wee hours.' He twisted round to look at the clock. 'It's not midnight yet.'

'Will yous not be missing your sleep?' said Robert. 'I don't want yous keeping watch with me if you don't want to.'

'We want to,' said Brendan. 'There's never been a wean born under this roof since I've been here.'

Robert felt himself flush. He wanted to reach out and grasp the hands of the men who kept vigil with him, but he didn't know how.

A prolonged scream came from upstairs and then a stunned silence, broken eventually by the distant squall of a cat. Brendan Kelly pushed back his chair and came round the table to clap Robert on the shoulder.

'You're a father, so you are.'

'What?'

'That's your child crying, so it is.'

'I thought . . .' Whatever Robert had thought was lost in the thunder of feet on the stairs.

'Mr McClure? Would you come up here now?' came a voice, and the feet thumped upwards again.

'On you go, so,' said Malachy. 'We'll wet the baby's head tomorrow, so we will.'

'Thank you . . . I . . .'

'Go on with you,' said Brendan.

Robert climbed the stairs faster than he'd ever remembered doing, though he gasped at the needling pains in his right leg. At the door of the room he paused, listening to the women murmuring within. He waited until there was a lull in the conversation, then knocked.

'Come away in!' He recognised his landlady's voice.

Three women filled the space around the bed. Robert had a blurred impression of bared arms, sleeves rolled to the elbow, wisps of hair escaping as though the women had been running against a wind, a whiff of oil lamps and vinegar and of something metallic that for a moment recalled a memory of pig's blood splashed behind the Lamont farmhouse. The figures parted like curtains giving him a straight line of sight to the woman propped against the pillows, her hair brushed back and her face sheened with healthy sweat.

'Robert!' Annie held out something small and whitish. He went forward, sat on the edge of the bed, peered. Behind him he heard the shuffle of feet, and the door opening as everyone else left. Then Lucy came back, grasping the rail at the end of the bed. The mother and father lifted their heads.

Aglow with excitement and a shiny-eyed fatigue, Lucy said in a stage whisper, 'You've to stay in here, for your breakfast, both of yous. I'll be bringing it up, so I will.'

Then she released her grip, and fled to the door before either could speak. Robert glanced down at the baby and then at his wife. He thought he'd never seen her so happy. He thought he'd never felt so happy himself, exhilaratingly and frighteningly so. How frail and new a feeling it was.

'What—'

'A wee girl.'

'Our wee girl. Can I hold her?'

'If you don't drop her.'

He took the bundle as if it might shatter in his hands. 'Oh Annie . . .' he said, looking into the crumpled and impossibly small face, with its perfect eyelashes and obstinate mouth. 'Kathleen Teresa,' he whispered, remembering Cairncross's laughter.

Robert saw two serious dark blue eyes looking perplexedly up into his own. Looking down at his daughter, he thought, *She's had no experiences, good or bad. Like a pool of clear water. What the stream musta been like before they built the mill.* He wondered at all the joys and sorrows that would mark her. *I'll not be able to protect you from all of it, so I won't. But I'll do whatever I can.* He found himself trembling at the responsibility, and held the child closer.

Kathleen frowned up at him, and started to cry. Helpless, Robert let Annie take the child back and watched her attempts to put her to the breast. Just then, there was a knock at the door. Before he could speak the handle turned and Mrs Concannon bustled in with the ewer and basin, washed and refilled, and clanked them down on the washstand. The woman was in her nightgown and a faded wrap, with curl-papers twisted in her hair.

He felt a managing hand on his shoulder.

'Come out of it just a wee minute, Mr McClure,' she said, 'till I show her what to do.' Robert got up and retreated to the end of the bed, as the woman leaned over Annie and the child.

'Put a pillow under her,' she was saying, 'and guide her wee head up that way. So's the teat fits into the roof of her mouth. The pair of yous will have it worked out in no time. Look, she's latching on already.'

'Where's the milk, though?' said Annie, bewildered.

'It's there, right enough. Only the baby's to make it come. Might be a day or so and then you'll have enough to open a dairy. There's nothing in life but you have to work for it, even when you're only an hour old. You'll be a grand wee mother, so you will. But mind you sleep when she sleeps. And a glass of stout every evening – send Mr McClure out for it. Keeps your strength up. I'll see yous in the morning – later this morning, I mean.'

Her hand on the doorknob, the woman turned back to the little group on the bed. 'The first six weeks is the worst,' she said, smiling.

Robert didn't know how he got through the next day. He kept telling himself it was only fatigue, but he felt he was hallucinating from fatigue. Every hour that night, it seemed, they'd been roused from uncertain sleep by that cat cry. Each time he'd woken he'd expected to find himself in the tobacco fug of the room he'd shared at Mr Spedding's with McKeown and the others – McKeown, who had vanished from Cleator Moor for days on end, as Robert knew he would.

Late morning, to wake himself up, he limped out to the wash-house. Checking the door was bolted, he poured the contents of a jug of cold water into a basin and, taking his shirt off, gasped as he splashed himself, following up with carbolic soap rubbed into a scrubbing brush. Every evening, returning from the mine, he'd doused himself with cold water before coming indoors, wherever he'd lived. The thought of living as married miners did, with a wife to heat water for a hip bath by the fire every night, seemed an unimaginable luxury to him. *That's something to aim for: a little house for just the pair of us.*

The cold water on his skin recalled him to the present. On a shelf were a towel and a change of clothes, along with the shoes he had saved for from his earliest wages. There were similar bundles for the other miners who lodged at Mrs Concannon's – a practical arrangement that kept the house sprucer, but also made the men who lived there feel some pride in themselves, at being able to enter their lodgings in clean clothes. Finally, squinting into the little mirror provided, Robert soaped his face and shaved, something he had done only in the evenings when he'd been underground. What was the point of going into that gloom smooth-faced?

He contemplated his clean cheeks, from which the iron-ore ruddiness had faded. It felt like a kind of innocence, a new life. *A bit like their confession. Being washed clean.* He tried smiling at his reflection, something he couldn't remember ever doing. *I don't want Kathleen to grow up thinking most men are stained red, the way they are here. They won't be in Barrow.* Running his hand over his chin he took comfort from the fact that he'd not be scratching the soft wax of his daughter's face with his stubble. *You'll do.*

He went for the door, this time kicking against a pail he hadn't noticed on the way in. Full of water, it stayed firm. He peered in: all he could see were white rags, the paraphernalia of a tiny child.

'Thon Kathleen is a wee dote, so she is,' said his landlady when he came in the back door into the warmth of the kitchen. 'Sit first and drink some tea, will you? I'll take hers up.' Reluctantly, Robert sat down, but drank his tea so fast that it burned, then followed Hetty Concannon upstairs.

Annie was awake, propped up against the pillows, though she'd fallen asleep again straight after eating breakfast while he held the baby and watched her. She held out her arms without a word. Robert lifted his daughter from the ancient crib that had appeared from who knew what corner of the house; the last child to sleep in it he'd been told had been Lucy. Kathleen was wearing a knitted simmet and bootees Robert hadn't seen before.

He noticed that his wife smelled of carbolic and that the front of her nightdress was damp. The room was warm, and its faint cloying scent reminded him fleetingly of Lamont's cows – the pancakes he'd hopped around in the field, to be precise. He marvelled at how a creature so small by the mere fact of her existence had caused the whole house to revolve around her. Kathleen quickly fell asleep again in her mother's arms, her tiny fists furled and her mouth open.

'I wouldn't know what time it is except Lucy comes in with food,' she said. 'Otherwise I think I'd'a forgotten to eat.'

'Your tea'll be getting cold. Will she wake if I take her off you?'

'I don't know. We could try.'

'Just a minute though,' he said, feeling big and clumsy in that room, rapidly filling up with things that hadn't been there before, like the pile of folded squares on the washstand. He went to where his jacket and cap hung on the back of the door. He took a bottle from an inside pocket.

'I went out for this when you were sleeping,' he said, holding up the stout. He returned to sit on the bed, leaning over Annie to kiss her gently. *How'll I be able to love her with a baby in the same room?* He reproached himself for even thinking about such a thing, but wondered if he and Annie would ever kiss again the way they had sitting on that rock in the field. The baby stirred as she was handed to him, but didn't wake. Looking down at her, he said, 'We're a family, Annie. Something I've never had.'

'Something I thought I'd never have again.' She put her hand on his arm. 'Lucy had a message from the Priory House. Father Clayton will call today, so he will.'

'News travels fast.'

'I'll have to get up,' she said. 'Lucy says we can bath her in the scullery sink. He'll want to know about the baptism.'

'Oh . . . right.'

'We can maybe do it here. I don't want to go to the church.'

'You can do that?'

Robert caught the slight hesitation in her voice. 'It'd be easier here, right enough. Only we'll need to decide on godparents.'

*

'It doesn't matter where it's done,' said Father Clayton. 'This is more than adequate,' he said, looking around the room that had been Robert's extemporised convalescent ward.

Mrs Concannon was putting out tea things on the table, refusing Annie's help.

'It's only right,' she put in, 'seeing as the bairn was born under my roof. I'd thought the next time there'd be a proper celebration in this room woulda been Lucy's wedding.'

'I hope I shall have a role on that happy occasion,' Clayton said, though he knew this would depend entirely on Father Hagerty. 'Thank you for bringing us tea, Mrs Concannon,' he said. The landlady took the hint and left the room.

The priest looked at the little family across a table he didn't dare rest his hands on for fear of leaving marks on its ferociously polished surface. Her back resting against her mother's body, Kathleen stared back at him with alert, but unfocused puzzled eyes, her booteed feet jigging.

Clayton laughed. 'I wonder what they see, when they're that small? She looks a healthy child, thanks be to God.' He cleared his throat. 'About the godparents . . .'

Robert sat up straighter.

'We were thinking Michael Nolan,' he began. 'We'd ask Philomena, to build bridges. Only we don't think she'd want it.'

'I think you'd be right,' said Clayton. 'I'll ask Michael on your behalf, shall I?' That way he knew Michael wouldn't refuse, yet he felt uneasy. *God only knows how that woman will take revenge on the poor fellow.*

'And I'll ask Lucy, will I?' he heard Annie say, her voice light with relief. 'She's been dropping hints the way other girls drop stitches.'

*

Clayton went straight round to the Nolans. 'Defer no time, delays have dangerous ends,' he told himself, a fragment of school Shakespeare he'd never forgotten and always sought to apply, though he was pretty sure there were dangerous ends no matter which way you turned where Philomena was concerned.

'He's to stand up there in the church and make them promises?' said Philomena before Michael could open his mouth to answer the priest.

Clayton turned back to Michael, as if he'd spoken instead. 'It wouldn't be in the church, no. Just quietly under their own roof.'

'Well, that's a mercy,' said Philomena. 'Hole-in-corner just like their wedding was. I'm surprised they didn't just ask the minister.'

'Mrs Nolan. There is never anything hole-in-corner about any of the sacraments,' Clayton said coldly, then had to rebuke himself silently for the pleasure her stunned expression gave him.

'I'd be honoured, Father,' said Michael. 'Let me know when I'll be needed.'

*

The reaction in the Priory House dining room wasn't much better.

'What were you thinking of? Sure wouldn't one of the other lodgers do them, without you having to make the grand gesture?' said Father Hagerty, reaching again for the Bushmills. Though he knew it was uncharitable, Clayton couldn't help thinking, not for the first time, that Hagerty would have made a good local politician, or an astute horse dealer. Was it a vocation or poverty had taken the man to Maynooth? Clayton made a mental note of another sin to confess.

That evening another letter was sent to Barrow-in-Furness containing the softest snip of silky hair folded about with a piece of paper. After he'd posted it for Annie, Robert called round at his old home, as he had done several times since he'd been able to hirple around with a stick.

'You've done a grand job of that old perambulator,' said Mr Spedding, watching Robert test for the umpteenth time the hood he'd replaced with new cloth, checking to see if it opened and closed smoothly.

'I'll maybe give the metalwork another wee polish,' said Robert, rummaging in his pocket for his tin of Bluebell.

When Annie saw the pram she burst into tears and threw her arms around his neck.

'Why are you crying?' Robert said, dismayed, thinking that she must have expected something new instead.

'Because I'm happy,' she said, her words muffled in his shoulder.

*

Six weeks later the pram was lifted down the steps to the southbound platform at Moor Row. There was a small farewell party: Hetty and Lucy Concannon and Father Clayton, who crossed the child's forehead with his thumb. Mrs Concannon wept and begged to be remembered. Lucy got from Annie a ready promise of a visit to Barrow 'whenever yous have your own place', and cried over Kathleen.

Clayton grasped Robert's hand saying, 'I shall miss you. My parish priest tells me I am an abject failure for not converting you to the faith. But I can tell you honestly, you stubborn Presbyterian, that I have enjoyed the discussions you and I had more than I ever have with anyone else. For that I thank you from the bottom of my heart.'

'And I thank you for your kindness to myself and Annie. Without you we'd have had no happiness.'

Then they were gone in the roar of the engine and a belching of smoke, and Father Clayton walked back to the Priory House feeling somehow poorer.

*

This time the entire family were waiting on the platform in Barrow.

'You've grown, you two!' exclaimed Annie.

'We haven't,' said Joe. 'Kathleen's awful small, that's all.'

Amidst the cries and embraces, Annie kept half an eye on her husband. He was talking to Elsie, quietly as was his way, but Annie was almost certain she heard him say, 'Thank you,' at which Elsie put her arms around him. Then as the little group moved off, Mark distracted her, tugging her sleeve.

'If you're our sister, does that mean we're the babby's uncles?'

'You can be her uncles, or her brothers. Whatever you want.'

'Uncles,' said Mark. 'We can't be her brothers because she's too wee to play with. But we can look after her.'

'Can I push her?' cut in Joe.

'Oh yes ... of course. Do you know where we're going to stay?'

'At a neighbour's,' said Thomas. 'A temporary arrangement with the widow who takes the boys in after school.'

'You've a job?' said Annie, turning to Elsie.

'I have so. In the jute works. I was a mill girl in Ireland – before I married, that is. You should see the place. It's bigger even than Ainsworth's. They'd take you on too if you wanted.'

Annie caught Robert's eye. 'Robbie'll be looking for somewhere too. But for himself. For the tailoring.' She realised it was the first time she'd said this to anyone but her husband. She didn't know if that made it more real or if she was tempting fate.

'We might have the answer to that. You'll see what I mean when we get to Hardwick Street.'

*

'Are you afraid of the dead, Robert?' asked Thomas. They were standing below the flat he and Elsie shared, in front of the window of what had been the undertaker's. Newspaper was taped to the inside of the plate glass and the door was padlocked.

'I'm not. I've had more reason to fear the living. You say the place is empty?'

'Completely. I helped them load the cart myself. The front shop is big and airy. It always had curtains across the windows, right enough, but without them there must be a lot of light.'

'North-facing is best for tailors,' said Robert, looking up at the evening sky.

'There's two rooms at the back – a good size. And running water.'

'I'll write to my mother, so I will.'

*

Crossgar
30th January 1905

Dear Robert,

Albert wrote this for me, so he did. You're a good son and wrote me letters regular and musta wondered why did I never write you back. Well it's because I don't know how only now you are a husband and a father I have to send you a line. I hope you are all three very happy. If you can get your photo took same as this one of me and Albert I would like one of the babby your wee girl also to see are you well and your wife. Mr Cairncross said she is very pretty. My picture and Albert's was took in Killyleagh so maybe there is a man in Barrow too.

I seen Mr Cairncross as you asked me and Albert seen him with me as I am a married woman now as you know and Albert has cleaned up your things as best he can and Mr Cairncross will send them by carrier. Wishing you every blessing my dear son.

Your loving mother,
Margaret Warnock (Mrs)

*

Robert looked long at the cross his mother had marked on the end of her letter. He imagined her taking the pen from Albert when he'd finished, not knowing quite how to hold it, though on those few visits to the Big House he remembered the deftness of her fingers as she shelled peas or rolled pastry. In his memories of her she was almost always doing something, for there had almost always been something to do – for other people.

He gazed at her image on the piece of card, stiff and unsmiling in her old-fashioned Sunday best. He could name the dark twill she wore – bombazine – and thought her lumpy hat with the crushed silk flowers ugly. He knew Kathleen would have tilted it to a more attractive angle. His mother looked older, but then Robert was starting to forget how many years he'd been in England. She certainly looked older than Cairncross, but then, he thought, if you'd had to give your own child to strangers to bring up would that not make a woman age?

He looked at his mother's husband, standing with a hand proprietorially on the back of her chair. He appeared to be staring into the middle distance. The photographer's backdrop showed rolling parkland, a Grecian temple and a little bridge. Looking at the painted landscape, Robert knew that neither Albert nor his mother would ever be permitted to stroll across such a setting in real life. Even though the grounds of the Big House where they both worked might be something like the painting, the Warnocks would never be allowed to do anything but walk round the back to the Offices or conceal their presence by going through the ha-ha. That ugly hat would never disturb the view the owners had from their drawing-room windows.

CHAPTER FORTY-SIX

Hardwick Street, Barrow-in-Furness, June 1905

> 'Whosoever, being married, shall marry any other person during the life of the former husband or wife, whether the second marriage shall have taken place in England or Ireland or elsewhere, shall be guilty of felony, and being convicted thereof shall be liable ... to be kept in penal servitude for any term not exceeding seven years ...'

> Offences Against the Person Act, 1861

The tea-time conversation was interrupted by not so much a knock at the street door as a blow, as though someone had fallen against it rather than used their knuckles.

'I'll go,' said Robert to the others around the table. He was leaning against the wall, for his leg got stiff if he sat too long in the evenings. Working the treadle turned out to be the best thing for it; the atrophied muscles had gained strength and suppleness. He creaked through the little parlour and down the narrow staircase, just as whoever it was knocked again. He heard a muffled blasphemy.

'Who is it?' said Robert, his fingers on the door handle.

'It'sh *me* should be ashkin' who *you* are,' said a voice. Robert heard a scrape of nailed boots, then the door shuddered against his hand – the caller had evidently stumbled against it – a full-bodied belch followed. 'Now will ye open up or am I to break the door down?' The boots shuffled and what sounded like the flat of a hand hit the wood. Robert wondered if the drunk man was simply trying to stay upright. To his relief, the uncertain steps moved away – but not far.

'Maybe a brick through thon window'd get be shome notish.'

Robert opened the door.

To begin with he was sure he'd never seen the man before, though he'd seen plenty like him: his cap, his collarless shirt (not very clean), the greasy and pulled-out-of-shape jacket, the workman's boots. The stranger was middle-aged, stocky and, from the look on his face, incredulous. *No, I don't know him, but there's something about him I know.* He wondered had he seen the man on the boat from Belfast.

'Jaysus,' said the man, 'ye're a bit feckin' young for her, aren't ye?' Then the astonishment turned to anger in the weathervane way of the drunk, as the man lurched towards Robert and took a swing at him. Robert sidestepped his would-be attacker easily, and the man teetered on the edge of the kerb as though he were six feet off the ground and not four inches. Beyond him, Robert saw people gathering, women with folded arms muttering in pairs, men in shirtsleeves with hands in pockets, smoking, children distracted from their games.

'My weans!' shouted the man, regaining his balance. 'You've my babbies, so you have . . . you . . . you *fornicator*!' With that, Robert knew who the visitor was.

'What's all this carry-on, Robert?' he heard at his shoulder. He glanced round into Thomas's anxious face and hissed, 'Fagan!'

The drunk peered at Thomas and then Robert saw the man's expression shift from anger to loathing.

'Well, it's yourself, is it then?' he said, in a quieter voice, loaded with menace. Fagan seemed to have suddenly sobered up, now that he'd found his quarry. 'A fellow has to go away on business for a wee while, that's all, only to come back and find the woman who'd promised she was going to be his forever has upped and gone with her fancy man. Well, ye can get out of it now, so you can. I've come back to claim my own!'

'Claim your own? You never sent a word, nor a letter, much less anything to put food in them wee boys' mouths, Fagan,' said Thomas.

'Didn't need to, did I? Their sainted mother gets her bed and board some other way, right enough. Just you and him, is it?'

The man's head swung towards Robert, who thought of the bull brought to service Lamont's cows, and how he and the other children had been warned on pain of a thrashing to go nowhere near the field he was held in. Then Thomas's first punch landed, knocking Fagan so that he fell hard on his hipbone against the shop windowsill.

The man slid down the wall roaring with pain and then tipped onto his back, where like a vast, dirty insect he struggled until Robert stepped forward and put out a hand. Fagan took it, allowing himself to be helped up, then shoved Robert to one side as lowering his head he charged at Thomas. Robert turned to watch Fagan's advance as though he saw him in slow motion. Beyond him he caught sight of Annie's frightened face in the doorway and frantically signalled to her, hoping she'd understand and keep Elsie and the boys out of view. But it was too late. As she bobbed out of sight, Joe took her place. Robert saw the moment the boy recognised his father, his shocked, widening mouth. The child disappeared back inside. Someone slammed and bolted the door.

Thomas shoved his attacker back with both hands. Fagan yelled his outrage and returned to the charge. Robert glanced round: a semicircle was forming around them, to watch a prize fight nobody had to pay admission to see. As Fagan's head slammed into Thomas's midriff, Robert ran forward and grasped the man's elbows from behind, pulling him back. Fagan's cap fell off, and his greasy hair rubbed in Robert's face. The man stank of drink, unwashed clothes and vomit, but he was strong, twisting like an eel in his captor's grip. Thomas, recovering his balance, punched Fagan again, and the force of the blow knocked his head back, bruising Robert's nose.

'Clock 'im again, mister!' shouted a voice.

'Two of you and only one of 'im! Not right, that!' cried another.

Fagan roared and shook his head, spraying blood from side to side. Thomas paused, getting his breath back, glancing at his knuckles as if not quite sure he'd landed those blows himself. From an open window in the flat above his workshop Robert could hear a childish wailing, and the anxious voices of the two women.

Just then the shrill blast of a whistle sent the crowd eddying in all directions. Robert let go of Fagan, who staggered to the windowsill, putting his hands to his bloody nose and moaning. Two policemen ran up but, before Robert could say a word, he felt cuffs click around his wrists.

'You're coming down to Rawlinson Street, the pair of you. You'll be booked for affray, mebbe grievous bodily harm if the sergeant feels like it, though Tim there is more likely to do harm to himself without your help.'

'Tim?' said Robert, astonished. 'Yous know him?'

The policeman ignored this. 'You'll have to come too, lad,' he said to Fagan. 'We'll need your evidence and we'll get the police surgeon to take a look at you. Not that they've made your face any uglier than it was already.'

In a daze, Robert was marched along the street, a policeman's hand on his shoulder. His father-in-law walked alongside him, his hands also shackled.

'It was the one thing I was always afraid of. Him coming back,' whispered Thomas.

'Quiet, you! No talking!'

'Sorry, officer.'

Behind them, Robert could hear Fagan's shambling tread, his whining protests. 'They set on me, so they did! I was minding my own business, doing nobody any harm . . .'

'I told you already, Tim. You're not under arrest. Not this time, anyroad. We just need your statement.'

The two handcuffed men exchanged wordless glances, as the explanation of Fagan's appearance dawned on Robert. He'd not gone back to Manchester after all, the place the family had lived before their sudden departure for Cleator Moor, so suddenly that Elsie assumed her husband must have owed money to someone. Fagan had chosen Barrow, perhaps thinking it would be easier to go back to Cumberland from there and batten on his wife again if he felt like it. His armpits clammy with fear and shame, Robert thought of those two little boys, the anguish in Joe's face. He thought of the funeral suits on the table in his workshop, half-sewn, that he would probably never get to finish, let alone on time, because of a useless drunk. *Them poor wee boys coulda run into him at any time. He musta gone up to Cleator Moor on the train. It'd not have taken him long to find out where she was. His old landlord probably told him for the price of a pint. But why now?* All Robert could think was that given Tim Fagan's wretched state he had decided to force his way back into the life of the woman he'd failed to support for the last two years, and get her to feed him. He looked down at his helpless wrists. *There's worse locks than these.*

Yet it was he and Thomas who'd been arrested. Not the shambling drunk the police were treating with amused tolerance.

*

'I'm sorry, Robert,' said Thomas an hour later. They'd been photographed, questioned. Separately, the whole story had been told. The young constable who had interviewed Robert had been sympathetic.

'It was going so well,' Robert told him. 'I was getting the customers. I'd stopped worrying was I going to be able to feed my wife and my wee girl.'

'The law's the law, I'm afraid. We've had Tim Fagan sleeping it off in our cells more times than I can count. He's had fines for being drunk and disorderly mostly, and another for exposure when he'd relieved himself where a young lady in the Sally Army could see him. But the pair of you attacked him. It's him has the bloody nose. I can see he's a shackle around the ankle of the lady your father-in-law thinks of as his own wife, but you can't go taking the law into your own hands.'

'Thomas isn't a violent man,' said Robert.

'A lot of them say that,' said the young constable, trying for an experienced air. 'All except the ones as are proud of it.'

'So what'll happen now?'

'The magistrates' court. You'll probably just be fined, if the beak believes you when you say you were holding Fagan back rather than holding him for Maguire to hit him. Of course it's always possible that when Fagan's sober he'll not want to press charges.'

'What about Elsie?'

'That's something for her and him to sort out, I'm afraid.'

*

'They've told me I'll not lose my job,' said Thomas, a week later. He and Robert were sitting in the little sitting room through the back of the tailor's shop. The bereaved family had got their funeral weeds in time, though Robert had had trouble with the work, for he'd found it hard to concentrate. He had accepted only basic alterations in the last few days, afraid of the looming court date and what might follow. Elsie and Annie were upstairs putting Joe and Mark to bed, though Robert knew the younger boy had started wetting himself again. It was obvious to him too that poor Joe thought being the eldest meant he had to put a brave face on things, but Robert could see the child was struggling. But what pained him even more was the anxiety in Annie's eyes.

'But I'll not be foreman anymore,' Thomas went on. 'The manager was nice about it. Said he'd wait until we were tried but if I'm found guilty he said I'll have to go back on the hod, even if all they give me is a fine. I'd have no authority, he said. The lads'd run rings round me if I tried any discipline on them. It's not that, Robert. It's what'll happen to Elsie and the boys, and you and Annie and Kathleen. I've let you all down.'

'You've not. It's not your fault. In your shoes I'd'a done what you did.'

'You know what? I think I'd hit Fagan again if I got the chance. Even though Elsie tells me he's not worth it.' He looked around his son-in-law's little sitting room. Robert's eyes followed his, noticing how his gaze dwelled on the smallest things: the fire-iron with the Kilkenny cat handle, Annie's National School sampler in its plain frame, the ubiquitous St Brigid cross.

'I seem to keep losing things. My boys to Canada. My little farm. My poor wife. And then I thought I'd lost Annie. She coulda gone from me forever if it hadn't been for you, Robert. And now Elsie and the wee boys. I love them as if they were my own.' Thomas's eyes shone in the firelight. He sniffed and wiped them. 'Will you look at me,' he muttered. 'Weeping like a woman. To think we've to lose all this because of that excuse of a man who'd near beat the daylight out of all three when he was in drink.'

'We could move again. Liverpool. Birmingham mebbe.'

'Oh Robert, just when you've your tailoring doing so well. Look what a good job you've made of Conway's premises, even.

A workshop and a home. But I thank you for that "we" just the same. I just wish they'd hurry up with the summons. So we can get it over with. I can't think why it's being dragged out like this.'

Then there was a knock at the shop door – two authoritative raps.

'Oh Jaysus,' said Thomas. 'Now we've to find out what he's like sober.'

Robert put out a restraining hand. 'Stay there. Better if *I* go, mebbe. Go out the back and call up at the window. Tell them to stay up there.'

Robert got up, as a further rap at the door made him jump. He limped through to the workshop but before opening up he glanced through the window. He exhaled slowly. The man at the door represented a different kind of danger. Robert turned the key and opened up, standing back to let the visitor in.

'Evening, Mr McClure. Is Mr Maguire at home too?'

'Come in, constable. He's just gone out the back. I'll get him, so's you can kill two birds with one stone.' He looked expectantly at the policeman. *Aren't they supposed to hand you something?*

The man wiped his feet on the mat and said confidentially, 'I don't suppose there's any chance of a nice cup of tea at this hour, is there?'

Robert stared at him in astonishment.

'No matter if there isn't. Yes, would you get Mr Maguire a minute?' The man removed his helmet and reached for a chair. 'In fact, bring the ladies down too. They'll be interested in what I've got to say too.'

*

'The charges have been dismissed,' said Constable Burch. 'I wanted to come and tell you myself. You see, it turns out Mr Fagan wasn't in a position to accuse anyone of anything.' He smiled at the four startled faces, enjoying himself. 'We've arrested him.'

'What for?' said Elsie.

'Bigamy.'

Robert reached for Annie's hand. Thomas got up and went to stand behind Elsie's chair, holding her shoulders. She lifted her hands to cover his.

Burch cleared his throat. 'I've a cousin on the force in Manchester, you see. In Ancoats. I got from Fagan that he – that is to say he and yourself, Mrs Fagan – had been living down there before he'd gone to Cleator and then come on to here on his own. He's been a bit desperate lately – well, you've seen him. He lost his job at the wireworks because of his drinking. There'd been a woman for a bit, but she left him. He couldn't keep himself so he thought mebbe you'd do the keeping of him, ma'am. Only when he went looking for you back in Cleator Moor, it was to find you'd been in Barrow some while, under his nose, so to speak. Anyway, I like to be thorough. Sergeant says I'm going places because of it. So I telephoned my cousin just to see was there any record of Fagan in Manchester. There was – an outstanding summons for a man of the same name, same birth date. He'd come there from Belfast, with a wife and a child, but had separated from them. The lady got an order against him for the girl's vittles, but he didn't keep up the payments so she got a summons – it was that or the workhouse for mother and daughter

405

otherwise. Only by then he was married to you, in a manner of speaking.'

'So I'm free?' said Elsie, her voice shaking.

*

A few days later Elsie and Annie sat at the table in the upstairs flat. Across the teapot Elsie said, 'He'll get two years at least, Annie. For the bigamy. Not for the beatings or for me having to clean up after him all those times. Not for him leaving us with nothing for to pay the rent. Not for the offence against God of me going to the sacraments when I wasn't a married woman at all.'

'Hardly a sin of commission, Elsie. And you will be a married woman in a month's time. That's if Robert gets all them clothes made in time!'

'I can barely believe it. I still wonder if we shouldn't wait until after the trial . . .'

Annie reached across the table and put her hand over Elsie's. She recognised that anxious expression. It was on Mark's face in the photograph of his class at St Patrick's. A look that had come back until Constable Burch had managed to convince the boy that Tim Fagan would not be taking him away. He, John Burch, was going to take care of that personally.

'We've been through that already,' said Annie gently. 'The bishop himself in Lancaster has given his permission. In fact did he not say something to Father Farrelly about it being a good idea to make things regular as soon as possible?'

Elsie nodded. 'You must think me a foolish woman. Tim was a charmer, so he was. When he was sober, anyway. That bit older and cleverer than me – or so he made out.'

'Dadda is older too though I don't know about cleverer.'

Elsie laughed, but as quickly her serious expression returned. 'Tom wants to make it official with the boys as well. Only I don't know will he be let. By Tim, I mean. He'd have to give his permission for them to be adopted, even if he is a convict.' She shivered.

'That I couldna say,' said Annie. 'All I know is that when they eventually let him out – of Strangeways or wherever they've to put him – and if he comes back here, the constable said he'd be taken up for affray, public nuisance, anything else they can think of. He'd have no claim on you, Elsie. You were never his wife.'

'You've got sense, Annie. Sometimes I think you're the older one of us two.' Elsie hesitated. 'There was something I wanted your advice about, only Robert's so busy. Joe and Mark are getting that excited about their new clothes. He's doing so much for us already it seems like a cheek . . .'

'Do you mean give you away?'

'That's if he doesn't mind. I mean, being a Protestant and everything he'd mebbe not want . . .'

'I think, Elsie, he's been hoping you'd ask.'

'Father Farrelly wants it to be done on the quiet. He's going to arrange for us to go to Ulverston.'

*

Robert shifted in the bed, easing his stiff leg.

'I'll need to get more Epsom salts and make you another poultice,' said Annie. 'You're going to have a fair bit of standing around on Saturday.'

'Thank you,' he said, pulling her in to his shoulder and kissing her forehead. 'Oh Annie, I'm the happiest man alive. When I saw you that day, up at the window, I could see you were special. And after, even with your back turned and you bravely ignoring McKeown and the others. That shiny black hair. I'd been so used to being alone. Even in the middle of the march that day. Maybe even more when I was surrounded by all them other men. But the only men I could really call friends were Jem Spedding, and John Trescatherick, God rest him. But now I've got everything. My wife, my wee girl. Mark and Joe. They call me uncle, but they're more like my wee brothers. Well, if Thomas is my father-in-law and they're his sons now, then that *is* what they are – brothers-in-law.' He laughed, and Annie thought how much she loved that rare sound. 'There was only me. Nobody's child. And now it'd take a book just about to explain all the family I've got – all because of you.' He kissed her again, and feeling the returning pressure of her lips, did it again.

'Will this life be enough for you, Annie?' he asked eventually.

'What do you mean?'

'A hirpling husband. Living at the back of a workshop. You helping me make funeral clothes till your eyes are tired.'

'As long as you're in my life, that's all I want.'

HISTORICAL BACKGROUND

The small town of Cleator Moor lies about four miles south-east of Whitehaven and about forty-three miles north of Barrow-in-Furness. In the nineteenth century large numbers of immigrants from Ulster came to work there, either in Ainsworth's flax mill or in iron-ore mining, leading to the nickname 'Little Ireland'. By 1871 thirty-six per cent of the population were Irish-born. Unfortunately, with the new arrivals came the sectarian divisions of their homeland. In that year the anti-Catholic demagogue William Murphy was assaulted in Whitehaven by Irish miners from Cleator Moor, following mob attacks on Catholic targets he had incited in other parts of England. Then in 1884, following a Twelfth of July Orange march in Cleator Moor which deliberately passed through Catholic streets and in front of the Catholic church, a seventeen-year-old postal messenger, Henry Tumelty, was shot dead. A number of arrests were made and John Bawden, head of the Cleator Moor Orangemen, a foreman iron-ore miner and prominent in the Co-Operative Society, was accused of murder. However, at the Cumberland and Westmorland Assizes that November, the judge directed the jury to find him not guilty due to conflicting evidence. An Orange band met him and his co-defendants at Whitehaven Station and a crowd of 800 to 900 people marched in celebration round the town while the band played sectarian songs.

As Catholic children, the Fagan boys attend St Patrick's School. The Church of England Montreal Schools (senior, junior and infants) in the High Street was built by John Stirling, owner of the Montreal Mine (coal and iron ore) in 1866 and featured a ninety-eight-foot-high clock tower. It is the chiming of this clock that reminds Annie when she needs to go and meet Teresa and Percy. Both St Patrick's School and the Church of England Montreal School still exist but in newer premises. The original Montreal Schools had to be abandoned in 1946 due to subsidence caused by the workings of Crowgarth pit, and were subsequently demolished.

Percy went to get his baptismal certificate from the Church of England mission church on Wath Brow. This little building is no longer a church and is privately owned. It was painted by L. S. Lowry, a regular visitor to Cleator Moor. The painting and the building were up for sale at the same time a few years ago, but the painting fetched a higher price.

My great-grandparents, Robert and Jemima Hutton, came to work at Ainsworth's in about 1908, bringing with them my grandfather James and his little sister, Louie. Robert was the illegitimate son of a servant at Rademon House, Crossgar. His was a mixed marriage; my great-grandmother was Catholic, though her marriage took place in a Presbyterian church. Louie died as a toddler, followed by her mother, who had tuberculosis; they are buried in Cleator Moor. Robert the widower and his small son then returned to County Down. James Hutton came back to work in England as an adult, at Vickers ship-yard in Barrow, having served his apprenticeship at Workman Clark in Belfast – what was known as 'the wee yard', distin-guishing it from the mighty Harland & Wolff. He refused to join the Orange Lodge and in some respects at least was ecu-menical; my grandmother said she always knew where he was when he was out late, as the 'Pat Club' and the 'Unionist Club' had late licences on different nights. I'm pretty certain he couldn't have done that in Belfast.

I have used some artistic licence around Ainsworth's Mill. Caesar Caine, vicar of St John's in Cleator Moor, in his 1916 his-tory of the town, states categorically that 'no weaving whatever is undertaken there' though he does say that 'towels and tapes' were once manufactured there. There is a chromolithograph of Ainsworth's Mill, made for advertising purposes in about 1900, which does, however, show the characteristic sawtoothed roofs of weaving sheds, as well as strips of linen laid out on a bleaching green. But the artist also depicts the mill as almost on the banks of Ennerdale Water, which it wasn't, so we can assume he was cheating as much as I have done in including weaving sheds in my story, making Annie's workplace more like an Irish mill.

Remaining buildings of Ainsworth's Mill were later taken over by the hat manufacturer, Kangol, but after seven decades the company ended its presence in the town in 2009. At the time of writing, after more than ten years of lying empty, there are now plans for redevelopment of the site, preserving the facade of the remaining part of the mill.

Frederick Cuthbert Clayton came to Cleator Moor as curate in 1904, so slightly later than he first appears in this story. He

411

became parish priest in 1911 and remained as such until his death in 1956. The parish of Cleator Moor was founded in the 1840s as a Benedictine mission (hence the priests' home being referred to as a Priory House and the priests themselves also being monks); the order's presence in the town came to an end in 1972, since when St Mary's has been served by diocesan priests. Father Hagerty is an invention, as he is not a positive character and it seemed a wrong thing to give him the name of the man who was Cleator Moor's actual priest and who was apparently well liked. I have also employed some artistic licence in making St Mary's Penitents a Catholic organisation run by the Sisters of Mercy, one of the orders which ran the notorious Magdalene laundries in Ireland. It was in fact an Anglican foundation.

As they have all but disappeared, an explanation of some of the jobs carried out in a flax mill might be useful. By the 1880s Ulster, the biggest European producer of linen, annually exported more than a hundred thousand miles of woven cloth. In 1920 around fifty spinning companies and around a hundred weaving factories housing around thirty-five thousand looms were recorded in the province. Eventually linen, as for cotton in England, declined in the face of competition from man-made fibres and cheaper foreign imports. Andrews' Mill in Comber finally closed in 1997.

A flax plant went through many stages before being turned into cloth to make something like Annie's blouse or a fine tablecloth. Firstly the flax was scutched to remove the skin and core of the plant, leaving only the fibres. This was once done by hand, using a scutch knife, and when mechanised, between flat wooden blades or metal rollers. Roughing, carding, combing and hackling followed, rendering the fibres as soft and fine as human hair (hence the origin of the term 'flaxen'). In a linen mill, roughing and hack-ling was usually done on the first floor, spinning took place on the next two floors with finally reeling and winding onto frames (requiring lighter machinery) on the top floor. Annie's task as a doffer in a spinning hall was to ensure that spinning frames were stopped at the right time, the filled bobbins removed (or 'doffed') and replaced with empty ones. By contrast with the barefoot doffers, for spinning was a wet process, the reelers got to wear shoes and stockings. Sawtoothed weaving sheds were separate buildings, referred to as factories rather than mills, that might or might not be part of the same complex or business; a weaving supervisor was known as a tenter. The woven product, which at that stage was known as brown linen, was then either bleached out of doors (on bleaching greens) or by a chemical process (using chlorine). Various types of processes were then employed to finish the cloth (depending on its eventual use), of which an important part was beetling, which consisted of wrapping the cloth around slowly revolving rollers while wooden blocks called beetles pounded it to tighten the weave and to bring out a glossy finish. Needless to say deafness was an occupational hazard of being a beetler, as was lung disease to anyone working in carding and combing, due to the inhalation of dust and fibres.

Places to learn more about the linen industry include the Ulster Folk Museum at Cultra, Co. Down https://www.nmni.com/Home.aspx, the Irish Linen Centre and Lisburn Museum https://www.lisburnmuseum.com/ and the Museum at the Mill, in the former Mossley Mill in Co. Antrim https://antrimand-newtownabbey.gov.uk/museumatthemill/

ACKNOWLEDGEMENTS

I'd like to thank, as always, my splendid agent, Annette Green and the tirelessly helpful team at Zaffre: Claire Johnson-Creek, Katie Meegan, Lucy Tirahan, Alex May, Eloise Angeline for their editorial and production help, Felice McKeown, Holly Milnes and Eleanor Stammeijer in marketing and publicity, and Laura Marlowe for casting the right voice for the audiobook edition and of course Jenny Richards for her beautiful cover design. As the first draft of this book was written during pandemic restrictions, my initial research had be conducted at a distance. There are a number of people without whom the book could not have been written, so I want to thank Tom Duffy, author of *Cleator Moor Revealed* and his son Sean Duffy, webmaster, https://www.littleireland.co.uk, Dr David Hume MBE, Orange historian, Father Richard Whinder, parish priest, Church of the Holy Ghost, Balham and Professor Donald MacRaild of London Metropolitan University. As I have not spoken with an Ulster accent since I was thirteen, fellow author S. P. McArdle checked my manuscript for dialect accuracy. Any mistakes that remain, historical or otherwise, are entirely mine.

Welcome to the world of Katie Hutton!

Keep reading for more from Katie Hutton, to discover a recipe that features in this novel and to find out more about Katie Hutton's upcoming books . . .

We'd also like to welcome you to Memory Lane, a place to discuss the very best saga stories from authors you know and love with other readers, plus get recommendations for new books we think you'll enjoy. Read on and join our club!

www.MemoryLane.Club

Dear Readers,

Thank you for reading *Annie of Ainsworth's Mill*. Annie and Robert's story was inspired by my great-grandparents, but once I started writing the book, my two characters made the story their own, as characters tend to do.

My great-grandfather Robert Hutton had no birth certificate; he was the son of a servant at Rademon, the 'Big House' in Crossgar, County Down. On his marriage certificate (in 1905) his age is simply given as 'full'. The clerk began writing Robert's father's name in the appropriate column, but two letters into the surname, stopped, realising of course that the name was different from the young groom's. Robert's father's first name, James, and those two letters, are scored through, and 'illegitimate' is written above. The two letters don't correspond to the name of the people who owned Rademon, so I have no idea who Robert's father was. I don't know anything of Robert's early life. He couldn't have been brought up by his mother, though, if she was a live-in servant, but what is perhaps unusual is that he knew his father, well enough that he called his own son after him.

Although the girl Robert married was brought up a Catholic, the ceremony took place in a Presbyterian church, and six months later my grandfather was born. Robert and Jemima met at Andrews' Mill, in Comber, and at some point went to live in Cleator Moor, where they were both flax dressers. Their little girl died there of whooping cough, and when my great-grandmother also died, aged twenty-eight, of tuberculosis, the widowed Robert took my small grandfather back to Ireland. My grandfather was initially more or less brought up by a Catholic neighbour he'd hoped his father would marry (I based the character of Kathleen on her). He didn't, unfortunately, and the woman he did marry was not kind to the little boy.

Most of this I didn't learn from my grandfather but from a cousin's genealogical research. The news that I had a Catholic great-grandmother didn't entirely surprise me, as I've two photographs of her and she looks like one; I realise that this probably makes no sense whatsoever to anyone who doesn't come from Northern Ireland. Someone in the family was probably also an Orangeman, as when I was a child there was an old sash in the house, though the only person I ever saw wearing it was my teddy bear. Nobody knew who it had belonged to.

Try as I might, I couldn't get my Robert and Annie to go to bed together before marriage. Even if a writer bases characters on real people, if characters are to convince both writer and readers, they have to become 'real' in their own right. It became clear to me that my two, both products of a pious upbringing though in different sects, were both too innocent and not a little fearful – something that clearly wasn't true, or not true enough, of my great-grandparents.

There was also the practical issue of 'where would they go?' living as they did in a town where both of them were in lodgings.

It's always so exciting to be sharing my new book with you and I cannot wait to tell you all about my next one. I'll not give too much away at this stage but I can tell you that Annie and Robert will be back, this time as supporting characters.

I hope you enjoyed *Annie of Ainsworth's Mill*. If you did, please do share your thoughts on the Memory Lane Facebook page ⬛ MemoryBookGroup.

Best wishes,
Katie

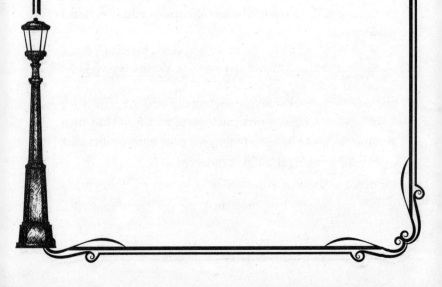

Soda Farls

I first ate these when I was a child, in a farmhouse near Kilcoo in County Down. They were baked on a griddle pan over an open fire – that farming family didn't get electricity until the early 1970s.

Preparation time about 10 minutes; cooking time about 20 minutes.

Ingredients:
- Two cups of flour
- Half a teaspoon of salt
- One teaspoon of baking soda
- One cup of buttermilk

Instructions:
1. Preheat a heavy-based flat griddle or skillet on low to medium heat.
2. Mix the flour and salt and sift in the baking soda. Make a well in the centre and pour in the buttermilk, quickly mixing to form a dough.
3. Working on a lightly floured surface, shape the dough into a flattened circle, about half an inch thick. Using a floured knife, cut into quarters.
4. Place the quarters onto your preheated griddle. After about ten minutes turn the farls over and leave to cook for a further ten minutes. Then when they're still piping hot, spread with butter and any other topping you want.

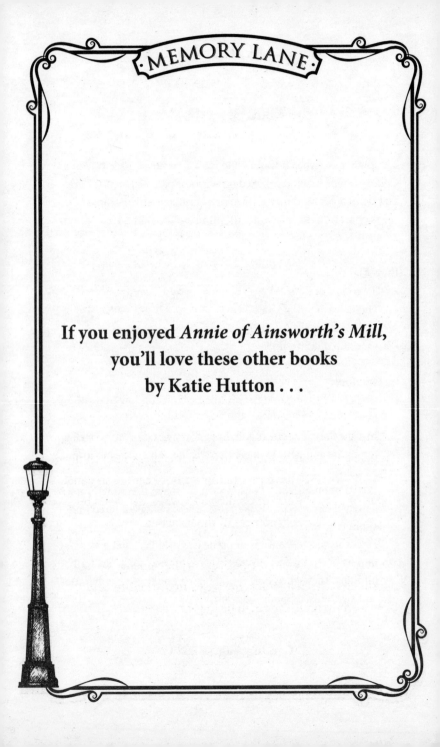

·MEMORY LANE·

If you enjoyed *Annie of Ainsworth's Mill*,
you'll love these other books
by Katie Hutton . . .

The Maid of Lindal Hall

Barrow-in-Furness, 1929

The days of the Barrow Union at Roose are numbered and it is due be closed, along with all the other workhouses.

Instead 'Cottage Homes' have been set up for pauper children, where they live in groups of twelve under the care of a resident mother and father. In house four, Robert and Annie McClure reside, tasked with taking care of a number of children. A skilled tailor, Robert trains boys to his profession whilst his wife prepares the girls to go into service.

Molly Dubber has been in the Barrow Union since the age of three. When a request comes in for a new girl to work at Lindal Hall, Annie, although worried, decides to put Molly forward. The Hall has a reputation for not keeping servants due to a moody and unpredictable owner, damaged by his experiences in the trenches.

When Molly takes up the position at the ramshackle hall, she finds herself with some unwanted attention and soon finds she could be in grave danger . . .

Coming August 2023

The Gypsy Bride

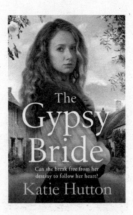

Oxfordshire, 1917

The granddaughter of a Methodist preacher, Ellen has her life mapped out for her. Engaged to the respectable Charlie, she is heartbroken when her fiancé is killed in the trenches.

But then she meets Sam Loveridge. Mysterious and unruly, Sam is from a local Gypsy community, and unlike anyone Ellen has ever met before. She is swept off her feet and shown a world of passion, excitement – and true love.

But the conservative world that Ellen is from can't possibly approve of their relationship, and Ellen and Sam are torn apart.

Is their love strong enough to overcome their cultural differences, or will the hostility and prejudice they face destroy their chance of happiness?

The Gypsy's Daughter

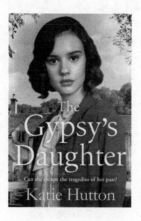

Kent, 1950s

Harmony 'Harry' Loveridge is growing up on a farm in post-war Kent. With a Gypsy for a father, she has had a somewhat unconventional, yet happy life.

But Harry has always hoped for more. And with ambitions to go to university, and a scholarship in sight, it looks as though she is about to get what she wants. That is until one fateful night, during the yearly hopping, when something happens to Harry.

Refusing to give up on her dreams Harry must draw on all her strength and courage as she embarks on her new life in Nottingham.

Will she be able to escape the tragedies of her past, or is history doomed to repeat itself?

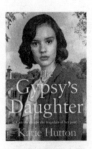
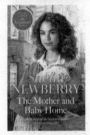

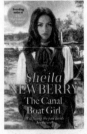

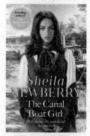

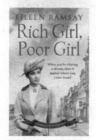